THE LIQUID EYE OF A MOON

THE LIQUID EYE OF A MOON

UCHENNA AWOKE

SCRIBE
Melbourne | London | Minneapolis

Scribe Publications
18–20 Edward St, Brunswick, Victoria 3056, Australia
2 John St, Clerkenwell, London, WC1N 2ES, United Kingdom
3754 Pleasant Ave, Suite 100, Minneapolis, Minnesota 55409, USA

Published by Scribe 2024

This is a work of fiction. All of the characters, organisations, and
events portrayed in this novel are either products of the author's
imagination or are used fictitiously.

Internal pages designed by Wah-Ming Chang

Printed and bound in the UK by CPI Group (UK) Ltd, Croydon
CR0 4YY

Scribe is committed to the sustainable use of natural resources and
the use of paper products made responsibly from those resources.

978 1 915590 07 7 (UK edition)
978 1 761385 91 9 (ebook)

Catalogue records for this book are available from the British Library.

scribepublications.com.au
scribepublications.co.uk
scribepublications.com

In memory of

my father, Edoga Nicholas Ugwokeja Awoke,
my mother, Obloko Rosaline Obeta Awoke (née Ijere),
my younger brother, Chijioke Awoke,
and my aunt, Monica Onyishi.

Till we meet to part no more.

THE LIQUID EYE OF A MOON

One

YESTERDAY IN MY MIND I REBURIED OKIKE, MY AUNT, in a proper grave, in a coffin my memory grabbed from Aku Road, a beautiful white box edged with a blue stripe, a patterning of hibiscus with yellow blossoms embossed on its lid. Sometimes I sneak out to Aku Road to see the coffins sampled outside carpentry workshops, edging the fine arc of the road, in all their colours and shapes. The road is a piece of artwork that I walk with my eyes, rising where it rises and curving where it curves. Even the Bishop Shanahan Hospital fence is artful in the way it curves then rises elegantly as if determined to hold those coffins back from strolling in and claiming their bodies waiting in the mortuary. I picture the coffin makers standing in their dusky workshops behind piles of their coffins with ambitious stares that call for patronage. Their bare bodies covered in fine powdery wood-dust and a sheen of muscle-gloss. But passersby always look the other way. Always focused on the curve of the Bishop Shanahan fence opposite, fear and repulsion rimming their eyes, like the dark lines of kohl around my mother's, as if by merely looking they are summoning death.

Okike's actual grave, in a garden near our house, has been overtaken by weeds, half buried in wild growth, umbrellas of mushrooms and small climbing-grasses sprouting wildly over it. My mother tells me that today marks a decade since her death. I am going to weed the grave neat in commemoration of her passing, and, one day, I will make Okike a tomb. My mother says Okike lived with us when I was a child. She looked after me. She and I enjoyed a special bond, my mother says. "Ahutubeghi m," she wonders at such closeness. "I have never seen a child that close to an aunt, even more than he is to the mother."

Sometimes I close my eyes and imagine Okike bathing me, soaping me all over, oiling my scalp and patting my baby neck and tender back with talcum powder, folding me in diapers and tossing me up in her arms, a happy, smiling, fat thing. But did I wear diapers as a baby? I can't seem to connect my small village of Oregwu, a remote, rural place in eastern Nigeria, with the townshipness of diapers, talcum powder, and coconut oil. Or this starved-looking boy that I see in the mirror to the round baby of my imagination.

Okike was my grandfather's lastborn. My mother tells me she drowned in the Ezenwanyi cave on the eve of Palm Sunday. According to my mother, she was plucked out of the water and hastily buried without a proper funeral. Her grave lies unweeded. Time has blurred its edges. I want to build a tomb over her grave, a beautiful tomb, to thank her for caring so much for me. But that will have to wait until I can afford it.

I was four years old when Okike died, and eight years old when my father took me to the attama—the priest—of Ezenwanyi. He took me there in secret because my mother, a Catholic, forbids her children from going near Ezenwanyi's shrine. My father might be the last proud worshipper of Ezenwanyi in our village. His face is probably the only one unfamiliar to the parish priest of the local church, Holy Trinity. But my father says the parishioners are hypocrites, not minding that my mother is one of those competing for the front pew during Sunday Mass. He says they bring nocturnal sacrifices to Ezenwanyi to seek his favours, and then they wear long scapulars to the morning Mass the next day to please the parish priest. "Pietists," he sneers.

"You must not tell your mother that I brought you here," my father whispered.

I nodded, excited to share a secret with him, a secret between men.

The attama is a tall, stooped elderly man who lives a few houses away from us. When he is not at the shrine he looks like any dried-up old man from our village, with a nose that dribbles snuff mixed with snot, who goes to work at his farm in the morning and spends the afternoon sitting on one of the huge old trunks in the village square. But he is a different man when he is seated at the shrine, distant and withdrawn, shrouded in dark mystery.

"My son here has been acting strange lately," my father said from across the square floor of the little thatch hut where we sat on a short bench. "He has been unsettled in his sleep. I want to know the cause of his strange affinity with my late sister, his aunt Okike."

The attama asked my father to get a stick, and to break the stick into the number of my father's siblings, and then name the broken sticks after the siblings. This my father did in secret outside the shrine. When he returned, he handed the broken sticks over to the priest. Holding the sticks in his crooked palm, his nose unusually clean and dry, the attama spoke a few words of incantation and cast the broken sticks onto the earth floor. They fell in a line, the seven of them broken into uneven lengths. He touched the broken sticks one by one with a short staff, back and forth a few times. And then he stopped, picked up the one to his right, and gave it to my father, who acknowledged that it was the very one he had named for my aunt Okike.

"She has reincarnation ties with your son," the attama said. "In other words, she is your son's ancestral benefactress. Their souls are tied together from the land of the spirits. Do not try to separate them or forcefully stop his predispositions towards her, no matter how strange they may seem. The connection between them is very strong, stronger than you can imagine, and that is why she comes to him in the dream, as a sign of that everlasting bond, a sign that she will be there for him if called upon in times of need or distress."

It seems the attama was right. For as long as I can remember, I have often seen a young woman drowning in my dreams. In these dreams, I always see myself standing by a riverside. The woman approaches the river in a bright yellow dress with floral patterns. She bounds up onto the rocky track, hesitates at the riverbank, her shoulders quivering, her face glistening with tears, frozen white. And then she trembles and walks into the water. She walks on until the water reaches her shoulders, her chin, her nose, her eyes. Finally, it covers her.

Later, my father took my younger brother Machebe to the shrine of Ezenwanyi for his mood swings and belligerence. The priest took one look at Machebe and revealed to my father that his second son was reincarnated from our forefather through the energetic village spirit Agubata. This is why Machebe is strong and hot-headed, and withstands me in a fight even now that I am fourteen years old, three years older than Machebe.

"The forefather he is reincarnated from was descended from the tiger spirit animal," explained the attama. "When the totem appears to Machebe, the tiger's passion and energy are released to your son the same way it happens to the masker." He gave my father a knowing look. "You understand what I mean."

My father nodded, but I was lost, and it wasn't until much later, when I learned about my father's masking prowess, that the cryptic message that passed between the two men unfurled to me.

"At least I am not reincarnated from a woman," Machebe sneered.

We argued hotly. I did not like the jeering note in his voice that suggested that being reincarnated from Okike was a stigma. Machebe and I were like water and oil, and I knew that he would act even more arrogantly now that it had been revealed he was reincarnated from the tiger.

My father walked in then and shouted us down. Such matters were sacred, and must not be profaned, he said. "And you must not mention it to your mother. You know her views on Ezenwanyi."

Two

MY VILLAGE MUST HAVE BEEN FULL OF NAKED TODDLERS without birthdays, or enlarged photographs of their childhoods taken in studios and displayed on smooth painted walls. I probably grew up the same way, naked and running around with poop in my buttocks. One of those potbellied, food-loving imps whose mothers would beckon the family dog over to lick them clean. I smile each time I indulge myself in those thoughts. But my mother talked about my childhood without nostalgia. She said I was a snot-faced child with nameless longings. I'd cry loudly, squealing like a squirrel baulked of a ripe palm nut. "Ibekazi," my mother would tease me. "You always preferred to be tied to the back of your aunt, and when anyone tried to take you away to ease the poor girl's burden, you cawed and fought like a crow, nearly clawing out their eyes."

When she said this, I hid my face and said nothing, feeling slighted that of all the pretty birds in the village, it was a crow my mother likened me to, but in her good mood I could ask, "What did Okike do when I squealed?"

My mother smiled. When my mother smiles, you catch a glimpse of distant beauty. It flickers and is gone, *fiaam*, like the dash of a glowworm. "When you squealed because you needed to suck my breast and I had gone to Ogige market," she said, "Okike plugged her nipple into your little mouth and sang for you until I returned and kissed away your snot and tears."

My mother said I sucked her like there was no tomorrow, and even suckled Okike's milkless breasts for comfort.

"Like seven famished puppies," she chuckled. "After you fed, you insisted on going up again on Okike's back, leaping with happiness."

So much for my mother's similes: first a crow, then seven famished puppies. But I was a big sucker, and that's the truth. I am amused, and sometimes angry, when my mother retells this story. Angry because I am embarrassed, amused because it is my love story, my childhood, the beauty that lies in not knowing the difference between breastmilk and breast, and because my mother never gets tired of it, this serial retelling.

"What kind of songs did Okike sing for me?" I'd ask my mother each time.

"She sang you baby songs." My mother would smile again even more broadly, and I'd catch a glimpse of the ghosts of her dimples, long receded into her sunken cheeks. Now they ornament my younger sister Usonwa's face.

"Sing me the song," I'd insist.

My mother would clear her voice, laugh a little as if shy, and then she would sing the song about the little bird: *Nwannununwannununta turuzanzaturunza nwannununwannununta turuzanzaturunza tukenekisiatu tunwokenikenike tunwanyinikenike tutumeropipiro piropirororo pi.*

It reddens my cheeks when I think of all this, now that I am an all-grown skinny boy who finished primary school at the age of fourteen after I lost one year to pneumonia. My mother says it was pneumonia, but now I think it was malnutrition, too much cocoyam and tasteless cowage soup. Some people say I laugh like water. Curiously, I find myself going to the creek in my village to listen to its ululations. Others say it is my father I laugh like, that it is his most telling feature, but most people agree that I look like my uncle Onumonu, my mother's brother, a primary school teacher, a man who reminds me of a squirrel. I can't imagine myself growing into a diminutive man in clothes that outsize me.

Let me tell you a little about my family. I am my parents' third child and their first son, if a boy like me being anyone's first son is anything to be proud of. So you know, about a year ago, I did pass my Common Entrance exam and raced home to flaunt my result.

"You are not going to secondary school," my father said in a parched voice. "Unless you will have me trade my manhood for school fees."

Heartbroken, I went to a corner to sulk. My mother came back and found me there, like a cat starved of affection. You have already met my mother, my heroine, the vibrant force in the family.

"Get up."

Her voice warmed my heart.

"Tomorrow you are going to the new school to begin your registration." My mother untied her wrappa, washed threadbare, one of the few pairs left on the clothesline. She reached for a grey pouch-like cloth bag she ties around her waist and emptied its contents, all her life savings. "I am sure I have enough in here to start you off," she said.

The next week found me walking the street proudly in the white and indigo of Community Secondary School. But after one term, my family could no longer afford the fees and I was forced to drop out.

"Nnam, don't worry. You will go back to school if I have to work my fingers to stumps," my mother reassured me.

I have six siblings—two elder sisters, Oyimaja and Ekete; my younger brother Machebe, my younger sister Usonwa; and the twins, a boy and a girl, Ebube and Ihebube—and you already know about my aunt Okike, my benefactress, and that I am her reincarnation. My father is my greatest critic, and I often feel he stands in my way. He has five siblings, but I know only one, my aunt Ogbom; the rest are either dead or lost. Sometimes my father talks about his father, my grandfather, a man my father says lived a lonely life. Ngwu is a white-haired little man in my father's last memories of him. He did not live to a very old age, and he was drunk more often than sober. My father talks of his late mother, my grandmother, too. He describes her as a tall, stern-faced woman with a glossy dark complexion and a strong will, the opposite of my grandfather. My father smiles brightly whenever he talks about his parents. He leaves me with a sense of guilt, because I don't think I smile, let alone brightly, when I talk about my father. He used to accompany my grandfather, a roofer, to work.

"A very good one when he was sober," he said, "but he was often getting into strife with those he disappointed."

I sense that my father had been proud following his father and making roofs with bamboo, raffia, and thatch, but ashamed of his father's drinking habit, as I am of his. I also don't believe making roofs is a great employment, even if my father treats this story as a delicate heirloom that, if allowed to slip and fall, would shatter like glass.

•

My father is now the second-oldest man in our village. He is not so old, but he has many strands of grey hair and a rough salt-and-pepper beard. He definitely looks too old to have fathered the twins, my last two siblings. I think it is because he hunches over in the sun to mould bricks. Maybe it was because his older brother Alumona chose to become a roofer like their father that he chose to make bricks instead. I hope that one day he will become the oldest man and thus the Onyishi of our village. Then everything—the hills, the caves, the land, and the trees—will be ours, and everyone will have to do as he says. He will superintend the slaughter of funeral cows at the village square and bring home a big lump of meat. And he will be respected. We will have farmlands to grow crops and drive hunger far away. My mother will become the Obloko, with more palm trees in her custody than any woman in the village. There will be money for me to return to secondary school, and to be reunited with Eke, my childhood friend. We desperately want to go to university and learn to speak big English words that fall from heights like breadfruit heads. And there will be money to build Okike a proper tomb.

But then I dream that my father dies on the day of his coronation.

"Dreams are nothing. They exist only in your imagination." My mother waves my dream away. But I know that my dreams about Okike are material, and I am overcome with a sense of foreboding.

The university I want to attend is just on the other side of the hill, so near that when the wind blows it fills my nose with the smell of learning: that hot, metallic scent of paper fresh from the mill. It is so close we can hear the sirens and see the helicopters bringing famous people to the Founder's Day ceremonies.

As children, we were afraid to enter that community of well-dressed English-speakers, where we were expected not to utter the Igbo language that is our mother tongue; their ground seemed too clean for our dirty feet. But our mothers would send us there anyway to fetch tap water in iron buckets during droughts. The cave dried up during those times, water trickling out of the rocks like breastmilk, but in the campus it gushed from the taps. We started to enjoy our visits. We helped the students carry water to their hostels. We cleaned their rooms in exchange for gifts. We gleaned their bins for morsels, but found nothing. "The university cannot afford groceries anymore, and it is the fault of government," my father said. "The students don't have enough to eat themselves, much less things to throw away."

Nowadays they fetch their own water and wash their own clothes, too. My father says it is the fault of government, and that tuition fees have jumped on top of the iroko tree. But that is for Eke to worry about. He is the one most likely to go to university.

To tell you a few truths about my small village of Oregwu, it is nice throughout the year, but sometimes December is brittle-dry, and March is warm, too warm. It is wet and cold in August. I like it in spring when the weather is cool and the grass is fresh and green, a time when it smells of nothing but new leaves and sweet loam. There are no storied houses in my village, but there are as many cement houses as there are those built of mud brick, the ugly type of brick my father makes for a living. The houses are usually squat or L-shaped. Most of them are unpainted. Hideous. Some have cracks where house lizards and geckos live and dash out now and again to snap up an insect. Nothing disgusts me like the guts of a gecko stained on a wall when the younger ones stone them to death.

In my village, every household with a man has a goat pen. In it you find more goats than sheep. The chicken coops belong to the mothers. The villagers mostly farm. Men plough and plant, women weed and cook, and children eat and play. But my father makes bricks, because he doesn't have many acres of land like his fellow men. There are a few drinking joints where men go to relax their muscles, enjoy palm wine, and chat about community happenings when they come back from the farm, like Madam Bridget's bar, with its crooked little signboard that says PALM WINE AND BUSH MEAT READY. A man might get drunk and slumber by the side of the road. He might wake up the next day soaked in his own urine and vomit. In the cold drizzle of the early morning dew, he might then sidle home to his irate wife and children. My father has done this many times. My mother does not speak to him for many days after.

When a baby is born in my village, children eat the insides of unripe palm nuts, and women yellow their foreheads with odo. They sing, and men drink palm wine and laugh in loud voices. They laugh like hyenas if the baby is a boy, even if he might grow into a village drunk like Oko. When a person dies, women weep and men cross their arms. A hole is made, and the person is covered with red soil. Dances are made, and after that everyone goes home. A tomb may be made for one out of three-score deaths and ten. I am not sure if we have ghosts in my village. People tell tales of them in Amalla Nkwa, a neighbouring town where human beings and ethereal entities interact between the spiritual and temporal worlds, but I am not sure if there are any here.

It's probably just moonlight playing with shadows.

Three

WE HAVE A FEW TOMBS IN MY VILLAGE. BUT THEY ARE
nothing like what I want for Okike. They are the usual blocks
of ugly dull masonry. I want the best tomb for her, a big, shiny
tomb, so I go in search of something similar. The villages that
make up our region of Ishiayanashi are all set up the same
way. They are connected by a twisted matrix of paths that loop
around farmlands and compounds. I know of many people
who've died: of old age, a fall from a palm tree, complications
from childbirth, convulsions, measles, malaria, or road accidents. But I find no more than a few graves as I walk through
the cluster of villages. Most of them have been ploughed over
and planted with crops.

I remember a grave in the village where people go to
Mass in a stone-walled building named Holy Trinity Catholic Church, where catechism classes are held outside under a
mango tree. On weekdays, the building is used as a primary
school. Ticks used to live in the broken floor back in my school
days. My mother would open up my big toes with a thorn to
free them of the large egg-white parasites imprisoned inside.
On Sundays, the classrooms disappear and an altar is set up.
The wooden benches are rearranged to create an aisle for the
bony parish priest to pace up and down. Sometimes, when angry for reasons known to only him, the erratic priest will hoof
around in a fit of bad temper. "Like a hyena that smells blood,"
I overheard someone say. The priest mandates the parishioners

to shun Ezenwanyi's shrine. "It is a heathen practice, and you must not allow yourself to be yoked with unbelievers," Father Matthew directs his congregation.

The damp morning is airless with the stench of rotten mangoes as I cross the church, which faces the cream-and-brown parish residence the congregation laboured to build for Father Matthew. My mother is saving for a general congregation levy to replace the priest's old, smoking 504 Salon car.

I finally locate the tomb I am thinking of on the roadside at the entrance to a long pathway up to a house painted in browns and dark reds. It is a plain, flat slab of cement whose occupant is depicted by a statue sitting at the head of the grave: a pretty young woman, showing a bit of flesh. Her skin is glistening with mist—a wet, plain-of-Bournvita brown. Her hair is plaited in a series of loops like the slender coils of akidi, the black bean pods planted in farms.

"Why are you touching that statue?" a harsh voice bawls behind me.

I had moved closer and stretched a hand to feel the statue's wet clay skin before the voice pinned me to the spot. I turn around to find a boy my age standing right behind me in a frayed black shirt and combat shorts. He is glaring at me. He looks troublesome, that I see at once.

"I am just admiring the tomb," I say in as polite a tone as possible, my eyes settling on his intimidating pectorals.

"Don't you know it's my mother's tomb," he says, bunching his fists and coming closer.

I take a step back. Anyone passing could stretch out a hand and touch the statue, that's how close the tomb is to the road, but for the sake of my teeth I do not want to argue with this boy in combat shorts with a strong chest and a bunched fist.

He quickly steps up to close the gap between us. We look at each other, his eyes flashing with anger and violence. I don't know what to say to him or do, if I should apologize or turn and take a sprint for it. He doesn't look like he cares about apologies.

Finally, I drop my eyes, my feet shifting uneasily. Maybe he sees my fear. He steps up and shoves me backwards, so hard I almost trip over. He waits to see how I will react, but my hands hang limply by my side. The insult rankles, but I know I don't stand a chance against him. If I want to do anything, it is to turn and tear off like a grasscutter doubling back from a predator, and then to show him my five fingers from a safe distance or even throw the whole ten at him in contempt. As if reading my thoughts he closes the gap between us again, so that I can feel his breath on my face like flame, his hands still tightened into fists.

"Hei, Ehamehule!" A man emerges from the house, his voice deep and rumbling.

The boy stops, loosens up, but his eyes are still on me, regretting the beating I may have been spared. It must be his father. I can see their resemblance. The boy has the man's healthy brown face and springy gait. In grey shorts and bare torso, the man looks well built, with good muscle tone, a clean-shaven face, and thick calves.

"Why are you fighting him?" the man says.

He approaches with brisk, springy steps.

"I caught him trying to dirty the statue," the boy says. His lie comes off so glib, like a clean breath.

"I didn't," I protest, my voice suddenly very loud and defiant. "I was only looking at the statue."

The man considers me briefly. The brown imperious eyes

move back to his son. "I have told you, if you keep fighting anyone who touches the statue, you will end up fighting everyone," he says in a voice full of reverence for his late wife or the artwork or both.

The boy walks away, still scowling at me.

On my way home, I run into Eke in the company of a dark-skinned, angular boy. Eke is my closest friend, and we are from the same village. We used to walk to school together, barefoot, eating unripe mangoes we stoned down and African olives we plucked from their trees like madmen. Eke is in his second year in the secondary school now.

The boy in his company looks like a snake, with small, loose limbs. He probably said something funny, because Eke is laughing in his dry, crackling way that reminds me of a quick bushfire. We shake hands like young men, the three of us, and then Eke and I watch the boy twist and dance down the road, his thin back arced like that of Bingo, our malnourished dog.

"Who is he?"

"My cousin. I was seeing him off. He came all the way from Lejja to visit us."

I glance back again at the boy's elongated form as we begin to stroll the other way, to Eke's family house.

I tell Eke about my run-in with the boy over his mother's statue.

"I know him. His name is Ehamehule, and he is the only child of the woman who died," Eke says.

Eke seems to know everyone. He lives with his mother and siblings in a house his father left them. His father made huge profits from groundnut storage and built their aluminum-roofed house before he died in a motorcycle accident. His mother is a warden at Holy Trinity Catholic Church. She doesn't like me all that much.

"I was so afraid, and then his father appeared, to my greatest relief."

Eke lights his crackling bushfire laughter. And then we arrive at the treed compound and settle down on a bench in the shadow of an orange tree in front of the large house. The tree is heavy with ripe oranges. At the back of the house are a goat pen and a chicken coop with low mud walls and grass roofs. A towering coconut tree carrying many seeds stands guard over the house.

Eke's mother is not home, and I feel relieved. She once called me "ohu ma"—a term I did not understand but knew was some kind of insult—even after the parish priest had said not to, especially to his wardens and the front-pew sitters. And then she swept away my footprints from her compound. I was in primary school at the time, barely nine years old. Eke and I were playing when his mother returned from the farm. I hurried off as soon as I saw her. As I made for the path that led home, I heard the quick, angry swish of a broom. And when I looked back, I saw Eke's mother sweeping the ground I had trod over on my way out.

Growing up, I had always sensed that something was wrong with my family. I knew that people whispered about us. I supposed that even my friends talked more freely amongst themselves than they did when I was around; sometimes I could not help but sense an air of reservation when we were together. When I visited my friends, I'd often have the feeling that I was being watched by their families. I walked into conversations that ended abruptly, suspiciously. I heard cryptic hisses and felt hard glares stabbing my back. I tried to talk to my mother about this, but eventually I gave up, because each time I raised it her mood changed. It brought sadness to her face. Words grew too thick for speech, sometimes ending in a flash of anger, so I learned to let go. I suspected it was because my father still openly went to that shrine.

"That makes you a coward, fleeing from a boy your age." Eke brings me back to the present, laughing long at my confession, his laughter crackling wildly and quickly, and then dying down in faint claps and pops.

"He looked like he was cast in iron."

"And you, what are you cast in? Apiti, a paste of loam?"

I chuckle at his joke. We pluck some oranges, peel them with a penknife, and eat.

"My mother says she was very beautiful, the boy's mother," Eke says. "She says the woman died the same day she made the pretty hair she wears in that statue, when Ehamehule was still a baby. Years after she was buried at the churchyard, they accidentally dug up her head when they were digging the foundation for the priest's residence. Her plaits were still as fresh as the day she had made them, untouched by dead-flesh mites. It was a big mystery, my mother says."

I vaguely remember. The story had broken one afternoon on our way home from school: a fresh human head exhumed at the churchyard.

I suddenly glimpse Eke's mother returning along the foot-path that leads into the compound from the main road in small curves and half loops. Sometimes the path makes me think of a necklace tossed carelessly on a table, curved here, twisted there. She is carrying a large basket on her head, a dark, robust, irritable woman.

I greet her as she crosses, a loudly whispered "Deje."

Stamping as if she bears a grudge against the ground upon which she is walking, she answers with a long sizzling hiss, stamps to a corner of the house, and tips the contents of her raffia basket violently. Something heavy hits the ground with a great thud and gives me a start. It is only a head of palm nut, but it sounds like an explosion. Some bush mangoes roll out of the basket with a familiar whiff.

"Eke!" she calls in a harsh voice that instantly sends me up on my feet and fleeing as Eke snaps a reply and rushes off to meet her.

Four

MACHEBE HAS BEEN LOOKING AT ME FUNNY. HIS EYES
are all over me this morning as I move around the house.
His stare unsettles me. Imagine a tiger incarnate with a hard
orange-brown stare. I can't take it anymore, so I walk up to
him. "Why are you looking at me like I am prey you are about
to pounce on?" I demand.

"That's exactly what I feel like doing, pouncing on you." He
puts down one of a pair of nice canvas shoes he bought yesterday and has been stroking all morning, carefully placing it
on a low stool beside the other waiting its turn to be caressed.

This is one of the many ways Machebe and I are different.
I spend the coins I make from load carrying at Ogige market
on snacks and soft drinks, on any ice-cold Coke that stares at
me from a hawker's plastic bucket. But Machebe will save up
to buy a pair of rainbow-coloured canvas shoes or a good shirt
with the profits he makes from basket weaving. He will hold
his hunger until food is ready at home, even if it is cocoyam
and grey soup. Sometimes he even hands his earnings to my
mother and says, "Take this to help with food." I envy him,
because I am not half as thoughtful. I have a weakness for
chilled soft drinks.

"Did you think I would not know that you fled from a boy
your age?" Machebe says.

So it's about Ehamehule. I don't want to argue with him.
I don't want to rouse the tiger. His jaws are clamped tight

already, his thews growing turgid. I know those tigerish signs, the huffing and snorting building to full tyrannical rage. I walk away with a hiss, ignoring his mocking laughter. My father always says that sidling is a clever way of dodging a combative bull without appearing cowardly.

Ogbuanya, our village head, dies the next day. A shrunken old man with two wives and many children. He dies in his sleep, after holding his position for almost a decade and half, our longest-serving village head.

"You were a few months old when he was installed," my mother tells me.

Cannons are fired to announce his death to the village.

"They remind me of the war," my father would sometimes say when he heard that sound.

"Spare us your gory details," my mother would cut in.

But my father will not stop talking about the civil war and the history of colonial Nigeria. "Nigeria was taken by the British Empire around the mid-nineteenth century. The colonialists left in 1960 when the country gained its independence. But the enthusiasm that greeted the new republic was cut short by accusations of corruption against the first generation of Nigerian politicians," my father says. "The first ever coup in the country was mostly executed by young, enthusiastic Igbo military officers from the east. The victims were mainly Hausa and Fulani people, including the prime minister, Tafawa Balewa. But the rebels failed to form a government, and General Aguiyi-Ironsi assumed power. The man was not even one of the coup plotters! He was a big military man— general officer commanding the entire Nigerian Army. But he was an Igboman, so it was easy for the aggrieved north-erners to jump and say it was an 'Igbo coup.' They plotted a countercoup and brutally killed him. They tied him to a Land Rover and callously dragged him along the road until he died. They didn't stop there, though; they massacred Igbo people living in the north in the hundreds of thousands, opening up the bellies of pregnant women. Odumegwu Ojukwu was the military governor of the eastern region. He wanted out of the Nigerian Federation because of the pogroms against his people. He called for a brand-new country, Biafra, so the military government led by northerners declared war against Igbo people."

My father was young and unmarried when the war came. According to him, the drone of warplanes and heavy shell-ing smoked our people out like rabbits from their warrens. They fled every which way, but they were massacred, children abandoned by their mothers for crying loudly and threaten-ing to give the rest of the family away, starvation feasting on their intestines, and kwashiorkor staring out of high, defined ribs and sunken eye sockets. My father's family fled to Agu Umabo to hide, a place covered with mangroves, where the sounds of the warplanes were distant. The enemy, deceived by thick expanses of mangrove forests, did not realize that they were thickly peopled.

"I escaped death by the whiskers," my father says. "Some-time in the middle of the war, as the drone of warplanes thick-ened and thinned in the distant sky, and as we ran out of food and more people died from kwashiorkor than the shelling, we snuck back into the village to find food, my friend Omeke and I, a trip that ended in tragedy. Omeke was shot at point-blank range after we were captured by enemy soldiers and herded into a hut. I tasted his blood and brains splashed all over me. I haven't forgotten that grim picture. I still wonder why the bloodthirsty soldier shot Omeke yet spared my life. But I know now that the great Ezenwanyi interceded on my behalf."

My mother would be an attentive audience to these speeches, nodding, shaking her head, and even shedding tears, but at the mention of Ezenwanyi she'd rise and walk out of the room. My father would then snort and reach for his snuffbox. He always reaches for his snuffbox when he is emotional, and if there's a story that drives him to the edge of his feelings, it is the Nigerian civil war. He'd take a large pinch in both nostrils, and the next minute, dark-brown emotions would start to trickle out of his nostrils. And then he'd calm again, like when you put out a fire with water.

"I was full of anger at Odumegwu Ojukwu," he would continue. "The man fled to a distant land to hide his beard. Yes, the man's beard is thick as a grove. He ran away in the fullness of the war, like a coward. He brought our legs out, exposing and abandoning us to the mercy of the enemy. But now I know better what Odumegwu Ojukwu stood for, seeing the turn of events: how our children can hardly go to school or get jobs, and how our kinsmen are still being manhandled in the north, all because we lost the war."

I spend a long time thinking of how Ezenwanyi saved my father, the terrible position the war put him in, and how our family's only hope is for him to become village head. Sometimes I wonder if he blames his failures too much on the war. But none of this matters anymore, because Ogbuanya has passed on, and so my father will be the next Onyishi.

My mother explains this all to us as the cannons fire, a flush brightening on her nose. She pauses to let it sink in, and

I can tell she's excited, too, even if she pretends to be sad about the old man's death. I do not know how she expects us to react to the news, whether to dance or jump up or start giggling. Or dash off to the neighbourhood to share the news with friends.

"There will be plenty of eating and drinking." She comes down to the level of the twins.

The prospect of feasting breaks on Ebube's and Ihebube's thin faces like a brilliant new dawn. They never let a morsel of food pass by them.

I ponder this shift in power, what my family will gain. My dream of going back to school comes alive. Perhaps I will even go to university and become somebody in life. I will dress in suits and ties, and sit in an air-conditioned office. Even Machebe, who has creative hands, will have enough raffia to make baskets and brooms, which he will sell at Ogige market. Or perhaps he will pursue his dream of becoming a mechanic. This opportunity has come at the right time. My father is no longer able to make bricks since dislocating his hip bone while he was working. My mother feeds the family. She picks things: wild mangoes, oil bean seeds, palm kernels, anything she can lay her hands on, and sells them to support us, but I feel this work is below her. When my father is crowned Onyishi, our patrimony will include arable farmlands and economic trees, enough to keep my mother's hands busy, and enough to bring wealth to the family. A better life. A fitting tomb for Okike. A future for me.

"The day is going to be ahum in the village," says my mother. "The deceased village head will be buried for your father to ascend the throne. The handover rite will be done before the burial by village elders and kingmakers from the nearby villages, making your father the official village head.

Your sister Oyimaja will receive the arua staff for your father because she is his first daughter. It will be kept in your father's custody for as long as his reign lasts, until his death, and only then will the patrimony shift to his successor. Your father will be addressed as Edoga whenever he raises a short, crooked staff to speak during his reign."

It is a nicely sugared chronicle.

My married older sisters, Oyimaja and Ekete, arrive, along with other relatives, hope brightening their faces, laughter on their lips. Their arrival sets the day's activities in motion. After a long trek their feet are dusty, their foreheads oily. Ekete's slippers have large holes in their soles. I would not be seen dead wearing slippers with holes. I would rather walk barefoot. My mother has returned from Ogige market, where she went to buy foodstuffs for a large feast. Drawn by loud conversations and laughter, neighbours and friends stroll in to eat and drink with us in merriment as the heavy percussion of Igede dance filters in from the village square.

"Hurry. We can't afford to keep the kingmakers waiting," my father says.

He is already dressed in his best, in his ishiagu: a long gown embroidered with a lion's wild, savage countenance, three rows of coral beads, and a black cap. A wrappa, tied around his waist and twined at his left hip the way it is done when someone dies, sways in rhythm with his uneven steps. I didn't realize he could still salvage some of his old good looks.

"I wonder what is keeping your brother Onumonu," he says to my mother. His manner is becoming impatient. "He is supposed to go with us to witness the handover ceremony."

"I am sure he will be here soon," my mother says.

I know my mother is not comfortable with my father

touching the arua staff, an object she considers heathen. She is not opposed to him becoming village head or her becoming Obloko, but she is afraid of what the parish priest will think of some of the traditions. Afraid of being banned from receiving the Holy Communion. Eke will probably not show up at the village square. His mother will kill him if he gets himself involved. His presence there would make headline news: the son of a church warden enmeshed in idol worship. Not only would his mother be forbidden from receiving the Holy Communion, but she would also be ostracized.

Uncle Onumonu arrives, to my father's delight.

"Have something to eat and drink," my father says to him. "We are running late."

Uncle Onumonu declines the food my mother offers him. It is clear from the look on his square face that something is wrong. "There is a situation."

The tone of his voice forces my father to take a seat. My mother is half dressed, her face taut with apprehension.

"I came from the village square. I went straight there, believing you were there already for the coronation. I met the kingmakers as they were leaving." Onumonu scratches his rough beard. "A new village head has already been crowned."

There is a deathly silence as the news sinks in. My father lets out a deep groan. From the village square Igede music floats in, providing an acoustic background to the booming of more cannons. The deceased village head is being buried, which can only happen after a successor has been crowned. Suddenly my father storms out of the room. I expect him to grab a machete and dash to the village square to confront the kingmakers, but instead he merely stands in the compound with his arms folded across his chest. His eyes are raised to the sky in a hopeless gesture. And then he lets out a long, strangled cry.

My family has never been thrown into such a deep mourning. It is as if someone has died.

"Amuta is the name of the man who was crowned the village head in place of your father," my mother explains after my sisters and the other relatives have left us alone in our sad, lonely house.

I know him, a man my mother says is several years younger than my father, a thickset man who goes around the village mostly without a shirt on, a machete or other farm tool always in his grip.

"Mother, if the headship of the village is not contestable, if it goes only to the oldest man in the village, then how could this happen?" I ask, wondering if the man took the crown from my father because he is thickset and goes around the village showing off his brawn.

My mother says, "Your father was robbed. The whole thing is a conspiracy, a wicked gang-up by the village against him." Pausing briefly, my mother appears to be caught in some sort of conflict. It's fugitive but intense, and I can feel her struggling with her inner self. And then her nerves relax in resolution as relief brightens on her face. "You are not such a child anymore," she says, almost in a whisper. "This kind of thing has never happened in this village before. It happened because of who we are, because of who your father is." My mother tries hard to smother a twinge of pain. "I want you to know that you are like any normal child in this village despite what has happened or what anyone may have done or said about you or this family. Because in this world people either like or dislike you. You should be able to identify people who truly like you and those who do not. Being careful how you associate with both, you must be able to manage your friendships and enmities. That's all I can tell you."

My hands ball into fists. I want to know more. I have a feeling my father was robbed of his right because he is "ohu ma": that mysterious phrase that people rarely speak in the village, that is taboo in our house, and that I sense is connected to Ezenwanyi's shrine. Perhaps it has something to do with my dream, too, with Okike and how she died. I have never heard of anyone else drowning in our village, ever.

But I have to be careful. My mother is touchy at the mention of my father's beliefs. I don't want to hurt her. I would rather let go of my curiosity than cause her further pain today.

Night falls with a sky strewn with a patchwork pattern, like a newly ploughed field. The moon is a slice of oiled yam hanging in the sky.

"Mother Nature's food for her children, because Mother Nature treats people equally. Mother Nature doesn't rob people of their rights," my mother sighs, sitting in the moonlight and singing to the twins, Ebube leaning his head on her lap, and Ihebube already asleep on the mat under the umbrella tree.

Her songs resonate with sadness.

Five

MY FATHER IS STILL IN SHOCK WEEKS AFTER HIS PUBLIC humiliation. He seems a broken man. He no longer swallows huge dollops of fufu with a deep noise in his throat like he used to; he now pecks like a bird. No matter how hard my mother presses him, he returns his meals almost untouched— to the pleasure of the twins. I wish he'd fight back, but instead he sits coiled under the umbrella tree, grinding his jaw and tapping his foot on the ground. He has vowed he will no longer go to any village meetings or gatherings, and has sworn never to set foot in the village hall. He drinks until he stinks of ekpetechi, and he tips snuff from his king-size box into his pinched palm, takes his time to dress it into a small black hill, and inhales in one furious and noisy sniff.

My father's frustration, his reluctance to rise and reclaim his throne, angers me, even more so because my hopes of going back to school have been dashed. The melancholic mood in the house is driving me up a wall. The silence sends me out to the street in search of some comfort. I yearn for Eke's company and head towards his house. I stop outside the aluminum house with its unforgiving yellow paint and crouch behind the skyscraping coconut tree swaying in a strong wind. I know his mother is home when I see Eke sidling out of the house slyly after I signal him with a whistle.

My father's shame blows like a strong wind across the community, I know. I see it in Eke's wide, solicitous face. But we do not speak about it. We are determined to remain friends, content to respect each other's privacy.

"I am going in search of a sample tomb for Okike," I say to save the embarrassing silence between Eke and me.

"I know where we can find a good tomb, but it is a long trek from here, in a village near Ohe," he says.

Eke and I have been to Ohe stream to catch crabs and tadpoles many times. My best catch ever was a guinea fowl, a pretty bird I tried to keep among my mother's chickens only to wake up one morning to find it gone—like Okike—even before we had a chance to learn about tender care and birdsong, those kinds of loving corners. We had even ventured up to Adada River to try to fish after school. Had my mother known this, she would have not only spoken to me with lemons in her voice but also called a family meeting.

"You should go to Lagos," Eke says as we walk. "You should tell your father to ask your cousin Beatrice to take you."

I have never thought of going to Lagos, but now that Eke has suggested it, I see the brilliance in his idea, even though I sense where it is coming from. Eke knows that my father is finished and has nothing left to offer me.

After walking for an hour and half, we find the tomb in a compound with a modest whitewashed house, a row of flowers leading up to its dark brown door. The tomb lies to the right, carpeted with dead leaves. There is no sign of life, but the air is warm. I can smell a bakery nearby. I move closer. The tomb is decorated with attractive bright blue tiles. It is the size of my father's bamboo bed. The floor around it is covered in costly-looking white stones.

"The owner of the house is a rich trader living in Onitsha. His father lives in the tomb," Eke says.

For a long time I stare in admiration, knowing I have found the right tomb for my aunt Okike. Moving closer, I catch the smell of old wet bark sharp against the cold morning air. My stomach rumbles, revolting against the familiar stench, reminiscent of a concoction my mother prepares with leaves and barks and forces me to swallow whenever I have a fever.

I don't understand why people take their dead to Bishop Shanahan Mortuary when all dead bodies will end up in the belly of dead-flesh mites.

"Don't put me in the *fridge* for too long when I pass on," I remember my father saying.

He doesn't support embalmment because it leaves dead bodies sallow-faced and unrecognizable if they are left too long in the mortuary. My father has a high opinion of himself, thinking the family will let my mother waste what little money she makes sending him to a mortuary.

I wonder if the man lying in the tomb was taken to Bishop Shanahan Mortuary. The coffin is probably gone now with the flesh, down the throats of famished termites. I imagine the white ants gorging themselves on his bulbous eyes, attracted to the delicious smell of death. Leaving two hollows where the eyes used to be, working their way to the ample nose and chunky lips, finally falling on the massive body. By the time they are through with him, nothing is left: only vermin, only the Catholic aura, and a set of teeth grinning at me from a hollow-eyed skull.

I shudder to think of Okike in the same way.

•

We pass Madam Bridget's bar on our way home. Eke insists we stop for a drink. He goes to the bar once in a while to grab a mouthful of alcohol and listen to men's talk. Madam Bridget's bar is easily the most popular drinking joint in the village. It is a short walk down the road from the village intersection, a wooden shed painted bright blue.

The bar is lively with loud highlife music and voices in animated conversation, accompanied by the wild guffawing of drunken men. The inside is littered with mugs, plates, and spoons. The tables and the floor are wet, covered with a whitish, foul-smelling substance streaked with black. Hanging in the air is the heavy smell of scum. Flies rise in their numbers as customers part the light wind-swayed curtain and walk in. We settle on benches to wait for our drinks.

"Dimkpa," Eke says, laughing in his crackling-bushfire voice as my bottle of Coke arrives instead of a beer, "when will you stop drinking sugar and drink a man's drink?"

The drunken men burst into laughter.

"I am not surprised," says Oko, who spends most of his day begging for drinks at the bar. "Ohu ma are not meant to enjoy things meant for people like us."

The bar explodes with their guffawing.

"Your father got what he deserved." Oko's affront is accompanied by a loud, drunken belch. "I would have my manhood cut off the day he became village head."

I feel anger rearing inside me like firewater corked in a bottle and vigorously shaken, but Eke taps me to calm me down.

"He is a clown, remember," he whispers.

Eke is right. It is better to stay clear of Oko's path if you don't want to get him permanently on your back.

We walk away.

Six

EKE'S SUGGESTION TO FOLLOW BEATRICE TO LAGOS FILLS my head like liquor. Beatrice is my father's niece. She has lived in Lagos for as long as I can remember. She lost her own father and buried him without entombing him, despite all her money, all her Lagosness. For this reason, I'm a bit wary of following her, but it will certainly be easier for me to raise money for Okike's tomb in Lagos. Though I am not sure my mother will let me go. It is such a distant city, I am told. I hear there is a sea in Lagos, and it is as restless as a cock coming back and running away again from a swarm of flies following its comb sores. Maybe Onitsha would be more acceptable to my mother, where people speak Igbo. If she lets me go at all, I think she will make me promise to keep away from the large river there. She has a phobia of flowing water. She would kill me if she heard that I sometimes travel long distances with Eke to swim and fish in a dark vernal pool where dead bodies of evil people are supposed to be dumped. I looked for those dead bodies my mother talks about the last time I went there with Eke, peering into hidden corners and undergrowth. But I did not find them, and I wondered if they had become ghosts since they were not interred, if they had migrated to Amalla Nkwa to live with the other ghosts. I have heard that all dead people go to Amalla Nkwa to become one big community of ghosts.

"I want to go to Lagos," I say to my mother.

"Lagos. O di ka uwaozo?" my mother hisses. "That place, is it on another planet?"

"It's where Beatrice lives," I explain to her relief. "I want to go there, make a lot of money, and become wealthy."

My mother laughs long and loud. "God will bless your ambitions, nna."

When you think my mother will pitch into you for saying the wrong things, she's suddenly all sweetness and light. I tell my mother that when I come back, I will take my family out of poverty and retrieve what was stolen from us. And then I will build a big, fine tomb for Okike. The very finest of tombs. I do not tell my mother that I also long to be far away from Machebe. He is strong and troublesome, and we fight every day. It is exhausting to have to fight a brother who is descended from a tiger. Even if I didn't have my mother's blessing, I think, I'd defy her opposition because there is no future for me here. But there is one problem. My cousin Beatrice has not come back to the village for many years, and we do not have her contact or address.

It seems the path to Lagos leads to a dead end. But then I remember what the priest of Ezenwanyi had said: *The connection between them is very strong, stronger than you can imagine, that is why she comes to him in the dream, as a sign of that everlasting bond, a sign that she will be there for him if called upon in times of need or distress.*

I did not understand then what the priest meant, but my father later explained that if I wished for anything and made my wish known to Okike with my hands raised to the sky, I'd have whatever I wished for. Since my dream is to go to Lagos and make enough money to take my family out of poverty and build Okike a tomb, I raise my hands to the skies and make a wish to my ancestral benefactress, willing Beatrice to come home.

My dreams of going to Lagos and working hard to raise money for the tomb fill out the empty days. Eke goes to school in the morning, and I go to Ogige market to carry loads, wheeling people's purchases in a barrow for coins to buy snacks and chilled Coke to stop the ache in my stomach and my craving for cold things. I have a sneaking feeling that my mother so quickly approved my going to Lagos because then she will have one less mouth to feed. My father, more dejected and passive than ever, will not be an obstacle to my plan. He consents to anything my mother approves.

In the afternoon, after Eke returns from school and I return from load carrying, we go to the only chemist shop in the village to watch men play draughts and talk about politics, the civil war, and Biafra. They sit on benches at the shopfront to gamble and talk in the enlightened way of people who have travelled a lot. They talk mostly about Biafra and the marginalization of the Igbo people. I like the way the gamblers push the squares and rounds about the board, and their dramatic reactions to wins and losses, especially the assured way that Patty Onah, the porcine fair-skinned man, smacks his seeds on the board and talks with confidence. Though he fools around a lot when he is playing and laughs with his whole body, Patty Onah is a genius at winning games. He is very mathematical and has a way of trapping his opponents with Greek gifts, then finishing off the game in a dramatic win. He raises his eyes when he has his opponent cornered and asks the watchers to chorus his name, and, when they do, he laughs, his body shaking like a well-fed sow.

I watch his cigarette-stained mouth and flushed features the same way Ebube and Ihebube will watch my mother's mouth when she is telling them moonlight stories. The gamblers talk excitedly about the coming sit-at-home order issued by a group championing the Igbo people called Movement for the Actualization of the Sovereign State of Biafra (MASSOB), a secessionist movement associated with Igbo nationalism. They hiss smoke down in their lungs and ponder the impact MASSOB's sit-at-home will have on the struggle.

"A lot," says Patty Onah. "You and I are rusting in this village, but when you go to the big commercial cities like Onitsha, Lagos, or Kano, you will see that we Ndigbo are controlling the commerce of this country."

"It is going to take more than sitting at home to achieve the struggle," Oluoha, his playmate and a grouchy little man, counters. He lights a cigarette. "Sitting at home is for women and children. Real men give expression to their anger, their agitation, in more practical terms. But this village is too dry, too effeminate. Nothing is happening here. I am going to try to establish contact with the leader of MASSOB." He sinks his voice to a whisper. "I am mobilizing young men for a protest march on the day of the sit-at-home. I am taking my time to pick only the courageous. We are going to storm the local government headquarters and tear the place down."

"This struggle cannot be achieved by violence," Patty Onah insists. "The war shows that. Yet this country will not see an Igbo president unless Biafra comes to pass."

"Tell me. What has anyone achieved in this country without violence?" Oluoha asks. "Is that not why we have Boko Haram in the north, Odua People's Congress in the west, and

Ogoni nationalism in the south? Why we even hear of al-Qaeda elsewhere in the world?"

"I am not in support of the struggle." The man speaking is grey-haired and widely travelled, a grizzled gnome of a man. "I know it is just a waste of time. What about the oil in the south-south and southeast of the country? Do you think the rest of the country will let go of that? What about our so-called south-south brothers? Are they not occupying our so-called abandoned property from when we fled?

"Before the war I was living in Port Harcourt. I had sacrificed my comfort, sleeping in a shop and starving myself in the most stringent conditions ever known to be able to save enough money to acquire a property. I fled Port Harcourt at the outbreak of the war. At the end of the war, I returned only to discover that my property had been occupied. Is it not foolish of our kinsmen who are still living in the north to refuse to come home in spite of the destruction the northerners are visiting on them? Are they not building mansions there to be destroyed in riots orchestrated by the northerners solely for that purpose, to keep us down? I tell you, brothers, Biafra is not the answer. Every Igboman building castles in the northern air ought to come home, and together we shall work at developing Igboland with our God-given talents and brains."

Stories of the civil war and the marginalization of my people resonate with me. The treatment of the Igbo people is a story of denial just like my father's story. My father accepts his loss and chooses to wither at home like a plant in the Harmattan, but the Igbo people will fight back. I feel anger stirring in me, equal with the dismay I feel against my father for his inaction. I find myself going back to the chemist shop to listen to the gamblers again. They argue hotly, these men who are going through midlife crises after travelling out of this community and spending years in the big cities, only to return again poor and frustrated. They were at one time owners of flourishing businesses in large cities. Patty Onah's textile business ended after insurgents burned down his warehouse in Kano. Each of them has a tragic story to tell. Left with nothing but their lives and families, they now carry loads at Ogige market and dig pit latrines for people to feed their families. Uwakwe, owner of the chemist shop, says some of them unjustifiably blame their failures on the violence against Igbo people in the north. Yet every afternoon they gather in his shopfront to smoke, drink ekpetechi, and gamble with what is left of their earnings.

"I want to know the full story, how the war started," I whisper to Eke.

"Then ask them." Eke nudges me.

"No. You ask." I return the nudge.

"How much are you going to pay for me to tell you what you want to know?" Oluoha lifts his eyebrows at me.

Patty Onah comes to my rescue. "Do you need to be paid to tell him how Muslim Hausas in northern Nigeria woke up one morning and started to massacre the Igbo Christians living in their place?"

Oluoha scowls at him. "Don't mislead the poor, ignorant soul. The Muslim Hausas did not just wake up and begin to massacre the Igbo Christians in the north. Something happened that preceded the massacre."

"Whatever happened cannot be a justification."

"The boy asked to know the reason, not the justification."

"What reasons can there be other than envy?" Patty Onah inhales his smoke. "Because of the fortune of the Igbo people and the opportunities we had created for ourselves in post-colonial Nigeria. General Aguiyi-Ironsi had meant well for everyone. His offense was that he tried to unify a country divided along ethnic lines. Because he was an Igboman, they saw it as a calculated move to establish Igbo dominance when he abolished regional governments and introduced a unitary one. Not only did they conspire to get rid of him in a coup, but they also found a reason to massacre our people. We had no choice but to fight back, to repeal their oppression and try to free ourselves. We may have lost the war, but we will continue to fight until we are free from their enslavement."

"They will never let us go as long as there is still oil left in the Niger Delta," the grizzled little man says, point-blank.

Sometimes I walk down the quiet stream alone, thinking of Okike, my mind creating blurry images of her from my mother's descriptions. "She was a rare beauty," says my mother, "your father's mother come back to life. She was your father's gourd of palm wine, and it broke, and your father started drinking ekpetechi after she died."

I sit in my father's compound and watch the days as they spend themselves pleasantly, with sunsets that leave behind them landscapes tinted with deep colours over the hills. I am enthralled by the spectacle, in that moment full of dreams, imagining a sovereign oil-rich Biafra nation and the good life that awaits us Ndigbo. The resonant voice of Patty Onah echoes in the hills: *We may have lost the war, but we will continue to fight until we are free from their enslavement.* Sometimes I lie down on my naked mattress, wishing my father could fight back, or feeling good and thinking of nothing, only a little worried that in a few weeks I will be fifteen years old.

Seven

SOME WEEKS AFTER I MAKE MY WISH KNOWN TO OKIKE,
my cousin Beatrice returns from Lagos. I don't believe my
mother when she breaks the news until my whole family goes
to see her in her fine cement house with brown paint, a black
corrugated roof, and a black gate, and I wonder about the
mystery of my reincarnation, truly awed.

"I think I know someone who needs a houseboy," she says.
"Dimkpa, I want you to amount to something. I hear that all
you do here in the village is go to Ote Nkwo wrestling and
Oriokpa masking festivals." She laughs. "Maybe you will put
that small muscle of yours to good use in Lagos."

I smile at her. She is fair-skinned and thick, with bulging
hips caged in linen trousers. She didn't used to be fair-skinned.
But Lagos has turned her into an agaracha who bleaches her
skin and dresses in men's clothes. An agaracha who refuses to
get married.

Beatrice is Uncle Alumona's daughter, that is, one of his
daughters. She used to run a sewing parlour in Ogige market
before she abandoned it and took off to Lagos without entombing her father, leaving without her little son, born without a father, because the man who made her pregnant rejected
her. Her mother's relative took in the little boy and has been
his guardian since. No one knows exactly what Beatrice does
for a living in Lagos or how she earned the money to demolish
her father's old mud-brick dwelling and replace it with a big,

modern house. People in the village hold different opinions of her. While the younger ladies envy her for her smooth skin and bold clothes, the older women frown at her agaracha lifestyle. As for the men, the bachelors won't approach her for marriage, and the old men look at her with pity in their eyes.

The night before my departure, I have my last supper with my family. Afterwards, we drink palm wine and chat into the night. I can't help wondering if it was palm wine Jesus Christ drank with his disciples or something softer. I promise to buy a ball for Ebube, and a ribbon for Ihebube, to cut short their rivalry before it degenerates to an argument.

"You are going to a place that's illuminated from heights; there's a lot to see, a lot to enjoy." My father laughs his water-running-through-stones laugh, and I sense that he is getting high on the wine, which is a gift from Beatrice. "But don't be carried away by the pleasures of the city."

I had gone to see Aunt Ogbom earlier that day, to tell her that I was leaving for Lagos. Ogbom lives in the hut my father built her after her failed marriage, the hut that smells of fresh clay polish. It looks clean as usual, daubed to a slippery shine. As a child, I would sit outside and smell fresh clay after a meal. I could not resist Ogbom's traditional foods, especially her uwuna or itipe or her cornmeal garnished with ilolo. Ogbom is the only woman I know who cooks her cornmeal with those winged termites. But it is not yet the season of ilolo; they are forerunners of the dry season, coming at a time when the mist coats everywhere in a translucent haze. They come in swarms that darken the linden tree at the hillside, but not now when spring is already edging out the dry season and ushering in the heavy rains.

"May Ezenwanyi protect you wherever you go," Ogbom prayed for me, her ashen face breaking into an affectionate smile as she pinched sand into my palm to consummate her prayer.

Machebe and I have a private moment on the old flattened mattress in the room we share. I realize that he has prepared for this talk.

"Lagos is a distant city." His voice is small and unusually soft, untigerish.

I agree with him, wondering where the conversation is headed. We are seated, our legs stretched in front of us, our backs against the wall, talking like two long-lost friends.

"You are going to be so far away from us," he says in a slightly husky voice.

"Yes," I reply.

A sound makes me look to see the money he rustles out of his pocket.

"Keep it." He pushes the crisp notes at me. "It's the money I have saved. You never know what might happen. Use it if you have need for it."

I have tears in my eyes when I say "Thank you."

Machebe can sometimes act like a decent brother when he is not behaving like the king of the jungle.

"I was saving for the future." His voice falters with emotion. "I might learn a trade. Our parents may not be able to afford the tools I will need, but you will need the money more. It's dangerous to go to a place so far away from home empty-handed."

We hug. I wish I had half his intuition, his willpower.

I lie awake thinking of his act of kindness. Machebe is already asleep. He doesn't snore, he roars. I think about the inexplicable stigma hanging over our family. Did it come about after my aunt's drowning, or because of my father's insistence on and subservience to Ezenwanyi in a village where almost everyone manages to appear in church on Sunday, wherever they have been the night before? Is ohu ma something to do with those stigmas, or is there a deeper mystery waiting to be unraveled like a parcel full of scorpions and snakes? I think of how to resolve these conflicts to better advantage my family as a rich young man who will have gained the exposure of the city. At the moment, everything looks hazy, but maybe time and success will see these thoughts settle like dregs at the bottom of a clear mug of palm wine. I lie awake, thinking of the journey to Lagos, small anxieties gnawing at me like a mischief of sharp-toothed rats.

My mother knocks on Beatrice's door at the first crow of the cock to deliver me to my cousin. Beatrice looks me over with disapproval. Hands on her hips and sleep in her eyes, she says I cannot follow her to a big city like Lagos with my things in the large tin box sitting on my head. Hearing her speak, you would think I have millipedes and worms in the box, not bar soap and a sponge made from wood fibre for bathing, and other personal things my mother has arranged for me. Beatrice prefers I take a few clothes in a plastic bag. My mother has given me a rosary, too, for protection.

Eke turns up, to my surprise. We had said our goodbyes the previous day. I know from his eyes he will miss me as much as I will miss him, and his expression also confirms my suspicion that he wants me to go to Lagos because he is doubtful of the prospects of my succeeding here, in a place that holds me in contempt.

Machebe's hug is not so tigerish, my father's is unexpectedly warm, but my mother's hug is the longest, the warmest. Her tears open the floodgates of emotions from Usonwa and the twins. The morning is cold, damp, and grey. Beatrice has arranged for an okada to take us to Ogige market, where we shall board a long bus to Lagos. My heart glows at the sound of the commercial motorcycle outside, driven by Arua, a townsman swaddled in a jacket. My mother and siblings wave goodbye with tears in their eyes in anticipation of a long separation, our first ever. I don't get a chance for a last glimpse of my family, because I am made to sit in the middle of the motorcycle, sandwiched in between Arua and Beatrice. Arua bathes me with his spittle, which he sprays generously whenever he opens his mouth to talk. I can smell his hangover through the dirt hanging thick on his jacket as he navigates a potholed road full of mud and water. A slight fear creeps up the small of my back, detached from a grain of nostalgia the picture of my family standing and waving at us has planted in my mind. Beatrice scolds Arua for his filth in her high-pitched voice, which sends my fear receding into the darkness. She spits into the emptiness. The man laughs, wryly. I can't see his face, but I imagine him blushing, looking like a stunned sheep.

"Between you and me, who is the filth?" He suddenly flays up, spraying more spittle, almost losing our luggage sitting on the tank of his motorcycle as we swim through the puddles.

I expect their quarrel to escalate, her mouth cracking open like a pod and words flying out and stoning Arua. But Beatrice allows Arua to rail, allows him to spout rivers of spittle and drown me in it. Eventually he stops, probably realizing he is getting no rejoinders from her, but he continues to drive like a madman. The market is not too long a drive from my village.

In Ogige market, beautiful things are displayed in shops in the glitter of their newness, and big women from the university come to shop for groceries—women who dress as if they don't poop—defying bad smells and flies that rise from the abattoir as they make their purchases. They wave braceleted hands at the load carriers and give them a few coins to carry their salad greens and bloody meat to their cars. The market is wearing a damp look this morning after days of rain. A musty smell clings to the air. A few people and cars are moving through the half-lit dawn. We stop at Ifesinachi Bus Station nestling on the shoulder of the market. Lying on the same arc with Aku Road, it sets off a fine sweep of valley—the Bishop Shanahan Valley—with a wilderness of rust-coloured roofs leveling out to the right-hand side and the Bishop Shanahan Hospital and Mortuary to the left. In the blue-grey light the trees that screen off the cathedral beyond look fake and ghost-like. Ghosts, moons, and dreams occupy my mind all through the wait, and even as the long bus finally noses out of the garage and swings into the road to begin the adventurous journey to Lagos.

I have a history with dreams. I always think of ghosts when I am alone in a dark room, so I sleep with the light on, but when I see a moon, even if it is shaped like my sickle, the first thing I remember is my old, sprightly grandmother, my mother's mother, a memory tied to moons and folktales.

I see Enugu, its urban periphery, in fleeting glances caught from the window at intervals when the bus enjoys the luxury of speed on the heavily potholed road. The driver mouths curses at the government for allowing dilapidation to overtake the road like a leg with festering sores. "What happened to the taxes they take from us?" he wonders.

The driver may have thrown out the question to provoke debate on corruption in the country, but some of the passengers are dozing already; others are awake but show no interest in the hackneyed old theme. Beatrice shoots me a glance. I must have been grinning, in conversation with my memory.

As we wade through Onitsha and the thick human and vehicular traffic, I am amazed by my first contact with a large city. There seems to be a set look in the face of every young man and woman pushing through the crowd. As we cross the Niger Bridge, the enchantment of water in receding expanses feeds my famished imagination, boats and canoes sailing far off in the brilliance of a midmorning sun. My village of Oregwu already belongs to a place I see now as the old world. I am more interested in moving into a new world, a large and dreamlike city. I remember Arua and his outburst—*Between you and me, who is the filth?*—but he only brushes across my mind and recedes with the endless stretch of deck and superstructure.

Onoyima walks up the bush track with a machete in his grip to find a man standing in his father's farm near a young palm tree, a man smaller than himself, with a machete raised over his head. Onoyima stops and observes the intruder, who is about his own age. At twenty, Onoyima looks powerful. He is brawny, with hair covering his broad chest. But this other man, he is a slight fellow. Onoyima takes a moment to size him up. The man is not familiar, and he looks ordinary, a no-match. Onoyima still holds the record as the youngest man to have killed a leopard in the whole of the community. Suddenly, the intruder brings the machete down, slashing through the soft stem of a palm frond, the grey of the steel shining in the midmorning sun, the frond falling, a slow, feathery, downward flight, covering the man. Onoyima bites his lip, flinching as if the machete had cut into his own heart.

"Who is this madman slashing things on another man's farm with impunity?" Onoyima's voice rumbles with the fury of a late-season thunder.

"I am not a madman," the young man says in a polite tone of voice, the hand holding the machete going slack, the other hand gently pushing the frond away to pave way for a better view of the man accosting him. "I am only a man looking for fodder for his goats."

Onoyima rushes forward instinctively, his own machete raised, barely holding himself back from cutting the small man down the way the man had cut down his palm frond. "That's not enough reason to kill a young palm tree," he thunders again, his anger threatening to rip his heart out.

"I do not intend to kill the palm tree," the young man explains, his voice soft but strong in denial. "I am only here to collect one or two palm fronds. It has been an unusually long season, my good friend. The sun has been strong and most unfriendly to the pastures." He waves around. "Look at how scorched and parched everything is looking. One can barely grab fodder for the goats."

"That is nonsense," barks Onoyima. "A man of your age should know that cutting the fronds of such a young palm tree could lead to its premature death. When you eat food, do you feed yourself through the nose instead of the mouth?"

"Do not make this issue bigger than it is, my friend," the man says. "You and I know that a palm tree no matter how young cannot die simply because you cut off a few fronds."

"You have no right to raise your voice in argument with me, little man," Onoyima says, growing even more furious, his machete going up again, threatening.

The young man backs away, raising his own machete in self-defense. The two machetes kiss each other with a grim resonance.

"You yellow monkey," Onoyima snarls. He makes to strike, misconceiving the intruder's instinct of self-defense for a challenge. "You dare to raise your machete at me, little man? I will make you regret being born a monkey. I will make you eat your own excrement."

"Body mass is not an assurance of strength." The young man squares up for a fight, angered by Onoyima's insult.

Onoyima drops the machete. He goes for him with bare hands. "It'd be unfair for me to fight you with a machete," he spits. "I am a man who detests inequity."

The young man strikes, the blade of his machete gleaming viciously. Onoyima parries the blow, but the razor-sharp blade grazes *his left shoulder. His thick, wide, grim face turns ashen at the sight of blood running down his shoulder. Onoyima strikes with his big, right fist, knocking the machete out of the intruder's hand. Fear and shock competing on his face, the young man turns to flee. Onoyima gives him a hot chase. He is fast for a man his size. They stumble over crusted farm ridges, tripping and falling, with Onoyima spitting threats, hot in pursuit. When he finally gets his huge hands on the man, Onoyima grabs his opponent by the nape of the neck, lifts and hangs him up in the air, his massive hands tightening around his throat. The small man kicks out in agony, his strangled voice rising in a great outburst of alarm and dying again as his body suddenly goes limp. Onoyima flicks the lifeless body down. He glances at his shoulder that is still dripping blood. Suddenly realizing he has murdered a man, he begins to flee the scene. He stops again at the edge of the farm, walks back to the body, drags it towards the far tree line, and dumps it there. He returns to get the two machetes from the farm. He looks around as though to be sure no one has seen him. He wipes the blade of the other man's machete, stained with his own blood, on scorched grass and steps quickly onto the path leading home.*

Onoyima arrives home to a large compound with three wattle-and-daub huts, a few trees scattered among them. He tries not to look ruffled so as not to give himself away to his mother, a large-boned woman sitting alone on the parched ground, legs stretched out in front of her around a thatch kitchen. Bare to her massive waist, she is cutting into wild mango balls to get to ogbono seeds, heavy breasts swinging with her motions like cow udders.

"Nnoo, nna." She doesn't look away from her chore as she welcomes him.

The air is fusty with the smell of the round, light green fruits.

"*Deje, nne.*" Onoyima returns her greeting in a surprisingly calm voice.

He leans his machete against the wall and walks into his own hut. The walls inside are covered with animal skins from his kills; from the deep tree-branch yellow of buffalo hides to striped hyenas, from the charcoal and white of pythons to the thick scales and bony plates of the alligator. The big one covering his mud bed is the striking hide of a leopard, with its dappling of solid black spots and golden patterns. Everything in the room speaks of a man of achievements. He settles on the bed to rest and feed snuff to his nose. A healthy black cat emerges from an inner room and rubs its long body against his legs before settling around his feet. After inhaling a few fierce pinches of snuff, Onoyima pokes his head through the door and blows his nose with a rasping noise, spraying the air umber. He wipes his nose clean with the back of his hand and rubs his palms together. He then picks up a hoe and, using the back door, walks all the way back to the farm, to the scene of the murder.

The place is still quiet and lonely the way he had left it. He marks a portion on the forest floor and starts to break the soil. It is hard on the surface, but soft and loamy beneath. His hoe rises above his head, sinks into the ground, and comes up with warm mounds of red soil. He works in silence, his strong biceps swollen and shiny with sweat, the hoe tearing the ground with a sound that travels through the quiet forest with a chilly echo. He stops and climbs out, bathed in his sweat. He walks to the body and starts to drag it towards the shallow grave. He rolls the body into the grave, wipes his sweaty face with his forearms, and begins shoveling the red clay back into the rectangular hole. He works until the pile of earth disappears. He then stamps the ground level again. He steps back to watch the grave that forms a sharp, startling red contrast to the rest *of the forest floor covered with fallen leaves. Bending, he rakes then spreads dead leaves over the grave to make it one with the forest floor. He then cleans his hoe, wipes the sweat on his brow, heaves a deep sigh, and walks hurriedly away.*

The next morning, Onoyima's father, Egwu, sets out with Onoyima to the farm with a raffia climbing rope around his left shoulder. A man of average build, he wears his loincloth firm around his small waist. He looks sprightly and moves with quick, nimble steps through the sunbathed midmorning along the lonely bush track, on his way to his farm to harvest his palm nuts. Egwu does not know of the murder his son has committed. As he winds the raffia rope around a palm tree and knots it where the two ends meet, he is unaware that he is standing a few yards away from the shallow grave his son dug only yesterday. Onoyima calmly watches as his father slips the rope over his head and around his bare scrawny back and begins to climb the tree, using his feet and the rope as pro-pellers, his machete tucked tightly in between his left shoulder and jaw, his small buttocks clenching and unclenching in his thin loin-cloth. When he gets to the top of the tree, he takes the machete from between his jaw and shoulder and starts to cut the palm fronds, slashing them at the base to create space around the head of palm nuts. Each frond slashed waves its long green many-fingered arm at Onoyima as it crashes to the ground.

As he raises his machete again to cut the palm-nut head itself, Egwu stiffens as his quick eyes meet the cold, lifeless eyes of a long black cobra, a spitting cobra. In his over twenty years of climbing palm trees he has encountered different kinds of snakes, from co-bra to mamba to adder to boa constrictor, but the spitting cobra is the most deadly. His reaction is mechanical and swift as the snake, hissing fiercely, pink tongue streaking like lightning, lunges at him. He attacks with his machete, aiming at the snake's head. Many of the snakes he has stumbled on before he would behead with one precise stroke of his sharp machete, though a few escaped, either dropping to the ground and slithering away to safety or disappearing into the thick plume of fronds, but now as he strikes at this cobra and misses it, the sharp edge of his machete slashes through the raffia rope. Plunging with a long, piercing cry, he lands, to Onoyima's horror, neck-first on the hard, dry ground with a sickening thud.

Like a wild Harmattan wind, Egwu's accident blows through Ejuona and is greeted with shock and an outburst of weeping and mourning. He is given a quick burial, and then a few days later, Igolo, Onoyima's robust mother, succumbs to a swelling illness. Her illness worsens, the swollen body breaking and maggots shimmering within the rot, emitting a horrible smell. And then she dies on the fourth day, and is buried, too.

"It is a bad omen for a widow to die in her blacks," says an elder in the family.

This run of tragedies cannot be ordinary: a man dying from a palm-tree fall and his widow following even while his body is still fresh and has not sweated in the grave. The elders are confused, and they ponder what to do. Finally, they agree to see a seer and set out at once to the seer's shrine, a clearing in a grove somewhere at the edge of Ejuona, where a little man sitting on a goatskin mat with horrid kaolin patterns sketched around his eyes receives them in a hut.

"Someone took what belongs to a goddess," says the seer after casting and studying his divination motifs, a pair of round husks strung together. "Murder!" the seer cries. "Look at it here. It is very clear." *He points to the motifs in front of him. "A man killed another man for nothing. The man who was killed happens to be the property of Ezenwanyi, a very powerful goddess in a distant, far-flung community from ours."*

The elders crane their necks, but they see nothing.

"For this sacrilege," says the seer, "the young man, the murderer, must take the place of the man he murdered at the shrine. The bodies of his late parents must be exhumed and taken to the shrine, too. They are also possessions of Ezenwanyi, including all that the murderer has. You must do this at once to forestall further deaths in that family."

The elders are stung by the news. They walk back home and swing into action, prodded by a note of urgency in the seer's message. That same day, four young men are sent to the graves of Onoyima's parents to exhume their bodies. Working in utter silence, palm fronds clenched in between their teeth, they exhume the bodies of Egwu and Igolo, his widow, and travel all the way to Ishiayanashi to rebury the corpses in Ezenwanyi's grove.

Eight

I CLIMB OUT OF THE BUS AND THE WHOLE WORLD TURNS yellow and mad.

Cars and buses are covering the motor park and lining the road in rows. I never dreamed of seeing so many people and motorcars crowded together in my life. It's as if an important man has died and his funeral is in progress. The percussion of revving engines and speakers reminds me of Ikorodo dance back home, the hooting of lorries like the dance's deep flourish of horns. My mind wanders to the half-dressed young girls dancing to the soft drumming and vibrant woodwind rhythm. The girls stand on their toes, bend their knees, and wriggle their slim waists. They always leave me scowling, itching to reach out a hand and pinch their breasts that dare to point at me in their skimpy costumes.

"Dimkpa," Beatrice says, startling me, her voice shaking me out of my mind trip home. "What are you staring at again? Oya, let's go."

Once again I fall in step with Beatrice as she meanders through the maze of crowds and yellow buses with liquid ease. I did not realize that I had stopped walking, that I was daydreaming, and now I am struggling to keep pace again, pushing against people weaving back and forth like armies of marching soldier ants. The last time I stepped into one of these dark columns, the ants hissed with anger and stung me mercilessly, their harsh smell fouling the air.

The streets are milling with people and cars, the sun burning the back of my neck. One look, one quick glance into the clouds and I bump into a woman in aso oke, her gele standing high on her head like a plume. She swears at me in harsh-sounding Yoruba. I don't know if it is my imagination, but the woman leaves a trail of the familiar odour of the soldier ants. I spit and wrinkle my nose at the smell, the sun burning harder, speakers screaming with music and reedy voices in ads, conductors and touts shouting for passengers in strident voices, hawkers clanging their bells and blowing their shrill whistles, molues and grim-faced bolekajas roaring and shitting exhaust fumes that sting my eyes and force sneezes out of me, the world going round and round, faster and faster.

A body is lying close to the road. I look at it with wide-open eyes, shaken by the sight of this dead man, riven and charred like roast yam. His face is pressed into the concrete of the sidewalk. Flies rear and swirl over him. Vultures are sidling, surveying the landscape. People who are passing either ignore the body or spit and go their way.

A hand grabs and pulls me away. "You better stop staring like a goat!" Beatrice screams at the top of her voice above the din. "This is Lagos."

"But I just saw—"

"Forget what you saw!" She tucks my hand into hers and tows me along like a dog on a leash as she rides the wave of the surging crowds. "You will see many more dead bodies, some pickpockets, some robbers, all burnt to death with petrol and tyres."

A shiver runs over me. Back home people treat the dead with respect. Women scream and tear their hair while men cross their arms in tearless grief when a person dies.

We walk through a market where the smell of ripe fruit mingles with dried fish and the sweaty odour of market women, the crowd thickening, and the smell so strong I retch. I have never seen so many people in my life moving all about me in a frenzy. It is as if the whole world has gathered here. Beatrice is elbowing people, and people are elbowing her, and I am struggling to follow. She is cutting corners and emerging again in places that look like where we have passed before. Clutching my polythene bag of clothes tighter, I allow myself to drift with the stream of cold, insensitive crowds.

"You are staring again, village boy," she snaps, nearly yanking my hand off, as I pause and stare at a woman fighting with a man.

A fleeing brown goat gets crushed by a speeding car as it tries to cross the road. We climb a pedestrian bridge. When I look at the thick crowds below, the human heads are like grains of sand in the distance. As we climb down on the other side of the road, around a bus stop where many people are waiting for molues and bolekajas, I see two young men trading punches nearby. They are stripped to the waist, sweat glistening on their bodies. They are throwing blows, real hot blows, and kicking and heaving with muscles that bunch on their arms and backs. As the fight goes on, molues and bolekajas are arriving, conductors shouting their destinations in a confusing blur of words, and bus-waiters are diving in. Some join the knot of spectators watching the fight. They cheer as the blows rise and fall, slower and slower. Others, like Beatrice, look away without interest as we wait for more molues and bolekajas to come.

"Will somebody not separate them?" I say.

"They will stop fighting when they are tired." She waves

her left hand, throwing them an indifferent look. "Nobody has the time to separate fighting touts in Eko."

No one tries to stop the fighters, whose faces are already swollen and bloodied. The crowd is enjoying the fight and cheering as the men wrestle each other to the ground and roll in the grey gutter water overflowing onto the sidewalk. They struggle again to their feet, their bodies covered with grime, their punches and kicks becoming slower each time, weakened by tiredness. They are almost finished, only leaning on each other, and throwing the blows sluggishly at intervals with the last sap of energy left in them. The yeahs and the oohs of the fight-watchers are also dying down. I watch with revulsion and a sense of savagery. More than being caged in by the mob of fight-watchers, the fighters are captives of their own ego, and neither of them wants to give up even at the risk of being killed, perhaps, to avoid being thought a weakling. So this is what Lagos turns people into, I think: cannibals and savages.

A bolekaja going to Palmgrove finally arrives with a toot that tears through my thoughts.

"Oya, let's go." Beatrice dives in, dragging me with her.

In the scramble to get on board, I step on the toes of a woman. She throws curses and pounds my torso, setting off an exchange of hot words in fleet-footed Yoruba with Beatrice. The woman has touched her venom, and now Beatrice is ready to sting. She is shouting and screaming like a madwoman.

"Don't let us tear each other to pieces in this bolekaja," she rails, thrusting her full breasts into the face of the intimidated woman, who decides to back out of a possible fistfight.

59

I find myself lost in the crowded wooden passenger compartment with one single entrance and exit point—a door at the back. The bolekaja is overloaded. Those who have no seats are standing along the aisle, holding on to the railing for support. At bus stops the bolekaja slows down to discharge and pick up more passengers, and then speeds up again. I find myself needing space and breeze, getting choked on a smell like that which wafts from a cow pen.

The woman I had stepped on causes a mild drama as the bolekaja draws close to the next bus stop. "Oloyun-po omo! Oloyun-po omo!" she yells several times in a loud voice, forcing the driver to fully stop for her to disembark.

"Oloshi!" the conductor shouts at the woman as she clambers down.

She rails back abuse in Yoruba.

The passengers laugh, but Beatrice does not, and I think it wise not to laugh, too. I don't know how she might see it. Besides, I didn't grasp a word of what transpired between the conductor and the woman, as I do not understand Yoruba.

"She lied that she had a baby tied to her back and was pregnant with another," Beatrice explains. "It is a simple trick that fat women who can't jump out use to force the drivers to stop."

I laugh, not because it is funny, but because I feel that Beatrice expects me to laugh. But then she frowns and looks away.

At each bus stop the conductor squeezes a note into the palms of touts to be allowed to pick up passengers; the touts with their menacing faces and bloodshot eyes, scowling and bellowing in their rough base voices as though they are the gatekeepers of Lagos. Sometimes the conductor tries to shortchange them. They end up exchanging hot words or even a few blows. Policemen standing at close intervals get their own share of the squeezed notes. Drivers drive against the traffic and scream swearwords at each other.

Lagos is madness raging like Harmattan fire.

Nine

WE ARRIVE AT A PLACE BEATRICE CALLS PALMGROVE, a quieter, saner area with clean streets and tall lampposts and fine cars cruising. We make our way along an avenue edged with trees. The sun has gone down and the streetlamps are on. They create soft shadows. I remember my father's words, *You are going to a place that's illuminated from heights.* Back home the poultry would be roosting about now. My mother's long shadow would darken our compound as she waits to make sure all her roosters and chickens are in.

"Evil bird," she would swear at a fowl that has gone feral, preferring to roost in treetops. "You are nothing to me but waste after losing whatever little flesh you had to flight."

She'd ask my siblings to go after the fowl. Once they caught it, she'd take it to Ogige market and sell it for nothing because it had lost its weight and value. Alternatively, she'd slaughter it and cook her favourite ogbono soup with its meat, suck her fingers with a loud smack, and beat off flies with a straw fan while relaxing under the umbrella tree in the middle of our compound. My father always gets the gizzard because he is the man of the house.

We stop in front of a large, beautiful house and ring a bell beside a huge black gate. Tall plants with drooping leaves line the walls of the gate, drawing level with the fence, some growing even taller.

"They look like Wonder masquerades." I draw Beatrice's attention to the plants.

She smiles. Tightly. At least I have been able to make her laugh even if in a stifled way. "They are mast trees, village boy," she says.

A tall, gawky man in a shabby grey caftan and an embroidered cap opens the gate for us.

"Sanu kyakkyawar mace." He shows a set of brown teeth on a ruined face to Beatrice in greeting as we walk into the compound.

The ground is shining like the breakable plates Beatrice eats with in her house back in the village. I walk on my toes so as not to stain the ground with my rubber shoes. Beatrice is walking ahead with measured steps, her hips swinging right then left. I can feel the gawky gateman's eyes following her. Trees with blossoms like bulbs that I would like to pluck and suck on are bordering the long paved drive. I want to ask Beatrice the name of the trees, but then I change my mind.

"They are cherry trees," Ejiro will later tell me, in a voice that lets me know how "bush" he thinks I am.

The balcony is shaped like a new moon. It hangs dangerously as if it might crash down anytime on the fine motorcars parked in the garage below it. A large tomb glitters white under the floodlights before we get swallowed up in the house, a tinkling sensation washing over me. A dog begins to bark, though I can't see it, so loudly the ground seems to shake as we climb the stairs. I can hear the hard, pointed heels of Beatrice's shoes echoing through the house *koi koi koi*.

A boy my age opens the door and greets Beatrice familiarly. I feel him sizing me up as he closes the door behind us.

I don't know why, but I have the feeling that he doesn't like me. We enter a big, shining room where a large fair-skinned woman is seated. She is half-dressed. As we enter, she hitches her wrappa up around her chest to cover herself with her left hand, the right one holding a mobile phone to her ear. She talks loudly into the mobile phone as she waves us over to one of the deep green cushions.

Beatrice walks into an open doorway while the woman is still talking. She returns with two soft drinks, keeps one for herself, and places the other on the glass table before me. While I drink the cold Coke, I look around the wide, voluptuous room. My feet rest on a thick milk-white carpet. The seats are even bigger and softer than the ones in Beatrice's house back home. Every other piece of furniture or electronic device, from table to shelf to curtains to television set, is twice the size of those in her house in the village.

The family photos catch my eye. A boy and a girl look down at me from pictures taken at different times in their lives, starting from their first birthdays to when they have become adolescents who wear tight clothes and shining makeup. The boy, older, has thin eyebrows and brown eyes like his mother. Their father appears in some of the photos, a thick-looking man in heavily starched clothes. In one of the photos taken at a much earlier time in their lives, he is standing shoulder to shoulder with the woman, who looks slender and very pretty in a brown wig and two rows of red beads.

"Sorry, Beatrice o jare," the woman says as she ends the call, laughing more than I have ever heard anyone laugh, her body shaking like cassava paste, her eyes all over me. "That boy can talk forever if I allow him, my son in America. He's such a mummy's boy and never gets off the phone."

Beatrice laughs, too, her eyes full of admiration for the woman.

"Is he the boy, Beatrice?" She pronounces the name *Bee-triss*.

Back home the villagers pronounce her name *B-e-e-a-trice*. Most villagers call her *Be-e-a-tie*. I squirm each time I catch the woman's stare.

"Yes, Mummy," Beatrice says.

In the big television set standing at the head of the room, two boxers bathed in their own sweat—one in blue trunks and the other in red trunks—are hammering each other. The one in the red trunks already has a ruined face. His left eye is closed, the skin covering the eye swollen and shiny, folded into each other like thick lips.

"What is your name?" the woman says to me.

I am startled. "Dimkpa Gbaghalu," I manage to say.

"Olodumare!" she cries. "Dim . . . what?"

I repeat the name more slowly.

"I will call you Dim and forget the other name that sounds like a thunderbolt." She waves away her frustration.

Beatrice chuckles.

The woman rises and turns, her eyes lingering on the fighters. She is heavier at the hips, the skin of her back paler than the rest of her body, her wrappa slack behind, showing deep furrows that ridge her hips. While she is in the other room, Beatrice tells me to be a good and dedicated houseboy. Like a stubborn creditor who refuses to go away until he is settled, she reminds me of the poverty waiting at home.

The woman returns with a wad of crisp banknotes and sinks back into her seat. "Your boy is in safe hands." She hands the money to Beatrice and throws me another brown eye.

"Thank you, Mummy." Beatrice stuffs the money into her jeans, hissing her drink down. Watching her, I have a feeling of being sold. "Dimkpa. I will be coming to see you from time to time," she says to me, and begins to walk out of the room, the house resounding with the *koi koi koi* of her heels hitting the staircase.

The boxers are still battling it out inside the television. A hollow feeling washes over me with Beatrice suddenly gone. I stare at the boxers, the rawness of the brutality, my feeling of hollowness turning into cold fear. My skin is pricked with goose pimples. It is obvious the one in the blue trunks is headed for a win. He is giving his opponent the beating of his life. The woman of the house is engrossed in the match now. She is all taken up, body and soul, her eyes alight and glistening with pleasure. I find this strange. Most women I know in my village dread violence. My mother cannot stand the sight of such a bloody fight. She once passed out in the heat of a fight between me and Machebe.

The boy who opened the door for us, who I will later learn is called Ejiro, enters, looking grumpy. He beckons to me to follow him, leads me into a room, and says it is mine. In the room there is a big rainbow-striped bed, a table and a chair, milk-white walls and windowsills. Everything is calm. I am still standing in the centre of the room long after he has left. It seems like a dream.

Later there are footsteps along the corridor. The door opens a crack to reveal the boy's meagre face again.

"Go to the dining room for your food," he says in a cold voice.

The door bangs closed, giving me a big start. I listen to his footfalls as he retreats. I can feel his irritation burning the soles of his feet. I imagine it catching fire, like petrol from a match flame, and the whole house going up in flames. I climb out of bed after the footfalls have faded and walk quietly to the empty dining room, where eba and soup are waiting on breakable plates. The dining table is made of beautiful square-patterned tiles in white and black, brown and grey. My image is reflected on its shining surface. I uncover the plates. The eba is the colour of the tall plants I saw outside in the garden. The egusi soup is tasty, filled with dried fish and stockfish, and other little things that keep my mouth busy. There is also a big dish of chicken. It is a king's dinner.

I finish the whole eba with a big belch, convinced I have never eaten anything so tasty, not even during Egba Nwachukwu or Ogonna festival, when women visit their birthplace with their children, bringing food prepared with washed hands. My mother would take us to her village, Amadim. My grand-father was an old man with shriveled arms and stiff long hairs pointing out of his nostrils like bristles. He would allow us a few sips of his palm wine. My grandmother was the kind-est and gentlest woman ever, light-skinned and delicate. She would fight to protect us from bullies with all her energy. They are both gone now, my grandfather with his height and wis-dom and hair sticking out of his nostrils, and my grandmother with her light skin and goiter.

I retreat into my room to lie on my bed and ponder what I consider my good fortune. I feel the bed's softness on my back and inhale its clean smell. My village will be asleep by this time of the night. Sometimes the voice of a drunken man will rise above the darkness as he staggers on his way home. If there is a moon, families will sit outside in their compounds and enjoy stories after dinner. Ogbom will sit alone chanting dirges in front of her hut. I don't like listening to her. Sometimes I keep her company, but her voice makes me sad, her lamentations piercing me like an arrow. A cock wakes me up every morning with its long crow.

I go to sleep without the background music of chirping crickets and droning cicadas, and wake up early the next morning to the sound of motorway traffic, vigorous clapping, and a voice chanting a slow dirge from a microphone. I didn't know that Lagos people also chant dirges, but it seems Lagos has no cockcrows. When I look through the window, I see men in long garments crossing the road into a round white house with a dome shaped like the black chieftaincy cap titled men wear in my village. The voice is coming from a big horn speaker on the roof of the house, but the clapping seems to be coming from neighbours praying in their flats.

From my window, the tomb shines. It is made of white marble, the same type as the floor of Beatrice's sitting room in her house in the village. The top of the tomb is rimmed with gold. It looks more beautiful in daylight. I climb out of bed and rummage through the wardrobe. There are clothes and shoes. There are a few books, too. They must belong to the houseboy who lived here before me, I think. I pick up one of the books, drawn to its unusual title, *Black Moses*, wondering if the former houseboy had read them, intrigued that a houseboy could read novels.

I return the book and go downstairs to take a closer look at the tomb, sidling close to the wall and stepping lightly so as not to attract attention. The house is so quiet that I wonder if I am the only one awake. I stop beside the tomb and try to read the name engraved on it, but I am only able to understand the year the occupant was born, which was 1934, and the year he died, 1999. The tomb must have cost a lot of money, I muse. I imagine that my aunt Okike is the one lying inside the grave, with her name written on it, and the tomb is lying in my father's compound.

I walk on towards the swimming pool, passing the garden, the two connected by well-trimmed hedgerows. The garden is blazing with rose, hibiscus, and sunflower bushes. They look like the ones from my primary school science textbook. I don't know the names of the rest of the flowers, but they are very beautiful, too. The garden is a feast of colours. Three cars are parked in the garage. I am not able to read their names, but they are coloured black, ash, and red. The name of my new madam is Bola Folashade, but I eventually learn that everyone calls her Mummy. I have a hard time pronouncing her name. I also learn that she is widowed and sits on a large estate left to her by her husband, the man lying in the marble tomb. She has a married daughter who lives overseas. Her son lives in America. She lives and cooks her meals all by herself, and maintains two male live-in servants about my age, and an older gatekeeper. She swims in the pool, naps on the lawn, watches men fight on TV, and sometimes goes for a drive. She has a paid gardener who comes weekly to tend to her flowers. The gleam that I saw in her eyes as she watched the boxers and the sheer brutality of the fight leaves a sinking feeling in the pit of my stomach.

Ten

BEATRICE WAS RIGHT. A TIN BOX HAS NO PLACE HERE, I think to myself.

Although I see no moon from my window, the night outside the mansion is shinier than a night of full moon in my village. This place has its own peculiarities, like jet planes screaming overhead, and constant motorway traffic buzzing like bees when they travel in swarms over my father's house towards the village backwoods and hills. Eke and I'd climb trees to harvest their honey in a clay pot. This noise of the jet planes flying past almost drives me out of my mind. In my village, I'd see an airplane only once in a while. As children, the distant drone in the sky would draw us outside. We'd gaze up at the tiny winged steel, appearing and disappearing in the far-flung clouds with a low, dull sound. We would wave at it, and appeal to its occupants to hurl down gifts to us. Here, the airplanes fly very low, as if they might crash into the tall buildings, the whole house reverberating like a continuous rumble of thunder.

At times the electricity goes off and plunges the mansion into darkness. Lagos will suddenly become quiet and mysterious. The woman I now call Mummy is not used to such troubled quietness, I can tell. It is like forcing a restless child to go to sleep against its will. Mummy's big, fierce dog, named Ogidan, a beast she lets loose at night, will bark. Then the generator will start with deep breaths like a giant waking up from a slumber, opening its shiny inhuman eyes, its breathing normalizing in a steady hum.

Back home I heard stories of what happens to village boys who come to cities to work as houseboys to rich families. They are treated like garbage. They take care of snot-nosed children and deal with their soiled diapers and stagnant hosts of buzzing flies. They spend the whole day cleaning the house, washing dishes, and laundering heaps of clothes and bed linens. And then they get slapped and kicked for dozing off while waiting for the family to finish a late-night movie. One houseboy ran back to our village with a deep burn on his back. His employer had pressed a hot iron into his flesh as punishment for some offense. But I have a different job description. There are no children to take care of here. The garbage collector comes from time to time to clear the trash, and the launderer comes for Mummy's clothes. Two weeks have gone by, and all we do, the other houseboy, Ejiro, and I, is clean the house and keep the garbage in the trash by the gate for the dustman. I should be happy living in the mansion and having very little work to do, but I keep fighting off a sense of foreboding. An adage my father often says hangs over me: "'Take it all' is never a gift."

First thing every morning, Ejiro goes to the gym to lift weights. Then he swims in the pool. "It's a ritual in this house," Mummy says, insisting I, too, cultivate the habit of training. So now I lift weights. I wake up in the morning, train at the gym, take a swim, and eat a breakfast of tea, fried eggs, and bread; a lunch of jollof rice and chicken; and eba and egusi soup for dinner. They are my favourites. I didn't eat eggs in the village unless I stole them. The neighbours' poultry some-times strayed into our territory to lay eggs, which I'd quickly grab and fry in secret. But now I have tea in the morning, eat rice in the afternoon, and then eba at night, and the next day I might go for a different menu from the assortment in the freezer. Mummy is a great cook. She likes to cook her own meals. It's a hobby for her. We only assist her in the kitchen. She sometimes spends a whole day making a variety of dishes. She then keeps them in the deep freezer from which we help ourselves.

With so little to do, I sometimes spend the afternoon watching cars cruising along the streets from my window. My eyes linger on the tomb lying beneath my window in its rich glitter of white and gold. I sit on it sometimes, close my eyes, and rub my hand over the smooth, cool surface of the marble slab, thinking of Okike. And then I come inside, lie on my bed, and feel its softness on my back. I inhale the room's clean smell with my eyes closed, pondering if the sit-at-home order has gained full momentum in my village. There is silence about it here; it seems like Biafra has no voice in Lagos. I am already missing the gamblers. Every afternoon I see Patty Onah and Oluoha in my mind locked in a fierce game of draughts. But mostly I miss Eke, and my family, and our moonlit meals. I wonder what my absence means to them. It might bring my mother relief, one mouth less to feed.

It is just the three of us in the mansion: Mummy, Ejiro, and me, not counting Abdul, the gateman, who sleeps in the small house built into the wall of the fence. The mansion is large, but Mummy is full of energy. Full of vitality. She fills up the emptiness with her loud Afrojuju music. Her friends visit now and again, women as large and energetic as her, noisy women who spend the whole day dancing, drinking, and shrieking. Maybe they are the ones she visits when she drives out in big lace clothes and high-rising headgear. From what I have seen so far, life in my village is hell. The hardest I work here is cleaning the house and helping Mummy in the kitchen. I even have access to the TV. The only time I watched TV in my village was when I could steal a glance through a neighbour's window. But after a few weeks, I start to wonder about my wages. I want to know what I am working for. Beatrice didn't tell me how much I would be paid as a houseboy. I want to know how long it is going to take me to gather enough savings to help my family out of poverty and build a tomb for Okike. I may even start a business of my own if I make enough. I don't know how to ask Mummy such a thing, so I decide to get it out of Ejiro.

"You are still on probation," he says with clenched teeth. "You will be paid well if you do well."

I want to know how long my apprenticeship will last, and what will happen if I don't do well, but he is gone even before I finish thinking. Ejiro is a pillar of wood. That is how best I can describe him. Nothing moves him. I am certain he doesn't like me. He never did from our first eye contact. I can see his dislike for me in every detail of his attitude towards me. On one of my first days at the mansion, I had remembered the rosary my mother had given me, fished it out of my bag, and pondered aloud about going to church.

"Church." Ejiro laughed until I started to feel stupid. "There's no talk of church in this house. It's a taboo. Mummy is Muslim. You are allowed only to be Muslim as long as you are in the mansion."

I told him that my mother would have a heart attack if I

switched from Christianity to Islam, the religion of the Hausa and Fulani. I had never even met a Muslim in my village.

"Your mother's opinion is not wanted here," Ejiro said, and stamped out, leaving me with that cold sense of trepidation.

Eleven

EKE MATERIALIZES IN THE MANSION LIKE A NEW MOON
in the sky. I look at him with big watermelon eyes as he approaches. He looks well, and so spruce I don't need anyone to
tell me he is now a senior student at the high school. I reach
him in one breath, shooting forward like a seed out of an oil
bean pod, but I end up catching the air as I try to hold him.
The light from the lamp beside my bed dazzles my eyes. I can't
sleep without a light. I open the window to allow the new day
to stream in and bring me back to the mansion, away from my
sojourn with Eke. I hiss. I am missing his friendship. I climb
out of bed, thinking about the dream as I brush my teeth and
change into my gym outfit, one of a set I found in my new
room. Ejiro says I can use anything I find there.

He is already in the gym when I arrive, working on his
forearms. The mansion gym has everything: pully bar, ab
roller, kettlebell, battle rope, deep stand, and other equipment
the names of which I find it hard to memorize. I am concen-
trating on my triceps. After more than a month of training I
can feel my biceps heavy and bulging even though I still look
the same in the mirror. I nearly gave up at the early stage. It
was as if my stomach was full of countless needles.

"Who lived in that room before me?" I try to strike up a
conversation with Ejiro while we are training.

He is doing a towel pull-up. He lowers himself down

slowly, his wiry body bathed in sweat. Throwing the towel around his shoulders, he walks away without a word.

It is maddening not to have anyone to talk to in the mansion, with Mummy busy entertaining her glamorous friends, Ejiro in his sulky mood, and Abdul determined to hate my Igbo guts. Ejiro hardly says a word to me unless he can't help it. His surly, unapproachable manner makes it impossible for me to dig into his background. But I know he is an Urhobo boy. I know he will wrong me many times to tempt me to smash his head with a bottle. I can sense it. We live like enemies. When I smile at him he answers with a glare. When I greet him in the morning he replies with a swearword. When we bump into each other on the doorway he steps on my toes. The way we are going, we could turn ourselves into those boxers fighting in Mummy's TV, but he will be the battered one in the red trunks, I assure myself.

After working out, I move to the pool to swim. Ejiro has already finished. He must be eating breakfast, scowling at the empty dining room seats. I remember how Eke and I swam in the Adada River, in the water looking cyan with algae. The mansion pool is shaped like a kidney, a stainless blue in the glorious midmorning sun, with the sky reflected in the water. I climb into the water instead of diving in, feeling like a shrew with a bad smell hanging on it, following it everywhere it goes. I spend a lot time in the water trying to wash off the bad smell.

After breakfast, I pick up *Black Moses*, deciding to kill time with the novel in the absence of work to do. I was a good reader at primary school, one of the best in my class. The first

name of the author of *Black Moses* is Alain, which I read with
ease, but the surname gets stuck like fish bone in my throat. It
is one of those names that has three or more consonants and
vowels following one another in a confusing syllable. I open
the book and read the first sentence, feeling its softness, its
ease and spirit. The words are ordinary, but they are full of
power. But the names of the characters are so long, it seems
one name can fill an entire paragraph. Somehow it makes the
book even harder, but more hilarious.

Mummy is in the big sitting room watching the BBC
News with interest when I finally come out. She is cursing
and swearing in Yoruba. I know she is swearing by the tone
and force of her voice. I don't quite follow the energetic, nasal
voice of the olive-skinned, long-haired BBC newscaster, but I
am able to make out that the MASSOB leader, a man named
Ralph Uwazurike, has been arrested in connection with the
planned sit-at-home only a few days away. He has been detained and will be charged. Some people are shown on TV
protesting on the streets of Lagos.

"Come here, Dim, Omo Ibo ajeokutamamuomi." Mummy
beckons to me, calling me the derogatory name in Yoruba
for someone from my tribe. She has worked herself to frenzy.
"Come and see your people protesting."

I watch the protesters as they are tear-gassed and battered
with batons and gun barrels.

"See how the police are beating them like dogs just because they want to go?" Mummy was furious. "Why should
they batter and brutalize anyone because they are protesting
and asking to be allowed to be on their own? Wo, Omo Ibo
ajeokutamamuomi. Do you know what I think? I think this
country should be divided. Our leaders are cursed. They are

thieves, selfish, and tribalistic; that's why things are not work-ing for us as a nation. I think the country should be divided into the three major ethnic groups. You Igbo people will go with your brother Ojukwu to Onitsha, we Yoruba will go with our Lagos, and the Hausa and Fulani will have their Kano."

I don't know what to say, so I linger in the room for as long as she rails, slipping out when I realize she has lost interest in me. I stroll to the tomb to sit and think about the things she said. They are not all that different from the arguments of the gamblers at Uwakwe's shopfront. I hadn't known that the Yoruba people have also lost confidence in a united country.

I hear about similar protests going on in major cities across Igboland in the following days. Women in Umuahia protest Uwazurike's detention half naked. The TV shows pictures of them as they storm the streets in only bras and shorts, fol-lowed by images of the police brutalizing and chasing the pro-testers, who are carrying placards and chanting the mantra "Enyi mba enyi."

I suspect from his recent attitude that Abdul has listened to news of the protest in Hausa on his transistor radio. Each time I take his meals to him he says sanu, thanking me, but when I turn my back, I hear him swearing, using strong Hausa words like *banza* and *nyamiri*, which are as contemptuous as *Omo Ibo ajeokutamamuomi*. I feel like talking to Ejiro about the protests. He is from Warri in the Delta, a territory the gamblers had said was mapped into the proposed Biafra nation. I choose a mo-ment when he seems to be in a light mood. He is even whistling one of his Urhobo songs.

"The police shouldn't have beaten those protesters like an-imals," I say to him.

He ignores me and continues whistling.

"They were not violent," I add.

"I don't care if their skulls were broken," he snaps. "I am not an Igbo boy."

I walk away, realizing how impossible it is to reason with him.

Twelve

I'VE BEEN LIVING AT THE MANSION FOR SIX WEEKS when, one afternoon, Mummy summons us out to the lawn, sits on a lounge chair in her nightdress, crosses her legs, and orders us to take off our clothes and fight only in our boxers. Confused, my eyes linger from Mummy to Ejiro, who is already tearing off his clothes.

"I asked you to strip and fight in your underwear," she snaps, her voice hostile, cruelty kindling like fire in her eyes.

Again I glance from her to Ejiro, who is almost down to his boxers already. Surely she couldn't mean what she has said. I remember the boxers on TV, and the rapture in her eyes.

Ejiro has finished undressing. He has a wiry, intimidating body. He takes a combat stance in his checkered green boxers, hands balled into fists, legs planted astride, face set.

"Stop staring." Mummy's voice startles me. "Go on. Take off your clothes and fight him."

I don't make a move; I only continue to stare in disbelief. Ejiro moves in suddenly and throws a punch, catching me on the jaw. His punch stings like hot wax. A pillar of darkness appears then vanishes. Mummy emerges from a galaxy of stars and dissolves again into the dark nothing of the lawn. Ejiro delivers another punch that explodes in my face, birthing millions of fireflies chasing one another.

"You better take off your stupid clothes and fight me or I am going to kill you." Ejiro's voice sounds faint and distant.

I cross my hands to stop the punches from falling on my face.

"Ohu ma!" He throws more punches.

The name hits me like a sledgehammer, but it is enough to set me off. I have never won a wrestling bout at Ote Nkwo festival back home. I enjoyed watching Eke, who would fight anyone he considered a fair match. He has won more matches than he has lost, whereas I have wrestled a few times and lost each one. So it surprises me how I react to Ejiro now as he rains his punches down. Spurred by the intense rage his insult provokes, more than the shock of hearing it from him, I suddenly dive low in between his legs and sweep him up like a crane that lifts weights up tall houses. Eke would do this to his opponents, and then he would throw them down, not too fiercely, but in such a way that their backs would touch the ground; that way he would win the matches. But now I want to smash Ejiro's back on the grassy lawn. I want to hurt him for calling me that name. But he is clever. He moves like a trained fighter, looping his left arm around my neck. We come down together, landing on the carpet of grass, his back down and my neck in the loop of his arm. Now that he has me, he tries to pin my legs to lock me in. If he succeeds, I could pass out, but I prove myself stronger than Ejiro could ever have thought. My unlikely new strength from working out every day and my capacity to endure pain from fights with Machebe keep both of us glued together in that jerking knot that (as I will find out later) fills Mummy with immeasurable pleasure. Her face, a glint in my fast-fading vision, is wreathed in a baleful smile, her cruel brown eyes glistening with sinister happiness.

•

I lie quietly in bed and mourn my defeat to Ejiro, his calling me "ohu ma," brooding over it and hating myself. I must have passed out. Mummy was still sitting in the lounge chair, all wrung out, when I regained myself and staggered to my feet. Dazed, I stared at her with bewildered eyes, my chin where I took Ejiro's uppercuts still burning as I retreated to my room. How is it possible, Ejiro knowing that phrase and everything about me within just a few weeks of my arrival?

Police sirens are screaming into the night, and Ogidan is barking. My mind is a complete blur. My body aches. My spirit craves a rematch. Ejiro enters suddenly without knocking. My breathing quickens at the sight of him, my hands balling into fists under the blanket. He walks in slowly and throws a wrap of crisp banknotes at me.

"Gift from Mummy. I got extra for winning, and for fighting in my boxers," he says curtly, and walks slowly out.

I stare at the money for a long time, and then I pick up the wrap and leaf through it, inhaling its brand-new scent. Confusion knots my face as I try to puzzle it out: the fight, and now the money, a lot of money. I have never in my whole life held such an amount of money. *Gift from Mummy*, Ejiro had said.

What is going on?

It is later spelt out to me in clear letters by Ejiro. When Mummy gets bored with watching boxing bouts on TV, she turns to her houseboys, forcing them to fight in her presence until they have no energy left in their bodies. "Mummy enjoys watching us," he says in his snotty manner. "I have stayed for the money. There is really nothing too hard about it. She pays well. I have a target, and I am fighting my way to it to take my family out of poverty. My parents are fishers in some polluted

Niger Delta creek, so wretched we can hardly feed because our land and water are poisoned by government-backed oil companies. You are worse off, the way I see you. I heard your aunt Beatrice telling Mummy about the wicked things the people in your village put your family through. It is up to you to decide whether to stay or be a coward and flee back to hunger and shame. Mummy will always find another boy."

Ejiro shocks me with his disclosure. Is that why he avoids me, hates me? I want to know more about what he overheard. What exactly did Beatrice tell Mummy? What does she know about "ohu ma" that I do not know? But Ejiro has once again retreated into his shell. His audacity rankles in my mind. I would not have stayed. I would have left. I would have resigned at once and gone far away from this fight-house. This evil house. But now I will do no such thing. I must have my revenge on Ejiro. I am not leaving until the scores are even again, until I have saved enough money to bring home. I don't want to return to my village as poor as I left it. If I have earned so much from just one fight, surely I will be able to save a capital. And then I will resign, return to my town, build Okike's tomb, and start a business. Maybe I'll sell coffins on Aku Road or even football boots in Ogige market.

In the meantime, I begin to plot my revenge. I hope that Mummy will ask us to fight again soon. But if she doesn't, I resolve to provoke Ejiro into another fight. He seems to be enjoying his victory. Since the fight, he has relaxed his hostility towards me a little. He is not exactly friendly, but he smiles at me, tightly, and we even manage to have a chat; he tells me about some things I didn't know, like the beautiful cherry trees outside.

"They are ornamental trees," he says sarcastically, his gaze meeting and locking with mine briefly. "They don't grow in a bush village."

Before the fight I had sought his eyes, his friendship, but the best I had got was his unfocused stare passing over me without interest.

"You knew about the fighting before you came?"

He laughs, dryly, skin taut against a square, bony face with a cleft chin. "I only knew about a rich woman who needed a houseboy."

I give him an open-mouthed stare.

"What is your fascination with graves? I've seen how you romance that tomb as if the man inside is your papa," he says, his voice like the laughing calls of the bush baby inhabiting my village backwoods.

"I am going to use the money I am paid here to build a tomb for my aunt," I say. "Please, Ejiro, when you heard Beatrice and Mummy talk about 'ohu ma,' what exactly . . ."

He doesn't wait for me to finish; he just walks out laughing, his laughter growing hysterical, like a demon.

Thirteen

THE DAYS DRAG ON. NOTHING HAPPENS BESIDES THE normal rhythm of life in the mansion: Mummy cooking elaborate meals, swimming half naked in the pool, sunbathing on the lawn, dashing out and in again in big cars, and throwing parties for big-bottomed, loud-laughing women to whom we serve food supplied by hired caterers. Once in a while, the thought of abandoning the job springs to the surface of my mind, but the money, the food, and my lust for revenge hold me back. I throw more energy into training for my next fight.

I have been thinking of Beatrice. I have not set eyes on her since the day she left me cold in the mansion and went away with a wad of crisp banknotes and a phony promise to come check up on me. It's been over two months. I wonder if she knew about the fights all along. Was the money she collected a price on my head? Will she ever come back to see how I am doing?

Less than two weeks after the first fight, Ejiro and I battle again. The match happens unexpectedly, as suddenly as the first time, with Mummy inviting us out to the lawn. I have been waiting for this. I rip off my clothes straightaway. Ejiro is quick to react, to throw off his clothes, too. The fury in me is so strong that I have no time to spar with him, no time to build up energy for the fight or give tactics a thought. I spring at him like a wounded leopard, throwing a wild swinging punch. It is a miscalculated move provoked by my rage and my quest for revenge. Ejiro ducks to avoid the punch and it sends me pirouetting. Using my momentum, he lifts me up effortlessly, then slams me down on the tuft. The impact leaves me stunned. Trapping my head in the crook of his arm and wrapping his legs around my midriff, he tightens his grip until I am gasping for air and the world goes dark.

I wince with pain as I climb out of bed, my body aching all over, as though I have been sledgehammered. I open the window. Sunlight floods the room. I remember stumbling back after the fight. I don't know for how long I have slept. The wall clock says it is 4:30 p.m. I fought Ejiro around midmorning. I can see Mummy at the pool through the window. She is reclining in the lounge chair in a yellow swimsuit. She watches Ejiro in the gym as he works on his muscles: dark, sweaty muscles looking menacing in the sun. How I dread those wiry muscles now. I am never going to give Ejiro the chance to put them to use against me again. I know he is training for our next fight, because the more we fight for Mummy, the more money she gives us, and he gets the larger pay for winning. When I close my eyes, all I see is Ejiro and myself battering each other: exchanging punches, wrestling and crashing into cushions. I see us locked in a mortal combat, rolling on the grass, scratching and biting, squeezing each other's balls, and groaning with pain while Mummy watches with a sinister smile, twisting like a python around its prey.

What does she gain from it?

I sit on the bed and consider my options. Ejiro is a monster. Money and fighting are the only two things that seem to matter to him. Again I picture us going at each other, not for sport, but for pride, for vengeance. I see the fight getting violent, even bloody and vindictive, weapons leaping into use, flesh tearing, bones cracking, heads being smashed. I might need money badly to pull my family out of poverty, but my father would say, "Only a tree waits when death looms, but a human being will flee for his life." My father's words, ringing in my head, help me to make up my mind. I begin to pack my things. I came to this house because I wanted to work as a houseboy, and to help my family—not to fight. I cannot stand to see myself fighting for money again. My loathing of Ejiro will never lead to anything good. I can feel it gathering intensity so quickly that I can see how it all will end.

I consider taking the red suede shoes I found in the wardrobe with me as I pack to leave; that's how I discover the diary, small and tucked into one of the shoes. Curious, I open it. Its owner had squiggled in sections in the book. Each section has a date suffixed to it. The word *fight* recurs. And then I see the word *wounded* in the section dated July 2. It appears also in the next section, followed by the word *sick*, dated July 4, and *very sick* two days after. This is the last entry. I lower myself onto the bed and flip the pages of the diary back to the first section. The first entry is dated September 12, although the year is not indicated. The next entry is dated October 2, with the following entries coming in intervals of two weeks, with slight variations except the last three. I ponder the last three entries, the closeness of the dates, and the recurring words. Even the writing looks pained. My heart stops beating. A sudden feeling of horror stabs me in the chest.

I pick up my bag and peep through the window again. In the sunlight, the pool water is a sparkling blue and the hibiscus blossoms are a startling peach, brighter and more beautiful than my primary school science textbook could ever have depicted them. I hesitate as doubts invade my mind once more. One doesn't always have the chance to live in such beautiful surroundings, but one needs to be alive to enjoy such things. I have tried my best to make it work. I like it here. That is why I have lingered and endured with the hope that Mummy might see that I am not a fighter like Ejiro and use me as just a houseboy, that she might look for another fight-loving boy to replace me.

I sneak out of the room. Abdul is loitering outside. I completely forgot about him in planning my escape. I duck behind a row of flowers lining the veranda. I watch as he lounges around the gate in that hideous caftan that stops below his knees, exposing his stick legs. A cigarette protrudes from his lips. There is something grim about him. It suddenly occurs to me that since coming to live here I have not seen Abdul leave his post. He never goes out. The farthest he moves from his gate is to the neighbouring gate to buy cigarettes from a fellow Hausa gateman. I wonder what he knows about the fighting houseboys. Is he part of some crazy arrangement?

After hours waiting for him to leave his post with no luck, I return to my room, drop down on my bed, and doze off. I open my eyes to a knock on the door as Ejiro walks in. I sit up quickly, wary and watchful. He stops in the middle of the room, frowning, his eyes lingering on the bag lying at my feet.

"What do you want?" I snarl at him.

"I want to talk to you about something," he says, coming to sit on the bed.

"You have never wanted a conversation with me."

"I wanted to say there's no gain without pain," he says. "You will get used to it."

I move away from him, angered even more by the smirk on his face. The fool! Whoever gets used to pain? I ignore him. I will not dignify his idiotic comment with a reply.

"I don't like Hausa gatemen." His voice assumes a serious tone. "I hate them because they drink ogogoro like water. And they are fond of fighting when they get drunk. They enjoy sticking their daggers into other men. Their women, too; they will pull at each other's hair until braids come off the scalp with flesh and blood."

I am lost.

"I don't know why Mummy decided to employ Abdul," he continues. "I don't like him for anything. He has a ruinous face and rotten teeth. His legs are like stalks of dry grass, and he won't let you out of that gate unless Mummy says so. But that's not the main reason why I don't like him. He hates anyone from the east because of the civil war. Because of Biafra. He cuts them at the slightest provocation. Have you seen him cleaning his dagger? Have you noticed how the blade shines with a luster whenever he cleans it?"

It is beginning to make sense.

Ejiro pats my shoulder and walks towards the door. "I keep out of his way. Because I don't want to get cut."

He walks out, his shuffling feet fading into the emphatic silence of the house.

I remember my father speaking about Aguiyi Ironsi: *They plotted a countercoup and brutally killed him. They tied him to a Land Rover and callously dragged him along the road until he died. They didn't stop there, though; they massacred Igbo people living in the north . . .*

Hatred, it seems, is our heritage. The message from Ejiro is clear. I undress, kicking my shoes off onto the floor and flinging my shirt to the end of the bed. I lie down and ponder the situation. Ejiro knows I had planned to escape. He will tell Mummy, if he hasn't already. Mummy will alert Abdul, who will make my escape impossible.

It appears I am trapped here forever. I moan.

Fourteen

MUMMY SUMMONS US TO FIGHT AGAIN AND AGAIN. SHE does this anytime boredom weighs heavily on her wide shoulders and hunger for excitement lines the rims of her eyes. On one occasion she summons us to the garden, where she is drinking with her friends. We are asked to fight for the three of them, each of whom is nursing a glass of wine and swaying to Afrojuju music blaring from an MP3 player, laughing and watching us beat each other without mercy. I often watch her with pity from my window or other cryptic angles. I am struck by her secret helplessness, her misery. She is a woman who has everything that life could offer yet lives in bondage. A prisoner of her own habits. I may be a captive in her house, but, hopefully one day, I will walk through that gate free; I only need to watch Abdul long and hard enough.

But the days flip into weeks, and the weeks roll into months and nose towards the end of the year. I have a pile of money in the wardrobe after many fights. I manage to win one. I am able to maneuver Ejiro into a lock that leaves him farting and gasping for his life. But I come out of the fight with a twisted arm. I savour my first big win with a period of convalescence reading *Black Moses*, struggling to make meanings out of unfamiliar words and sentences. I fall in love with the story after I find out that it is about a revolution, about conflict and tension between northerners and southerners in the Republic of Congo. It reminds me of our Biafra story. I come across a curious word, *imperialism*, which I first heard from the griz-zled little man at Uwakwe's shopfront. In one of their debates, he said that the colonial masters had preferred to hand over power to a northerner because they didn't want the southern-ers, and especially the easterners, whom they thought bright enough to recognize their suspicious intention of continuing to take advantage of their former colony. Eke and I had be-come so excited about the word *imperialistic* that we resolved to go to university to learn more words like it.

I also fall in love with the character Moses even though his surname is a whole paragraph that I have to skip after almost chewing my tongue trying to pronounce *Tokumisa Nzambe po Mose yamoyindo abotami namboka ya Bakoko*. I probably like him because he reminds me of my brother Machebe while I see something of myself in the character of his friend Bonaven-ture, a weak, cringy, cowardly boy who dreams bad dreams all the time of people dying. He is paranoid, hates his name, and depends on others to fight for him.

After I finish *Black Moses*, I start to read the second novel I find in the wardrobe, *The Catcher in the Rye* by J. D. Salinger. I quickly warm to the story, picking up the book whenever I find myself in a bad mood to amuse myself. He is so hilari-ous, the protagonist Holden Caulfield, so confused and disil-lusioned. I don't think I am half as mischievous as him, and even if I was, who could blame me? Anybody would do the same in my position.

I'm at the part of the novel where Holden goes home. Where he gets cold outside and sneaks in. He inspires me. I know my family will be unhappy with the way things have turned out in Lagos. Machebe will be mad at me, the same way Holden's sis-ter, Phoebe, snubs him, but I can always start all over again, just as Holden plans to apply himself at his next school. So I walk up to Mummy in the back garden, where she is eating apples and nodding to Afrojuju music from her MP3 player.

"I want to leave, Ma," I say.

She takes a bite at the apple. "Leave? To where?"

"I want to go home."

She bursts into laughter, her shoulders shaking, her mouth full and buttery, and then she stops laughing. "Why do you want to go home?"

"I can't fight anymore. Ejiro says you can get another boy who can."

She laughs again. "Yes, he is right. I can get another boy at the snap of my finger. But I pay you well, don't I?"

"I don't want the money. You can have all the money you have given me. I haven't spent any of it."

"Don't be a coward." She swallows neat, smacks her lips. "Ejiro is a boy like you. Don't let yourself be intimidated! You'd be a fool to abandon a home like this for the poverty of your village. I know your family needs the money."

"I would rather be poor than die fighting," I insist.

She stares at me long and hard. "Okay. Go, if that's what you want. I am not stopping you, but I will not be held responsible for whatever happens to you at that gate."

She turns her back on me and resumes eating her apples and nodding to her music as I walk away crestfallen. Abdul's ruinous face appears and vanishes again in my dew-eyed vision, his stinking brown teeth bared in scorn.

I try a hunger strike. I figure she will let me go if she realizes I might starve to death. I go to bed hungry yet determined, but then I wake up in the middle of the night with an ache in my stomach. It is so acute it drives sleep far away from my eyes. I sit up the rest of the night listening to the choir of worms in my stomach. In the morning, I hide behind the dining room door and swallow my spit as Ejiro eats a breakfast of scrambled eggs, in that surly manner of his. Later, the smell of lunch sets my whole body on fire. I can't take it anymore, feeling I might go mad if I don't eat, so I rush into the kitchen and polish off a large plateful of rice and chicken.

I sit on my bed in my room and revise my escape plan. I can see Abdul from my window beyond thick ixora hedges. He is holding his transistor radio to his right ear and nodding to some flute-flavoured Hausa song. Every morning, he sits there by the gate and cleans his teeth with a long chewing stick. And then he smokes, and listens to his radio, his mouth moving furtively with kola nut. He says "Sanu Nyammiri" and scowls at my back if it is my turn to take breakfast to him. After eating, he smokes again and again. Sometimes he naps on the bench. But he is restless in his sleep, scratching and yawning, swatting at flies and waking at the littlest noise.

He spends the rest of the day in more or less the same way: eating, smoking, and napping lightly, so escape during the daytime is out of the question. I explore the nighttime option. The surroundings are too bright, too well illuminated at night to go unnoticed. But then I remember the powerhouse. A young mechanic comes once in a while to service the generator. There is a control switch on the side wall that, if turned off, disconnects the automatic changeover switch and renders the transfer of power to the generator impossible. There is a ladder always leaning on the wall of the powerhouse. Ejiro uses it if there are any minor repairs to the house that require a ladder. It's tall enough to take me to the top of the wall. With the alarm disconnected from the central control system, it will be easy for me to scale the barbed-wire fence in total darkness and land on the ixora hedge on the other side. But there is the dog to watch out for. I had completely forgotten Ogidan— aggressive, with a big black head, wide shoulders, and narrow hips. He is shaped like a lion. He has an ugly face and long overlapping ears. I don't want to think about his teeth. Ogidan may not recognize me in the shadows. What he is capable of doing to an intruder is better left to the imagination. It is too dangerous to try to scale the high fence. Even if I succeed in disabling the central control system, and in beating Ogidan, I will still face the risk of being shot by one of the neighbours. It seems that every landlord in the neighbourhood has a gun. Mummy has one, too. She fires warning shots into the night every now and again to deter robbers. I realize how impossible it is to get away from this place unless providence smiles at me. But then a sudden idea brings me to my knees.

Raising my hands high to the ceiling, I cry out to Okike, imploring her to take me out of this hell disguised as a mansion.

After a few moments, a woman walks into the room and offers me a white handkerchief. She walks out again into the corridor. I must have shed a few tears of frustration. There's something familiar about her floral-patterned lace dress. Her steps are light, almost immaterial. On her way out, she leans against the door frame and begins to slide down. Her body is racked by spasms, like that of an epileptic in the pangs of a seizure. She foams at the mouth. And then she stills. I stare on in shock as she rises to her feet again and smooths out her dress. And then she hurries down the corridor.

I wake in my bed. Rising, I walk to the door and peer down

the empty corridor. No trace of a woman in a lace dress with floral designs. I walk back into the room and sit on my bed. She was so real. Suddenly an idea leaps into my head: feigning epilepsy. I am up on my feet again and pacing the room. What if I pretend to have epilepsy to frighten Mummy? She might panic and get rid of me. I know how much epilepsy is dreaded. Someone in my class had it in primary school. Everyone avoided him because it is believed to be contagious, deadly, and without a cure. But I will have to practice how to fake a fit like the woman in my dream without hurting myself.

My arm has healed. Mummy gave me painkillers to aid my recovery. And Ejiro is too engrossed with training to care about what I am doing. I guess he is trying to come to terms with my victory in the last fight. The look I see in his face says, *Enjoy your victory while it lasts. I will make you eat lawn grass in our next bout.*

I start to practice a fake fall, standing at the centre of the big bed and letting myself down on the mattress the way I had seen my epileptic classmate drop in his many fits, clumsily at first, but more deftly after many rounds of rehearsals. And then I move the rehearsals to the floor of the room. I find the foaming at the mouth repulsive, but I have to do it to be convincing, letting drool ooze disgustingly down the corner of my mouth. After days of practice on the floor of my room, I perfect the skill of sliding to the floor and jerking spasmodically, saliva drooling down the corner of my mouth.

The opportunity to display my new talent arrives when Mummy calls for a glass of water at the lawn, where she is luxuriating in rich afternoon sunshine. The glass of water tumbles from her grip as I set the drama in motion, twirling then crashing suddenly. A small scream escapes her throat. The next minute, she is shouting Ejiro's name as if a big long snake has loomed into sight. Ejiro's frantic approach is heralded by the quick stamping of feet. I give them some minutes of melodrama before I slow the spasms, and then still. I open my eyes and notice they are watching from a distance. I sit up and wipe the saliva gushing out of my mouth.

"Are you telling me you have had epilepsy all this while you have lived in my house?" Mummy asks.

I nod a reply, feigning shame and fatigue.

A look of disgust leaps into her eyes. "Does anyone else have it in your family?"

"No. I got it in primary school. A boy in my class had it. He farted during one of his fits, and I caught it." I had also rehearsed the lie.

"Are you saying it's really contagious?" The wrinkled look of disgust turns to wide-eyed alarm.

"My teacher said it can be contracted if you breathe in the fart of a victim when he is having a fit."

With a wild flare of her hands, she asks, "Are you sure you did not fart just now when you were having the fit?"

"I don't know. Maybe."

She slumps into a seat. "Maybe?"

I bring myself to my feet and walk inside to wash myself and have a good laugh. Ejiro is waiting in my room when I return from the bathroom.

"You scared Mummy," Ejiro says. "But you did not fool me. I know you lied. You don't have epilepsy. I would have known long ago if you had it. You lied so Mummy will send you away. Deny it."

I stare at him, dumbfounded.

"Mummy may have believed you, but she doesn't let go easily, especially if a boy is strong and resilient. You are a strong boy. One of the toughest I have had to fight, which makes it more exciting for Mummy. She will not let you go just like that. She will bring a doctor to make sure you really have epilepsy. I have thought about telling Mummy that you lied to her, but I am not going to betray you." He pauses to savour the suspense he has created. "I want to help you even though I think you are a coward. If they divide this country into three, the Niger Delta will fall into Biafra, so we are . . . well, brothers. Mummy believes everything I tell her. I will tell her you really have the sickness if you give me the money you have saved."

Ejiro's proposal is a tsetse fly that settles on my scrotum. If I strike it, I will crush my testicles; if I let it be, it sucks my blood.

Obochi, a pretty maiden from Idu village, sets out in search of snails with two friends, not knowing it will be the unhappiest day of her life. Obochi enjoys snail meat, although her mother, Ijedi, despises it because it leaves a sour taste in her mouth, especially now that she is expecting a baby, and her father, Omenka, thinks that only gluttons eat the unclean, slimy meat of a snail. Obochi doesn't care how her parents feel about snail meat, doesn't care that her mother forbids her from using the house pot to cook her snails. All she cares about is combing the bush with friends on her free days in search of snails, and then cooking and enjoying the crunchy taste of the meat. Sometimes she returns with a good harvest, sometimes with little or nothing for her troubles. When the harvest is good she cooks and eats some of the snails, and then she sells the rest at the local market and saves the money. Today happens to be her worst harvest. The girls have been roaming the bushes with little to show for their efforts.

"Let's go home," Nnedi says, pouting with frustration. "I am tired."

"Me too." Obeta, fair-skinned, is flushed with exhaustion.

"Girls. Why don't we search a little longer?" Obochi says in a persuasive voice.

After a long, sweaty trek, her brown skin flushes a smooth, wet loam. Slender with coils of red and black beads around her waist, Obochi thinks herself very beautiful, breasts pointed like spears, a ripe and desirable maiden. Her friends are sweaty, too, and tired after hours of walking from one bush to another, peeping into damp corners and turning over fallen leaves for hidden snails. They are torn between going home and continuing the fruitless search in the hot sun. Obochi is in the mood for adventure, so when her friends turn and head back home, she merely giggles and continues her search. She walks on in the burning sun, resting in the shadows and moving on again until she arrives at the edge of a large forest. She has never come this far in search of snails before, passing the last village in her community and crossing the boundary into another. She contemplates the dark, grim forest, her sense of adventure feeding on the cries of shrews, the babbling of monkeys, and the chilling laughter of hyenas. A snail hunches its pointed brown shell at her as she tilts the first leaf. She reaches down and quickly picks it into her sack. She tilts more dead leaves and finds more snails. For every damp leaf she upturns with her stick, a fat snail is hidden beneath it; every tree has one stuck to it. A squeal starts in her throat, but she clasps her mouth to smother it as she grabs the snails with both hands, throwing them into the sack quickly until it fills up, and she has difficulty tying its mouth to keep the snails from spilling. She barely manages to lift the sack to her head as she begins to trek home, sweating and groaning under the weight of her incredible harvest. The snails are so many that she decides she will take the surplus to the market to sell.

By the next day, she is counting the coins she has saved from her harvests, which multiplied with yesterday's sales. Over and over again she counts, whistling with surprise at how much she has been able to save over the weeks, peeping outside to make sure her siblings are not watching her as she tucks the money out of sight somewhere in the wattle of the hut. If her brothers see her hiding the money, they will surely steal it from her.

"Nne dalu," she says to her mother as she sails outside to where Ijedi sits under a walnut tree in the small, shadowy compound

peeling cassava roots, her belly protruding out of her scrawny body.
"You are working too hard, Mother."

"Ke maka afia." Her mother's voice is thin and inaudible. "I
trust that market was good."

"Market will never be good with those middle-women blocking
us from selling directly to the white men." Obochi settles on a stool
and starts to wash the peeled white cassava roots into a pot of water.
The roots will be left in the large clay pot for a few days to ferment.

Ike, her mother's lastborn, a naked toddler, is busy wandering
the compound. He picks up a fallen leaf, walks to Ijedi, and stretches
his little hand towards her. Ijedi takes what he offers her and smiles
her thanks. Encouraged, Ike then scoops up some sand, walks back
dutifully, and empties the sand into Ijedi's palm. He then takes off
again in search of another gift, ignoring her protests.

"You should be thankful that the women are there to buy the
snails and take them to the white men in the city," her mother says.
"How many people in this community would eat snails, not to talk
of buying them?"

Obochi shrugs with despair. She is the second of six siblings: four
boys and two girls. When her mother was pregnant with Ike, Ob-
ochi had hoped her mother would have a girl. When she had Ike,
Obochi had been disappointed. While Ike is only a sweet baby now,
she hopes the child her mother is carrying in her womb is a girl
and not another brother, another rascally boy who will grow up
and use his strength for mischief rather than to help the family, and
who will attract endless complaints from neighbours whose trees are
robbed or whose children are fought.

"I wish you would have a girl to strike a balance, nne."

"I'd love to give you another sister." Ijedi's voice is conspirato-
rial. "But it's almost certain it's going to be a boy, the way the baby
is kicking at me."

Obochi's lips form a pout. But then she spies her father as he walks home wheeling a bicycle up the long approach to the compound in a shade of trees. He is returning from a long meeting of his kinsmen with a flushed face, one of the few men in the village who owns a bicycle. Ike waddles towards him. He gets himself lifted up onto the frame of the bicycle and rolled in.

"Nnam ukwu," Ijedi says. "What kind of a meeting would keep you out all day on an empty stomach?"

He apologizes. "Too many issues to be resolved among obstinate kinsmen."

Ike whines in protest as he is lifted off the bicycle, and then he breaks down in tears. It takes a coin gift from Obochi to silence him. Omenka leans the bicycle against the kitchen wall and walks into the house.

"Go and serve your father his food."

Obochi returns to continue the conversation with her mother after serving her father his meal as Ike comes back with yet another gift, the bicycle fuss receding with his short attention span. This time he picks on Obochi, whimpering to get her attention. She reaches out a distracted hand and collects the gift with a cold, crawling feeling in her palm. She looks down sharply and finds a baby chameleon swaying in her palm. With a cry she flings the reptile away.

"What on earth are you doing with a chameleon?" she scolds.

Startled by the harshness of her voice, Ike bursts into tears.

Ijedi hisses, says chameleons are a bad omen. At this stage in her pregnancy, all she does is hiss, snap, and scratch her hair. Her belly is almost touching the ground, growing out of her small-boned body like the bill of a pelican.

The chameleon disappears in the carpet of fallen dry leaves at once, blending into the surroundings—a rich, saturated tone of grey.

The next day, as Obochi settles down on a clump of dry grass to watch her father eat the food she has taken to him at the farm, her mind wanders again to the chameleon her brother had picked up, and her dream the night before in which her father was bitten by a snake.

"Esogbula." Omenka eats slowly, dunking each slice of yam into salted palm oil in a calabash vessel before taking a bite. "Dreams are nothing."

Obochi looks skeptical.

A few bites of the yam are enough for Omenka. In the evening, he will indulge himself a few shots of ekpetechi to release his knotted joints, to prepare his muscles for work the next day. Now and again he takes a long drink of water.

"I will be back." Obochi decides to go fetch firewood. "You have to finish the food, though," she says, her tone mandatory.

Omenka grins at her. "I will try."

She moves to the other side of the farm to gather firewood. A bunch of berries, brown and luscious, catches her eyes. She walks over and plucks them. They are something for Ike when he comes bounding towards her at home, shrieking his welcome. Her skin tingles as her fingers come in contact with the berries people call "ram testicles." She chuckles as she puts the berries away, giggling to herself, thinking that they look exactly like a boy's balls.

She walks back with a handful of firewood tucked into the crook of her arm. Her father has finished his meal, to her delight.

"Thank you for finishing it."

"It was a good, delicious meal," he says.

She turns pink in the face. She always feels excited when her father praises her cooking. She begins to pack the clay dishes into a raffia basket along with the firewood. She lifts the basket onto her head and begins to walk home.

Ijedi is sitting half naked in her accustomed position on a raffia mat under the walnut tree tearing her hair when Obochi returns from the farm. Obochi takes a stool and joins her.

"My father praised my cooking," she says, blushing.

"It means I taught you well." Ijedi rips at her hair.

Obochi moves her stool closer. She probes into her mother's hair with her fingers in search of lice. "You are tearing it to pieces."

"I feel like getting rid of the whole thing."

"It is badly infested." She plucks a louse, crushing it between her thumbnails. "I will have to treat it with faifai."

"You will have to wait for the baby to come first. I can't stand the smell of faifai."

Obochi can tell that her mother is almost due by her mood swings, her weight loss, her drooping eyelids, and the way she drags herself around the house almost naked. They make little conversations. Ijedi talks about the weather, complaining of the heat, and the long-awaited rain.

"I'd like to have the baby before the rains start. I don't want to leave the weeding of the farms entirely to you and your siblings—" She finishes her speech with a sharp wince as she snatches up her outstretched left leg with a suddenness that alarms Obochi.

"O kwa agwo," Obochi screams when she sees the snake getting away, a thin, green tendril slithering towards the garden.

Her siblings rush back home at the sound of her alarmed voice. Her voice also attracts some neighbours, mostly women, for the men are at the farm working.

"*Go bring Odo. Mother has been bitten by a snake!*" *she yells at her brother.* "*Tell him to bring his snakebite antidote right away. Hurry, and do not come back without him. Run!*"

The boy tears off.

"*Her water has broken,*" *observes an old woman.* "*Somebody should go fetch the midwife urgently.*"

Obochi dashes off.

Fifteen

ASKING DIRECTIONS ALONG THE WAY, I FINALLY AR-
rive at a bus station in the heart of Lagos. Thankfully, I still
have Machebe's money, which Ejiro never got to know about.
The streets are humming with traffic, car horns, and police
sirens serenading the vastness of the night, lively and illuminated. I walk to a yellow kiosk and ask a light-skinned girl
with lips painted bright red for a ticket to the east.

"You are lucky," she says, smiling at me. "You are buying
the last ticket."

I don't consider myself lucky, but I forgive her ignorance.
I pay for the ticket, sure she is the one in luck. I can see she
is relieved to be going home. She looks fatigued. The bus is
being loaded with travelling bags and sacks of goods. A long
yellow-and-green bus. Touts are making a lot of noise, and
people are shouting to be heard. It is getting colder. I walk to
a tea shop and order a dinner of tea and bread, watching as
the Hausaman shovels spoonfuls of Milo, powdered milk, and
granulated sugar into a plastic cup. He pours the tea into two
cups and passes the liquid between them a few times to cool
its hotness before passing the cup to me. The tea has a syrupy
taste, not at all like Mummy's rich creamy tea, but it warms
me, rekindles my last memories of the mansion, which I will
take with me to my village. From the tea shop I can see the
bus driver. He interests me. He is standing away from the bus,
smoking and watching it being loaded, a light-skinned man

in khaki shorts, black sandals, and a towel hanging around his bare shoulders. He is tall and fleshy. Folds of flesh ring his belly and his neck, not in any way that is obscene, but in a way that shows he is *eating* money. In a way he reminds me of a long-range agric pig.

We begin boarding the bus around 10:30 p.m. The driver's name is written on a copper nameplate above the wheels: AKUBUILO. We take off around 11:00, Akubuilo easing the long bus into the road, flowing into the sea of darkness spotted with yellow floodlights like a tributary. The traffic is heavy and drags along like a snake with a broken spine. Hawkers of bread, sachet water, and soft drinks move up and down the long lines of vehicles like scroll bars on Mummy's computer as they stop and push their wares into car windows at passengers. I sit quietly and watch the scrambling going on all around me, knowing that at this time my village will be asleep. I entertain my eyes with the psychedelic neon signs advertising businesses: insurance companies, banks, shipping companies. Mummy's children overseas would send her things through FedEx and DHL. Enormous billboards of pretty ladies in ads and politicians with double chins recede into nothingness as Akubuilo's headlights swing, picking them out.

The traffic eases up. Akubuilo moves smoothly, slowing down and swerving this and that way to avoid potholes. Cars coming from the opposite direction appear so small that it seems he will crush them like a big foot dragged over an ant. The passengers are mostly Igbo traders travelling to the east with heavy sacks of goods. The journey is flavoured with Osita Osadebe's highlife music. I shut my eyes and allow his fine, throaty voice to sandpaper my ears, the voice that blends with

the wailing engine, the roaring road, and the heavy thud of
percussion instruments.

Machebe is standing outside the front of the house when I finally reach our compound at sunrise the next day. A lightning
bolt of anxiety tears a path through my stomach. I did not
expect that he'd be the first person I'd see upon my shameful
return. He watches me with a blank expression as I approach.
My mother emerges from the house to my relief. Upon seeing
me, she stops. And then Usonwa and the twins come tearing
out as my mother shrieks a loud note of surprise at seeing me.
And then my father appears and stands in the doorway, his
mouth curling in a mocking smile. I can see from his stance
that his hip injury has slightly disfigured him.

"Come quickly inside." I didn't realize my mother would be
so dramatic. "I don't want the neighbours to hear you."

I know the neighbours well. They are like the swarming
termites drawn to the light of the oil lamp; one by one they
will fly in until the compound is carpeted with their water-
colour wings. I know that at the sound of my mother's voice
they will come nosing into our compound. The moment the
story of my sojourn drops from my mother's mouth to the
ground like a crumb of food, they will swoop on it like ants,
take bits from it, and carry it elsewhere to share with their
friends. Some will have the crumb salted and peppered to
make it more delicious.

Dinner is cocoyam and akworakwo, a peppery sauce.
Ugh! This homecoming, I am beginning to feel bad about it,
about the cold walls of my room and the mattress that's so flat
it feels the same as lying on the hard, bare floor.

"Lagos is a swarming mass of ants, and you can't tell a red ant from a fire ant," I begin, narrating my well-rehearsed story to settle everyone's curiosity, about the mansion and the luxuries of life in Lagos, the delicious meals of chicken and mutton and beef.

The twins stop eating to mope at me, noses beginning to run from the hot pepper sauce. I can feel them savouring the chicken dish in their imagination.

"You should see my madam," I say. "Mummy is what we call her. She is beautiful and an amazing cook. We have the mansion to ourselves, Mummy and I, and the other houseboy."

"She doesn't have a child?" my mother asks.

"Her children live overseas," I explain as Bingo comes sniffing around me in the company of flies.

I ignore the sickly-looking dog, counting her ribs at a glance. We have always had a dog in this house—from Ugodu to Ekuke, and now Bingo, who eats shit with glee, with a body covered in scabies. She once defecated into our pot of soup. My father beat her until she lost her voice from crying, and then she sat away from us afterwards, and watched my father with sad eyes.

"Bingo is not at all like Ogidan, Mummy's dog," I say.

"What kind of name is that for a dog?" Usonwa says. The most excited about my return, she eats absent-mindedly, staring at me with bright little awed eyes.

"Ogidan is as big as a lion. His body is covered in hair as soft as cornsilk. He won't eat any food if it is not fresh or if it has a sour smell. In the morning, we feed him a whole bowl of milk, which he quickly laps up before a breakfast of beef or mutton."

"Beef and mutton for a mere dog?" my father chips in.

The best meal that Bingo gets is soured food from my mother once in a while, if Usonwa forgets to warm a meal and it becomes dangerous for us to eat. Otherwise Bingo survives by eating excrement and hunting lizards and mice.

"Yes," I say. "That's not all. The first thing you see as you step into the mansion is a big white marble tomb that tells you Mummy's husband is sleeping in heaven."

There's a moment of silence while my family digests the incredible story of social imbalance.

"Dimkpa," Machebe says, speaking directly to me for the first time.

His voice, like the jarring notes of a cracked gong, unnerves me. He has never been the talking type. Tigers don't purr, they roar.

"Let's say you have had the chance to live in a mansion with a gorgeous woman who lets you do nothing but eat, swim, and feed milk and mutton to a dog that is almost a lion. My question is, why did you come back home? Or are you just visiting?"

I have dreaded this question. I can't tell anyone the real reason I fled Lagos; I'd only be advertising my cowardice. How can I justify running away from a house filled with luxuries simply because I was scared of a boy my age, and then coming home empty-handed? I'd be taunted forever.

"We were enjoying all that, and the luxury of watching TV and sleeping in a bed that is as big as a hut, and as soft as cocoyam paste," I start in a tone so unnatural I almost resent my own voice. "I even read novels and worked out in a gym, if you know what that is." The pauses in my narration are deliberate. I am careful not to sound too glib. I can imagine Machebe's hackles rising, a tiger about to leap on its prey. "And then all of a sudden Mummy puts the mansion up for sale, because she is relocating to America to live with her children."

The room hisses into silence, like a burning cigarette dropped in water. I can almost hear the soft crackling-fire sounds of my mother's ochanja. And then the only sound is of my mother scratching her hair in obvious disappointment.

Sixteen

I LEAN AGAINST THE UMBRELLA TREE IN OUR COMPOUND and watch the trees, the houses, and the livestock moving about. I have had a long sleep. I feel better waking up and eating the breakfast prepared by my mother. Just eating my mother's food and looking around my father's compound is a comfort. My eyes wander to Okike's grave.

"Mother, how can you allow weeds to grow on the grave?" In my absence, it has become completely overrun again.

My mother and siblings have been working all morning, hulling boiled okpeye seeds and preparing them for fermentation. In a few days, my mother will grind the fermented cotyledons into paste and mold the paste into fingers of raw umber seasoning, a fetid smell thickening in the air.

"You and graves," she hisses. "I have more important things to do than weed graves."

The avocado tree my father planted to mark the head of the grave has grown taller than I am; that is how long Okike has been gone, and that's how much the distance between us has grown. I stroll over and stand near the tree, determining to weed the grave, to pull out the tufts that wedge between us.

I wonder how they could have allowed such ruin to befall Okike's resting place as I reach down. I picture her, pinned on all sides with spikes and nettles, suddenly regaining her space, her freedom, and breathing freely again. I imagine her smiling at me with gratitude. I regret not coming back with money for a tomb. I have failed myself, and my family. I couldn't even buy the toys I promised to the twins, and I wasted Machebe's money on my ticket home. Ejiro called me a coward, a weakling. Maybe I shouldn't have fled Mummy's house that easily. I know I will soon get tired of eating cocoyam and cowage soup in place of the mansion's pantry full of butter, corned beef, Geisha, sardines, juice, and confectioneries.

I spend my days indoors to hide my shame. The village is boring without Eke. I'm told he left shortly after I travelled to Lagos. No one seems to know why he made the decision to abandon school and take off to an unknown place. Patty Onah and Oluoha are also gone—both in police detention for mobilizing protesters who went around town carrying placards after the MASSOB leader was arrested. The police stormed the village, traced them to the chemist shop, and arrested the two of them. The place is deserted now, the whole village silent and apprehensive.

For a few days I enjoy the lull in my life: eating, sleeping, and waking up late in the morning. I no longer eat with my younger siblings on the tray with peeling paint on which my mother dishes a large quantity of food for the children to share. Since I have returned, she has been serving my food separately on metal plates, and speaking to me only in her sweet tangerine voice. My father is down and hasn't bothered me about fetching fodder for the goats. The pain of his dislocated hip bone worsens after my return. My siblings help him out to a mat under the umbrella tree in the middle of our compound and back in when he gets tired of lying outdoors. Machebe thinks I am a failure. He is the most critical of me, taking over the role of my father while he is bedridden. He resents that I am being treated "like a king," scowling when my mother serves my food on a separate plate.

"Why is everyone licking his buttocks?" he flares up when he can no longer bear it. "He came back with nothing. He won't go to the farm, he won't fetch fodder for the goats, he won't do anything. He just sits around and eats from the effort of other people. Are we celebrating his failure?"

I swallow a retort. I am trying to avoid a fight. He has the right to be angry with me for wasting his life savings. My father sides with Machebe as usual, his voice sharp, and when my mother rebukes my father for not sparing himself even in his sickbed he says, "I dislocated my hip bone, not my voice."

My mother says nothing. Usonwa is silent, but I sense I no longer have even her sympathy. I know when I am defeated. And Machebe won't stop. He is all bunched up for a fight. I may be older, but he is bigger. He inherited his impressive stature and muscle from my father's side. I look more like my mother's people. If I had won any fights with him in the past, it was not because I was stronger, but because my sense of being older prevailed. Because it made me more resilient.

Suddenly we are exchanging blows. I hit him first for his spittle that touches me, for the memories of my brawls with Ejiro that flash in my mind and prod me to rise up. I hit him on the jaw. Square. It is unexpected, and I feel his bone shift as he cries out with pain. He staggers back and falls, although he doesn't go down completely, landing on one hand like a swimmer taking a backstroke dive, using the same hand to lever himself up and spring back to his feet almost at once. He charges at me. I step back, neatly dodging him. He must realize how much my skills have improved. But then I trip on a nearby bench, sending my plate of food crashing to the ground. I struggle to rise to my feet, my left leg getting hooked to a short curved framework on the side of the bench, frustrating my efforts. The rest is easy, and Machebe is all over me like a famished tiger. My mother and siblings scream for help. My father watches silently.

I feel small and ashamed after the fight. Things are how they used to be before I went away, when I woke up every morning to the same tepid view of the hills, feeling trapped inside the village; when my life revolved around helping my father with bricklaying and breaking the soil with a hoe; a life of eating cocoyam and cowage soup, and millipedes crawling over everything. Ugh!

Machebe carries himself around like a peacock. His life seems to have more purpose since I left. More rhythm. He will be apprenticed to a good mechanic when the family finds one. I know I am never going to have the patience to learn a trade under a master for so many years. I cannot go back to load carrying after returning from a large city like Lagos. I consider it demeaning. My family cannot afford the capital to start me off with a business at Ogige market. My dream of erecting a tomb on Okike's grave is fast fading. I am a butterfly on a purposeless flight.

But the fight with Machebe shakes me out of my trance and renews the impulse to dream big once again. I remind myself of the task ahead—to pull my family out of poverty and stigma—and know that until I have completed Okike's reburial, my soul will know no rest. I have to leave this village again somehow. I know I cannot make the kind of money my family needs here. Before going to Lagos, I made a wish to Okike, and it came to pass. In Lagos the idea of pretending to have epilepsy was obviously planted by Okike. So once again I raise my hands skywards to make another wish.

Eke shows up in the village two days later.

Seventeen

HE IS WEARING A NEW SHIRT, AND A NEW WRISTWATCH, and glossy black shoes. He has started to grow a beard. Memories of the old times come flooding back as Eke and I walk down the road chatting. I tell him briefly about Lagos, about the crowds that are like swarming masses of ants, the cars, and the fights; Lagos and its weird community and speed of light. I edit the parts of the story that are not favourable to me.

"Your Mummy is a very strange woman," Eke says. "That boy, Ejiro—I should have a little bout with him." He squares his shoulders. "You shouldn't have fled."

I wince with a stab of regret. Eke is one of the people I have failed. Going to Lagos was his idea.

I ask why he is no longer in school.

"I left because my mother spent the money my father had saved for my school fees on my sick sister and told me to drop out," he says with a sad smile. "I work with Micheletti Limited, a large construction company in Awka."

The name of the company has a metallic resonance that impresses me. "I am happy you came back. I was going out of my mind with boredom."

"Let's go grab a drink at Madam Bridget's." He reaches for a wallet in his back pocket. It's full of cash. He counts crisp notes and hands them to me.

I have seen only Mummy handle this amount of money before. Eke's cash is sweet-smelling. I imagine a site full of overalled, helmet-wearing construction workers going to and fro.

"I am tired of this village."

Eke laughs his combustible laugh, fishes out a cigarette, lights it, and takes a draw, not minding the eyes of the passersby. I didn't know he had started to smoke, and publicly, too.

"I am serious."

He hisses smoke out. He is still the same lean, dark boy with something melancholic about his looks, something that starts from his innocent dark eyes, brushes past his short nose and high cheekbones, and hides itself in his small mouth.

"We are not eating rice and chicken there, so you know," he says.

"Am I eating rice and chicken here?"

We laugh as we enter Madam Bridget's bar, happy strains of a melody that belongs only to our friendship. The place is full as usual. The customers are engrossed in a rowdy argument on issues ranging from politics to Biafra to music. We settle on benches. Eke orders pepper soup and drinks for everyone in the bar. He gets an ovation from the beneficiaries. They praise him loudly before returning to their talk.

"Listening to their music is like eating an unripe mango," Nichodemus, a bony man with sunken cheeks and a widely travelled panache, says of contemporary musicians. "If you wish to savour the real juice of a ripe mango, then listen to the oldies by Oriental Brothers or Oliver De Coque or Osita Osadebe. Or even Felix Liberty's hit track 'Ifeoma.'"

A funny-looking man who probably enjoys being at variance with everyone for nothing insists the best highlife musician is neither Oriental Brothers nor Oliver De Coque nor Osita Osadebe. "It is Paulson Kalu, and if you doubt me, go listen to his hit track 'Okwudili' again; it's not only a song, but meat in a song."

The room rumbles with argument.

"I don't care about highlife." The bar falls silent at the sound of Eke's voice. He sips his Golden Guinea directly from the bottle and smacks his lips. "But to me GG is the best beer ever."

I am amazed at how much Eke seems to have matured, how much silence and respect he commands among the customers, many of whom are older, the power in his voice, and how like a bell it at once captures the attention of the house.

"Monarch is the real beer," a roly-poly little man says. He runs his tongue over his dark lips deliciously after sipping from a glass cup.

I have noticed how Roly-Poly keeps following Madam Bridget with greedy, drunken eyes as she walks in and out, shaking her waist. Madam Bridget is a mother of two, a playful, pliant, and robust young woman. Her bar is the most patronized in the village. I don't know if men patronize her because her palm wine is better and her pepper soup more delicious and spicy or because of her big, curvy hips. They keep staring as she walks. Occasionally, a man will get drunk and aim a playful smack at her backside, but she never flares up when the smack lands on its target with yummy softness. She simply looks at the man in mock anger, giggles, and then walks away, knotting her wrappa more firmly around her waist. I have never seen her in a bad mood, although I don't often go to her bar except when my father sends me there to buy palm wine for an important guest.

"GG, Monarch, they are all poison and can't be compared to palm wine," says Ogbu, a rock of a man drinking palm wine from a mug.

I imagine him fighting Roly-Poly because Roly-Poly insists

Monarch is the better drink, him blowing air at Roly-Poly, and Roly-Poly melting and becoming a soft mass on the floor. I feel so awkward to be the only one drinking Coke. It makes me a little nervous, gives me a sense of déjà vu, but my insecurities seem safely masked by the aura around Eke.

"I was surprised to come home and meet our Biafra detainees still in prison cells." As always, Eke's voice throws water on the fire lit by the drunkards.

"That is a high level of impunity," Nichodemus says with a clear belch. "Don't we have freedom of association any longer in this country?"

"Most troubling is that the detainees are going to be left there indefinitely in the most inhuman conditions." Ogbu spoons peppersoup into his mouth.

"Many will be victims of extrajudicial executions," Nichodemus says, his panache swelling.

Eke and I exchange nervous glances. I know that he is thinking what I am thinking, and Patty Onah and Oluoha are the themes of our overlapping thoughts.

"Can we change the topic, please?" Roly-Poly spoons peppersoup into his mouth, his voice muffled by either the pepperiness of the soup or the hotness of the subject. "I want to enjoy this meal and beer in peace. I do not want to be thrown into jail."

At home, we talk about my plan to follow Eke to Awka. My father is indifferent to the idea, Machebe seems to be shooing me away with his eyes, and my mother is skeptical.

"I don't like this idea of you going to live in Agbenuland with all those stories of rituals and blood money there," my mother says. "I hear that in every household there is an adult with the brains of an infant, an imbecile with saliva running down her mouth, because her brains were offered for a money-making ritual in some occultic underworld altar."

My mother has this impression that most wealthy young people are money ritualists whose mothers or other close relatives are mummified corpses vomiting banknotes in some secret chamber in their mansions. But nothing anyone thinks or says will make me change my mind. I overhear my father speaking to invisible gods alone in his room.

"Ndi nwe ana." He makes reference to the deities of Igbo pantheon. "My son is about to make a trip to a land where humans eat their fellow humans. Do not let any harm come to your son. Protect your son from danger in a foreign land. Makana nwaeze adi efu n'mba."

I imagine my father nipping bits from a lobe of kola nut onto the floor as he whispers his prayers in private. My mother asks for the rosary she gave me when I went to Lagos. I haven't used it since I left. I can recite only a few lines of the litany that I remember because of the poetry of the language describing the Virgin Mary as a Mystical Rose, a Tower of Ivory, an Ark of Covenant, a Morning Star, a Mirror of Justice, a Seat of Wisdom, and a Vessel of Honor.

I lie awake far into the night, musing over Eke's glittering new life: his packet shirts that bear inside their lines of newness an aura of good living, his shoes that mirror my image and his necklace that catches the light, the power in his voice that drowns all other voices in Madam Bridget's bar. My desire to follow him to Awka turned into an obsession when he said that he even worked with white men. My eyelids twitch at the prospect of earning the salaries white men earn, in hard currency.

Eighteen

WE SET OFF TO AWKA, EKE AND I. WE TRAVEL THROUGH
Enugu in a bus driven by a boy not much older than we are. He
looks wild, hair dirty and uncombed, and has a voice like metal
scraping against metal. He keeps two souvenirs: one is a tooth
knocked out of its hole, and the other is a long scar running
across his temple. Maybe he got them from a fight, maybe from
an accident, but either way they give him a severe look. Midway
through the journey, he rips off his shirt, leaving the passengers
with no choice but to gaze at his back with its ugly scales left by
skin infections. In Enugu, we change buses. The driver of the
blue-and-white bus marked ENTRACO who drives us to Awka
is the opposite of the first driver. He does not swear at other
drivers. He does not bump suddenly into potholes and throw a
retort to anyone who complains of his rough driving—"Am I the
government that refuses to pave the road?"—or turn his head to
glare at the passengers as if daring anyone to challenge him. The
drive to Agulu, and then to Anukwu, a remote community near
Anaocha, where Eke lives, is mostly quiet and bushy. We seem
to travel in arcs—we have done almost the full circumference of
the region by the time we arrive—but it's still a much shorter
journey than the one to Lagos.

We arrive at a large, uncompleted house with a bleak veranda. An earth-coloured grave fills a wide space in the courtyard. Eke says the house belongs to a widow. Her husband
passed on, leaving her a shell of a home and his own grave.

I throw it another glance, wondering why the widow did not think to entomb her husband, who died before seeing their house complete. Eke leads me through a large, dark living room with a high ceiling, heavy columns, and windowless walls to his room. I see now that he lives in two skins: the one he wears here in this bleak one-room apartment and the other he puts on when he shows up in the village glistening like a rainbow. This place is a dark and well-protected secret, tucked away under the tarmac of a road stretching for miles.

His room, like the other rooms in the building, has nothing within its cold cement walls but a mat, a kerosene stove, a pair of pots covered with thick layers of soot, a few plates and spoons, and a few old clothes. He hadn't washed the dishes, which still contain dirty water and remnants of food from his most recent meal before he travelled home. They are shimmering with maggots and houseflies, and give off a bad smell. The other rooms are all occupied.

"This place is a jungle," he says that night as we lie on the mat in his cold, bare room, tired from travelling. He is naked, stripped of those secrets that enshroud him like darkness, now unfurling like daylight. "I never worked with Micheletti Limited," he confesses. "I am a day labourer. Here it is survival of the fittest—this is the real world." His voice is suddenly apologetic. "I am sorry I lied to you. It's what the people back home believed, and I didn't want to change the narrative. Besides, I didn't want to discourage you. You needed to leave." He paused. "I believe we will make something out of this place if we work hard."

Eke's revelation hits me like Ejiro's punch.

The house is packed full of labourers who live in threes and fours to a room. The living room is empty, and doorless, with huge columns that seem to belong to the Middle Ages.

This is where we will sit on mats and chat on Sundays with the other boys who do the same work, while a radio is playing, Joe's radio. Joe sits on a bench on the veranda or leans against a pillar, sipping a beer and humming along to a highlife tune by Oliver De Coque.

"He is as deeply attached to the radio as he is to Premier beer," Eke says. "He keeps it by his side when he is cooking or having his meals or when we are chatting after a hard day's work. He seems to draw strength from the music."

I watch Joe with interest. Dark. Muscular. Soft-smiling. Watching him, I at once become fond of highlife music and Oliver De Coque. I know I will eventually like Premier beer as well.

I wake up the next morning itching all over with bumps from tick bites. I don't have time to dwell on it, though, because as soon as we are up we must hastily wash our faces, pick bitter leaf stalks for chewing sticks, and set off to work with spades and shovels. We pass beautiful houses buried in thickets, some unoccupied, looking lonely and sad. We arrive somewhere Eke calls Ogbo-Mmanu, an open area near a small, ramshackle market. The space is starting to get busy. Boys of my age in tattered work clothes appear with spades, shovels, head pans, and other tools, and fill up the space. Breakfast is served to the labourers by a food vendor, a thick, dark woman with a grouchy male voice sitting on a stool beside a wheelbarrow in front of the provision shop. She picks the okpa from a large bowl sitting in the wheelbarrow; uncovers the waterproof wrapper to reveal a steaming, delicious-looking yellow cone; and slices it onto a plastic plate for Eke and me.

"There are no gentlemen here," Eke says again, his mouth yellow with okpa.

I watch Ogbo-Mmanu as it bustles with labourers, eating, talking, and laughing. They are scattered in groups, every sentence laced with humour, shovels and spades and head pans kept within a snatching distance.

Akata is a clownish boy with a wicked sense of humour. We share the same apartment. He entertains the labourers both at home and at Ogbo-Mmanu.

"Don't make the mistake of bringing your head out first if robbers knock on your door at night," he says to Uwoma, whose big head outsizes his spindly legs. "If you do, they will hit you real hard, thinking you are a big, strong fellow. But if you show your stick legs first, they will think you are a little boy and deal you light blows."

The labourers roar with laughter. But I notice their alertness in spite of Akata's jesting—every pair of eyes lingers on the long stretch of tarred road, waiting for the sight of a contractor or a tipper.

"To survive here you have to be fast, strong, and ruthless if need be," Eke says to encourage me.

But hearing him talk like this leaves me with a feeling of dryness in my mouth.

"Loading a tipper truck with sand or laterite is not as hard as it seems—you only have to learn the techniques and tricks involved. You really have to sprint fast, because the first three or four persons to jump into the tipper truck are the ones who will get hired. But you have to be careful. Someone once slipped off the bucket and landed face-first on the tarred road. You will know how these things are done with time, though. There is always the softer work of serving the masons at building sites. The contractors don't know you, so it is going to be hard to find someone to hire you, but I will use my contacts to give you small-small jobs. With time it will get easier."

I answer with a nod. Everything looks strange. And scary. I am quietly watching the rowdy scene as the labourers abandon their food and conversations midway, snatch their shovels and spades, and sprint towards a contractor who shows up, a tipper truck that looms into sight, or a car that stops with a hand beckoning. In this way the small crowd steadily thins down. By midmorning, the eagerness begins to wear off, and a sense of frustration envelops the remaining labourers. If in the end they don't get hired, they will walk home in a melancholy vein.

I spend the first few days following Eke around. The quarry is a steep, fast-receding prominence that feeds laterite to building construction sites in the neighbourhood. I sit away from the excavation site and watch boys and men dig with muscles that Mummy would have loved to sit half-naked near the pool and watch. They shovel the laterite into the bucket of a tipper truck with powerful, sweaty thrusts. In between loading the tipper truck and waiting while it races to a construction site to unload and return for more, they smoke and make conversation. I'll learn that the saying "one-man show" was coined from the greed of labourers who will take on the loading of a tipper single-handedly. "Like a nosing rat who feeds itself to death on poisoned crumbs," Akata sneers. The quarry looks dangerous. The labourers will dig and deepen its soft base until it hangs like a precipice. Like it might cave in under the weight of the peak and crash down on the labourers.

And crash down it will, and bury some of us alive.

Ijedi is no longer lying on the mat where the elderly women had surrounded her when Obochi returns with the midwife. She has been moved into the hut. The old woman who sent Obochi to the midwife is wrapping up two bloody bundles in banana leaves as Obochi and the midwife hurry in. The snakebite has forced Ijedi into labour. She has birthed a set of stillborn twins and lies groaning and writhing on the bare floor.

Obochi is stunned by a scene outside as she turns to flee the room in terror. Her father, swaying on the shoulder of the young man who found him unconscious at the farm, is being brought home.

"They offended a goddess," says a tall, angular man, a seer who unrolls a tiger skin, nestles down on it, breaks a lobe of kola nut, throws the four parts into a gourd filled with water, and peers intently into the gourd as if it were a screen that played back hidden events.

"Someone in the family, a maiden, went to a forbidden territory to pick snails belonging to a goddess, and now the goddess wants the young woman as a bride as retribution for her trespass," explains the seer. "There will be tragic repercussions if this penalty is not done at once. Every living thing in that family will lose breath: humans and livestock. Hurry! Find out who amongst their daughters did it,

and then take her to the shrine of Ezenwanyi, the offended goddess in Ishiayanashi, beyond the thick forest that stretches to the boundaries of our community. Do this before sunset today to avert the tragedies that are looming."

Nineteen

THE EARLY DAYS ARE INTERESTING, AT LEAST. I FLOW with the daily rhythm of my new life. It is exciting working and living all by myself, drawing my budgets, listing my priorities, cooking for myself, and managing my freedom. Now I know why Eke left the village for this place. He could have learned carpentry, painting, or any trade back home, but he obviously wanted to manage his own life without his stern mother breathing down his neck.

I take my first beer and smoke at Mama Obodo's bar, where Eke and the others go to drink away their lives, their savings.

"Hei, Dimkpa," Eke says, laughing, as I mark time over the bottle of Premier beer. "Why do you squeeze your face as if you are drinking bitter leaf juice?"

The barroom is bustling with people, and now they explode with laughter. It reminds me of Madam Bridget's bar and her disparaging, inebriated clientele.

"He is an ohu ma and will never fully savour the taste of a good beer," a cruel, familiar voice slurs.

I grab my seat tight to hold myself from falling as a nervous feeling streaks like lightning in my stomach at those words: *ohu ma*, again!

"Take a few puffs of cigarette, Dimkpa, and it will whet your taste buds for Premier beer." Joe's voice startles me.

I blink with suspicion at the half-drunken barroom crowd

cheering in support of Joe's suggestion, wondering if I had imagined the cruel voice.

"Eke's right." My glance moves from Eke to Joe, whose love of Premier beer crinkles in his eyes. "The beer doesn't taste like bitter leaf juice, it tastes like acid."

The barroom cracks up with laughter.

"Let Dimkpa be," says a drunken old man whose oily beard is stained with a paste of his thick mucus. "He is chicken-brained. If you force him to smoke and he bugs out, you will be blamed for it."

"Give me a stick of cigarette." I wave at Mama Obodo, feeling insulted and emboldened by the old man's mockery, not certain that the voice I heard earlier wasn't an echo of my fears.

Mama Obodo, as round and goggle-eyed as an owl, serves me the cigarette from a gold pack. Eke lights it for me. A puff sends me into a spasm of coughing, and others into convulsions of laughter. But this puff initiates me into the clique of smokers, and into many evenings of boozing and squandering at Mama Obodo's bar. As sour-mouthed as she is thick, Mama Obodo literally drives us away to close up every night.

"Leave my shop, you pigs from Wawaland," she spits at us when one of us gets too full and throws up beer and morsels of manioc all over the place.

A round of guffawing shakes the barroom as she forces the fellow who has thrown up to clear his vomit, which he does by scooping it with his hands.

Mama Obodo continues to rail. She calls us all sorts of names and says we are good for nothing except working as houseboys, maids, latrine diggers, load carriers, hawkers of chewing sticks and toothpicks, that we are speakers of a dialect that doesn't sound at all like Igbo, impoverished and slaving for the rich Agbenuman who pays us nothing for battering our bodies.

"There's dignity in labour," a dark, leathery fellow named Nwodo retorts. "Don't look down on me because you see me in your barroom. I am a graduate. I studied psychology. I am only here because there are no jobs in the country and I don't want to be a burden to my family after they struggled to train me. I am only here to save money to go back to university to become a lawyer and self-employed."

The barroom swells with a deep grunt of doubt.

"I am saving for a house of my own and a pretty wife, so you know," says another fellow I have seen at the bar a few times. He speaks in a half-sneering, half-serious voice.

"What woman will look the way of a poor, dirty concrete-casting church rat like you?" Mama Obodo hisses at him. "At the rate at which you are guzzling alcohol, you will end up living the rest of your miserable life in a wattle-and-daub hut, with the soaring cost of building materials in this country."

The barroom roars its laughter.

The fellow who has vomited returns to his seat and asks for another drink after clearing the mess, but Mama Obodo ignores him.

"This body will break down if I don't refuel it," he moans.

"As for the aspiring lawyer . . ." Mama Obodo seems determined to send us off with her foul tongue so she can close. "I am sure what you have inside that head of yours now is a jar of alcohol, not a brain."

The barroom laughs into the skies.

"What I don't understand is where the Agbenuman is

getting all the money to build his skyscrapers in these hard times." Akata's voice is unusually sober, a knowing smile planted on his face.

The barroom hisses into silence like a doused fire. Glances are exchanged, throats cleared, and beers sipped in that interval of uncomfortable silence. I remember what my mother said: *I don't like this idea of you going to live in Agbenuland with all those stories of rituals and blood money.*

Coiled on my mat, lightheaded with beer, I take stock of the day, every letter of that hateful phrase *ohu ma* still echoing in my head. Who spoke it, I wonder, or was it actually my imagination? The labourers are mostly poor migrant workers from northern Igboland under an umbrella body called Wawa. Eke tells me that the group holds a meeting once in a while to discuss working conditions and welfare. Mama Obodo was right: the Agbenuman is rich and exploits our bodies to erect his skyscrapers, and then she sucks our pockets dry at her bar to keep the vicious circle going. We are nothing but tools, used to build their mansions or line their pockets. The moment their projects are standing, tall and proud, we are discarded like old rusty shovels and head pans.

I think of Ejiro, who is stuck in the mansion, fighting to entertain Mummy. "I have stayed for the money," he said. How can he be sure that he will come out of the mansion with a kobo of his savings, or even with his own life? I must not forget the purpose for which I came all the way here. I promise myself that I will not be sucked into that whirlpool of beer and smoke in Mama Obodo's bar at the expense of saving for the future, and for Okike's tomb.

•

Sometimes, we are clearheaded enough to discuss politics and our ambitions. Eke wants to be a politician someday.

"I have been thinking about it for some time now." Eke is wearing a crumpled face. "Politicians have sucked this country dry. I'd like to go in myself, to grab my own share. I am sick and tired of being sacrificed."

I look at him, confused.

"Money ritual is not only when they slaughter you at some altar and harvest your human parts; labour exploitation is another kind," he says to settle my curiosity. "We won't be able to do this kind of work forever. That's why I've joined MASSOB, to secure a position for myself when Biafra comes."

Akata laughs in his usual satirical way. "I see that you want to spend the rest of your miserable life in prison."

"If I join politics, it is not because I want to steal from the country," Joe says. "It is because I don't like how the northerners are treating us easterners."

"I am not interested in MASSOB or Biafra," Akata says. "If we have our own country, how do you know the Agbenuman will not play god over the rest of us his tribesmen, just as the Hausa and Fulani do to us now? We are better off as Nigerians than Biafrans, if they restructure the country to give other tribes a chance at being president."

"Who dash monkey banana," Eke says, not in Igbo, but in Pidgin English.

I have been drawn to MASSOB from the first time I heard of the movement from the captive gamblers in Uwakwe's shopfront, so I follow Eke to the next meeting, which is at a football pitch. Abada, the leader of the group, is also a football coach. He is middle-aged, athletic, bow-legged, and a little hunched.

He begins to address us as soon as we are settled in the grass. "Let me first of all welcome the new boys amongst us. This is our seventh meeting since they took our indefatigable leader, and our agenda today is to update you regarding his arrest."

Eke is staring at Abada with hands wrapped around his knees, forehead veined with interest when I glance at him.

"MASSOB is a peaceful group, and we do not understand why they have taken our leader on the accusation of violence." Abada scans the sweaty faces of the young men just out of training. Anyone watching us from a distance would think he was just a football coach. "They may have taken our leader, but I want to assure you that it is not the end of the struggle for Biafra sovereignty. You shouldn't panic. Our lawyers are working hard to get him released. We cannot be part of a country that treats us like slaves."

We sit listening to Abada's long and impassioned speech. It fills me up like food fills a famished man. On the way home, in the company of Eke and Nwodo, I ponder all that Abada has said. I am particularly intrigued by his claim that those who support MASSOB to a victorious end will be made councilors, local government chairmen, or even commissioners. "You will be leaders," he said, "over those brothers of ours who have distanced themselves from the struggle."

"Abada is right," Nwodo says. "They drill our oil and leave us to die in poverty and pollution. He is right about the network of good roads in northern Nigeria, and the dilapidation of federal roads in the south, and airports that are in ruins and out of use. He is right about everything."

I throw him an awed glance.

"I was stuck in university at the age of thirty, all because I am a southerner," he says. "They made me sit the entrance exam five times before they offered me admission. Yet someone who sat the exam along with me the first time scored fifty marks less than my aggregate, but he was accepted and had long graduated and was working in the ministry before I finally was admitted. He was a northerner, of course."

Nwodo is a hurting, bitter man; I can feel it. He goes on to rage about how the NNPC lost its autonomy under the watch of the leaders; how more than half of Nigerians are living below the national poverty line in a country that is one of the world's largest oil producers, with more than fifty billion dollars in earnings from oil exports per year; how the universities have to increase tuition fees, yet students receive lectures while sitting on the floor in overcrowded lecture theatres or even standing outside the classroom windows; how the roads are dilapidated; how he has to work menial jobs after graduating from the university—in a country where the average legislator's salary is more than fifty times the country's GDP per capita.

I stare at Nwodo with mouth wide open, truly amazed by his intensity, his knowledge. He looks calloused, as if braided by his anger, his resentment of the state of the country.

"I am blaming them, our leaders, for all that went wrong," he says.

I feel even more motivated after listening to Nwodo. Abada's promises have reignited my curiosity and interest in Biafra, and I spend the evening with my friends at Mama

Obodo's bar nursing a bottle of Premier beer like a delicate dream. I imagine myself a councilor or a commissioner or a local government chairman. I will be in charge of the Nsukka administrative area. My village of Oregwu and its fraudulent Onyishi and his stolen little stool will be under my control. He will be forced to vacate the throne. It will be the end of poverty and shame in my family. And then I will build Okike a gargantuan tomb.

Twenty

CHRISTMAS IS APPROACHING. I CAN'T WAIT TO VISIT home and see my family again. It's always a wonderful time of year in my village. Carols play on the radio, stirring mixed feelings in the dusty winds of Harmattan. The songs always make me smile to myself in reminiscence, and in anticipation of Christmas clothes. The season throws my father into a grouchy mood. New clothes are luxuries he cannot afford.

But I am elated every time I hear carols playing from Joe's radio, because I have enough savings already not only to buy Christmas clothes for my siblings but also to finally build Okike's tomb, pay back Machebe, and regain my pride of place in my family. When I come back here after Christmas, I will work even harder and save even more money for the future.

I dream of convoys, and sirens, and wake up late full of hopes as I walk to Ogbo-Mmanu. The square is deserted. Most of the labourers are off to work already. Two men approach me minutes after my arrival. They are flustered and out of breath. One is in a bright blue shirt, the other in a mango-juice-yellow shirt. They come hurriedly towards me.

"We want you to catch someone who is sick," Blue Shirt speaks, touching his head to indicate that the "someone" is mentally sick and has probably escaped from a psychiatric hospital.

I jump at the offer. It sounds like the kind of job that pays well. I might even expand my Christmas budget to include funding a petty trade for my mother at Ogige market to stop her from foraging.

"You will need a partner," says Yellow Shirt.

I throw a look around Ogbo-Mmanu. It's pretty empty, so I settle for the only boy within sight, a small fellow named Uba, with an elongated head and a funny face.

We haggle with the men and finally arrive at a favourable price, but it is not only about the money; it is also about the excitement of capturing an escaped madman, one who is dangerous and perhaps wields a machete. It is risky, but it is the risk that makes it exciting, like something in a film.

"Show us where he is." I want to impress our hirers with my confident tone. I would have preferred to do the job with someone stronger than this boy with a head shaped like sweet mango, but I can't rob him of his luck now.

The men lead us towards a house not far from Ogbo-Mmanu. On our way they explain that the lunatic strolled home and, indeed, grabbed a machete after his escape and chased everyone away.

"We will get him," I assure them. I am thinking of what else I could do with my share of the six thousand naira. I could erect a statue for Okike after entombing her.

"He goes on and on about his nunchaku," Blue Shirt says as we approach a black gate.

"What's that?" I say.

"He used to be an expert in karate," Yellow Shirt explains. "He almost killed a man with his nunchaku. They sent him to jail, and from there to a psychiatric hospital, but he escaped. He's been asking after his nunchaku since he showed up."

A cold shiver of fear knocks me sideways.

"Are you scared?" Blue Shirt squints at me.

"I am not scared," I say, and sneak Uba an impotent smile.

"We are not afraid." He returns a tight smile as we walk through the black gate into a compound that feels like a trap.

The sight of the madman stops me dead in my tracks. The compound is large. He is standing in the sit-out of a cream bungalow. He is a big fellow, bigger than either of us, naked down to a pair of greasy boxers. He looks wild, with knotted hair, which tells me that it must have been a while since he escaped. A machete with a glancing blade is leaning on the wall next to him. He is muttering incoherent words. My heart nearly jumps out of my body.

"Be careful," one of the men whispers from behind.

It looks like the house is empty. I imagine the chaotic scene upon his arrival, the madman bursting through the gate and grabbing a machete lying about, the first person to see him raising the alarm, the house emptying of women and children who fall over one another as they scamper to safety.

I take a few steps closer and crane to hear him better. I see more details. In the hollow where his eyes are supposed to be, what I see are smouldering embers. They dilate with violence at the sight of us. He seems to sense danger by the way the embers keep shifting to the machete leaning against the wall. I know he will get to it in a few steps if we try to grab him. That would be suicidal.

Blue Shirt and Yellow Shirt have withdrawn to a safe distance. Uba is cowering behind me. The impulse to turn and bolt becomes tempting. *Six thousand naira*, a voice says within me. And then an idea flashes through my mind as I make out something of what the madman is saying. The best thing to do is to try to lure him away from the machete and then grab him from the back. I quickly cook up a story.

"We are friends, and we come in peace," I begin to explain.

His ember eyes shift from me to Uba to the machete.

"It's about your nunchaku."

The word has a magical effect on him. He stiffens to attention, the wild combative look fleeing from him.

"Why not take us into your room," I say, "so we can talk about your nunchaku?"

He begins to move away from the wall into a long passage. We follow at a safe distance, Uba cowering behind me. The madman stops again, probably sensing danger, maybe realizing he is walking into a trap. We stop, too. The madman throws another glance at the machete, and then at us, and mumbles, "Nunchaku." I make sure to keep a safe distance. I will be out the gate like lightning before he gets to the machete. I used to be a good sprinter back in primary school. I am sure Uba is also sharpening his feet, but then the madman continues walking down the passage again, all the time mumbling "Nunchaku."

Everything suddenly looks easy and smooth. Now is the time to swing into action, as the madman's back is facing us. My heart beats fast. I exchange glances with Uba. I can see fear in those small eyes of his, which resemble the black dots on a dice. Fear seems to have chased his ugliness to the surface. We wait for who will make the first move. The men who hired us are nowhere within sight. The house is quiet, ominous. I signal Uba to move first, but he returns the favour. I wonder if we are the only people in the courtyard as I begin closing in on the madman. The air stills as I braze up to lunge at him.

Maybe I should have waited for him to go inside or even become tired and lie down before grabbing him. The madman is quicker than I could ever have imagined. He reacts the moment I grab him from behind, pivoting on his heels and lunging at me. I feel the rush of sticky liquid down my side as he sinks his teeth into my left ear. Pain sears through my body, drawing a wince from me. It all happens with electric speed. We heave and sway, but his strength is bewildering. Already I can feel one half of my ear gone, probably down his throat. I have to fight to stop him from eating up the rest. I try to hold on for as long as it will take Uba to look around for a weapon, but I can feel the madman's strength bearing down on me, overpowering me, and I can hear the stamp of feet. I know then that Uba is fleeing the compound, leaving me at the mercy of the madman.

With my remaining strength, summoned from the instinct of self-survival, I kick out at him, targeting his groin. I hear a thunk, a howl of pain, and then I feel his grip on me relaxing. I make my escape, tearing through the gate and down the road, making a trail of my own blood.

I am told that I was found in a pool of blood by the roadside. I must have passed out. I wake up at St. Anthony's Hospital, my eyes bulging with panic. St. Anthony's is a hospital in the neighbourhood people avoid for its expensiveness. I managed to escape with half of my ear bitten off, the tissue barely hanging, but Dr. Onodugo says it cannot be stitched back. I was brought to the hospital too late. I have lost half an ear to a madman, and all the money I'd saved to the hospital bill.

I take some time off work after my discharge. I spend the days alone lying on my mat after Eke and others head to work, mourning my misfortune, my lost half ear and my savings,

wishing I weren't so greedy. We didn't get a kobo from Blue
Shirt and Yellow Shirt, and I haven't seen them again since
the incident. I wonder what became of the madman, if my
kick was hard enough to cause damage to his groin.

With my savings gone, I resume work just under a week
after I am discharged from the hospital, with a bandage still
wound around my ear, my emotions heavy.

"Don't you think you need a little more time to recover
fully?" Eke says.

Eke had spent days at the hospital looking after me. He
has been of great support. I am still frail, but Christmas is fast
approaching, and I have to pay my weekly MASSOB dues,
which Abada has introduced. "They are needed to quicken
the release of our leader," he says. "We want to hire the best
lawyers, so you see why you have to be consistent in paying
the dues. Up-to-date members will be given priority." He will
be travelling to Okwe from time to time to remit the dues
at the headquarters of MASSOB, and they will be used in
funding the lawsuit.

"You have to be more careful," Eke says when I insist on
resuming work.

"It's the fault of that mango-head, that coward, Uba. He
ran away."

"I have heard that many times from you. Just be more
careful about what work you do. That madman could have
slaughtered you with a machete. What would I have told your
family?"

Sometimes Biafra seems like a ripe fruit that I could pluck
with a mere stretch of the arm. Sometimes I wonder if I am

wasting my time with politics. I tell myself I must learn how not to give up so easily. I don't want what happened in Lagos to happen again. Often I wish I had stayed to slug it out with Ejiro rather than coming here to face this harder life. At least I ate good food in the mansion.

The months of September and October are dry, so dry one considers himself lucky to be hired twice in a week. I wonder if I'll be able to save enough to return home for Christmas. It will be my first Christmas since coming to Anukwu, and I don't want to spend it in a foreign land. I want to spend it with my family. But the work drought seems to worsen as we enter the first week of November.

Twenty-one

I NEVER IMAGINED SPENDING CHRISTMAS AT A graveside. I never imagined that while others were eating rice and meat in their homes and drinking palm wine with their families on Christmas Day, I would be digging a grave in her little garden behind her house in which to bury her, the woman who killed a god.

I begin the day with a smoke as usual. I smoke first thing every morning. I enjoy it, lying in a relaxed posture, hissing smoke deep down in my lungs while thinking of the day ahead. When I am not in the mood for work, and I have some money for food and beer, I often lie on my mat all morning, smoking and listening to music on Joe's radio. I go to Mama Obodo's bar to spend the afternoon and return late and drunk. But if I don't have money, I am the first to show up at Ogbo-Mmanu, and I will carry buckets of sludge to empty a pit latrine as long as someone will hire me.

Lying quietly on my mat, I ponder a lonely Christmas without beer and cigarettes. An oil lamp turned low, daylight stealing in through the door, and a bird singing at my window have become familiar sights. Finally I get out of bed. Emptiness echoes through the house. Almost everyone has gone home for Christmas, including Eke, and the house seems colossal, frightening. I may as well be at work.

I step outside and hug a draft, a white morning dyed a partial blue. The bird at my window is yellow-chested, a weaver bird. I ignore it and walk into the pit latrine. I like to smoke in the toilet, squatting over the round concrete hole with eyes closed and enjoying my cigarette as much as the latrine fumes that warm my anus. I pull my grey shorts down to my knees as I lower myself. I have constipation, so I have to push with a lot of strength and groaning to get anything out. I wonder what I ate that has tightened my stomach as things I could have stoned somebody with finally hurtle out. My anus feels like it has been rubbed with pepper.

I wash my face, dress in my work rags, and hit the road with my spade. The scent of Christmas combs the street, intertwining with the Harmattan haze coating Anukwu. The road is busy with adults and children heading to church in their Christmas attire. I pause for a moment to ponder my religion. I haven't been to church since I came here, and long before that even. But I have been to a Christmas church before, and listened to the choir sing Alleluia Chorus. I am tempted to walk in, but my desire to make money pushes me along.

Mama Obodo's bar is open. I stop to ask for a stick of cigarette. Two men in dirty shorts and singlets, Okute and Nwude, are nursing a shot each of nkwu-oku, the locally distilled hot drink that has already jaundiced their features. They are sitting on a short bench at the mouth of the barroom, all pale and red-rimmed with hangover. One is a mason, the other a carpenter. We live on the same street, and they both are regulars at Mama Obodo's.

"Happy Christmas," I say to them.

"Happy Christmas," they grouse a chorus, lifting sagged faces to peer at me, their voices husky.

Mama Obodo is leaning on the counter, chin cupped in hand, with a face like mud.

"Happy Christmas, Mama Obodo," I say, grinning at her. "Give me a stick of cigarette."

"I am not going to begin the morning of a Christmas Day with debt," she snaps, sensing that I am broke.

"I will pay when I come back from work," I say in the softest of voices, knowing I won't get the cigarette if I return her insult.

She looks away. "I wonder who hires a labourer on Christmas Day."

I stare at the bottle of nkwu-oku and a squat porcelain shot lining the counter with packets of Benson & Hedges, Gold Leaf, St. Moritz, and Marlboro, and I swallow hard. A radio is playing Christmas carols.

"Give the poor fellow a shot and a stick of cigarette, and add it to my bill," Okute, the carpenter, says, scratching his fat yellowed nose, and posing as if he is doing me a great favour. I swallow the drink, light the cigarette, and thank Okute even though he is only paying back a debt. I buy him a drink sometimes, and I take exception to being referred to as "poor fellow" on Christmas Day.

I walk away with my spade while humming along to "The First Noel" playing from Mama Obodo's radio. It reminds me of *A Christmas Carol* by Charles Dickens, which I read back at the mansion, and Mama Obodo reminds me of the book's miserly protagonist, Ebenezer Scrooge. How can anyone hate Christmas? I miss my routine of reading at the mansion. I don't have anything to read here, and even if I could get my hands on a book, I'd be too exhausted to read it after a hard day's labour.

At the end of the road, St. Emmanuel Anglican Church resounds with more Christmas hymns. The church is festooned with decorations: tree, lights, balloons, and flowers. The congregation straggles to the premises. The spire is standing proud and tall with the birth of Jesus Christ. I know my mother will be in the local Protestant church in my hometown, singing hymns and speaking in tongues, asking God to bless me, Dimkpa, her first son. I heard she left the Catholic Church because the God there had refused to prosper me when I went to Lagos. Now she wears a lemon vest and wanders off for days with a Bible, just as my mind wanders back through the months. Still I have not saved anything to help my family out of poverty. Still I wake up with a hangover every morning. Still I have a piece of my left ear missing, and a small round bald spot on my scalp I got from lifting concrete up a flight of stairs.

Ogbo-Mmanu is quiet, deserted. No labourers jostling for work. No tipper trucks and no contractors. A boy my age is leaning on a spade beside a locked provision store. He looks hungry and broke, too. I wonder if he has a hangover. Maybe they hesitate to sell things to him, too, if he can't pay for them. I am tempted to cross over and ask him for a stick of cigarette, but instead I sit on the paving of a locked grocery shop and rest my chin on my spade. I know I am just wasting my time sitting here waiting for work on Christmas Day, but I can't stand the loneliness of my cold, cheerless room. At last, overcome by my hunger for a cigarette, I walk over to where the boy is seated. He looks Nwaba, a scurfy, timid individual.

"We seem to be the only two around here." I keep my voice low and casual, the way we do when we address them, the classless, dirty, razor-blade-selling, dialect-speaking Nwaba boys. I hate it when people like Mama Obodo yoke us together just because we both are from northern Igboland.

"Yeah." He looks like a rabbit ambushed in its hole. They always look wary, and intimidated.

"You have a cigarette there, eeh?" I look away into the distance for effect. The road is dusty, coated with Harmattan haze. The market and its lock-up shops are looking very strange, lonely. Much of the world beyond can't be seen.

He fumbles in his shabby trousers pocket and comes out with a squeezed packet of Three Rings. "Here," he says.

"I don't smoke this." I make a face but grab the packet still. "But the shops are closed for Christmas, so I have no choice."

I pluck two out of the four sticks left in the pack. I light one and take a long, famished draw. "Everyone has gone home for Christmas." I toss the other stick into my pocket. "You didn't go home. Why?"

"No money," he says.

"Money is not my problem." I have to let him know we are not on equal terms. It is called packaging, an exaggerated way of life we try to learn from the Agbenu townspeople. "I didn't feel like going home. I would be bored out of my mind sitting back in the house. That's why I am here."

He says nothing, and I wonder if he knows.

The road gets busy again towards midmorning, with people driving or walking home from church, and noon is thickly perfumed with spices that wake hunger pangs in me. Now the streets are full of boys with fried hair and perforated ears, cruising around in SUVs. The haze is gone. A car stops. A fat hand beckons me over. The hairs on my body raise themselves to their full height with hope as I hurry across the road to the big man on the wheels. There is no competition with everyone gone home, so no need to sprint. Nwaba drags himself behind me at a respectful distance.

"We need a grave, and some people to help us bury a body," says a man with a crew cut and a plain black T-shirt from behind the wheels. His companion is a smaller man wearing a starched green shirt.

A ripple of excitement spreads inside me. This is not a regular job like casting concrete or loading a tipper truck or serving as a building hand. It sounds intriguing, even more adventurous than catching an escaped madman fisting a machete.

"How much will it cost us?" Starched Green Shirt says.

I glance at Nwaba. "Pay us five thousand."

I should have asked for more. Crew Cut waves us into the car without bargaining. We are whisked away with our diggers and spades. The drive to the place is a quiet one. I am sitting at the back with Nwaba, in quiet contemplation. Crew Cut's voice keeps repeating itself in my head: *We need a grave, and some people to help us bury a body.* In my village a dead person is buried by his relatives. This man must have a lot of money to be hiring people to bury his dead for a whole five thousand naira. But he doesn't really look rich. He doesn't have a large stomach, his hands are not beefy or hairy, and he is not bald. He doesn't even have a full beard. I can usually identify a rich man by his voice and his laugh. I haven't heard this man laugh, though.

Christmas masquerades are now out on the road, drawing spectators out of their homes. Growing up, I had a Christmas Igariga mask back home. We arrive in a sleepy little village and stop outside a small cement house with a rusty tin roof. The house is enveloped in a sad silence. A small group of mourners sits outside. A fetid smell seeps through the tight Harmattan air as we come down with our tools and are led into the house past the mourners dressed like a church congregation. A wrecked wooden door leads into a small dingy passage. I feel the smell swell and seep into my pores as we turn right into a bare room where the body is lying. They have let it slide into a terrible state of decay. I glimpse a face bruised and drawn taut in the agony of death. I can't discern the sex of the bloated body lying on a soiled mattress in the unpainted room. My stomach turns. On the cement floor by the bed is a roughly made coffin. I suppose I wasn't expecting to see a body swaddled in clean, laundered sheets or lying in a varnished pitch-pine coffin.

Crew Cut leads us to the back of the house and points to a small garden where the grave will be dug. He returns to join the mourners. I wonder who he is to the dead person. There is a small backyard and a kitchen. A low shrub fence separates the compound from another compound with a bungalow. I notice people living in the next compound peeping at us through the fence as we dig the grave. They are looking at us as if we might bury ourselves in the grave right after digging it. We work without cigarettes, in silence, after we share Nwaba's last stick. He is a human excavator. I watch him dig, his body dark and shiny, pure wire-hard muscle. My mind wanders to Mummy in Lagos, but my wandering eyes catch the gaze of a gawky teenager standing in the neighbouring compound as I straighten to stretch myself.

"I will be back," I say to Nwaba. I walk to the shrub fence to meet the boy, who takes a few steps back as I approach. "We were hired to dig this grave and bury a body. Who is he?" I say to him.

"She killed a tortoise. She's an osu," he says and glides out of sight.

I stiffen to attention. *Osu* is the Agbenu word for "outcast."

I have a creeping feeling I am about to unravel a mystery, but the boy is gone like a flash of lightning. I walk back, sit on a heap of red clay thrown out of the grave as Nwaba shovels, and watch a white-chested bird perching on a shrub at the head of the garden as it suckles at a flower, beaking some grey insects to death.

"Check if it's okay," says Nwaba, wanting to know if he should stop digging.

He actually says it a few times before I hear him. My mind is busy trying to work out what has happened here. I consider asking the men who hired us as I walk around the grave with hands tucked into my pockets like a supervisor in some important ministry.

"Okay," I say, after asking him to mend this angle and dress that corner.

When it is time to box up the body, we move towards the room where it is lying. I ease behind to allow Nwaba to go first. After the experience with the madman, I have learned not to go first. I sense Nwaba's fright. We both hesitate at the door, but I win. He suddenly enters, startling flies. A fat fly stones the upper side of my mouth on its way to escaping. The smell in the room has gone from dry to a sticky, sickening wet. Nwaba throws a soiled blanket over the body and jerks his head at me. Together we haul it into the coffin and slam the lid closed.

The slow nasal hymn of the small congregation singing with wrinkled noses escorts her to the grave:

Not a burden we bear
Not a sorrow we share
But our toil he doth richly repay
Not a grief or a loss

Not a frown or a cross
But is blest if we trust and obey

Elizabeth-Marie, the woman we buried, founded Jehovah Kingdom Mission in Anukwu in 1981 and died childless, Crew Cut tells me later.

My face must tell him that I want to hear more.

"Everyone in this village believes she was killed by some deity because she accidentally killed a tortoise. Can you imagine that?"

"It's unimaginable," I say. My father once told me that Ezenwanyi took the form of a snake. People had seen the snake sunning itself on a rock surface in the cave. The snake would not harm them. It simply withdrew for them to fetch water, prompting villagers to announce their presence before entering the cave to avoid stumbling on the goddess's serpent incarnation.

"Of course the people in this village foolishly believe this tortoise is their god incarnate . . . You and I know that tortoises are tortoises, and so did she, but these people wanted her to perform expiatory rites, and when she refused . . ." At this point, his companion strolls up and interrupts our conversation.

My eyes scan the small, impersonal crowd, the choir singing Psalms, her congregation according her a full funeral liturgy even after the villagers refused to get involved.

Laying Elizabeth-Marie in her coffin was an ordeal that left my hands oily. They are still sodden with her fluids even after washing them with hot water and detergent. My memory holds nothing and my eyes see nothing but her bloated figure—even after smoking countless sticks of cigarette and drowning myself in alcohol at Mama Obodo's bar.

Twenty-two

EKE AND I GET HIRED AFTER HE RETURNS FROM THE village with stories of Christmas and how my family has missed me and wish I had come home, too. My mother even wrapped spices and asked him to bring them to me. She now carries a new Bible, Eke says, that's as big as my tin box. Eke met my father sitting under the umbrella tree when he went to our house. My father wanted to know if I had sent him something for his snuff and ekpetechi. Eke ended up oiling his palm to make him stop groaning. My father laughed, blowing air from his nose, and Eke was sprayed umber. I cherish hearing stories of the village from Eke: my siblings whining about how they have missed me, Machebe's curiosity to know the real reason I did not return like everyone does at Christmas and how Eke lied that the white men had requested me to do a special job for them, and Madam Bridget's bar swarming with drunks who went wild when Eke showed up like a rainbow in their sky.

Eke and I are hired along with two other labourers to fill in the foundations of two new, large buildings in early January. What a lucky break! Eke figures it will take slightly over a hundred and fifty buckets of the tipper truck to complete the work, and about one week and a half to finish the contract if we manage to do sixteen trips a day. We are going to be paid a lot of money for this job, and Okike's tomb is long overdue on account of the setbacks I suffered. If all goes well, I will be visiting home after we finish the contract to take care of the tomb and see my family I have missed so much. I don't tell Eke about the woman we buried, though. I don't want him blaming me for accepting the wrong kind of job even though it helped me to recover financially after the attack from the madman.

"She had been an outcast for many years," Mama Obodo had said after hearing the story. "She became one after she killed a god reincarnated in a tortoise, or so they say."

"I don't understand," I said.

"You are foreigners, that's why you were hired to bury her, as any indigene of that community who gets involved in her burial would be cast off, too. Her children would have been contaminated if she'd had any. They would belong to the god now."

On the first day of the contract, Jerome, Nduka, Eke, and I manage to do fifteen trips, working from dawn to dusk. As usual, we spend the evening at Mama Obodo's, to release our aching joints for tomorrow's work. The next day we are back digging and hauling, smoking and chattering. We take turns to dig, to deepen the soft base of the quarry, leaving a peak hanging dangerously above us. A large powder keg sitting next to a fire.

I am in the pit digging for our ninth trip of the day when suddenly a large cube of laterite breaks off from the sagging peak and cascades noiselessly down. I experience momentary darkness. I have only seconds to puzzle it out, to haul myself free and out of the way of the avalanche before its arrival. I barely manage to escape being trapped. But we are excited by it. Tons of laterite falling at our feet like manna and quail falling from heaven for the people of Israel make our work easier for the day, as we do not have to dig and only have to shovel it into the tipper truck.

On the last day, we work until the sun labours up the hill and begins to ease down west, a red ball of fire the size of a large breadfruit head. We have worked fourteen trips, and we have only a few more remaining. Eke was almost perfect in his estimation of the number of buckets the project would gulp. In all, we have done a hundred and forty-six trips in ten days. We are sitting in the pit, fatigued, smoking and waiting for the tipper truck to return. Already the evening is looking good, as beautiful as the orange wash of the sunset.

Suddenly a deep crack tears my mind away from our evening at Mama Obodo's bar back to the quarry, a cleavage so loud and sudden the earth appears to have fractured. The ground heaves from beneath us, whirling like a massive roller coaster, the heavens engulfed in a great blanket of darkness. It's a nightmare in which the earth disconnects from heights and a landslide plummets from the skies. Dazed, I stare at death as it fountains down on us. I have the sensation of being pulled into an abyss, of drowning in a dark sea. We are a stampeding herd of buffalo, Eke, Jerome, Nduka, and I, as we scrabble in what will soon be our graveyard. For a fleeting moment I glimpse the face of Ezenwanyi's priest and hear his deep voice: *The connection between them is very strong, stronger than you can imagine, and that is why she comes to him in the dream, as a sign of that everlasting bond, a sign that she will be there for him if called upon in times of need or distress.*

"O-ki-ke," I cry out in a voice as loud as the great deep bellow of the sky now falling on the earth. And then I make a lunge for safety, diving, balling, and rolling away like wheels as the monstrous apocalypse arrives.

As soon as I come to, I relive the horror again in painful snatches: How everything around me went quiet. How the valley sat back after the deep, colossal belch like a tired old man full with food, and the quarry was covered in a mountain of laterite. How the tipper truck crashed into a copse across the road, knocked into motion by the impact of the avalanche and sent flying over the way into the clump, battering its face on a huge tree.

I see the driver now as he emerges from a haze, bleeding from the forehead and limping. I remember him sitting on the wheels of the lorry while we loaded. He usually takes a stroll or stands away and watches, but this time he had waited impatiently on the wheels, eager to be done with the job. Eke is nowhere to be seen. Jerome and Nduka are missing, too. A wave of panic grips me after the driver and I make a few frantic calls without reply.

And then somewhere from beneath the rubble comes a deep human groan. My heart stops beating. We scramble around for diggers and spades, but they are buried. I fall on my knees and dig with my hands to free him, them. I claw away like a pangolin desperate to burrow a hiding place. I imagine voices, police sirens screaming, the wailing of an ambulance.

And then it all goes black.

Twenty-three

THE DAYS FOLLOWING EKE'S TRAGIC DEATH, AS I AR-
range to bring his body home, are melancholy days, and they
fill me with a deep sense of loss. I have never before lost someone so close to me, watching them die. Realizing that Eke was
buried in that graveyard of laterite forged the lethal tool, but
hearing his deep groan speared my heart. I lie exhausted on
my mat, limp as a leaf lamed by heat, less from passing out at
the scene of the accident than from what lies ahead as I con-
template a life without my friend. I can't stop the tears from
flowing. I try to shake off the fear that stalks my paths. Eke's
memory is everywhere in the half-finished house, his ghost
looming in the large, empty corridor.

The bodies of Eke, Jerome, and Nduka lie cooling in a mortuary. The Wawa community makes donations to take care of
this and the ambulances that will take their bodies to their
hometowns. The tragedy seems to unite the migrant workers
from Wawaland even more and fill them with a sense of duty
to the dead. I am going to ride all the way home with Eke's
body. I had thought of going home to announce his death be-
forehand, to warn his family, but I cannot leave Eke's body
alone in a foreign land. The community here needs me in their
plans, too, as his closest kin.

Home is a sour grape I have to eat. There is not much to
pack. Two shirts, a pair of trousers, a comb and a mirror, a
packet of Tiger razor blades, my new Kchibo radio, and a

pair of slippers—they make up my household property. But I also have to take Eke's things. I am going to give them to his mother, plus his share of the money from the contract. The full impact of Eke's tragic end hits me as I take one more look around the room. I let out a sob as I lock the door and slip the key under a doormat where I always kept it for Eke, as if expecting him to come back from work and find it as usual.

I follow the shortcut, the side of the fence where the low brick wall has crumbled, instead of the old gate whose rusty hinges groan like a sick man when it is swung open. The track runs through a grove to the wide road that connects Ogbo-Mmanu. I turn to look at the large, unpainted house for the last time. Some crows are up on the roof scratching and clamouring in their harsh, annoying voices. I consider stoning the evil birds away, but then I turn and begin to stride down the road, leaving them in their uproar. Ogbo-Mmanu is quiet, still trying to come to terms with the tragedy. The whole Wawa community gathers as the ambulances arrive with a convoy of three chartered buses to escort the bodies of their fellow labourers home. Eke's memory fills the space in my mind on the drive to Agulu through the same road that brought us to Anukwu. Death is all I think of as we depart Anukwu, rolling in between a depressing mesh of greenery.

We arrive at Ogige market around sunset. Nothing has changed in the hilly town of Nsukka under the dull chrome of a sunset. Ogige market still exudes that familiar unidentifiable damp smell, but the smell of fresh leaves and barks banish the Ogige market–flavoured stench as we head towards Oregwu. The roads are muddy, the houses old; the ones that are close to the roads are streaked with red mud. Everything unwinds like a bad dream. Sad and scary. The sound of the ambulance as it approaches the village brings people to their housefronts, panic on their faces. Hell is let loose as it noses its way to Eke's family house, and as Eke's body is lifted out and taken to his mother without warning, a mistake I will live to regret.

The arrival of Obochi is the most exciting thing to happen to Onoyima since he was forced to relocate to the shrine of Ezenwanyi.

Obochi had first fled to escape her fate. "I would rather die than become the bride of any goddess," she had vowed. But she hadn't got far. Her parents passed on before sunset, as forewarned by the seer. A few days after their deaths, her older brother fell from a tree and broke his neck, forcing her out of hiding. She walked straight home and surrendered herself to prevent the deaths of her remaining siblings. She was escorted to the shrine of Ezenwanyi by relatives. They walked miles and miles into the forbidden forest, finally arrived at Ishiayanashi, and were received by attama Ezenwanyi, a haggard old man sitting in his large polygamous household filled with humans and livestock, overseeing a community of outcasts.

Onoyima works all day at the farm. He leaves his hut at dawn and returns at dusk. Surprisingly, he likes it. It means less time to brood over his misfortune. It would have been less hurtful if he had been captured by the slave raiders from Aro and Nike terrorizing the villages and sold to the white people who came to their land through the seas. Knowing that he fell to the powers of the famous Ibinikpuabi and his own weakness as a man would have appeased his anger and self-reproach. But he realizes how important it is to accept his fate with calm and bravery, and not dwell too much on the good home life he used to have when he was still living with his parents and six siblings, though he misses them greatly. "I am forever estranged from them," he laments, and there and then he vows *to dump the name Onoyima and henceforth go by Gbaghalu, imploring their forgiveness and severing the last link with his family.*

Obochi is frightened in the early days of her arrival. Gbaghalu had felt the same way in his first few weeks, like a lonely little bird in the wild. He keeps her company and makes conversation to reassure her. Sometimes they sit in tense, guilt-laden silence. She senses in him a man struggling to overcome his past. He notices how heavily the guilt of her parents' deaths and that of her brother weighs down on her. Now the bride of a goddess, a few weeks ago she had been a beautiful and happy maiden, obviously desired by all the eligible young men in her community. It was killing him, too, his guilt over the deaths of his parents by his own hands.

"The attama is Ezenwanyi's physical agent," he says to her. "He guides her worshippers and looks after her belongings: her outcasts, her livestock, her farmlands, her forests. Her universe."

Obochi listens to him with her chin cupped in her hands, lines of anxiety etched on her forehead.

"But it is safe in the shrine," he assures her. "We are sacred and untouchable beings." He inclines his head and says in a thick voice, "I killed a man from this shrine. I wouldn't have touched him, no matter the level of provocation, if I had known he belonged to Ezenwanyi."

"What happened?"

He told her the full story of the fight and murder at the farm.

How different their stories are. He killed a man, but she only picked snails.

"You are only a victim," he says, concern and sympathy in his voice. "Would you like to hear the story of how Ezenwanyi came to this community?"

"Yes, please," she whispers.

He begins to narrate the story of how the community fell to intervillage warring a long time ago, losing many of its citizens to death and enslavement, while others fled to distant places for safety. The few survivors, in order to protect themselves from the slaving and warring activities of enemy neighbours, installed a powerful, protective deity. Ezenwanyi, a female warrior goddess, has the responsibility of nurturing and protecting the citizens in order to repopulate the community. She enslaves people who trespass into her territory and claims their belongings as part of her rebuilding mission.

Obochi's eyes light up with a new understanding of the structure of Ezenwanyi.

Gbaghalu takes Obochi around the shrine, showing her the other outcast huts. He points out one with a pillar of smoke rising from a fire just outside. A man and a woman can be seen in front of the hut. The man, shrunken and old, is sitting a short distance from the smouldering fire. He is warming himself in the cold of the forest in his loincloth. The woman is tending a clay pot. She is thin, her shriveled breasts stretched like fibres on her bare chest, but it is easy to see from her height and her litheness that she was once a woman of great beauty.

Gbaghalu stammers an explanation. "The man I—I accidentally killed was their son. He was their only son. He had been running an errand for his father on the day of our bloody encounter, but he was attracted to the shimmering green plume of the young palm in my father's farm on his way home."

Obochi listens in calm, horrified silence.

"The old woman, his mother, is a promise made to Ezenwanyi a long time ago," he continues. "There was a deadly famine in her place of birth. Her father had to come all the way to this shrine on

pilgrimage. He made a deal with Ezenwanyi to dedicate his fairest daughter to the goddess in exchange for prosperity, to save the rest of the family from starvation. His prayer was answered. He gave her up in fulfillment of his promise. Her husband, then a charming young bachelor, saw her and fell in love, but his family was not in support of him marrying an Ezenwanyi 'dedicate.' He insisted on marrying her, took her bride price to the shrine, dropped it on the altar, and made his intentions known to the goddess. By doing that, he secured the permission of Ezenwanyi to marry her. But for getting involved with an outcast, his family disowned him, because he had become a contaminated man himself. He relocated to the shrine, and they have lived together here ever since."

A fresh wave of sadness envelops Obochi.

Obochi steps out of her hut and into the rain. Standing under the shaggy eaves, she lets the water stream down on her. She shuts her eyes as it seeps into her soul, finds her guilt, and begins to cleanse it—the guilt of causing the deaths of her parents and brother, and mortgaging the future of her siblings in the hands of others. Every time it rains, she strips, walks outside, and gets a good drenching. And after, she enters into a long revitalizing sleep, and feels better when she wakes up. This is, for her, an act of penance. It is, more importantly, therapy.

One day, while she is in the middle of her outdoor bath, she becomes aware of someone watching her. The forest seems to have grown a pair of ogling eyes. Though her own eyes are closed, she can feel the intensity of the stare, like a rig drilling a hole in her nakedness.

"Who is there?" Her voice is tentative, wavering between uncertainty and a tepid confrontation.

The forest replies with silence punctuated by birdsong.

Later on, as she searches around for clues, she finds footprints, and they are familiar. She sits in front of her hut wondering, mourning her lost maidenhood: the fancies, the pretenses, and the daydreams of growing up, and of falling in and out of love.

Gbaghalu emerges from his hut. He walks towards her, his male whiff and brawny features stirring desirous feelings in her. But she is incensed nonetheless. She had before that afternoon in the rain seen him as a responsible young man, a leopard killer, but now as he strolls over for the ritual of a chat, she watches his slow shuffling gait, debating whether or not to confront him. She does. He squirms, brushing an imaginary speck off his arm, his reaction betraying his guilt.

"You have no excuse," she snaps, incensed that he tries to excuse his mischief, his act of indignity as male weakness, a shameless peeper like him.

"I am sorry." His feelings of remorse tighten on his face.

Somehow she likes it that a reason to hate him has presented itself. He has been making things too comfortable for her in the shrine.

"I want to be left alone," she declares.

"Your idea of penance," he says.

He is right. She shouldn't be heard laughing at his jokes. By laughing, she desecrates the memory of her parents and brother. She should be mourning instead of spending time in the company of a man whose every action betrays a deep adoration for her.

"I have done something terrible and shameful," he says. "Something inexcusable. I will take whatever comes to me as a matter of atonement, but to sit here and wallow in self-pity, I will not let you."

She stares icily at him.

Twenty-four

MY FATHER'S COMPOUND IS A TAINTED GREEN CARPET, covered with moss. It drizzles all night, as if the skies are mourning Eke, the air thickening into a solid frozen lump. I think of Eke sleeplessly: the years we spent together, the friendship and laughter we shared. I replay the horrible memory of Eke's mother banishing me from his funeral and my mother blaming me for it. "You acted like a child," my mother said. "You should have come home to break the news ahead of the body arriving as his closest kith and kin in that foreign land." The village is still in shock. Eke's mother is heartbroken. The Anukwu community that escorted the body home left after the burial, but I have resolved not to return to Anukwu. I am done with migrant work. My mother took one look at my wrecked body, my mangled ear, and broke down in tears.

The ground is soaked this morning, blending the smell of wet loam with the stomach-churning odour of decayed wild mangoes and goat dung. My gaze wanders to the garden by the side of the house, the grave catching my eyes, flourishing green with cassava, pumpkins, and spinach in the genial morning sunlight. Eating breakfast with my family, sober, feels unfamiliar. My youngest siblings are excited to see me, and they bug me with questions about my ear, but Machebe's jaws are clamped tight. He knows there is nothing to celebrate about my empty-handed homecoming. Once more I have failed to help my family out of the poverty we are mired in. But I have resolved to build Okike a tomb as a token of my gratitude to her for saving me from imminent death, even if I have to spend my savings down to the last kobo. It's not much, the bulk of it coming from the work that took Eke's life, but it is enough.

Eke's mother is out of her mind with grief. I don't really blame her for reacting the way she did, for charging at me like a wounded beast. Beyond blaming me for bringing her son's body home unannounced, I sense a resurgence of the old hatred, some sneaking suspicion that Eke died because he had stubbornly refused to dissociate himself from me. But I forgive her. It is easy to do that when I think that it could easily be me lying six feet below, putting my mother in his mother's position.

"It's not a bad idea," my father says when I mention my plan to start work on the tomb. He also believes it is Okike, my ancestral benefactress, who saved me. But my mother is sure it is Chukwu Abiama, the Christian God-of-the-Selected, who tucked me in his giant lemon wings and whisked me out of the way of the massive earthfall.

"For taking care of her grave, your aunt will continue to protect your interests from the world beyond," my father says.

"It's a heathen belief," my mother says, shaking her head.

"Okike has been giving," my father insists. "It has not been a good season for plants, with greenflies all over the place, but the plants in the garden where the grave is remain untouched by the aphids. The spinach grows from nowhere. Harvest it today, tomorrow it sprouts again."

"Did you ever kill a tortoise?" I hear myself saying.

My father snorts as he often does when asked a dumb question.

I rephrase the question. "Is it a sacrilege to kill a tortoise?"

"Well, it depends." He begins to explain as my mother walks away from what he is about to utter, from sin. "While it is not a sacrilege in this community to kill a tortoise, it might be elsewhere, in places where gods incarnate themselves in certain animals. Ezenwanyi is one such goddess. But she takes the form of a serpent."

I tell him the story of the woman we buried in Anukwu, but in the third person, as if it happened to someone else.

"I feel for this woman, assuming she actually killed the tortoise accidentally," he says, with more cool than I had hoped. "But she should have gone ahead to perform the expiatory rites. It—"

"That's blasphemy." My mother flying out of the house again interrupts him.

"Well then," my father says. "Would you have preferred to die?"

"For doing what pleases my father, yes," my mother says with hands fisting her hips, fight in her posture. "And to take my place in his house in heaven."

I leave them to their argument.

As I approach Okike's grave and see the plants blossoming green on this clear and calm morning with its bank of grey clouds, anger rises in me like hot Saharan dust. I shouldn't allow rage to defile my mourning, I tell myself, even if my family has thoughtlessly ploughed my benefactress's grave. I have decided I will not start work on the tomb until after twenty-eight days of mourning Eke, the traditional period for close kin. I go to bed every night hoping Eke will come to me in my dreams, but instead I have nightmares, violent and stark, depicting his end. I realize that I don't have a single photograph of him, and my feelings of despair deepen. It's only days since his death and his features are already receding in my memory, kindling the fear that his image might continue to fade until it becomes a pale blur, and then only just an idea.

I sneak out to his gravesite one night. The grave is in his father's compound, next to the tree where we used to sit and peel oranges, and where Eke would call me a coward and laugh in his crackling bushfire voice. I must cut a lonely figure standing in the cold darkness, whipped by the rain, lit by streaks of lightning. I choose a stormy night because his mother is more likely to be indoors. Lying six feet below the ground, Eke must be cold, too, and wrapped in thick layers of darkness. I do not leave the graveside until I'm thoroughly damp and shivering. As I walk home on the orange path paved by lightning, the feeling that Eke and I are on equal terms again fills me with relief, but then I am ashamed of the self-centredness of my thoughts.

After twenty-eight days, I send Eke's things to his mother through my father and set to work.

It is easy for me to harvest the cassava. The ground is soft and wet after weeks of rain, and the thin, immature roots of cassava follow each effortless pull without any grudge. My mother watches me with a pout. "I don't understand why you have to destroy those plants in these hard times all because of a tomb. Can you not wait until they are harvested?"

"I don't want to spend the money budgeted for the tomb on something else," I explain.

She walks away with a hiss.

I weed the grave neat after harvesting the cassava. The

avocado tree my father planted to mark the head of the grave has matured. I rush off to Ogige market to buy cement at Commercial Avenue, near a smelly abattoir where the butchers wield curved carving knives with glancing blades. I can't help but feel for the cattle as I imagine all sorts of grim possibilities. I have worked out the cost of building the tomb. The money I returned with covers the cost of cement and tiles. Some of my father's bricks are lying around in the compound, so I won't need to buy blocks. I will fetch sand from deposits along the village road for the construction. I know it won't be anything close to the Folashade gold-rimmed tomb, but it's all I can afford, and I hope Okike understands.

I form the tomb with the bricks and raise a wall at the head of the grave to the height of my waist, and then I fill up the rectangular brickwork with sand and cover it with the white tiles. It takes a long time to construct it, maybe two hours, maybe three, because I do a clean job. Finally I wash the tiles clean and stand back to admire the shining white tomb, filled with a sense of achievement, imagining Okike's statue seated on the short wall at the head of the tomb in lace, beads, and a purse, her ichafu rising on her head in poetic folds.

Satisfied, I wash, eat lunch, and stroll down to the cave, thinking of the woman we buried in Anukwu. My father has talked about the healing powers of the cave's spring, its waterfall provoked by euphoria at moments when Ezenwanyi is in a benevolent mood. He has talked about Ezenwanyi's protectiveness, and how the goddess blesses her favoured. I ponder the mystery of my survival at the excavation site, realizing that my mother should not have forbidden us from Ezenwanyi's cave or waved away my father when he said our destinies were tied to a reptile goddess, a crowing crested cobra.

Two groves lean away from each other on the broad sweep of hills. The cave is buried in the womb of one of the groves, the thicker of the two. At this time of the season when the rains are relentless, water ambles out of the caves and strolls down the valley into the second grove with ululations that beguile, with the devotion of a mother feeding a child. The view is breathtaking, but the scene is nothing in the dry season after the hills have been licked by tongues of orange flame, leaving a charred, soulless ridge. And then the caves dry up completely, with cakes of dirt collecting at their bottoms. The entrance to the grove is a dark corridor pierced by shafts of sunlight. Everything seems quiet, not a bird chirping, so quiet the ululation of the water is unusually audible, pure melody, reminding me of okanga, a dance of drumming and fluting performed by the old men of my village when they celebrated Ezenwanyi with music before the arrival of Holy Trinity Church and Father Matthew, according to my father.

Everything seems to have gone quiet in this part of the grove, where Okike's body was found, as I was told. I wade across to the spot where they found her body wedged on a tree. It seems no one comes this way to fetch water or do laundry or wash breadfruit any longer for fear of being cast out by Father Matthew. Years of water washing over the base of the tree has bared its thick root. The grove is full of spots and beautiful patterns of sunlight. I sit on a looped branch, one of several spiraling down all the way from the treetops, and begin to swing forth and back with eyes closed as I try to reconnect with a feeling, the energy building up. The story is that Okike drowned in the cave at a time when it was full and flowing. She was there alone in this lonely grove for three days before they saw her body. She may have let herself into the bowel of the cave, her body floating down the broader side of the channel to this place where the creek is narrower, becoming wedged on the tree.

The branch suddenly snaps, perhaps with the weight of my thoughts and feelings, and I see myself easing down into the water. I step away and hug the tree in gratitude, my arms ending halfway around the huge, leathery trunk. But for the tree my father might never have found Okike's body. She could have been swept away where my father would never have found her. I kiss the tree, the smell of its bark filling my nose like the caffeine I always smelt in Mummy's coffee in Lagos. But I am startled by a sharp pain that needles my chest as a black ant, which has smuggled itself into my shirt, unleashes its fury at being crushed: a tendril of pain that spirals through my body, ending in a bubble of liquid at the tip of my penis. I let go, moving away from the tree, pondering its name. It has the leathery grey bark of an oak, but it is not an oak. It is not a banyan, either. It is the Tree of Life and Death—the phrase appears suddenly and fully formed in my mind.

I glow at the new name, Tree of Life and Death, at this flash of inspiration, as I undress for a bath, stooping and scooping water with cupped hands, throwing each scoop over my shoulder and shuddering as it falls on me with a chill. I dress after the bath and walk out of the creek as the sun sinks below treetops, low and red in the sky, and the day slowly fades like a scene in a boring film as I walk home.

At home I stand afar and admire the tomb again in the blue-grey light of a dusk skimming with bats and swifts. I have a feeling that Okike is very pleased with me. Dinner is yam and salted palm oil. The room is illuminated by the big round flame of my mother's ochanja, but we eat outdoors in the moonlight. The tomb is chalky under a cool lunar glow. After the meal, while my family enjoys a post-dinner conversation, I lie on the tomb beside Okike, face up and looking into the big liquid eye of a moon. I imagine myself in her arms, my little teary face pressed into her breasts, and my small mouth tightened around her milkless nipple as she pats my small shoulder and croons me a soft song: *Onyemurunwanebeakwa, egbemurunwanebeakwa, wetuzizawetose, wetamaraneluofe, kumunnunurachaka, egbeoo egbeoo.*

Twenty-five

AFTER SEVERAL WEEKS OF CONFINING MYSELF TO THE house, I stroll to Uwakwe's shop one afternoon only to find the place deserted. The gamblers are no longer there. The whole place looks dry. Uwakwe is sitting on the same bench the gamblers used to sit on in front of the shop in a frayed singlet and worn-out boxers.

"I have not seen you for years." He smiles broadly at me. He is so dark you could bump into him in a corridor, mistaking him for darkness. A broken fragment of solid darkness.

"I have not been around, but I don't think it has been that long." Truthfully, I have been away for nearly three years if I add up all the time I wasted in the mansion in Lagos and working in Anukwu.

"You have changed a lot." His eyes wander to my left ear. "What happened there?"

"It was an accident." I wonder what Uwakwe will say when he realizes that, besides missing half an ear, I now smoke Benson & Hedges and drink Premier beer.

"Oh. I am sorry," he says. "Speaking of accidents, I didn't see you at Eke's burial. I heard you were living with him when it happened."

I figure he is only feigning ignorance. He would have heard that I was banished from the funeral. Oregwu is a small village. People are known to each other. They know what the next household is having for supper.

"I was there when it happened."

After I finish the tragic story, Uwakwe stares at me with arms folded across his broad chest.

"Poor boy. It is a terrible thing to be buried alive," he says with a gesture of revulsion. "Surviving such a close shave with death is a sign that you will live to become the custodian of the village patriar . . ." His voice trails off, his thick, soupy face draining of colour.

I feel sorry for Uwakwe after his slip of tongue. He looks so guilty, so pathetic, like a boy caught stealing meat from his mother's soup.

"I was bored at home, so I came to watch the gamblers." I change the subject to save him further embarrassment.

"They no longer come here to play draughts," Uwakwe says in a whispering voice. "Patty Onah and Oluoha are still in detention. The police come here every once in a while to sniff around. Everyone is afraid of being arrested."

I am surprised they are still detained even after the release of the MASSOB leader. I heard of his acquittal from BBC Igbo Live on my radio.

"The man has been silent," Uwakwe hisses. "He is doing nothing to help those who were detained alongside him. Some say he has backed down from the struggle out of fear for his life. Others say he collected a large sum of money from the government, a payoff."

"Too bad, if what they say about him is true. How could he abandon his supporters for money?"

"His silence is like the silence of a mother duck whose ducklings are snatched by the hawk," says Uwakwe. "The land is shaky with uncertainty. There are even rumours of a new group called the Biafra Zionist Movement, which will pick up where MASSOB has failed, but people in this village are only talking about it in undertones."

I ponder this new movement. "I would like to know more about this group."

"It's still being talked about in whispers," he says. "I know that it's a pro-Biafran group, that's all. But I have my ears to the ground. I will let you know as soon as I hear of a meeting or anything."

I wonder what will become of Abada's group if the MASSOB leader abandons the struggle. Eke's death and my relocation to the village cut short my membership, the dues I paid now wasted. I walk away to allow Uwakwe to attend to his customers.

It's twilight when I arrive home. I eat an early dinner and lie on the tomb. When I tire of this, I wander off again to the cave, climb down rock ledges, and yell like a madman to wake echoes and set off cascades. But nothing happens. I walk away, disappointed, angry that the cave refuses to yield to me. My father is probably wrong about Ezenwanyi's powers.

Then, soft, beguiling woodwind rhythms of Ikorodo dance wafting in with a mild wind lure me to a bustling village square in a neighbouring community. The dance is performed by beautiful girls my age and younger in a V-dance formation at the centre of the crowded square: lean, swarthy, brown, bare sweaty shoulders, slender arms, and smooth thighs. Breasts like spears.

"What's the celebration?" I ask a boy in the crowd in a loud voice.

"It's a reception ceremony for the first university graduate this village has produced." He whoops with excitement.

Presently the celebrant arrives. He alights from a big black car, a man of impressive height and panache, in a well-tailored suit. His tie is a startling red, his skin the dark brown sheen of a guanabana seed. He smells of education, walks with dignified steps, and speaks English in a low and refined voice. The crowd applauds his arrival. The dancers pounce on the music, dancing with a measured sway of their ample hips, their bodies gracefully suspended above bended knees, their feet clasping the ground at the toes while they wriggle their waists. The vocalist's well-oiled voice is raised in eulogy above the percussion, a dapper little man dignified by his talent. He praises the educated man, calling him the fluted pumpkin that reaches its vines afar to claim ownership of the farmland. He calls him the migrating swallow that returns an eagle. After a few delicate dance steps, the educated man raises a big wristwatched hand to call for silence. The music and the voices peter out. He speaks in a voice full of power. His laughter resonates, punctuating his speech. And then he reenters the car and is whisked off, but the dancing and celebration continue.

A man, quick and lithe, breaks into the circle of spectators and positions himself in front of the dancers. I can see the man's talent is legendary from the way the crowd reacts to his appearance. He is a man who wins beautiful women with his dance steps, says the vocalist. The dancer glances from the tamarind tree standing nearby to a swift-flying red-crested woodpecker cruising across a stainless blue deregulated space. He scans every happy face in the crowd and pushes the air this way and that way, to the delight of the crowd. He is being careful with his prelims. The prelims are the kernel of any dance if well handled, the rest is a matter of energy, asserts the vocalist. The crowd roars in wonderment as the dancer begins to wriggle to the pulsing drumming in agreement with the feline, female dancers. The whole arena is set alight as more people from the spectators break into the circle to wiggle, hop, and twist to the dance. An old man tries to scratch something out of a hip-bone injury probably sustained from a palm tree fall. He reminds me of my father. But my father has healed, enough to stroll to any of the drinking spots in the village if a little money enters his hand, although apparently not enough to return to his work.

Silence screams at me when I open my eyes to find that I never left the tomb, never went to Ezenwanyi's cave again or to the celebration. The cold slab of the tomb digs into my ribs as I muse over this dream and the educated man: his aura, his panache, and his rhetoric skill. I want to be educated like him, rich, impressive, and polished. I see myself returning to the village as an important man, celebrated by pretty dancers, my success drowning our hardship. I rise from the tomb and grope my way inside. But the dream is waiting for me in the room. It forms a beam of light as I lie awake on my mattress and wait for sleep to claim me again.

Growing up, I dreamt a lot about food and hunger. And then I would see myself flying over mountains and canyons and rivers, sailing smoothly and effortlessly. When I told my mother about it she hushed me up, saying, "Don't mention it again or people will think you are a wizard." But I had a dream about my father, where he slumped and died on his coronation day, and it came to pass when he lost the crown to another man. I dream of Okike still, my protectoress, and every time I watch her drown, I see myself cheating death.

This new dream ushers me into a new day with a new thought, a fresh idea that soon ferments like my mother's manioc as the emptiness of the days stretches out before me, filling me with boredom. Hot-hot days filled with flies and sunshine and dust. I can't sit on the tomb because the sun heats it. I resign myself to the company of the Tree of Life and Death in the loneliness of the creek, and to sitting under the umbrella tree in our housefront, just sitting and staring. Every morning, I watch students of the Community Secondary School in their white-and-indigo uniforms as they cross ways with Queen of the Rosary girls looking like cerulean angels. I stare at them with envy, pondering my wasted years. I watch them as they come back from school on afternoons that are colour-washed white and sky blue, feet dusty, and tiredness blooming on their foreheads. The youngest amongst them are between twelve and thirteen, the oldest and the ones wearing trousers or braids are anything from sixteen to seventeen. I will be eighteen in a matter of weeks, with a wisp of unfamiliar beard. I would have been one of those blue-trousered boys had my father not lost his throne.

The educated man is everywhere in my head again. I can feel his presence, strong like a well-brewed burukutu. My dream comes back to haunt me again and again. Oregwu doesn't have a university graduate. When most girls finish primary or secondary school, they get married; others learn braiding or sewing at Ogige market. The boys learn motor mechanics or carpentry or masonry. Others go to Onitsha or Kano or Lagos to get apprenticed to big traders. I want to fill that empty space. I know it is a tall ambition to achieve, but I want to become the first graduate ever to come out of my little village, Oregwu.

Twenty-six

I FINALLY SUMMON MY FAMILY AFTER WEEKS OF SLEEP-
less nights pondering how to broach the matter. I try to control my trembling voice. My heart is beating so loudly I can
hear it. My eyes are watchful, noting every nuance of expression. My father's face is a cold, blank mask, but I can sense his
disinterest, his lack of confidence in me. My mother looks at
me as if I were about to climb Ugwokanyi Mountain and jump
off the summit. Machebe thinks the dream, the whole idea
of returning to school, is laughable, senseless. We have done
nothing but exchange red eyes and expand the vocabulary of
curses we throw at each other in the last few weeks.

"I am not in school because there is no money to train me,
and I will be spending many years as a motor mechanic apprentice," Machebe spits in protest. "But now after wandering
all over the place he comes back with half an ear and says he
wants to go to school."

My father brings out his snuff box, a large tin that could
take enough snuff to go round his estranged kinsmen, those
tobacco-smelling greybeards who call him Agala—a nickname that came from his masking prowess—instead of Egwu,
the name his parents had given him, and who turned around
to stab him in the back when providence smiled at him.

He snorts. "From where do you expect your mother and me
to raise money for fees?"

"I will not let any of my children kill me before my time,"

my mother says painfully. Her crow's feet are so long and so close they could pierce her eyes. "You should be talking about learning a skill: motor mechanics or carpentry or bricklaying, but instead you choose to hang your laundry at impossible heights."

I wasn't expecting my family to succumb easily to my wish. But I will not give up without a fight. My dream was so vivid that I know it's a revelation, but I figure I should cover all bases. I go to the tomb to petition my ancestral benefactress, feeling guilty and ashamed to face Okike. For as many times as I have failed and betrayed every wish she has granted me, she must feel disappointed. I have grown to understand the ways in which she passes an idea across to me, mostly through dreams. So I know what message she is passing when she walks away only to turn around again and smile at me with my sister Oyimaja's face. I know then that Oyimaja is the key with which to unlock my father's closed heart. She's the oldest in the family, and her opinions are respected. She lives with her husband, Joseph, and their six children in Igugu, a neighbouring town. They live in a crowded house: two small rooms built by Joseph. He has a carpentry workshop where he makes stools, but he is also an assistant catechist in the local church. I resolve to involve them.

I set off to Oyimaja's house early one morning, travelling on foot because I don't have the money to transport myself. It's quite a long trek, and I arrive around midmorning. They are both home, but their children have gone to school. The youngest is a sleeping baby.

"Ala, welcome," Joseph says for the eleventh time within just a few minutes of my arrival.

He is a small man. I have always wondered if his size has anything to do with why he makes stools and small pieces of furniture instead of big chairs and cushions.

"I hope you did not lie to me when you said that Father and Mother and everyone is fine at home," Oyimaja says with somewhat of a note of anxiety over my sudden, unannounced visit.

I had rehearsed my lines, but now that I am sitting across from them, the words grow thick and heavy in my mouth. I stare at their wedding photograph hanging from a nail on the wall.

I finally spill it. "I want to go back to school. I know that Father and Mother will not give their consent. So I came to ask you to talk to them."

I have passed the burden, and I can feel my older sister groaning with the weight of it. A large dried palm-frond crucifix from the previous Palm Sunday is tucked in the corner of the room where she sits.

"They will not consent to it because you have let them down," she says, an edge to her voice. "And they are not the only ones you let down, wasting so many years and returning a failure each time."

Her words hurt. They force things out of me before I can stop myself. I would have been killed in a fight if I hadn't fled Lagos, I burst out. And I didn't want to come back from Anukwu in a coffin like Eke.

"Why did you keep what happened in Lagos to yourself?" Her voice drops, flailing like a dead leaf and settling with a softness at my feet. "Why didn't you tell our parents about it?"

"It's better kept from them," Joseph says, his voice a tiny spurtle. "Telling them wouldn't have changed anything, and it is best to spare the old folks the psychological trauma."

At least for once I have someone's support in the family, even if he is a poor and diminutive brother-in-law. I wonder why they did not consider their smallness, their sameness before getting married, to avoid having an elf out of story-land for a child.

"I will think about it," Oyimaja says. "I will be home this weekend to discuss it. By then I will have made my decision."

In the wedding photo, she is cradling a bundle of lantanas the same way you would cradle a sheaf of fodder collected from the bush for goats. The wedding gown looks as if it was passed to her by a much larger woman who had worn it, someone of a matronly size, but despite being the smallest in the family, Oyimaja's voice is the strongest.

A few days after my visit, Oyimaja arrives with her last baby strapped to her back. She looks haggard, dry, and thin. The baby's nose is filled with thick yellow snot as if it is suffering from a cold. She unstraps it, puts her mouth to its nose, and sucks the snot noisily. I watch her as she spits it out, sick to my bone marrow. Ugh!

"I am in support of Dimkpa going back to school." She wipes her mouth with her dirty wrappa.

The silence that greets her speech is intense. I glance at my mother. She reacts to Oyimaja's suggestion as if someone has pinched her hard. For supporting me, I at once forgive Oyimaja for her grossness.

"How shall we raise money for his school fees?" my father says in a heavy voice.

My mother takes the baby from Oyimaja and rocks him on her lap.

"Sell our land if we have to," Oyimaja says.

The room whirls. Her voice sounds like my mother's, soft

but powerful in effect. Among us siblings, she looks the most like my mother. I'd sometimes mistake her voice for my mother's when she was living with us, quickly straightening myself out, thinking my mother was back, if I was up to any kind of mischief.

My father gives a low snort. "Are you saying we should put up for sale the family's only piece of land? Our only inheritance?" he says.

"You lose one thing to gain another," Oyimaja maintains. "The family needs to take a bold step; otherwise, we will remain sunken in poverty."

The tiger in Machebe growls, my father tips snuff into his left palm with a darkening brow, my mother rocks the baby in her arms with a vigour that hurts the baby and provokes a whine. There is silence that is as sticky as earwax. My father clears his voice, says the silence is a chance for the spirits to contribute their views to the discussion, a statement that seems hollow, but it helps to relieve the tension. Ihebube enters and insists on taking the baby from my mother. I watch her as she struggles to shoulder him with the help of my mother, a shudder of revulsion passing over me as I remember the snot-sucking. It grows into a retch when Oyimaja dunks the drinking-water cup into the large water receptacle in a corner of the room. I watch her as she lifts the cup to her lips and gulps down the water. Ugh! I am never going to drink from that side of the cup where her repulsive snot-sucking lips have touched it.

The piece of land Oyimaja has suggested we put up for sale is the only one my father inherited from his father, the same land where his father was buried. My father snorts and sighs again. He shifts in his seat as Oyimaja recounts my dream when my father lost the crown.

"His dreams have a way of manifesting themselves in reality." Her voice is soft, and beguiling.

My mother gives a wavering smile, probably not because she believes in dreams, but because she lacks the willpower to oppose her first daughter, her double.

In my father's eyes is a look accusing the women of conspiracy, the look of a cornered prey, a look blaming my mother for betraying his hiding place.

"I cannot object to the decision of the family, as hard as it is for me to lose my only heritage," he says in a vanquished voice. "I would send all my children to school if I had the means. Education is good." He scowls at me. "I will put up the land for sale, but I hope you realize that to whom much is given, much is expected. It is your responsibility, as the first and privileged son, to strive to be successful and ensure that your younger ones also get their share."

Excitement riles inside me like liquor in a drunken man's head. I can feel Machebe's eyes singeing my back. I don't blame him. He goes to his master's workshop every morning dressed in mechanic's rags. I will soon leave the house every morning looking like a swan in the whites of St. Teresa's College.

"Don't fool yourself." He lashes out at me when I mention St. Teresa's College as my first choice. "I know you can't pass their entrance exam, ever."

Machebe is right about St. Teresa's College. The community school is less elite, more like okrika, the used clothes that I can bend down and select from a heap at Ogige market for little money, but it's still school. Every night I lie awake, invoking a buyer for the land. And then I wake up the next morning feeling a step closer to my dream.

Twenty-seven

I WAKE UP AT THE FIRST COCKCROW ON THE BIG DAY and set off to school before sunrise, too excited to eat breakfast. Machebe says I look funny in my undersized white-and-indigo school uniform. I will be starting in SS1 Class. Machebe insists I am too old to return to school. But I don't care. It is my big day, and I will not let anything soil my mood. I did my best to look younger. I got rid of the wisp on my chin with a new razor blade.

The school is a trek of five miles each way, along a path that weaves through village squares and compounds, ultimately bringing you to a signboard with COMMUNITY SECONDARY SCHOOL printed in white lettering against a blue background. Each time I pass people who know me, their whispers and suppressed laughter wither my pace. It brings a flood of relief, the sign that stands by the entrance to the large compound fenced in with wire gauze. A small man with a stern look is manning the gate. He is old and half deaf. Next to the school there is a football pitch with rusty whitewashed goalposts and two huge African olive trees on either side, under which students either watch football practice or lounge in the shade. It is the same pitch where Eke and I used to play football before I dropped out. Eke was good, almost at the same level as I was. We were a threat as a team, and archrivals as opponents, but an image that will haunt me, which almost feels like a betrayal as I reenter the school without Eke, is of us always strolling off the pitch with hands linked at the last whistle.

There are four identical classroom blocks, two either side, with stained cream walls. Their roofs and eaves have been partly destroyed by woodlice and hostile winds. Many of the windows and doors are broken. Behind the school, beyond a garden planted with cassava and spinach, is bush where villagers relieve themselves.

I am proud to be standing erect at the assembly ground with other students, facing the sunrise and singing the national anthem. I try to ignore the furtive glances and the giggling going on around me as the principal addresses the assembly from the stairway. Besides being new, my age and tight uniform mark me out. And my half ear. The other students had better get used to it, I tell myself, because they will be seeing more of me around. People always stare at first, but they eventually lose interest.

The principal is plump, short, and light-skinned. She reminds me of an owl with her voluminous wig and bulging eyes. Her teeth seem to be struggling for space in her mouth; one worries she might bite her tongue when she is talking. The vice principal is a small man with a pointed face. In his shabby coat and hat, he makes me think of the gnome in my picture book. The teachers are beaming behind the principal and the vice principal in wigs and spectacles.

After the morning assembly I walk with a sense of déjà vu into a squawking classroom that smells of chalk. It is crowded with lockers and chairs. And dominated by girls. We are twenty-one in number: seven boys, the rest girls—a shrieking flock of beautiful birds. The arrival of a teacher throws cold water onto the flames of my imagination.

There are bright students eager to raise their hands and answer questions, and dumb ones who stare and clap their hands when asked to by the teacher, and others like me who secretly pray that the teacher will not call on them to answer a question. There is a thin, awkward-looking girl who raises her hand to all the questions and answers them brilliantly, and a noisy, rascally boy sitting in the same row as me. The girl sitting two rows in front is pretty and restless. She and the rascally boy are punished now and again for disturbing the class.

I enjoy the first few classes, especially geography. We read the atlas and learn about places with exotic and rhythmic names: Antarctica, Mississippi, Pacific, Eastern Europe, Eritrea, St. Vincent and the Grenadines, British Virgin Islands, New Hampshire, Botswana, Puerto Rico, Mauretania, Kampala, Cambodia, Dominican Republic, Equatorial Guinea, El Salvador, Madagascar. The list is endless. I try memorizing the names of oceans and seas and lakes and rivers. My classmates make a song to help their memory: *Nile Niger Senegal Congo Orange Limpopo Zambezi.*

I enjoy the noisy intervals when one teacher walks out at the end of his class and another is awaited. The class has nicknamed the mathematics teacher Nza, like the bird, because of his small stature and spindly legs hidden in tight trousers. He is not the only teacher with a nickname. The principal is nicknamed Lioness for her harshness, her aggressiveness. The vice principal is called Cat for the bowler hat that never leaves his head.

The class splits at break time, everyone tearing out to the field to play. I am still a good footballer. I was once in the school's junior team, but most of my teammates are now graduated and gone, so I am happy to watch others play.

The final lessons are slower. There's relief in the faces of my classmates as school finally comes to an end for the day. I trek home musing over my first day back in school, the staring eyes, the furtive giggles, and me trying not to be self-conscious about my age and my half ear.

My mother's lunch of rice is waiting for me at home to celebrate my first day. The beginning of my journey to becoming the first ever graduate in Oregwu. Beyond secondary school, I will study to earn a degree and become a good politician, and, when Biafra comes, I shall be amongst her first crop of leaders. And then I will buy back my father's ancestral land and tenfold more.

Twenty-eight

I HAVE ALWAYS HATED MATHEMATICS. I SCOWL AT Nza as he paces the classroom, stopping by the blackboard to write numbers and symbols with chalk. And then he starts to explain them away in his sharp, loud voice, but I only get more confused listening to him spout so much numerical gibberish. It almost drives me mad. In one of his classes, he walks towards me, ignoring everyone else, all the raised hands. My heart beats fast. He stops and points at me.

"You. Tell us the LCM of 4, 6, and 8?"

I curse myself. "But I didn't raise my hand," I say in protest.

The pretty girl giggles; the whole class joins her.

"I know. Stand up and give us the answer," Nza insists.

I raise myself slowly to my feet and remain like that. The class giggles again.

"Your name first," he says. "I can see you are new in my class."

"Dimkpa Gbaghalu." Saying my name sparks off another round of giggles, maybe because of the thick consonants or its sheer virility. I have always wondered why my mother chose such a strong masculine name for me. It would have better suited Machebe, who is muscled and driven.

"How old are you?"

"I am eighteen years old."

The class roars again.

"Quiet," the teacher bawls, and the noise tapers off. "Give us the answer, Dimkpa."

I stare at him, my mind blank.

"Come on, give us the answer." He looks outraged that an SS1 student doesn't know the answer to a common arithmetic question.

I remain silent with my head bowed in shame. The class is quiet now, my classmates sitting in disarmed silence, their unsettledness finding expression in feigned coughs and paper rustling.

"Come forward, kneel down, and raise your hands if you don't know the answer."

I do as I have been told, coming slowly round to the front of the class, and kneeling down with my hands raised.

"If anyone in this class answers the question correctly, he will give you six strokes of the cane," Nza says.

A wilderness of fingers shoots up into the broken ceiling. He settles for the long, thin fingers of the pretty girl, Grace. She answers the question correctly, smartly, and gets applauded. Nza insists I lie down on my locker and take six strokes from the girl on my buttocks in front of the class. I do as I have been ordered. Grace takes the stick from the teacher. She hesitates.

"I will ask someone else to flog you instead if you don't do it," warns Nza as Grace dillydallies.

Emboldened by the fear of being flogged, Grace raises the stick and delivers a weak stroke across my buttocks.

"That's a lame stroke." He grabs the stick back from her, orders her to stretch out her palm, and hits her hard. Girls are not flogged on the buttocks.

She yelps as the cane sinks into her palm.

"That's how hard I expect you to hit him."

She takes the stick back from him and unleashes hot strokes on my buttocks, fear driving her energy and courage. The class shrieks with excitement. After delivering the last stroke, she drops the stick and flees the class.

"You are quite old for this class," the teacher says as I walk back to resume my seat on his orders. "So I expect you to work hard or I will have you demoted still."

I trek home in the harsh sun after school, nursing my shame and resenting the teacher for disgracing me before the class, for causing my classmates to give me the nickname "Papa." Nnamdi Adaka, the rascally boy, coined it, and at once it found an echo with the class. The average age of the class hovers between fourteen and sixteen, so at over eighteen I am easily the oldest.

I arrive home tired, hungry, and angry to meet a lunch of cocoyam and grey soup again. My mother has cooked a lunch of cocoyam and grey soup all week long. Who does that on her son's first week at school? I make sure she sees the anger and frustration on my face. I don't care if it spoils her mood, if it takes the tangerine off her voice. I had expected her to cook something delicious for lunch. I consider rejecting the food, but I am famished, so hungry I could eat cockroaches.

I stroll down to the cave after lunch. The sun is strong and hurts the back of my neck. The sky is blue, as stainless as steel, an expanse that looks surreal against the bright green of the afternoon hills. But in my mood I don't care if there is no sky at all. I look out at the kerosene hills not caring what they might contain. Since my childhood, I have heard people say that the hills are filled with kerosene, and that one day the government will come and start drawing it out, bringing electricity and pipe-borne water to the community. Each time I see the wooden electric poles lining the village roads like figures of distress, some hollowed out or inclining dangerously, I remember the kerosene hills and the government's promise. The poles were raised by the villagers who had to tax themselves heavily in their failed project to draw electricity to the village. Yet every season the ridge of hills gets covered in fine, thin blades of green grass that wave in the breeze like a boy's spiky hair. Every season the grass ripens to a golden colour, and the villagers fetch it and use it to cover their roofs before mischievous boys set the hills ablaze, yet the government is nowhere to be seen. Maybe somebody made up the story at the gambling den.

I feel humiliated, and in a foul mood. I am too old to return to secondary school. I am sure now that going back was a bad idea. I didn't understand anything of what that maths teacher had explained. Everything was puzzling and blurry, like Oshodi market crowds. Why didn't the English and literature teacher ask me a question instead? I am sure I would have done better with a question on those subjects. And now I am off on the wrong foot.

I jump down, landing in the cool water with a splash that startles a sparrow into a panic flight. I am never going to like school or Lioness or Nza or Cat. I am still trying to decide who between the two I dislike most, the principal or her vice? I see the principal again in a tight green gown patterned with black symbols resembling inverted commas, reminding me of how inverted my life is. The gown strains on her belly, which bulges like that of a pregnant goat in my father's pen. I see her pacing the assembly ground on high heels, a robust, hairy hand fisting her hip, calves bunched. The heels of her small, neat feet are polished to a clean, flush-coloured shine. I see her as she walks proudly around with an easy and slow swing of her hips.

I am tired of eating cocoyam and grey soup, tired of living in a chicken coop. I am tired of seeing the wrinkled old tobacco-smelling faces of my father's treacherous kinsmen in our house, tired of hearing them call him out to an evening in an ekpetechi spot. "Agala, Agala," they call from the approach as they stroll in, wary of my mother's reproachful eyes. I am tired of hearing my father talk about his youthful valour anytime he has had one shot too many. He remembers his times as a young wrestler, and how he had battled the biggest and the fiercest of wrestlers from other towns; his times as a masker, the Omabe festival, and the mystery surrounding the leopard motif. I am tired because it all amounts to nothing. Because when the time came for him to be village head, they ripped him off. No one remembered his talents and contributions to the masking cult, his patriotism, and the risks he took to wrestle dangerous opponents from other villages to uphold the pride and dignity of Oregwu.

Why did I even think of school as an option to making money for my family, all because of a mere dream? I should have realized that my dreams happen in opposites. If I dream of eating a large plate of delicious food, I will wake up the next day with nothing to eat. If I dream of riches and prosperity, I will wake up in the destitution and pennilessness of my father's hutch.

I walk back home, my mood worsening with my father now

in the picture, and my heart growing as cold as a dog's nose. I am tired of seeing the self-righteous faces of those old, boring church women who come to our house to look for my mother. They talk about tithing when we have nothing to eat. Everything irritates me the way pepper irritates a man with sores on his tongue.

Machebe is waiting at the door. He demands to know why I threw his clean shoes down on the dirty ground. I had found Machebe's pair of brown moccasins on the tomb earlier when I returned from school. He had washed and placed them upright on the tomb to dry in the sun. My anger had fumed like petrol poured in a fire at the sight of the shoes on the tomb.

We exchange red eyes and a few hot words.

"You are eaten up with envy because father sold some land for me."

He sniggers. "It's not about returning to school. It's about passing your exams, about achieving something to justify selling our only parcel of land for you."

"Stop, you two," my mother says in a frustrated voice.

I ignore Machebe and walk away. I don't want any of his tigerizing this hot afternoon. He is the least of my worries now.

Twenty-nine

I WAKE UP LATE THE NEXT MORNING. MY MOTHER pulls me out of bed, nagging about my oversleeping on a school day. Grumbling, I begin to get ready in a slow, unhurried way, refusing to bathe in protest, washing only my feet, my arms, and my face. Breakfast tastes like bamboo.

"Nnam Jisieike," my mother says, addressing me as her father to encourage me, but in my mood I don't think it's a compliment to liken me to her dead, hair-sticking-out-of-nose father. "You will get used to school again, ooh."

Her words draw a hiss from Machebe. "This is what happens when a full-grown man with a beard is treated and pampered like a little boy," he spits.

I decide that it is too early to start arguing with him and set off to school with a note my mother squeezes into my palm. Machebe irritates me like a mosquito buzzing close to the ear, returning after each vain, painful slap.

The principal has finished conducting the morning assembly and classes are in full swing when I get to school. For coming in late, I get six lashes of the cane that should sting, but I feel nothing as they are being delivered on my buttocks. And then I am shown a portion of the garden to weed during break as additional punishment. I sit moping through maths, in a violent mood.

But then the English and literature teacher strolls in, a cheery soul in a washed-out grey coat and ivory tie. He asks me, the new student, to read aloud from *Black Boy*, a novel I have already read in the mansion in Lagos. It's about a boy named Richard Wright who accidentally burns down his family house and gets beaten unconscious by his mother. His father abandons the family to live with another woman, and, without his financial support, the family falls into poverty. School is hardly an option for Richard, so he does whatever odd jobs a child can do to support his family. Not surprisingly, he gets into all sorts of trouble, spying on people in outhouses and becoming a regular at the local saloon—and an alcoholic—by the age of six.

Richard's father is just like mine, I muse, as I read through the novel with ease to the amazement of my classmates. Maybe he would have run off, too, had my father found a woman who accepted him. He didn't even raise a finger in objection when I went off to Lagos. He was so quick to offload me. Does he know I almost got killed in Lagos? Does he know what it feels like to be punched up for sport every day? And what it means to have your left ear bitten off by a madman or to bury a de-composing body, a body whose peeling skin stains your hands with oily fluids, whose smell violates your stomach?

I manage to get myself into trouble again when I sneak out to a joint near the school for a shot of monkey tail with the money my mother gave me to cheer me up. The school's dis-ciplinarian, a boy named Obi, smells alcohol on my breath and reports me to the principal. She is furious and orders fifty lashes of the cane to my buttocks. As the school's disciplinar-ian, Obi has been given the power to nose out unruly students and punish them. Four strong boys are asked to hold me down on a long table. Obi comes forward wielding a big, long stick, face set. He is used to things like this, enjoys it. He devours me in the full view of the school. He sets my buttocks on fire to the excitement of the students, leaving scars of broken welts. I howl with pain until I lose my voice.

I virtually crawl home at the end of school. I have no appetite for lunch. Night throws its blanket over the village with one deft swing of its arm. Dinner tastes like stalks of dry grass even though it is only boiled water yam and palm oil. Sadness and anger compete inside me with athletic zeal. I feel like sinking my teeth into somebody, Machebe or Ejiro or Nza. The tomb is the only place where I find comfort. I lie on it, face up, and gaze at a half-clouded moon, my mind dreading school the next day, my thoughts many small moons imprisoned and freed again in rolling steel-grey clouds. I think of a piece of my ear lying in a foreign land, in the bush at Anukwu where I had thrown it away after a doctor certified it dead and useless. I wonder what happened to it, that part of me in Anukwu. Maybe a dog strolled up and made a lunch of it; maybe it went down the throats of dead-flesh mites. I think of the woman we buried, who killed a sacred tortoise, a god incarnate. I think of her congregation that sat aloof and sang hymns, the neighbours who distanced themselves and watched us foreigners bury her through shrub walls with pity in their eyes, because if they got involved they themselves would become contaminated like the woman. I think of Lagos and all the burnt, decomposing bodies of madmen, pickpockets, and innocent thieves; the fighting touts and the weird gatekeepers; Lagos and its smell of decayed dreams. Broken dreams. I wonder if another lean, muscular boy has taken my position at the mansion—Ejiro had said that Mummy always managed to get another boy. I imagine the new boy and Ejiro locked in a sweat-slick brawl on the lawn, and Mummy watching from a lounge chair, mirrored in the sparkling blueness of the pool water, and I am lying here sad but safe. I think of the Folashade tomb in its gold-edged, pelican-white beauty, and all the nice foods that I see only in my dreams now, and I conclude that I am a big fool. I am one big, indolent coward.

Finally, I think of Okike lying here with me beneath this beautiful tomb. For a moment, I feel at peace with the world, a feeling banished almost at once by a riot of thoughts. Okike had spent a few days at the creek before she was found, which means that her body had started to decompose. Had she started emitting fluids like the woman in Anukwu when they found her? Was she buried by strangers? I hadn't asked my mother. Were the hands of those who buried her stained, like mine, with fluids that cannot be washed off?

I fall asleep on the tomb and dream of riches and shops stocked with goods from ceiling to floor. My mother comes out and wakes me up in the middle of the night.

"Enigmatic child," she says, cupping the flame of her ochanja to prevent it from dancing atilogu dance in the wind. "I don't know what you have in common with the dead, but I know I should not have allowed you to rebuild this grave."

The night is deeply spent. It is quiet, dark, and cold. The moon has gone to bed. I follow my mother into the house. She continues to swear and accuse me of dangerously clinging to my convictions as a sloth clings to decaying wood. I lie on my mattress feeling warm, like a candle flame in my mother's cupped hand, protected from the wind.

Thirty

EVEN IF I SWALLOW THE INSULTS THE TEACHERS AND
my classmates heap on me and continue with school, I will
be studying for many years. I am over eighteen. I may very
well be an old man by the time I finish, and Machebe will be
running his own workshop full of apprentices. I must drop
out, but how do I face my family? How do I look into my
father's eyes and tell him that I am withdrawing from school
and wasting his only inheritance? My head is in a whirl. My
family expects me to go to school on Monday morning, so I
have until Sunday evening to think of something. I wish Eke
were alive. I have had no one else to confide in or turn to for
help since his death. I am friendless.

The tomb is a mess, grained with chicken droppings, but I
have too much on my mind to bother about cleaning it. Maybe
my mother is right. I have given the grave too much attention. And in return I have ended up with one frustration after
another.

"Aren't you going to clean your bedroom?" Machebe's voice
is heavy with sarcasm.

I ignore Machebe and the tomb he calls my bedroom and
stroll to Uwakwe's shop to clear the cobwebs, to see if he has
news about the Biafra Zionist Movement. On my way, I see
children returning from church in their Sunday clothes, and
a man pedaling a bicycle and whistling. And then a familiar voice comes floating over in the gentle afternoon wind.

Inyinya pops up. He is walking alone. Inyinya is the teacher who writes hymns for the Holy Trinity church choir, a fine middle-aged man in a well-ironed, short-sleeved white shirt tucked into grey trousers. He is singing a hymn, a file tucked under his arm. At a closer range, I see something I have never seen before on Inyinya's face. He is radiating happiness. I watch him as he ambles down the road, crooning. Nothing else seems to matter other than the hymn and the flow of blessedness oozing out of him. I watch him until he branches off into a corner out of sight. I have never seen anyone with such an aura of innocence.

"I have nosed out a secret place where the new group holds meetings," Uwakwe whispers with a crooked smile.

I flinch to attention.

"I am already a member." His grin broadens.

"Can you take me there?"

"Of course. They need younger men like you. Zealous young men who can keep secrets. Meet me here tonight. I will take you there, but you are expected to pay weekly dues, and you must remember to keep it a top secret. You don't want the police harassing us at this early stage."

I promise my discretion even though I am not sure how to raise dues on a weekly basis.

The news makes me restless all evening. I sneak out after dinner back to Uwakwe's shop. He is waiting for me. He has already locked up and is sitting on the bench in front of his shop, in utter darkness. It's easy for him to meld into the darkness, becoming one with it like oil and Bambara flour when my mother mixes both with water to make okpa. We set out to the venue with torchlight. The meetings are held at the primary school classroom at night. We arrive as things are just getting started. The men are sitting in absolute darkness.

"There are spies stationed in the dark premises to watch out for danger," Uwakwe had warned me.

Someone points torchlight in my face as Uwakwe introduces me as a new member. "He is young," says a whispery voice. He makes it sound like a demerit.

My eyes ache from the light.

"Tell us your name, age, and what you do for a living." The voice speaking now is deep and authoritative, the torch still pointed to my face.

The men asking the questions seem to relax after I finish introducing myself, explaining that I was once a member of a MASSOB group in Anambra State. The light is withdrawn, leaving me completely blinded.

"Sit down," he says.

I grope my way to a seat.

"You are young, but because you were once a member of MASSOB, you will be given consideration," he growls. "We are admitting you not because we share the same ideologies with MASSOB, but because we will not let this zeal, this enthusiasm burning in you, die for nothing."

My eyes get used to the darkness. I make out more than a dozen men seated in the class like school pupils. Many of them are not familiar, but others are people I see every day. The man addressing me, Ikuku, is not known to me. Though small, he seems full of enthusiasm and speaks in a strong, motivational voice.

He picks up the thread of a speech he had started before we arrived. "The MASSOB leader is a selfish man who is only after what he can make for himself from the struggle. He accepted a payoff and abandoned the struggle, and all those who were detained with him. Our leader, Benjamin Onwuka, will not abandon any of us, no matter the situation. He is dedicated to this struggle, and will give his life to see it succeed. Like I said, he is an international lawyer with the right connections to deliver a fresh Republic of Biafra to us at no other cost besides our steadfastness. Only those who endure to the end will be rewarded. They may laugh at us now. They may call us loafers or any names they choose to call us, but we shall have the last laugh." His eyes rest on me again. "You should study hard. You have more potential as an educated man, and better chances of making it to the hierarchy than most of us when Biafra comes."

A few other men also make speeches hinting at the same points he had raised. And then dues are paid, and the meeting ends.

"Try and pay your dues by the next meeting," Uwakwe says as we make our way home through the dark and silent night. "The payment determines your membership."

"I will try." I can't tell Uwakwe that unless I steal the money from my mother or lower myself to the indignity of load carrying at Ogige market, I will not be able to raise the weekly dues of one hundred naira.

In bed I lie awake, fighting a maelstrom of thoughts. Ikuku says that I will have more potential than most as an educated man. I muse over a new Republic of Biafra where I am a ward councilor or even a commissioner. I see myself pulling down my father's chicken coop of a house and building a mansion. I will send my siblings to school and open a big grocery business for my mother at Ogige market. There won't be any need for her to roam in the bushes picking things to sell to feed the family and pay tithes. My mother is becoming more and more religious. She treks about four miles to a church way up in the Ikeagwu Hills, a small congregation that meets four times each week to sing, clap, and condemn Catholics for their use of images and reverence of the Virgin Mary. My mother says it is idol worship, the use of images. I will make sure that my father has sufficient snuff and palm wine always, and will not need to go to any of his treacherous kinsmen. My self-respect, which I have almost lost, will be restored.

I just have to persevere with school.

Gbaghalu cannot sleep. He is filled with self-reproach for hurting the woman his heart throbs for so violently. Obochi is the only reason he hasn't taken his own life. His world had been a dark void before she came along like a waft of breezy sunshine and filled the space around him with light and a soft scent.

Obochi has been avoiding him, her anger worsening every time she remembers that, aside from peeping at her nakedness, he also killed a man. He claims that the man provoked him. How true is this? Where is the evidence that he was actually provoked, and that he did not murder a man in cold blood? He seems good at making excuses. They used to walk together to the fields, chatting and laughing, but now she walks without him and keeps the company of other outcasts in his place.

Work is tedious. Ezenwanyi owns acres of farmland, and the attama is using the outcasts to push back her endless stretch of forest. The outcasts do the work of producing the crops, which they store in barns for the use of the attama and his subjects. In return they are allowed small portions of farmland to make food for themselves. Gbaghalu and other men of the shrine work tirelessly to raise large mounds of earth and sow yams into the mounds. Obochi and other female outcasts plant maize, melon, and other crops. Work goes on endlessly, season to season: from yam to cocoyam to cassava to

*potatoes, from ploughing to planting to weeding to harvesting, su-
pervised by the attama.*

*While they are working, the outcasts share their sad stories to
reduce the drudgery of labour. Nweke, a beautiful young maiden,
became Ezenwanyi's bride after buying a trinket that had been
stolen from the shrine.*

*"Ezenwanyi is a goddess of moral conduct with the ability to
detect when theft has been committed in her territory," Nweke
moans. "But I did not know that the trinket was stolen. I fell sick
after the first day I wore it. The illness grew stubborn. I had only
just finished seeing my first blood, but the strange illness ceased it
again, and I did not see it in the following months. My father took
me to herbalists, but they found no solution. And then I started to
recover, my blood coming again. Suitors started to come, attracted
to my beauty."*

She walks around with a pout, swinging her hips.

*"Please finish the story before the priest catches us fooling around
in the middle of work," one of the maidens scoffs at Nweke play-
fully. "I don't want to be punished because you are flaunting your
outcast body."*

*Nweke laughs a hollow laugh. "I married one of them," she con-
tinues. "The sickness returned as soon as I moved into the man's
house. My blood fled again. My husband got frustrated, thinking
I wasn't going to give him a child. He started to mistreat me. We
fell apart, and I went back to my father's house, was healed, my
blood returning. The cycle started: I got married, fell sick, got healed
again, and my blood came back the minute I left the marriage back
to my father's house. The villagers started to call me a witch, but
upon investigation by a seer, it became known that the trinket I
had bought some time in the past had been stolen from the shrine
and sold to me at the local market. And, as penalty, Ezenwanyi*

demanded to have me as bride as the only condition for my healing. This is how I ended up as an outcast."

"But what happened to the thief?" Obochi asks after listening to Nweke's story.

"I don't know. He is not known to me," Nweke explains. "I went to the market, saw a trinket that caught my fancy, and bought it. How was I to know that it was stolen? But I know that nobody steals from Ezenwanyi and gets away with it."

Obochi finds Nweke's story pathetic, and similar to hers. Obochi had fallen in love once. His name was Odoja, and he was a fine, lanky young man. Odoja and Obochi's brother, Ugwu, had been close friends. Odoja would visit her brother, and, while they were sitting outdoors and chatting, Obochi would hide in the hut and watch him as he flicked his thick eyebrows up and down while talking softly. She liked the luxuriant way his hair grew close to his forehead, his bright dark eyes and soft cat gaze. There was something feline about him, an aura of masculinity beneath a supple exterior. She had watched him in secret, a strange sensation forming a lump in her chest. She had imagined him alone with her in a hut filled with his virility, and that sweaty odour of men her brother sometimes secreted. She had become so prepossessed with him that she had found herself comparing him with her suitors, seeing flaws in every suitor. Odoja's charm was so great it exposed the incompleteness of each suitor. Gbaghalu and Odoja are opposites, she thinks. Where Odoja is graceful, Gbaghalu is rugged. And where Gbaghalu is brawny, the strength Odoja exudes comes from within. Where Gbaghalu's laughter threatens to rupture the fabric of his voice, Odoja's laughter gathers and crumples in his eyes, and then it lingers in a light dance to the soundless rhythm of his voice.

As the maidens work and gossip, Gbaghalu's laughter, that violent rupturing, is carried on the wind across the field to them. He at once becomes the subject of their gossip as he materializes farther afield.

"He is by far the most handsome man in this shrine," says one maiden.

"He is good-looking in a cruel kind of way," says another. "I heard he killed a man of this shrine, but overpowering and killing a fellow man makes him all the more attractive to me."

"I would give everything to have him," chips in a third maiden. "I wish more young men like him would come here to claim us."

Obochi is tired and does more listening than talking as the ladies carry on with their praise of him, their gossiping and giggling. She has had a hectic day. Night is fast approaching. It is beginning to dye the fields in indigo, with smears of pink and orange in the sky. Obochi is relieved when the day's work finally draws to an end.

At home, she is overcome by a feeling of sadness, weighed down by a sense of loss. The night is warm. The sun had been intense all day, sucking the moisture dry. She sits alone outside for fresh air, her gaze wandering now and again to Gbaghalu's grass hut. He is nowhere within eyeshot. She hisses, walks to a pepper fruit tree, and leans against it. Maybe he is tired and has gone to bed early. The light from his oriona is still on. She lets out another hiss. Could she be missing him? She savours the evenings when they sat together in front of her hut, chatting. Maybe she overreacted. For days she has been sulking, refusing to talk to him, and resenting him.

It is dark and the sounds of insects fill the cold, still void of the night. Suddenly, she notices a sidling movement among the trees.

A thief!

She opens her mouth to scream but holds back. She has never heard of an incident of stealing in the shrine since her arrival. She follows the figure with her eyes until it melts into the looming *darkness outside Gbaghalu's hut, but not before she has seen that it is a woman's figure.*

In bed she cannot sleep, suspicious that one of the maidens in the shrine may have snuck into Gbaghalu's hut in the night. "What is she doing in his room?" she wonders, realizing at once the folly of her question. What would a full-grown woman who sneaks into a man's room in the night be looking for? She blames herself. The gods had given Gbaghalu to her so cheaply. He is strong and handsome, the dream of every woman, but she has spent too much time resenting him. And now she has succeeded in driving him into the arms of another woman.

She bursts into tears on her bamboo bed.

Obochi's uriri burns brightly, illuminating the sinewy frame in the doorway when she opens her eyes. A scream starts and dies again in her throat.

"You startled me." She sits up.

"I didn't mean to creep in on you." Gbaghalu stares at her briefly, a wild, hungry look in his eyes. He had arrived at her door, unnoticed, like a thief.

She summons him in with her eyes.

"I came to say I am sorry again." He moves in fully, sits next to her.

She stares at the fingers of ripe pepper fruit in his outstretched palm with wide eyes.

"For you, as a token of my apology."

"What have you done?" she whispers. He would be whipped mercilessly if caught plucking the fruit. The attama had ordered one hundred strokes of bullwhip scourge on one of the outcasts for plucking oranges. He was whipped by his fellow outcasts before the entire village.

"No one saw me."

She accepts the gift with a fair amount of reluctance, savours the strong taste of one, and puts the rest away. He places a big hand on her lap. She lets the probing hand linger, lets her body warm to his touch. Sure of the chemistry, she forgets in that moment of heaven when the big warm hand in her lap wrapped around a man's throat and squeezed the life out of him.

"You are so pretty, I couldn't help myself." He confesses as they lie side by side, united in a splotch of her blood on the mat, a shy smile of guilt playing on the broad estuary of his face.

She laughs and buries her face in the forest of his hairy chest. "You don't have to apologize for making a woman out of me," she says sweetly.

"Thank you for giving me the honour and privilege."

Suddenly the thought of a pregnancy clouds over her feelings of pure bliss. Hereditary characteristics always show themselves, her father would say. She could have a murderer for a son, an ogler, or a rebel who robs fruit trees.

"What are you brooding about?" He notices her withdrawal, her recoiling from him.

"You could have impregnated me."

The prospect seems to entice him. "We will get married. We are permitted to do so."

By enslaving offenders and allowing physical relationships among the outcasts, Ezenwanyi cleaned up the society and freed it of vermin, carried out her responsibility of protecting the village and continuing her repopulating and expansionist mission, and made available outcasts for human sacrifices to strengthen her own powers. But he doesn't want to scare her with too many details.

"*We will speak to the attama about it, tell him we are in love, and perform the necessary rites. I am sure we will have children and a happy home.*"

"*Who talks of love and a happy home in a place like this?*" she moans.

If he was hoping the promise of a marriage and a happy home would clear the frown from her face, he may have succeeded in driving her fears and doubts deeper. She would love to marry him. His presence always fills her with a sense of safety in this odd new world, but her fear is about the future, about the children they would have together as a couple.

"*Have you thought about our offspring?*"

His face broadens in a smile. "*Our children will be the very definition of beauty.*"

"*They will grow up as ohu ma.*" She groans. He had misunderstood her by a wide berth. "*Like me. Like you. The girls will grow into old, haggard women who have reached menopause without husbands because they are outcasts, stained and untouchable. The boys will grow up with stigma following them everywhere they go like the dung-stained, fly-infested tail of a cow because they are the possessions of a fierce and overprotective goddess, and decent society has no place for them.*"

The truth sinks in, draws a sigh from him. He pulls her closer and tries to shake her out of her low spirits. "*We should make the most of this moment. Somehow we find ourselves in this situation by an unfortunate conjunction of circumstances.*" He strokes her hair. "*Please accept my proposal as the happy-ending story of its conquest.*"

She hesitates.

"*I accept.*" She snuggles closer to him.

Thirty-one

I STILL HATE MATHS AND THE LONG, HOT TREK HOME.
But I determine not to quit. Ikuku's words—*You have more
potential as an educated man*—have reinforced my belief in myself, and rekindled my hopes of catching up in school. English
and literature and history are my best subjects. Lioness, with
her toothy way of talking, becomes one of those curiosities
that make school bearable. Nza's genius at mathematics and
chemistry now fills me with awe, though I am still nursing my
anger at him for humiliating me in front of the class. He still
skips about like a wren and caws like a crow.

I visit the cave sometimes when I return from school to
spend time with Okike. Time and time again, she has unlocked the door when I thought it had closed against me.
I often sleep on her tomb until my mother wakes me up in
the middle of the night and insists that I come inside. My
evenings, weekends, and holidays are spent picking oil bean
seeds and palm kernels, which I sell to pay my weekly dues
to the Biafra Zionist Movement. The group is growing. At
the last count, there were more than fifty members. I attend
their meetings regularly and pay my dues religiously. I also
forage the bush for the seeds that break out of their pods
in the intense sun with a clapping sound. It is not stealing
when they are picked in this way. I sell them at Ogige market when I collect a good quantity. I use the money to buy
secondhand clothes, football boots, and other little things,

but when I need money for something big, I climb a tree and steal its pods.

I still smoke and drink alcohol in secret whenever I have the money to buy them. I can't stop going to Ogige market to carry loads because of the gnawing hunger that torments my stomach. When they see me, my classmates laugh at me at school the next day. They call me onye eburu for carrying groceries and other purchases for the university women or heavy sacks of goods for traders who are returning from the large market in Onitsha. I steal from customers, a careless customer or a fat one who cannot keep pace, as I have seen other boys do. I navigate in between the aisles that appear the same to those who are not very familiar with the market. In this way I can confuse the customer, lose myself in the crowd, and rocket out of sight to safety with the load the moment I come clear. I then sell the items later or take them home and lie to my mother that I bought them.

School would be even better if not for Nnamdi Adaka, the rascally boy in my class, a late bloomer like me, though no one dares call him names. He is younger than me by at least one year, and burly. A bully. Every student fears him. He makes it his business to know everything about anyone who cuts his interest. He has formed a gang of boys who make mischief. They drop things they are holding in front of the classroom and pretend to pick them up in order to peep at girls who are not properly seated. They sneak into the bush behind the school block to smoke and drink alcohol, and to kiss and fondle girls. Nnamdi tasks the junior boys to pay dues to him from time to time. He doesn't care how they get the money, if they steal from their parents. He issues threats should the boys fail to pay or summon the courage to report him. No one dares say anything to the teachers, who are afraid of him, too. Rumour has it that he is a cultist. A teacher was once shot at with a catapult. The stone grazed his temple and missed his left eye. The culprit was not caught, but it was believed Nnamdi Adaka had shot at the teacher in retaliation for a punishment. And, unfortunately, he despises me. The mere sight of me irritates him. He is a very clumsy footballer, but each time we have training practice he bullies his way into the opposing team. He almost always ends up in blows with someone. I worry that one day it will be me.

I look forward to the holidays and sing with gusto:

Holiday is coming!
Holiday is coming!
No more clanging bells
No more teachers' whip!
Goodbye, teachers. Goodbye, scholars.
We are going on a jolly holiday!

Girls: A jolly—
All: Holiday!
Girls: A jolly—
All: Holiday!

Thirty-two

I HAVE JOINED THE SCHOOL'S MAIN FOOTBALL TEAM, and have played well in the interhouse matches. It has helped me to blend in. We have been training for the Unity Cup final match in a competition that involves all the secondary schools in the region. I helped my school qualify for the final match. There's excitement in the air as the match approaches. Lioness, the teachers, and the students are all talking about it.

At last the day arrives. The whole school empties to Government Field, the venue of the match. The crumbling pavilion is filling with spectators as we dress in jerseys and warm up. Soon we are at it, playing with tenacity, like it is a World Cup final. I assume my usual position in the attacking midfield. Every contact I make with the ball is greeted with shouts of "Etim Esin!" by the fans from my school, after the famous midfielder who played for the Nigerian national team.

The ball sails across to me from an aerial pass, a perfect telegraph sent by Ife after he spots me alone and well positioned towards the edge of the right flank. Ife and I always make a good pair, like Eke and I did. We understand each other, and it is easy to destroy opponents when we both are playing. I gain control of the ball, lifting high above its flight to chest-trap his delicious pass in that easy and elegant way that always triggers ovation from the fans, especially the girls. A defender from the other team charges forward to stop me from making a dangerous incursion into his team's eighteen-yard box. I tap the ball smartly, rolling it in between his legs and skirting around him neatly to collect the ball again. My clever move sets off another sky-high ripple of applause from the spectators, and more shouts of "Etim Esin!" Our boys are howling their support and motivation from the touchline, the girls screeching with delight, trying to outshine the rival school's fans. And then I set the stadium on fire as I dribble past the defenders and drive the ball hard into the far corner of the opponent's goal.

My goal gives my school victory. I enjoy a ride high up on the shoulders of the fans at the end of the match, and a bear hug from Lioness. The victory is important for the school, the first time we have won the cup. The celebrations last for days. A lesson-free day is granted.

Suddenly, I am the toast of the school.

Weeks later, I'm sitting by myself in class at break time, nursing my ankle after a game. I've been playing almost every day since my victory, pushing my body to its limits to maintain my status at school.

"Does it hurt a lot?" she says, coming to stand near me with hands on her hips, Grace, the girl who gave me six strokes of the cane on my first week.

I stare at her, surprised she would stoop to speak to me, with all her prettiness and her posturing.

I'd hurt myself playing against Nnamdi Adaka, limping off the field back to the classroom to sit alone and think of what lay ahead for me: the long, painful trek home. And then she'd appeared.

"I am sorry." She sits close to me, making me feel awkward alone with her in the empty classroom.

My leg is swollen and I dread the hot water my mother will use to treat it. She has a particular way of treating wounds. The day I stepped on a nail, she held my leg to her lap with the heel pointed up. While my siblings held down my hands, she dunked a red-hot kitchen knife into a tin of palm oil buried in a smouldering charcoal fire, lifted the knife, and carefully dropped the shimmering, hissing oil into the wound in my heel. I saw open white expanses of pain.

"But why don't you stop playing football to avoid injuries like this?"

I stare through the window framing the football field to hide the feeling of shyness that my face must betray. Grace is one of the sly, intelligent girls—the school's prettiest girls— who gossip and giggle all the time. The field is a confused blur of blue and white as students are kicking balls around and engaging in other playful activities. My glare rests momentarily on Nnamdi Adaka for inflicting the injury on me. He was furious at the shameful way I'd dribbled him, envious of my new fame. The spectators had booed him, so he'd given me a hot chase. I'd felt his anger like the cutting edge of a knife on my back just before he unleashed a sliding tackle from behind. I'd been expecting it. I'd leapt out of harm's way, neatly dodging the tackle that would have cut me like a machete blow. The crowd had booed again, inflaming him the more, and then he'd charged at me, and this time he'd caught me at the right ankle.

"What will you do now? How will you walk home?" She breaks into my train of thought.

"I will manage. My mother is going to treat it with hot water."

She makes a face. "But won't you go to the hospital?"

I almost laugh. I want to tell her that I have never been to a hospital besides when a madman bit off my ear. As a child, my mother would oil my body with palm kernel oil when I got feverish, and when I got really sick, when I started vomiting and shaking violently, she'd summon Uwakwe, who forced me to swallow big white tablets and long capsules. He'd drive a long needle into my buttocks. I got well again after the injection, but sometimes it resulted in an abscess, forcing me to walk like a stooped old man. Then my mother would invite Uwakwe again to cut the big, ripe boil with a short knife to release thick yellow pus that spattered everywhere like custard cream.

"I am sorry." Her voice is whispery, the words falling softly like a feather. Suddenly, she is not the same rebellious girl shrieking and giggling in class. "I should not have answered the question that day, should not have beat—" The feather drops.

She flees the class.

The trek home could not be more painful, with the sun sharp and biting. I think of Grace's unexpected apology. She couldn't possibly have guessed how much I cherished her soft, feathery words, her gentle scolding, and her company. I spend a long time on the road, arriving home with a leg twice swollen. My mother and I go through the ritual of hot-water-palm-oil-swearing massage.

"What I will not condone is your going to school and bringing back injuries like this," my mother protests as she presses a cloth soaked in hot water to my ankle.

My mother's scolding worsens the pain. Injuries like this

make me wonder if I will ever play football again, but I see myself returning to the field as soon as it heals. Ebube and Ihebube return again and again to say ndo to me where I am relaxing on the tomb after the treatment.

Thirty-three

IT'S A LONG, PAINFUL WEEKEND. I CAN'T GO TO THE stream. I can't go anywhere. Okike's tomb and Ralph Ellison's *Invisible Man* are my only companions. The novel is a gift from the ever-smiling, coat-wearing English and literature teacher, who knows my fondness for novels from my performance in his classes. He probably noticed I was craning to catch the title of the book in his grip.

I pour myself into the book now, relaxing on the tomb. The story is set in a Negro college. The narrator's experience when he arrives at the hotel ballroom where he is to give his speech, where he is informed by the white leaders of the town who are smoking and drinking together about a boxing match—a "battle royal" fought between black classmates of his in which he is invited to take part—reminds me of my time at the mansion, and how much people are willing to exploit other people's bodies for their entertainment. Buried in the novel, wondering how much more of me is still to be discovered hidden in a book, I only notice her presence on the novel's page, in the umbra of her shadow.

The tall, slender form of Grace is not what I expect to see when I look up, outside our poor mud house of all places. Her sudden appearance leaves me speechless. I have never seen her in a dress other than the school uniform. She looks prettier than usual in this pink round-neck dress that flares at the hips. She has long, graceful arms, and her skin is the soft brown of cowpea in the dull Saturday afternoon sun now passing over the tomb.

I don't want to take her inside. It is bad enough her coming here and seeing the outside of our rat hole. I don't know her family, although she strikes me as someone who lives in a good house, as someone whose father trades at Ogige market, sells jewelry or Echolac bags. She hesitates when I ask her to sit on the tomb with me.

"Whose grave is it?" she whispers.

"It is my aunt's."

She is silent, fear shadowing her thin face and mounting a flush to her cheeks as she sits down with one buttock.

"Ime aga?" I can smell her soap's pear taste as I ask after her well-being.

"I am good." She brightens. "What are you reading?"

Showing her the title of the book, I say, "I got it from the English and literature teacher."

Eyeing me, she replies, "I didn't know you read novels as a hobby."

I quickly list the novels I have read, to impress her.

"I am sorry about your aunt," she says after we talk a little about novels and poetry, and how Chris Okigbo's "Elegy for Alto" is her favourite, a poem about the onset of the Nigerian civil war, in which the poet bemoaned the disintegration of the country and the bloodletting to come. I could see the English and literature teacher performing the poem in class, feet firmly planted and hands at his sides. Of a particular poignancy to me is the poet prophesying his own death in the war, his dying as he fought on the side of Biafra, that we may live and have honour.

"My mother says I came to Okike to suck her breasts and

cried when I didn't find milk in them." I bring the conversation back to my aunt.

She giggles, looking shy, then intrigued. I can see she is endeared by my closeness to Okike, but the part about sucking her breasts makes her fidget nervously.

"It was naughty of you sucking your aunt's breasts."

I don't know how she might react if I tell her that I am Okike's reincarnation. "My mother says I was a big sucker."

She giggles again. "Boys are big suckers. My brother sucked his teeth milk yellow."

"My brother sucked his rust red."

She laughs.

I laugh.

"Is he home, your brother? Do you look alike?" A flush of curiosity warms through her.

"He looks finer. He has the muscle of a man and the skill of a spider. He used to weave baskets he sold at Ogige market. Now he is a motor mechanic apprentice."

"How nice!" She smiles, nervously, her eyes leading me to Bingo sitting on the doorway, fighting off flies from her sores. The dog is doing it in rather a repulsive manner, catching the flies in her mouth and grinding them. Ugh!

I think she is going to retch. I stone the dog away.

"My mother is not home, either," I say, sensing her anxiety, her discomfort. "I have a sister like you, but she has gone to see my other sister at her husband's place. The younger ones are playing somewhere in the neighbourhood. I am home alone."

"Oh!" she says lightly, but I can feel her relax beside me. "Where has she gone to, your mother?"

"Church. My mother is a Protestant."

"Oh." She relaxes on the tomb. "You. What are you?"

Her question startles me. "Catholic." I couldn't possibly tell her that I visit Ezenwanyi's cave. She would see me as a pagan.

"I am Catholic, too."

Silence.

"They cry a lot, too, boys." She returns to the original conversation. "They sap their energies crying, and then they suck like there is no tomorrow."

"I was a big crier, my mother says, a snot-nose." I pick up a stone and throw it at a goat that has wandered out of the goat pen behind the house; the animal doubles back.

"You must have been such a horrible child." She laughs. "Oh, what a shame! I came to know how your leg is healing, and here we are talking about other things."

I stretch out my leg, which looks ripe after the massaging and oiling, for her to see.

"It must be very painful. Can't you stop playing football?"

"If I didn't play football, would you be here talking with me?" I say this softly, because I can never be angry with her. "Would you have even noticed me?"

She looks at me with a somewhat guilty expression.

"I was a good-for-nothing student who couldn't answer a question in class. Papa. Have you forgotten all the giggles, the gossips, and the name-calling?"

Silence reigns again. I feel like telling her I almost quit, but I don't dare. She is my guest. I wouldn't dare even if the circumstances were different. She looks so pretty, delicate, and fragile.

"My mother caught me crying." The feather in her voice alights. "I told her about the lashing. She insisted I apologize, but I . . . I . . ." A back-and-forth flight of the feather in that irregular rhythm. "And then you hurt yourself. I had to take the chance when you were alone. I came to know if I have been forgiven."

There's nothing to forgive, I tell her.

"You surprised me with your football skills." She is relieved and glowing again. "You look really good in a football jersey, and you play elegantly. I was proud of you when you scored the goal that won our school the cup. But then you became too big a star in school to notice someone like me."

"That's not true." I grin, amused by her mischief. "I am not a big star. And I doubt I'll ever become one, because of you."

"Me? How?"

"Don't you want me to stop playing?"

She hesitates. "I don't know. You get hurt. Look at your leg, so swollen."

"It's nothing." I want to say more. I want to tell her that everyone gets hurt sometimes, one way or another. But they get better and play again, that's the only way they can become a star. I want to tell her that my father is a failure because he refused to confront the people who stole his crown. That more than nurturing the conspiracy against him to success, his silence stripped him bare and left him a penniless weakling.

We sit in silence, falling back into our thoughts.

"Have you lost an aunt or anyone close to you?" I say, to fill the emptiness.

"I lost my grandmother."

"I am sorry. Did your father build a tomb for her?"

She shakes her head.

What a shame! I could tell her that I built this tomb for Okike, but I don't want her to know how Okike drowned. The shame of it. I begin to drum on the tomb. And then I stop, scratch my hair, and throw stones to fill up the silence.

"I miss her." She purses her lips. "I took after her. I was named Egoyibo after her, but Grace drowned my native name."

"Egoyibo." I gasp for the love of the name.

She giggled. "She kept poultry and insisted that I alone eat their eggs."

"What happened to her poultry?"

"They went feral after her death. She came in a dream and scolded my father, and then he replaced them."

I draw silent parallels between her grandmother and my aunt.

"Tell me about your ear."

Suddenly I feel her hand on my bad ear like electric shock. No one except my mother has ever touched my bad ear in that tender way.

"I am sorry you had to go through all that," she says after hearing the story of the madman, which made her giggle, frown, grimace, and then shed a tear.

The silence becomes awkward.

"I shall leave." She rises, the setting sun falling on her, glowing on the cowpea brown of her skin. "You don't have to see me off if you can't."

I insist.

We talk about school and the exam on her way out. About Lioness, and Cat, and Nza. I manage to walk her to the village road and watch her bound ahead, as light and free as a butterfly. Suddenly she turns and looks back, and then she waves at my silhouette before vanishing at the village intersection.

I may have told Grace that I am Catholic, but the truth is, I can't remember the last time I went to church. "No son of mine living under the same roof with me will end up a pagan," my mother would swear at the top of her voice each time I failed to go to church. "It's bad enough that your father worships idols and those other worthless gods."

I turn around and begin to hop towards home with a big smile, my mind rewinding the name over and over again like a beautiful song, lyrical and poetic.

"Egoyibo."

Thirty-four

PATTY ONAH AND OLUOHA ARE OUT OF DETENTION. The news spreads through the village. People rush off to see them as if they are creatures in a zoo. They come back broken, looking malnourished and sickly, with hollow cheeks and sunken eyes. Still, they entertain their guests—friends and relatives who visit them—with distressing stories of the life of pro-Biafra detainees in prison cells across the country.

"I advise anyone who will listen to me to keep away from any kind of pro-Biafra activities," Patty Onah says in a faint, sickly voice, his porcine features gone. "We saw hell in detention these past few years. The food is terrible. They dumped and forgot us there, ten men packed in one tiny, infested cell. We slept with an epidemic of mice and ticks, and woke up with the smell of our own stool right there in a bucket next to us. The soup looked like diarrhea, tasteless and watery. The garri was as hard as stone, and a meal was hardly sufficient for a little child, not to talk of an adult. At times we were not fed for days. Four men lost their lives in the cell where I was incarcerated. Their families did not even see their corpses." He shook his head. "They abandoned us there to die, the same people we were loyal to."

But Oluoha has a different story. "They did not abandon us," he insists. "The government was hell-bent on breaking us. It is not even the inhumanity of government that is the issue; what is heartbreaking is that our brothers have turned around to stab us in the back. The leaders of Biafra Zionist Movement are traitors. They are self-centred people trying to reap where they did not sow. They don't deserve the support of any well-meaning Igboman."

They may have been freed, but they are terribly malnourished and jaundiced, and no longer have the strength to carry loads or dig pit latrines, and their wives face the huge task of nursing them back to life. The fear of being arrested and detained in such inhuman circumstances jolts me. Their grim and conflicting accounts of their lives in detention fill me with horror and doubt. Ikuku says the leaders of MASSOB are traitors. Oluoha says Biafra Zionist Movement is a fraud. I figure they did not make the decision to abandon Biafra alone; it was made in agreement with the ticks, the spiders, and the cockroaches that shared the cell, crept out at night encouraged by the silence of sleep, stopped to listen, and then inched forward again drawn to filth and the smell of blood.

They probably would not have ticks feast on them if they had money. The warders would allow them to sleep in the VIP section of the prison yard reserved for people with the right connections. They might even swap their names and get released, but all of this depends on the size of your "Ghana Must Go" bag or your big-big connection. I didn't know that politicians took stolen money home in "Ghana Must Go" bags and hoarded them away in underground vaults until I heard it from the gamblers who have slowly returned now to Uwakwe's corner.

"Yes. The warders can do anything for you," explained the wizened little man. "They can swap your name with someone else's name—that's to say that someone without connections or money for bribes can be substituted for you. All you have to do is drop out of sight long enough for attention to shift. And trust Nigerian leaders to have the attention span of a two-year-old child. And why not, when they are busy chasing oil money and bribes they hoard in household strongrooms. The warders can do that for you even if you are on death row. They can make someone else die for your crime the way Jesus Christ died for our sins."

My head reels with conflicting thoughts. The nocturnal meetings at the primary school are becoming more frequent, more interesting. I always sit in the front row to watch Ikuku as he speaks to his ever-growing audience. Sometimes he sounds like a historian. He tells us how the Igbo ancestry is linked to the ancient Israelites. He recounts the biblical story of events in the eighth century BC when the Assyrians invaded Israel's northern kingdom, forcing ten tribes into exile. Ndigbo, he says, are descended from those "lost tribes" of Israel.

Gad, the seventh son of Jacob, had three sons: Eri, Arodi, and Areli. They settled in Igboland and fathered clans, established kingdoms, and founded the towns of Owerri, Umuleri, Arochukwu, and Aguleri. That is why there are many similarities between Igbo rituals and customs and those practiced by Jews. Traditional practices such as circumcising male children eight days after birth, refraining from eating taboo foods, mourning the dead for seven days, and celebrating the new moon.

But the idea of a brand-new Republic of Biafra recedes into the background of my life as school terms come and go. I am now a senior student studying hard for the West African Secondary School Certificate Examination. Anytime I remember the exam, I get lightning streaks in my stomach. I have to pass to shame those who robbed my father of his inheritance.

I have to pass to silence my critics, especially Machebe. But each time I try to study, my thoughts keep drifting to Nnamdi Adaka's bullying and my feelings for Grace. Nnamdi Adaka is the proverbial horsefly on the scrotum. Grace is like a pageant, parading the close periphery of my mind, her soft laughter lending to the emptiness a sure feeling of her presence.

I keep having premonitions about Grace. What if she gets knocked down by a car or even an okada while on her way to Ogige market to buy things for her mother? What if a snake bites her or if some jealous girl who resents her beauty throws acid into her face? I keep imagining all sorts of things happening to her, and, after each long and boring weekend, I run off to school to see her face.

I walk her home after school one afternoon. She lives in a small, shadowy village buried in the woods, where birds and beetles welcome you with their songs. You can hear owls hooting and see millipedes and earthworms slithering around in damp corners. The houses, some tin and some thatch, nuzzle up against one another as though to keep each other warm in the chill and silence of the wood.

"You ought to be going back now," she says after the long trek. "I am almost home."

We stop and link our hands, hers as soft as warm cornbread, and in that moment we seem to conquer our small universe: the quiet conspiracy of the woods, the nyala's spiral-horned curve of the road, and a bicyclist who looms into sight at the far tree line.

Snatching her hand away, Grace gestures towards the approaching bicyclist and whispers, "He looks like my uncle."

I look up the curling vista, amazed at how the road braids itself impeccably then curves out of sight where the bicyclist has emerged.

"It's him," she says as he pedals into a recognizable distance. And then she's gone like a butterfly, in a lilting, fluttering flight.

I turn towards home, passing the pedaller: a scraggy old man in a raffia hat with a basket of cassava roots tied to his bicycle.

Grace is not in school the next day, and, worried she might be in some sort of trouble from yesterday, I go back to the woods. She had described her father's house to me, but the compounds here look confusingly the same. Luckily, I run into a little boy.

"I am looking for a girl named Grace," I ask the little boy.

He frowns, and then, remembering, points towards a newly renovated house in a small compound with a few shady trees. A kitchen with a crumbled side wall and a roof hanging askew faces the main house. In front sits a girl. I can see the inside of the kitchen: the soot-blackened back wall, three large stones set in a heap of ash for cooking, a pot on the fire. The girl sitting in the compound under a small orange tree has her legs stretched out in front of her. I can see her short skirt, her bare arms. My heart beats fast as I recognize Grace in the lively company of goats and poultry bleating and clucking. A black goat with white patches takes her by surprise and grabs a mouthful of grains drying in the sun. I can see that she has been keeping an eye on them and only glanced away for a moment. She shoos the goat away distractedly, her eyes fixed in my direction. I watch as the other goats suddenly determine to take their share, drawing her up on her feet, and, whilst she chases one goat away, another one helps itself. I admire her self-conscious grace, the poetry in her movements.

I'd not have seen the large new house in the background if I hadn't caught a glimpse of its fiberglass roof and sliding windows. The house is hidden in a lattice of branches. I know that only a few rich men around here can afford such a luxurious house. Grace probably forgot to mention the house, but every other thing is as she had described it: from a clump of trees by the side, to a banana bush carrying huge bunches of green bananas, to a coconut tree. She signals to tell me she has seen me. I slide out of sight to wait under a tree, straighten myself out, confident in jeans, T-shirt, and a face cap. The face cap is pushed to an angle to hide my half ear.

She comes tripping towards me like a butterfly.

"Egoyibo." I stare into her eyes to see how she reacts to my calling her by her native name, which means "banknote."

She blushes, then giggles. I can see she likes it.

"What are you doing here?" she asks.

"You were not in school today, so I came to know why."

Her dress is off-white, with a skewed neckline, and her dark eyes are creased with worry, her hair flecked with ash. She has a dark smudge on her left cheek, which she brushes off with a shy smile when I draw her attention to it, making me wish I had summoned the courage to reach out and brush it off her. She takes my hand and herds me down the road.

"You smell of onions and crayfish and smoke," I say, smiling at her.

She giggles again, then balls her fist. "I think I should smell of anger instead."

I am lost. "What do you mean?"

She laughs nervously. "It is good you did not come inside. My father is at home, and he is in a temper. He would have caused a huge scene."

I let out a sigh of relief for being spared of the wrath of a father in a temper.

"Let me see you off. We can talk on the way," she says.

We walk down the path. "What happened?"

She hesitates, her eyes shifting. "There was a quarrel between my father and my mother."

That stops me dead in my tracks. Had her uncle seen us holding hands?

She walks back and takes my hand. "Not about you," she says. "The truth is, my father wants to give my hand in marriage to a wealthy man who lives in Kano."

Something shrinks inside me.

She glances at me with a mischievous smile. "You don't want me to go? You are going to miss me?"

I have noticed how the atmosphere becomes charged when I am alone with her. I want to be with her morning, afternoon, and night. "Do you want to go?"

"No," she says. "That's why I was not in school today. The truth is, my uncle did see us yesterday and told my father. To avoid you getting me into trouble, my father then resolved to give my hand to this suitor who has been pestering me." Pausing and giggling again. "He thinks you're going to impregnate me!"

I sense myself scowling, then blushing, then wondering why she is making light of a situation as serious as this.

She takes my hand again. "But you know what? I am not going to marry him. My mother is angry with me for refusing.

My stubbornness has put her in a very awkward situation with my father. He accuses us, my mother and me, of conspiracy to deny him a rich son-in-law who has already helped in building his new house and promises to do more if he convinces me to accept his proposal."

I don't know what to say, but her story is crushing.

"I fled the kitchen in the main house to my grandmother's old kitchen to be in the company of her goats and poultry."

I had judged her wrongly, I realize then. A proud person would never leave that stately home.

"I always slept with my grandmother in the old family house. She did not want to abandon the old house, where her husband breathed his last, to move into the new house with everyone. I kept her company. The poultry and goats are still in the old house."

A thick cropland precedes us on both sides of the path that leads out of the village. Tall reeds rise along the edges of farmland and encroach on the path. In the mild wind, a reed assumes the posture of a striking cobra, now thrusting forward, now withdrawing.

"We are all alone here." She laughs to ease the awkwardness of the moment. She's all butterfly again, eyes sparkling with many small lights. "The only companions we have are the farmlands and the bushes around us. If a lion were to suddenly jump at us from the bush, what would you do? Run away and leave me here to be devoured or stay back and defend me?"

The answer to her question sticks like gluey cocoyam fufu in my throat. I am not sure I would stay if a dangerous animal were to show up here, say a mad or hungry dog. Maybe I am a coward, but that is the truth.

She laughs again, sliding her slim fingers between mine,

her hand that feels warm and tender. "I got you there. Don't be scared. I was only joking. We don't have lions here."

"As if I didn't know."

We laugh, and walk in silence, hand in hand, her breast brushing against my body, sending a ripple of excitement flowing up my spine, making me wonder if it is by accident or design. But I am enjoying it whichever way. We talk about the fast-approaching exam. Her restless eyes are settled again, dark and calm, like a sea after a storm has passed.

"I have some grains in the sun and at the mercy of the goats," she says suddenly. "Thank you for coming. I will see you in school tomorrow. Bye."

Her departure seems abrupt. I watch her tripping back home, fingers holding her dress at the tips of the flare to free her movement, each foot lifted clear off the ground, each step measured in that graceful way that girls skip. In that capricious way that butterflies swim the air. I muse over her on my way home. I am happy she will not marry her suitor. Tomorrow she will be in school. And the next day, too. I cannot imagine her going away, not seeing her ever again. She killed me when she said, *He thinks you're going to impregnate me!* in that plainspoken and mischievous way that spread warmth in my stomach. I didn't know she was already thinking of us in such conjugal terms.

That night, as I lie on the tomb with my thoughts drifting to her, a strange feeling possesses me in low waves of sadness.

Thirty-five

I NOW PLAY FOOTBALL AS SPARINGLY AS POSSIBLE, not because my injury is preventing me or because Nnamdi Adaka is boasting to his friends about sending me to a bone-setter when next we play against each other. Grace wants me to stop to avoid hurting myself again. My classmates have started to notice my attachment to her. They call me *woman wrappa*. Because I don't want them taunting me, I dash out to play when Grace is not looking, shooting to the field and back in again like a restless tongue unsettled by a sweet taste sticking around the mouth.

But I will never have the courage to ask her for sex, as my classmates are urging me to. What I do now, which I learned from Eke back in Anukwu, is sneak into the bathroom with soap and water if I feel heavy in my groin. I will close my eyes and imagine a girl's supple body with an oily sheen stroking my erection until a slimy, snot-coloured matter jets hotly out, leaving my body racked with spasms. It is usually accompanied by a muffled groan that I try to keep within the dark dungeon of the bathroom.

One evening, during the Biafra Zionist Movement meeting at the primary school, something unexpected happens. I almost don't believe my own eyes. I think it is his ghost when I see him there, and, throughout the meeting, we don't say a word to each other, though our eyes meet now and again. I'd never have expected it, but Nnamdi Adaka does embody the qualities the group wants. He is strong and plucky. I think about it all night in bed, what having my bully there means, with goose bumps washing all over me.

I walk to school the next morning like a wet hen and sit distracted through my classes after I catch him scowling at me. I find him waiting outside the classroom at break time. He probably sensed I would try to give him the slip and intercepted me.

Drawing me aside, he demands, "Are you pretending you didn't see me last night?"

"No."

"What's no? You did not see me or you are pretending?"

"I am not pretending."

"You are a liar," he says. "I am sure you were pretending not to have seen me because you didn't want to pay dues for the both of us."

"That's not true."

"Are you calling *me* a liar?"

"No."

He considers me with suspicion. "How long have you been a member?"

I tell him, hoping Grace will not see us together.

"I will see you at the next meeting." He begins to walk away, and then he stops and turns to look at me with sincerity in his eyes for the first time since he tackled me. "I am sorry for your injury."

With wide staring eyes, I watch him walk away.

•

The final exam is drawing nearer. I begin to study in the night with my family's oil lamp, but it doesn't take long before sleep conquers me.

"Is this how you are going to study for the big exam, dozing off even before you open your book?" Machebe sniggers in front of the family as we eat together.

"What business of yours is it?"

"Your education is family business. It became so after you were given what belonged to all of us. I am one of the shareowners."

Machebe makes it sound like I've stolen from him personally. Truth is, I haven't paid him back for the money he gave me when I left for Lagos. I may pretend to ignore him, but he leaves me with a huge sense of responsibility every time he talks that way. And he makes my heart lurch each time I remember the exam.

"I heard you have been sneaking out to secret meetings," my father says.

I throw Machebe an accusing look. I am sure he has told on me. "I have not been going to any secret meetings."

"That's a lie," Machebe says brusquely. "You have been there many times."

"How do you know that?" my mother snaps at Machebe.

"It's an open secret in this village," says Machebe. "Some people have joined a new pro-Biafran secret organization."

"What is this about you and Biafra?" My mother flares up, turning to face me. "Have you forgotten how those who were arrested were dehumanized? The trauma still hasn't left their bodies. Who will bail you out if they throw you into detention?"

"As a father, it is my duty to speak out when I notice any of you derailing. If Biafra will be, it will be, but not because you are a member or not of any so-called group. You better leave the scratching for those who have fingernails."

I had thought I would bluff my way out of their accusation. I know I am never going to stop going to the meetings no matter how upset they are with me. Not at this time when momentum is building. This time when frustration is growing and public resentment of the government is deepening. When the smell of a fresh country is thick in the air.

A brand-new Republic of Biafra that belongs to the great and resourceful Ndigbo, Ikuku says.

Sometimes I am able to study deep into the night, and I manage this on the eve before the first day of the exam, but then I wake up late the next morning. I grab a bucket of water, wash my hands, my face, and my legs. And then I put on my school uniform. I will not eat cocoyam and cowage soup for breakfast on the morning of my first exam—that kind of food could give me bad luck—so I take off to school on an empty stomach.

Teachers are moving about briskly, papers in hand, and students are standing in small groups. Around ten o'clock, a white van with a team of invigilators and the exam papers speeds up like a politician's convoy. When it stops with a screech of tyres, the invigilators jump out like military men and women. The movement of the teachers becomes frantic. Around eleven, we are summoned into the exam hall and given our papers.

"You have until one thirty to pass your papers," says an invigilator, a middle-aged man with a stern look. "That means you have an entire two and half hours. Begin."

Grace is also taking the exam. I can see her sitting in front of me. Her bride price has been paid by the rich man despite her protests. He is waiting for her to finish her exam to complete the marriage ceremonies and whisk her away. The speed with which everything has happened has left me dazed. I talked to my mother about Grace, but she warned me to avoid any kind of intimacy with her if I did not want to be heartbroken. "Forget her, because her parents will never like you," she said, point-blank, then added, "Being with her amounts to fornication in any case."

It was hard for me to do what my mother had asked. I have never before liked any girl as I do Grace. I did not tell her what my mother had said, but I did nothing to help her fight for our relationship after that. I stopped going to her house, making sure we saw less of each other, lying to her that my mother would make a big scene if she caught us together, for religious reasons. I had to frighten her to stop her from coming to our house, to restrict our seeing each other to the school. She must have realized that I was avoiding her.

The exam period is a full month. I will see Grace every day. Her suitor drives her to school in the morning in a big car. He comes to pick her up in another bigger car. I often watch them with jealous eyes from a distance, but I wish her well in her marriage. She may think she has a crush on me, which I consider odd because I am only a poor boy from a poor family, a boy with one ear and a half, and I am nothing compared to that charming man who smells of money.

Christmas is coming again. The marriage between the coming Christmas and Harmattan births dust, cold winds, and mad rush. People will start chasing money about like it is a ball they are trying to kick. Money they will spend buying Christmas things. Business will pick up at Ogige market, with traders bringing in more goods from Onitsha and stocking up their shops. A week before Christmas, the market will explode in frenzied buying and selling. The university staff will spend their December salaries buying what they'll need when they travel to their various hometowns. Girls will braid their hair and paint their nails so that they will look attractive to young men who will be returning from large cities with a lot of money. Farmers will bring their harvests from remote villages to sell and will spend the money on clothes and shoes for their families. There will be more business for load carriers, many of whom will be caught stealing, then beaten thoroughly. In Lagos, crowds will set them on fire with tyres and petrol.

I sneak out to go to one of the nighttime meetings at the primary school. I have not been able to attend any since the exam period began, but now I have only a few papers left. Ikuku says a brand-new Republic of Biafra will be declared at the next United Nations meeting, and I don't want my membership to be put to question on account of poor attendance. "Biafra is as sure as precipitation in the rainy season," he says. He raises the stakes whenever he speaks like that, so that membership almost always soars by the next meeting. I can feel the breadth and intensity of the struggle rising. I can smell Biafra like crayfish in my mother's fried stew. But each time I remember the warning from my family I tense up, a nervous feeling now snowballing into a premonition. The feeling gets stronger and stronger. And then one night, while we are waiting for Ikuku to arrive like pupils in a class, something happens.

There is no moon. It is so dark that Uwakwe is a mere phantom. Suddenly we are covered in a flood of torchlight as gunshots rend the night air. The group breaks up, fleeing in all directions. I head to the door, aware of people stumbling and falling, others climbing walls. I realize that the building is surrounded as a harsh voice orders me to put up my hands. A shove sends me pitching forward, followed by a kick to my buttocks. They push me roughly into a van. Uwakwe and a few others are sitting in the van already, in handcuffs. They shove in more people, and then they whisk us away, driving past a sleeping Ogige market down the valley of Bishop Shanahan and up a small hill, where the police station sits in the company of tall mango trees. And then they push me in, leaving me cringing in the middle of a cold, dark cell, and startled by the rasp of steel meeting steel as the savage-looking police officer locks the cell bars.

The strong, unpleasant smell of feces welcomes me as I wait for my eyes to get used to the darkness. I smell humans, too, the rancid odour of unwashed, sweaty bodies. And then six inmates are staring hungrily at me as if I were a delicious plate of rice as vague shapes begin to outline themselves in my vision. All six men—excepting one who is lying down, a thick, keloided man of middle age—are squatting around the space that at best is the size of a cubicle, giving the impression of a crowd.

My greetings are met with silence and twelve brutal eyes devouring me, not even a sit-down gesture. The mistake I make is going to squat without being permitted. My buttocks hardly touch the floor when a massive hand slams a welcome blow to the top of my head. The blow quickly sends me back up on my feet. Illuminations form stars as big as moons. The stars fade into sable savannahs as I slowly return from the Milky Way back to the tiny republic of seven inmates now including me. I realize that the man lying down is speaking to me, or growling at me rather.

"Abeg, move back!" barks the voice in Pidgin English. He doesn't sound like he is from my tribe. "Wetin be ya name, sef?"

"Dimkpa."

"Which kain name be dat, sef?" He cackles. Others laugh, too, as if they are mandated to laugh when he laughs, and not laugh otherwise. "Oya. Go salute kodo."

It's one of the many cruel treatments given to a new inmate, forcing them to punch the image of the skull and crossbones sketched on the wall of the cell.

"And you beta punch am hard if you no wan collect beta punch from somebody to show you how hard you suppose punch," says the man they call Presido.

They make me punch the wall again and again until my knuckles are burning. It is part of my initiation rite, and also my punishment for daring to come into the cell without "something" for Presido and his republic, and then for allowing myself to be arrested too cheaply and on such a cowardly excuse as attending a meeting. And because I am a disgrace to Odumegwu Ojukwu, the founder of Biafra, who was such a fine, gallant soldier.

"Abi lion dey born dog?" growls Presido.

My position and work in the republic are made known to me after my initiation. I will run errands for my older inmates. They make me stay awake and fan Presido with my shirt while he snores through the musky cell heat. It is also my duty, as the newest inmate and the most cowardly, to dispose of the shit bucket every morning. Presido is the oldest and the "president" of the "republic." He got locked up for stabbing and robbing a man. Other inmates' crimes range from rape to robbery to murder.

The cops are just as villainous. "Small Ojukwu," says Opurum, the scraggly, sneering man who is my investigating police officer. He taunts me ceaselessly. "You tink say wetin Odumegwu Ojukwu no fit do, na you go do am jus like dat? Muscle you no get like me. See ya chest like dat of the bird nkele."

Opurum's taunting, the acts of wickedness I am being subjected to by fellow inmates, and the thought of being whisked off to a prison cell and dumped there to await a trial that might take forever to come fill me with fear. I become even more terrified when one of the inmates gets violently sick. It is clear the sick man will die if he is not rushed to a hospital, but no one makes a move to save him. The inmates can do no more than press a wet cloth to his burning forehead. The thought of watching someone die in the cell next to me frightens me.

It is now three weeks and there's little hope of my getting out anytime soon. I have been worried about my remaining exam, wondering about Uwakwe and the others who were also arrested and put in different cells. If no one comes with bail for me, I will be taken to court and remanded to a prison cell indefinitely. I know that my family cannot raise the kind of money the police will demand for my bail. The best they can do for me is the food my mother has managed to smuggle into the cell a few times, which Presido seizes for himself anyway.

Opurum shows up one morning after a month of my

incarceration. He cuts a grumpy figure as he fiddles with the cell locks.

"Oya, small Ojukwu, follow me," he says casually.

A cold chill washes over me. It descends on the other inmates, too, that familiar feeling that something terrible is about to happen to me, to one of us. It has happened before, an officer arriving casually at the door and saying to an inmate, "Dem wan hear ya case today. It fit be ya lucky day. As I see am, sef, dem fit to discharge you if the prosecution no get strong evidence."

The inmates would jubilate and hug the lucky inmate, the pain of losing him eclipsed by the hope of freedom. But is there freedom? Is there even a court sitting? The manner with which the officer slams the door and the angry rasp of irons as he locks up the cell raise questions. The answers are obvious. The ruling party is hell-bent on retaining power in the coming elections. So they set out to intimidate their opponents, and there's no more savage way of achieving this than by extra-judicial political killings. Abandoned inmates without connections or "Ghana Must Go" bags are smuggled out of their cells and murdered at strategic locations.

The attama passes on.

Obochi considers the passing of the Ezenwanyi priest. She decides it doesn't take away or add to her sorrows: her othering and this thing sitting right in front of her. She hasn't managed to refer to it in human terms, to relate to it as a parent since she gave birth to it seven months ago. Its conception ruined her relationship with Gbaghalu. It provoked her first big fight with him, its tiny kicks vocalizing her resentment of him and causing her to spit every rush of nausea into his face. She starved herself, eating only those things meant to flush the fetus out, poisons that became nourishments.

Finally, it slipped out of her like wind.

The baby is screeching on the floor, bathed in its own snot and tears, eyes begging for her motherly affection. But affection is a luxury she cannot afford. It's hard enough on her to have to breastfeed it. Bad enough that she has to take it in her hand.

Gbaghalu hurries in, alarmed by the baby's sobs.

"Show this child some love." He picks the baby up from the floor and croons to him on his wide shoulder, his voice more asking than upbraiding her.

The baby stops squealing and nuzzles up against its father, breath coming in convulsive gasps, its sad eyes following her to the door as she walks away from the claustrophobic scene. Everything—the house, the baby, Gbaghalu—is driving her out of her mind. She did warn him of dire consequences, but he persuaded her to consummate their relationship.

He comes outside with a sulky face and sits with her after feeding his child and putting it to sleep. He has just returned from where the male outcasts were summoned to dig the attama's grave.

"That boy needs your affection. How long are you going to deny him that?"

He looks even more attractive when he sulks, she muses. Over the months since the birth, he has alighted from shouting his protest over her attitude towards the baby to coaxing it, and now he talks about it with hurt in his voice, sounding utterly exhausted.

"When will they bury him?" she asks about the priest, not desiring to talk about the baby. Had the attama not passed on, they would all have been out working in the fields all day with the thing tied to her back, shrieking itself red in the face from the harsh sun.

His frustration with her finds expression in a deep sigh. "The ekwe, timber drum, will summon us," he explains. "It is not a good time for the outcasts. One of us will be buried alive today with the priest."

She almost tumbles off the bench.

He wishes he hadn't mentioned it, seeing her reaction, how terrified she looks, but he had to warn her ahead of time. Ezenwanyi's outcasts are sacrificed to the goddess in a periodic ritual to strengthen her powers. The village elders have decided that, since it's the year of the sacrifice, which ritual involved burying the sacrifice alive, it's only proper to bury him with the late attama.

Falling to her knees and grabbing his hands, she says: "Let's run away. Let's flee to a distant place where we will be free from this evil life."

"There's no escaping from Ezenwanyi." He realizes how hopeless *and helpless he must sound. Ezenwanyi will cast afflictions on anyone who tries to run away. He will be cursed with madness, blindness, leprosy, and wandering. He will end up a corpse for the vultures to feast on.*

He doesn't want to scare her more by telling her that the goddess usually makes her choice of sacrifice from outcasts who were enslaved because they took another life. Sometimes an outcast perceived to be rebellious is chosen. The goddess might also instruct the attama to sell such rebels to merchants from other clans, who then decide how best to use their slaves for different kinds of ritual sacrifices or for economic purposes. But he tells her that the new attama is consulting to determine the outcast the deity has chosen to be buried alongside the late attama. The timber drum will be sounded to summon the outcasts to the burial, where the victim will be made known.

They set off to the burial shortly after they hear the deep tones of the timber drum. The baby is a koala, and Gbaghalu is sure he will sleep through and will still be drowned in it when they return. He is too young to be taken to the scene of so much cruelty. Once the sacrifice is named, the rest of the outcasts will breathe a sigh of relief. And then the undertakers will prepare the sacrifice, gagging, blindfolding, and tying him up naked to be lowered into the grave side by side with the attama's slatted raffia coffin.

Thirty-six

OPURUM WALKS ME THROUGH A CORRIDOR TO THE counter where Nnamdi Adaka is waiting, the last person I expected to see. He laughs at my stunned silence.

"Small Ojukwu. You get beta friend wey come bail you from dis wahala," Opurum says with a note of sarcasm. "If you like go do Biafra again. Dem go charge you for treasonable felony. May be you no go get dis kain luck nes time see person wey go bail you."

I walk hand in hand with Nnamdi into the still morning air. The vendors are opening up for the day's business to begin the sale of stationery, beer, cigarettes, provisions, and items of confectionery outside the police station. It feels very strange walking with Nnamdi down the treed road and hearing him explain that he bailed me out with the money he hoarded from other students.

"But . . ." I search for words. "I mean, why did you do it?"

"You didn't want to come out?"

"No! That's not what I meant," I say quickly.

"I did it because we are one," he says. "We are all part of the movement now."

"Thank you," I say, stunned.

I wish I didn't have to face my family. My mother takes a long, sad look at me as I approach and cries out, "Nnam, have you been eating the food I brought to you? Why do you look so skinny?"

She says I look like something meant for others to wipe hands on after a meal. I know I look thin from hunger and sleepless nights, and from those bloodsucking bugs, but I didn't know I had become a hand wipe. I wonder how Patty Onah and Oluoha survived living like that for so long.

"They took the food you brought," I say.

"Don't worry, nnam. We have some beans and crayfish. The general overseer of my church shared foodstuffs out to poor members."

I have an aching feeling that those things were meant to be shared out to poor widows—that my mother had pretended to have lost her husband. But home feels like Mummy's mansion after weeks of enduring hunger pangs.

"We have to meet this friend of yours who plucked you out of the jaws of a lion," she says about Nnamdi Adaka.

My mother pampers me, feeding me with yam, beans, and crayfish. Machebe stamps all over the place, furious at the reception I am getting from my mother, reminding me of the story of the prodigal son I had read from the Bible in school.

Weeks after I return home, the exam result is released. I am full of dread, knowing there is no way I could have passed. While I was in detention, I missed the English Language paper. It is compulsory to pass English, and, even if I pass all other subjects, the result is nothing without English. I will be able to retake the exam next year, but before then I have my family to reckon with.

In school, when I reluctantly go for the result, I see

classmates I have not seen since I was arrested. I had hoped to see Grace, but she is not there. She has gone away with her new husband. I'm told they left soon after the exam period to the big city of Kano, where he lives. I miss her. I hate the fact that he has taken her to Kano, which Ikuku says was one of the sites of the anti-Igbo pogrom. More than half a million Igbo people were believed to have been massacred, leading to the Nigerian civil war.

Lioness is sitting in her office, all roundness and teeth. I hadn't liked her at first. I had considered her a wicked principal, but now I am leaving her school with a sense of loss and remorse for all the times I thought so.

She hands me my result, watching and half smiling as I walk out of her office.

The way home is the same—through a footpath that cuts across village squares. We used to cut corners, sometimes following crusted farm ridges with towering palm trees that end in a crown of leaves. Suddenly, I am aware of it, an individual scent provoking a powerful memory—the haunting, hunger-provoking Congo music and the burning sun.

I struggle to fight a clutch of melancholy deep in my belly.

My mother is anxiously waiting for me. She promised to slaughter one of her chickens and use it to cook pounded yam and ogbono soup to celebrate my success. My father promised to get some palm wine for the celebration. Everyone is eager for me to return.

"Is everything well?" My mother tries to read my expression as I walk into the house. She can get very anxious, always renouncing that inevitable dark moment when something really terrible will happen to us, her children, not because she is not prayerful, but because it is destined due to my father's sabotage, his conspiracies with small, insignificant gods.

I put my result away and eat my food; dollop by dollop the huge cone of pounded yam goes down until it disappears. I fall upon the lap of chicken my mother has put in my soup. I have been given the biggest portion: a lap and the neck. I sink my teeth into the lap and chew slowly with my eyes closed. My father's palm wine tastes sour, but after I drink many cups of it, it begins to taste like honey. Oyimaja arrives for the celebration with her four-year-old son and her new baby girl sitting on her hip, her clothes thin and shapeless as usual. My mother had sent for her to be part of the celebration since the whole idea of going back to school was hers.

Boyi, Oyimaja's son, eats himself silly. His cheeks balloon with food. His chest gets soiled with soup. He walks around like a pregnant duck, his belly protruding against high-defined ribs as he swallows and shoots out his tongue again to lap up the snot that oozes down his nostrils. Ugh!

Uncomfortable with too much food, he bursts into tears. Oyimaja unclothes him down to his little black penis, hooked to his groin like a thick thumb. Without warning he sends a jet of shit spattering to the floor. It is followed by a long sigh, as if he has climbed down a height, and then he falls back on the food.

I am getting lightheaded on the wine already, and I am not too interested in Boyi or Babie, his little sister, or Bingo, who, drawn to the smell of shit, wanders in with a swarm of flies. I don't care that the dog laps up Boyi's shit and licks his anus clean, or that Babie is busy sucking her mother's flaccid breasts to fibers on her chest, but I am worried about the trouble that will come when the truth about my results is made known. I feel guilty eating and drinking in merriment, but I feel I shouldn't spoil everyone's mood by announcing a bad result.

I watch my father laugh with a note of triumph as he downs more cups of wine. Lately, we haven't been hearing much of that no-holds-barred laughter of his that makes you want to laugh, too. My supposed success has come as solace for him from all that has happened to us. The evening goes pleasantly until he clears his voice and says, "Dimkpa. We have eaten and drunk to your success in the exam, now is the time to let us know in detail how you were able to ambush the lion in its den and return home with its carcass."

"I have a better idea." Machebe cuts into any explanation I might have to give, his voice belling away with mischief. "How about he shows the result round? Allow us to see things for ourselves?"

His suggestion stuns me more than Nnamdi Adaka's vicious tackle catching my ankle, or his bailing me out. I rise to my feet, and, swaying slightly, I wander into the house to fetch the result from my tin box. I know that I can't bluff my way out this time. Machebe may not have gone to secondary school, but he can tell the difference between a "P" and an "F" on a result sheet, and I failed my English Language paper with a capital "F," because I missed it while I was in the police cell. But I know they won't accept that as an excuse. What was I doing getting myself thrown into a police cell in the first place?

It's painful watching my family as they struggle to come to terms with my bad result, the fact that failure is their reward for selling our only land to send me to school. My mother is too shocked and angry to speak. She ignores me completely as if I cease to exist. There is no punishment greater than my mother sulking and not speaking to me when I misbehave. She sings a melancholy song, the one that resonates with sadness anytime she sings it, her mood almost driving me out of my mind.

The days pass slowly; quiet days filled with dust and heat and liquid sadness.

Thirty-seven

THE HARMATTAN TIGHTENS ITS HOLD ON THE VIL-
lage, now brittle-dry, now peppery. Sometimes the mornings
are calm and cold, but they build up to howling afternoons
and hammering nights. Lips get cracked and then broken.
Cold baths become an ordeal. Wounds become taut and painful, but they heal faster, and tight braids get torn loose by
eager fingers to ease off the pain girls feel. The wind unclothes
trees, creates dust devils, and gets artistic with the fine red
dust rearing and spiraling skywards over the village roads. The
whole thing leaves me hollowed out. I should have hired a
wheelbarrow as the Christmas season closed in. I should have
braved the scented, cold Harmattan mornings and set off early
to Ogige market to carry loads, and not have succumbed to
this strange lassitude. It is driving me nuts. My family's poverty and my mother's broken-heartedness aggravate me beyond words. When I am not sitting on the tomb scowling into
the afternoon sunshine, I ogle the village women: the new-
lyweds and the mothers of one or two whose buttocks have
filled out with flesh and whose bodies bear the fresh allure of
honeymoon or lactation. I resent the old women who go about
bare, exposing their flaccid breasts, which disgust me.

Christmas is dull, affected by the mood in my family as a
result of my failure, although we eat rice and meat, and drink
wine like any other family in the village. Ihebube and Ebube
have to forgo their Christmas clothes for lack of money. My

father slaughters the last goat in his pen to make up for this. He does not want the twins sneaking over to the neighbours to salivate. My mother cooks stewed rice. She fries the stew many times over because it keeps catching fire each time she tries to bleach the palm oil. Finally, it hisses aloud with onions and sends a strong scent to the neighbours.

The empty days bore me out of my mind. My obsession with young, fleshy mothers becomes one crazy, monolithic animal instinct to ogle Enujioke, the pretty wife of Odo, the nagged little man who whistles each time he crosses in front of our house on his way to his bicycle mechanic workshop. If whistling were a sport, Odo would win Olympic medals. Nobody in the village whistles better than he does, with clear resonant notes that can be heard from a distance. Enujioke is young and full of energy for a man of Odo's age. She is a mother of two, nursing a seven-month-old baby. She walks around swaying her hips in a suggestive manner. She always stops to smile at me, her gestures provocative.

Only a shrub wall separates my aunt Ogbom's hut from Odo's compound. Pretending to visit Ogbom, I hide in the shrub fence and watch Enujioke after Odo goes to his workshop every morning. She is mostly home alone with the children. When she is not idling around in the compound, she wanders from house to house with a bowl of melon seeds tucked under her arm, gossiping and making new friends or enemies, her laughter spiraling over the village.

Today I know that Odo has gone off to work when I hear him whistling by our house on his bicycle. I wait for the silvery notes to fade in the distance before strolling over to his compound. I have to summon the courage for what I want to do with a swig of ekpetechi stolen from my father's bottle hidden under his bamboo bed. Some children are playing in the wide compound enclosed in a shrub fence. The children always smell of dust, sweat, and sores. Enujioke plants herself at the door with a smile, a hand fisting her hip, which is arched invitingly. I bring soap and water with me. The shrub fence screens off my little act of pleasure. I must have shut my eyes in momentary ecstasy.

Suddenly Enujioke's loud voice startles me out of half orgasm. I open my eyes to find her standing right before me, looking scandalized. I may have made groaning noises that gave me away. Growing up, I used to dig rat holes with Eke. The sound of our digger would tell the rat we were closing in on it, and in panic, it balled out of the hole and triggered a hot chase from us. I take off now like a rat ambushed in its hole as Enujioke's screams rend the air.

I know that a big scandal has broken. I know that Enujioke will tell the whole world how she found me touching myself, and, for many days, I will be tied to her laughter when it spirals high over the village. For days she will toss me about like a paper in the wind.

Thirty-eight

I LIE LOW. I HAVE THIS FEELING OF BEING NAKED, AND the only way I can hide my nakedness is to keep indoors and curtail from parading my shame around the village; that is the only way to stop myself from being mocked and laughed at, from being held in a cold and silent contempt by the neighbours for humiliating myself with a married woman. I spend the days brooding and running down a review of my failed life. I think of hunger, which now only seems to get worse with my father's physical and emotional health plunging, leaving my mother toiling endlessly to provide food; I think of my reputation, which I have succeeded in tearing to shreds; and I think of my dream of pulling my family out of poverty, which is fast slipping away from me.

My mother picks up bad news on her way back from church on Sunday. Ehamehule, the boy who fought me over his mother's tomb, is dead.

I had forgotten about Ehamehule.

"He left school to become a highway bus driver. And then he got into an accident." My mother weeps until her eyes are reddened, swollen.

I remember Ehamehule's father with his deep, rumbling voice and the body of an athlete. I imagine him seated with sympathizers in a cushioned room, his face tight, and his muscles pulsing with sorrow. Will he build a tomb or even raise a statue for Ehamehule like he did for the boy's mother?

Everyone is talking about Ehamehule's death, how heartbroken his father is, ought to be.

"He will have no one to carry on his name," my father says.

"He could remarry," my mother says. "He should have done that long ago after his wife passed on."

"He is old and may not withstand the demands of a much younger wife," my father laments. "He might not even have the strength to get a woman pregnant anymore."

Everyone is talking about it, saying what they think. I ponder this man's tragedy, but from a different angle. He lost a wife, erected a tomb and a statue for her, something his son had guarded jealously, even fought over, and now the son, his only child, is dead. Should he die in a few months himself, this man who has lived a foolish life in the eyes of the villagers, but who happens to be my idol for his devotion to his wife after her death, should he die of a broken heart, of loneliness, that would be the real tragedy of his little, censured, self-sacrificing life, because there would be no one to entomb him.

In the meantime, paled by the tragic death of Ehamehule, my encounter with Enujioke slowly fades, greying like a dying day. There is little to do to fill the emptiness of the days. I get tired of sitting at home listening to the neighbours as they pound their fufu or a woman as she calls out in a strident voice to her child who has wandered off to play. Obodike, our neighbour, is always hitting his wife. Machebe and Usonwa are always fighting. The rivalry between us, Machebe and me, has shifted somehow, dislodged by my self-alienation and Usonwa's ascension to maidenhood. Their voices clash like a pair of cymbals whenever they happen to be home together. They fight over little things. They drag the clothesline,

Machebe kicking her bucket down, and Usonwa screaming abuses and lunging at him in retaliation.

I get bored and walk down to the creek and spend the afternoon there. I stroll along the far countryside, hungry and angry and in dire need of a little excitement, a little money for snacks and my favourite chilled drinks. The trees are also looking bare and bored, the ground parched and thirsty after weeks of wild Harmattan. The whole place is aflame with the tang. The sun is up and staring wearily down at me, like a weak infected eye, as I walk from tree to tree checking for pods I might be able to steal. Most of the trees have nothing on them. After a long search I find one, an oil bean tree heavy with pods. I can't believe my luck, but then I notice ants with big red heads and small black bodies crawling all over the tree. I look up again at the long black pods, determining to get them even if there are snakes on the tree. Some of the pods are broken, a sign that the seeds are very ripe. The broken pods look like a pair of brown palms coming together for a clap. These red-headed ants are vicious and may have been the reason the owner of the tree has ignored the pods until now.

I begin to climb the tree. Sensing an intruder, more ants pour out of a black nest gummed to a branch of the tree. They look scary with their big red heads and grim little bodies. I have to be fast to avoid the ants, but then I have to pluck the pods with my bare hands since I do not have a machete to cut them down. It really slows down the process. I do not bring a machete when I am coming to rob trees, to avoid attracting attention; someone might get suspicious. I pluck the pods and hide them in the bush, then come back with a bag to collect them under the cover of darkness. The next day, I take them to the local market in a neighbouring community to sell. I usually leave for the market before daylight to beat nosy eyes. These pods are fully ripe and easy to pluck, but the ants are vicious. I keep rubbing my feet together to crush them, to stop them from climbing beyond the knee into my private area.

"Come down quietly." A harsh voice, similar to a goat's bleat when it chokes on its tether, startles me, nearly pushing me off the tree.

Ogbareka, the owner of the farm, a bull of a man, is standing at the foot of the tree when I look down. I stare at him with startled eyes. I didn't hear him sneak up on me. He has a machete. Bare to the waist, broad and callused like a chimpanzee, he is glaring up at me, his beefy nose flaring with anger and his great fist tightened around the machete. Every time I see his wide nostrils, I imagine a game in which I jump into his head through his nostrils and out again.

"Come down right away."

I get a big ant bite at the tip of my penis and let out a wince, almost falling off the tree with the pain. The man tries to hide a chuckle. But still I refuse to climb down and have myself sliced like vegetable.

"If you must get me, then come get me up here, old man."

The ants are all over me with their ferocious, conspiratorial bites. I know I won't last much longer up the tree. He probably knows it, too, which is why he is patiently waiting for me to give myself up. Around him are the scattered pods I have plucked and thrown down, a sight that infuriates him all the more. I think of jumping. But people are in their farms working. I can see them bent over in the distance. The man is still yelling at me to come down. They will hear his voice and come rushing over with their machetes; they are bound by a keen sense of communal living. If I jump now and he catches me and takes me to the village head, I will deny stealing his pods since there is no witness, but if someone else comes along, not only will he have a witness but my chance of escaping a chase by two people will be very slim. The machete in his hand catches the sun and glances wickedly, dulling the pain of the ant bites.

"All right," he says suddenly, throwing the machete down. "Come down. I am not going to hurt you since you haven't made away with any of the pods. Your punishment is going to be a simple one. You will come down, gather these pods into a bundle, and take the bundle to my house."

His sudden change of mind seems suspicious. Is this a bait to lure me down? I could take the chance; after all, I cannot last much longer up here with these ants all over me. But then I think of the humiliation of being dragged into the village with pods tied around my neck and waist the way they do to thieves.

The man suddenly squints up at me, his left palm shading his eyes. "Wait. Are you not the son of Agala?"

I curse him under my breath for recognizing me.

He grabs the machete again, his fury suddenly taking a monstrous leap, making a wild beast of him, like a famished lion with a caged prey in sight about to be released to it for a meal. I recoil from the violence escaping from the holes under his nose in hot steam. "Yes. I am the son of Agala," I yell at him. "I am the son of Agala, his first son who will soon go to the university to study. Do you have a problem with that, you lousy fat-nose?"

"Me! A fat-nose!" He fumes.

"You are not only a fat-nose, you are an ugly chimpanzee." I suddenly do not care anymore.

"Chaii!" he laments.

"What are you going to do about that—rob my father of another title?" I rail at him. "Do you know that you are not qualified to mention my father's name because he is a better man than you despite your oppression? I am sure you don't have a son who is going to the university soon, or do you?"

"I am going to kill you today." He makes wild gestures that scare me. He is trembling with fury.

I reach out, pluck a pod, and fling it down at him. He ducks as the pod hurtles down towards him. I reach out for another pod, and another, and another. The man keeps dancing this and that way to avoid the pods, but I determine to stone him with the pods until he flees, and then I will have a chance to jump down and run. A man in a work hat and farm clothes emerges. He begins to race towards us. The noise of our skirmish must have attracted him. The man has a machete, too. The sight of him activates my clogged brain. Again I survey the distance that I will need to jump. The tree is a very tall one and I might as well be jumping from the top floor of a two-storied house. I look again at Ogbareka, howling like a mad dog at the foot of the tree, hate and anger making a pathetic wretch of him. Suddenly I let myself drop, landing on my feet and then rolling a few times to cushion the effect of the fall.

Ogbareka lunges at me with the machete.

The baby startles awake. Finding an empty house, he lets go a loud wail. The baby yells until his voice fades to a whimper. Exhausted, he sits in sobbing spasms, in his urine and excreta.

Obochi finds him in this state when she storms in. The child stares at her, apparently too weak to be startled by her sudden arrival. His stuttering breath tells her he has been awake a long time and has sobbed for all of it. They look at each other fixedly, fear and mistrust in the baby's eyes, hers still dilating with the horror of watching as its father was named the sacrifice. As they bound him, tightening the rope until spasms of resistance wearied out. And then they gagged his voice and blindfolded away the fire and spirit in his eyes. The first hoeful of red soil took a downward flight into the grave, landing on his broad chest with a thud. It paved the way for many hoefuls whipping his recumbent body and smothering out the small, muffled voice of history. She clutched her chest, heart ripped through with pain, face raked and twisted, and let out a wail. She tore herself away from the gruesome scene that replays itself now with the same cruelty, the same savageness.

Suddenly she dives across the room for her son. She holds him to her chest, crushes him to her bosom and smothers him with kisses, snot, sweat, tears, excreta, urine, and all. He gasps, and his body rebels against hers, asking questions: will a lifetime of cuddling be enough to make up for the injustices of denying him his right to motherly affection, the lunacy of referring to him as a thing in place of giving him a name? As she presses him tighter and whispers his new name, Gbaghalu, she imagines the cadaver expanding in time, and the blindfold ripping apart. She pictures the bulging eyes as they summon termites that make a meal of their terror, and then the seed decaying in the soil, bringing forth a new tendril.

Thirty-nine

MY MOTHER AND I TREK TO HER CHURCH AT HER IN-
sistence, to see her pastor for my deliverance. She is worried
about the many troubles that I have been getting myself into.
They are as many as the white mushrooms that sprout at the
waterside, she says, there for everyone to see, the latest being
my theft.

After a long walk we finally climb up a gravelled road that
leads to the church. My mother's church is a woodwork structure with a tin roof standing on Ikeagwu Hill. The compound
is painstakingly clean. Someone swept thoroughly and took
time to weed the wild morning glory that sprouts everywhere.
I'm reminded of early mornings when my mother leaves
the house with a hoe and a broom. A small signboard reads
THE LORD'S SELECTED in white lettering against a lemon
background.

I spent a few days at my sister Oyimaja's place after escaping Ogbareka and returned when I sensed that tension had
subsided, only to be told that Ogbareka had been to our house
with a machete to look for me.

"He accused you of stealing his pods. Did you?" my mother
questioned me.

My silence told her that I was guilty. I have a feeling that
Ogbareka was going to forgive me for stealing his pods and
then he suddenly changed his mind when he recognized me,
the son of Agala. My father did not become village head

because he was the son of Ngwu. It is a legacy of hate that had us, Ogbareka and I, stumbling over farm ridges, now falling, now rising again, until he got snagged to a cobweb of thorns and crashed down like a cow with a deep groan and lay flat on his belly.

"We may not have money, we may lack food, but I did not raise you up to steal from anyone, especially people who hate us so much and are looking for the slightest opportunity to humiliate us," my mother lamented.

Ogbareka dragged my father to the village council of oha to be shamed and fined for my offense. Too angry to say even a word to me when I returned from my flight, my father walked away with agitated legs, his thin back shrunken against me. He will need to provide two large jerry cans of palm wine to cancel the one jerry can Ogbareka had given to the council of oha when he passed the adjudication of the case of theft to them. My father will most certainly lose the case. He will be heavily fined if he loses, and given a deadline to pay up. They will fence his land off with omu, the tender palm frond that symbolizes sacredness and casts the spell of mystical authority in the community, to restrain him from farming on it until the fine is paid and the sacred motif taken down. The land may be sold to recover the money should he fail to pay by the deadline. But as our only piece of land has been sold, he runs the risk of losing our house, all on account of my idiocy.

We enter the church and sit on old plastic seats. Everyone is wearing a lemon vest, including the pastor, who is wearing his over a grey jacket. He stands on a platform curtained with blue linen like a photographer's studio. He is talking in a big, amplified voice. Sometimes he breaks into tongues, his wide mahogany face bathed in perspiration. The congregation is small, but the entire church is bustling with tongues. He begins to move from one person to the other. He lays a hand on their foreheads and causes them to fall on the dirty lino-leum floor, supposedly shoved down by anointing. The whole drama seems unreal to me. A few enthusiastic ones take it to really dramatic heights, screaming and rolling forth and back on the floor. When it comes to my turn, I wait for the pas-tor, excitement roiling in my head like wine. The pastor lays a clammy hand on my forehead. My heart beats fast in an-ticipation of being swept off my feet by a powerful force. The church is buzzing like a swarm of bees roused in their hive. I know my mother must be watching us with anticipation, with half-closed eyes. But nothing happens after some minutes of the pastor holding my forehead and praying in tongues. His hand tightens around my forehead, waking in me a suspicion that he is going to try to trip me as he steers me backwards like a car in reverse. But I hold myself rock-solid against the steering. I can feel anger rushing to the tips of his fingers, dig-ging deeper into my flesh. He is wasting his time reinforcing, I tell myself, but then I realize with a sense of panic that if he kicks me down, his congregation will not know the truth, because their eyes are tightly closed. They will believe that I was felled by the Holy Spirit in the man overcoming the dae-mons in me. I clutch the ground tighter with my feet. It is fine if an invincible force knocks me down, but I am never going to allow anyone to muscle me down and claim the credit. We scuffle from one end of the wall to the other. And all the time the church resounds with more tongues.

He stops, exasperated. We look at each other like two wrestlers who are equal in strength, panting, trying to recover our breaths, to explore the other's weakness.

"Brethren." He dabs his sweaty face with a handkerchief.

The church stills, voices fading away in a dying echo.

"Nine daemons have taken possession of this brother's body."

A murmur of horror passes through the congregation.

He begins to count the daemons while the congregation screams, "Holy Ghost fire!"

The daemon of disobedience
Holy Ghost fire
The daemon of drunkenness
Holy Ghost fire
The daemon of fornication
Holy Ghost fire
The daemon of lying
Holy Ghost fire
The daemon of stealing
Holy Ghost fire
The daemon of idolatry
Holy Ghost fire
The daemon of affinity with the dead
Holy Ghost fire
Ogbanje daemon
Holy Ghost fire
Mami Wata daemon

The church is rumbling by the time he exhausts the list.

"Brethren, open your mouths wide, shut your eyes tightly, and pray for him in your loudest voices."

The church explodes again in tongues as he resumes his little act of deliverance, redoubling his pressure to bring me down, kicking, punching, and shoving, his frustration turning him into something of a monster. The praying grows into hysteria, everyone jumping and howling. I begin to feel for my mother. I have avoided looking in her direction. I know she is humiliated. I know she is willing me to overcome the daemons and succumb to the will of God. A burst of *alleluia* rends the air as I allow myself to be felled, sliding onto the linoleum floor for my mother's sake. The pastor heaves a deep sigh of relief.

"Thus says God: therefore if anyone is in Christ, he is a new creation. The old things have passed away; behold, the new has come into being."

I lie down on my back, feeling dizzy, wondering where nine daemons were accommodated in my small body, where they fled to now that I have been delivered. And then I allow myself to be helped to my feet by the pastor.

"Young man, you have your mother to thank for bringing you to a living church," he says. "Go home and sin no more. Brethren, let us not forget to remember our brother in prayer."

I straighten out and survey the congregation and my mother's illuminated face as Sisters are embracing her for a successful deliverance, and Brothers are shaking her hands, a feeling of conquest in the air.

We hardly arrive home from the church before it starts raining at a most unlikely time of the year. The village gets soaked, looking grey and fragile from my window. The rain recedes, then comes again, starting a fresh cycle of violence each time, with lightning flashes and explosions of thunder. I think of the creek that must be overflowing, the farms that must be swamped, and Ogige market, which must be flooded out. Heavy rains will come every season. We'll hear stories of people being carried away by floods after a downpour. They'll get swept all the way down to Alor-Uno, where they'll be fished out dead.

The rain finally recedes around late afternoon after a hard downpour, but the sky is still roaring, still grumbling like a lion baulked of its prey. It is cold through and through, and my body yearns for the warmth of a woman, for raw flesh. With my reputation in the village—an outlaw who lusts after married women—no sensible girl will agree to go out with me. My penis will grow turgid, and then it will go limp again, like a weed in the Harmattan.

I set off well after twilight. The road is full of mud water and darkness. I pick my way with the help of torchlight, but Ogige market is full of yellow headlights that swallow my own little light. Peace Park is sitting in half darkness. It is empty, but the emptiness symbolizes dozens of commuter buses conveying travellers to and from other parts of the country. It is quiet as if recovering from the exhaustion of the day, like a lunatic chained down after hours of frantic madness. I cross suya spots manned by caftan-clad Hausamen snuggled close to crackling charcoal fires. They show their kola-nut-stained teeth at passersby. Patronage is low because of the rain. Old Park is full of roast chickens, red and inviting in their coating of chili pepper and tomato, in the glow of oil lamps. Their sellers, swathed in thick clothes, are huddled behind their tables like economic refugees.

I cross the road, looking left then right, and then I enter the shortcut that leads to Lejja Park. I avoid small areas lit by electric bulbs in front of shops that have not closed, docking and sidling like a creature of shadows. I don't want to be seen by anyone from my village to avoid another scandal a few hours after I was delivered from the old ones. I negotiate the end of a wall and come face-to-face with a dark-skinned lady. On seeing me, she hitches her body up against the wall, raising one high-heeled leg, her miniskirt sliding back to show me a fleshy lap. Her lipstick is so red that it highlights her glistening dark skin. She is wearing a pink spaghetti-strap top. I can see the straps of her red push-up bra with her protruding breasts. She flaunts a full-lipped pout at me with her head tossed back, knowing that her hook has caught a fish.

I slide into the room after her. It is my second time coming here since Nnamdi Adaka initiated me into the bordello, but the first time I have the courage—or the desperation—to face any of the pouting, half-dressed women lounging around. The room is narrow and dimly lit by a coloured electric bulb. A six-spring iron bed with a thin mattress is covered with a light blue spread. A clothesline hangs low with the weight of her clothes around an old cream wall, with cooking items crowding the right corner of the room. The smells of alum and shampoo fill my nose. She throws her arms around me. I am taller. She looks up at me with a questioning smile. I know the rules from Nnamdi Adaka's schooling. First one is "Pay before service." She lists the rest: "Six hundred naira for full-strip without condom, five hundred for half-strip, and additional one hundred for delayed orgasm."

They all have price tags like products in a supermarket. I go for half-strip without condom. Nnamdi has told me that he hates condoms, that they don't give you full satisfaction. She hitches her skirt down, my body trembling for her as she lowers herself on the bed. I unzip my trousers to free my erection and step up for the check, another rule I learnt from Nnamdi. It nods repeatedly with impatience, my penis. She grabs it and toys with it, hissing her disappointment at its smallness. At full erection it is no longer than the squat red banana that grows in the garden behind our kitchen. Her touch sends electric currents through my body. She presses expertly, forcing a sob from me. She is very professional, mechanical. Satisfied I have no STD, no milky pus obeying the will of her hands and rushing up to the tip of my penis, she lets go, leaving me a gasp away from coming in her hands.

"Remember. If you stay too long, you will pay extra hundred," she says curtly as I kick out my trousers.

"No problem."

She moans to acknowledge penetration, widening then contracting again. A few famished thrusts and it is out, quick and gushing. It is all over, as casual as a chicken dropping its dung and moving on. She shoves me away, suddenly hostile, but Nnamdi had told me that side of them, hustling you out so they can bring in another customer. I step into my trousers overcome with tiredness, with disgust.

Forty

THE RETAKE EXAM LOOMS LIKE A DARK CLIFF.

My sister Oyimaja and I had a long talk when I fled to her house to escape from Ogbareka. "You are destroying the image of this family." Her breath rasped in her throat, her slow, lingering gaze falling on me, withering me.

I had not been so scolded in a long time.

"You are going to retake the exam." She panted with exhaustion from scolding me. "Right now our mother is very angry with you. I made inquiries and was told you can sit the General Certificate of Education in place of the West African Senior School Certificate Examination you failed, which would require a lot of money to reregister for. The qualifications are the same. I have stored palm oil I was going to sell for my children's school fees. I will give you part of the money to purchase the forms."

The exam is only two weeks away now. The closer it gets, the more anxious I become. I remember Amechi, a fellow who forged my transfer letter back to Community Secondary School when I returned, a 400-level undergraduate of the university. Uwakwe had introduced him to me. Uwakwe had told me that he also helped students to cheat in exams. "He is an orphan and trains himself with the money he makes."

Now that I remember Amechi, I rush off to Uwakwe's shop to fix a meeting with him. I don't care if I don't sit the exam myself as long as I pass. I am desperate to make things right again. But I also have to think of the risk of failing if we are caught.

Amechi puts me at ease.

"You have nothing to worry about," he says as he stuffs the money I pay him in his shabby jeans pocket, his manner impatient, his eyes shrewd. "We will buy off the invigilators if they get difficult. Don't worry. You will get value for your money."

On the day the exam starts, a blowy February day, I set off to the Girls' Comprehensive School with anxiety niggling at my mind. The season has been full of winds and dust smells, but it is now settling, the Harmattan almost quiet. I arrive at the girls' school, which is separated from the Seminary School by a high fence. They raised the fence to high heavens, maybe to restrict girls living in the dorm from getting mischievous with seminarians and would-be priests. I walk through a rickety gate into a large and unkempt school compound full of old buildings and weeds. The school smells like a latrine, the Harmattan wind blowing the smell in waves across the exam hall from the surrounding bushes, where the villagers relieve themselves after pulling down the wire gauze fence.

The school compound is crawling with mercenaries hanging about, waiting for the exam to begin. The first person I look for as I step into the premises is Amechi, my mercenary. I spot him leaning against a cashew tree. His presence should be reassuring, but I'm filled with unease. I walk over and edge a little to the other side of the tree so that I can watch him from the corner of my eye. He is about my height, about my size, and about my age, probably a little older. I should have already graduated like him but for the years I lost as a sickly child with pneumonia, as a fighter in Lagos, and as a migrant worker in Anukwu. My eyes linger on him, from his white sweatshirt to his blue jeans and a pair of red loafers. Everything looks so new he probably got it all with the money I paid him.

We are supposed to get started around eleven. The mercenaries will throw in the answers on pieces of paper through broken windows. They will try to outsmart the invigilators, who will wear mean faces and chase them around. But then the tension will ease off as money exchanges hands. The scowls will then vacate the faces of the invigilators, and the mercenaries will work in a friendlier atmosphere.

"Meche," I say in a low, resolute voice, using his nickname. "There's something I want to say."

He turns an inquisitive face towards me.

"I'd like to write the exam by myself," I hear myself saying. "I am not asking you to refund anything. Keep the money, but let me do this alone."

He stares at me for a long time. "Are you sure?"

"I am."

"Fine, if that's what you want." He shrugs and starts to walk away, then turns around. "You really think you can do this?"

I assure him that I can, and watch him amble towards the gate and out of sight. And then I walk into the exam hall. The decision to write the exam by myself flew into me like a virus.

The exam period stretches into its third week. By the end of it, I am thoroughly exhausted. But I am happy it has ended, and I go out celebrating on the day I write my final paper, coming home drunk and slumbering on Okike's tomb, waking up at dawn wet with dew.

"Are you celebrating another bad result?" Machebe hisses at me, but I know when I should pretend to be more mature than he is, so I ignore him to avoid the fight his chest is thumping for. In any case, I am so dizzy with hangover I know I won't achieve anything in a fight.

The hangover worsens into a headache, forcing me to go to Uwakwe's shop for a dose of Panadol. Uwakwe is sitting alone in his shop. He is leaning his muscular arms on the counter and whistling to a clear tune from his radio, chin cupped in hand. Around him tablets and capsules are displayed in dusty packets on shelves, but I know that many of the packets are empty. Just over his shoulder a doorway with a thin threadbare curtain conceals a bedroom I know to be crowded with bottles, cups, plates, clothes, and other household items. The curtain is skewed, and I can see another curtain of the same light blue colour and thinness, the same degree of dirt cordoning off an iron bed, a sort of theatre where girls lie down to have their fetuses plucked out of them. His peak season usually begins a few weeks after Christmas. His victims are the gullible village girls who succumb to young men returning home for sex, misled with promises of a tangible union. Many of them end up impregnated and dumped. They flock to Uwakwe's shop and grace his theatre bed when they miss their monthly cycle long after the young men have left the village and gone back to the city.

"Have you heard?" Uwakwe whispers to me from across the counter.

My ears prick up for a piquant bit of gossip.

"Ikuku bought a new car, an okwuotoekeneze, and members are wondering how he raised the money."

"Are they suspecting that he used the collections to buy the car?"

"Yes. As we speak, someone has been sent to the headquarters to find out if he actually remits the collections to them as he claims."

The news upsets me. I find it hard to think of Ikuku as a cheat, a corrupt leader. But then a strong sense of relief floods over me. I am happy I summoned the courage not to cheat in the exam. All the same, my dream appears to be crumbling, my life disintegrating. I walk back home feeling restless, the headache gone, giving way to anxiety and despair. Even after making a wish to Okike, I find it hard to rid my mind of my feelings of insecurity.

Forty-one

I RESOLVE TO GO TO MASS FOR THE FIRST TIME IN A long time to pray for a good exam result, but not at Holy Trinity Church. Once in a while I am drawn instead to the Chapel of the Resurrection at the seminary school to see the young rector with a Roman nose and laughing eyes celebrate a lively Mass, and to hear the silky-voiced Reverend Sister sing.

"Heaven helps only those who help themselves." Machebe's sneering voice follows me to the seminary.

I walk through the high security gates into a large, pine-scented school premises enclosed in a prison-high wall. And then I walk up a paved drive fringed by an orange orchard and a patchy football field where cows are grazing. One cow looks up, sees me, and scowls at me as I cross. I stop and scowl back at her; we lock our stares like two boxers. After a while she loses interest in me and returns to grazing. I go my way, feeling like a winner.

The first diversion to the left leads to the Chapel of the Resurrection. It is screened off by flowers and tall pine trees with long green pins looking as threatening as Uwakwe's needles. A gentle wind whispers in the pines, blending with Handel's Alleluia Chorus. A marble statue of St. John holds my stare for a while in front of a cream-and-green house adjacent to the orange orchard; this is the rector's residence. The house overlooks another diversion that dips into a landscaped courtyard, rising gently again to the shoulder of an eminence seated by a cashew orchard. The orchard hems another green football field. The ground below the orchard is in soft shadows. An atmosphere of divine presence rules the premises, with birds fluttering about noiselessly. A cow mooing once in a while disturbs the governing saintliness. Smoke pluming into grey skies over the kitchen roof seems to transport the hymn to the high heavens. The Chapel of the Resurrection is as beautiful inside as it is outside. It resounds with the hymn beautifully rendered by students dressed all in blue. I feel myself drowning in a vast volume of voices, my eyes following the pretty Reverend Sister everywhere in the church. She is wearing a blue habit that startles today. I shut my eyes and think about heavenly angels as she sings in her faultless voice, which stills the candle flame and moves everyone to sing lustily along. I imagine the heavens opening and the Holy Spirit descending upon her in a flock of doves. The more she sings, the more the heavens open wider to release more doves into the church in a fluttering of white wings. When she stops singing, the doves stop fluttering their wings and silence falls on the church. A white and still silence.

"She has many skills," whispers a woman sitting beside me as if reading my mind. "She decorated the altar."

My eyes move to the altar covered with table frills—white, soft, and delicate, set with exactness—and I nod and smile at the woman. I haven't been to the confessional for how long I can't remember, and I know that my sins are as red and bloated as a baboon's butt, but I couldn't resist the temptation to have the beautiful Reverend Sister feed me with the Holy Communion. I avoid the priest's line for hers, my heart leaping with excitement as she draws closer to me. When it is my turn, I stick out my tongue, showing her only the tip of it because I want her fingers to touch my lips. Her fingers are warm and delicious. I waste a bit more time on the queue to inhale her clean linen. Her eyes are beautiful, with heavy lashes and pupils so dark and so penetrating, complementing the golden chalice of her skin.

"God took time to create her." The man who speaks is sitting in front of me.

He probably noticed I was staring. The man has a big nose, but it fits him. He has a big voice that startles me, a voice that is so loud a few people will cast glances in our direction whenever he speaks, so loud it drowns all other voices when he sings along with the choir or when he recites the Credo. There is a little extra to everything he does, like when he grips my hand tightly during the Peace Offering; his big, rough hand is clammy with sweat.

The result of the exam is released sooner than I expected, but I am afraid to go see it. I cannot imagine another bad result.

"A real man doesn't celebrate and get drunk," Machebe swipes at me again. "He is bold enough to go face his result."

We end up exchanging a few swearwords and hooking each other by the collar, dragging each other this and that way.

I resolve to go and check the result, hoping to spite Machebe with a possible success. My heart beats fast as I approach a cybercafé at Ogige market. I have to pass this time. I cannot face Machebe's taunts if I fail again. And I cannot disappoint my family a second time, my sister Ekete especially. My legs are shaking. I can feel my bladder full to bursting. I stop to urinate into a gutter, feeling the hot singeing urine as it whizzes through my pintle. Cold sweat breaks out everywhere on my forehead. My brain feels fried.

Suddenly, I turn and beat a hasty retreat. Maybe my maths teacher was right when he called me "a big irony." I did not know what Nza meant at the time, but I knew it wasn't good, because I had failed all the questions in his test. Failure is not the character of someone who is valiant, which is the meaning of my name; a valiant person would walk into that cybercafé and boldly pick up their result.

Determining to play the valiant even for once in my life, I head in. Three girls and a young man my age are seated at desktop computers in the illuminated room. The luminous blue light of the computer screens fill me with fear. I approach the young man. I don't want the girls checking the result for me and laughing at me for failing. I figure guys are supposed to be more sympathetic to one another. I pay for a scratch card and I sit down to wait while the young man fiddles with the mouse. He appears to be wasting time, his palm clasped over the mouse while he moves the cursor around annoyingly.

"No internet," he says. "You have to wait."

My fear pounds my heart to fufu in my chest as I wait for the internet to come back from wherever it's gone to. Why has the stupid thing chosen today of all days to wander away? I will flee from home if I don't make it. I do not know to where I will flee, but flee I must; perhaps to my sister Ekete's place in the mangroves of Unadu. My mind lulls at the thought. It takes ages and leaves me as soft and done as my mother's cocoyam by the time the internet dawdles back, dragged in by the mouse.

"Congratulations!"

I don't realize the young man has spoken to me until he says it a second time.

"Congratulations! You cleared your papers!"

Startled, and overcome with joy, I gape at the result sheet that slides out of a printer. I allow the tears to roll down my cheeks as I drop to the floor on my knees to thank my aunt Okike, my mother's God-of-the-Selected, my father's pantheon of gods, and all who pulled together to make my success possible. I want to do things as if by magic, I think, as I walk away from the cybercafé. I want to sit behind blue screens and churn out good news and make all right in the world again.

I race home.

My mother smiles at me; we embrace each other, and, watching us, the younger ones giggle with joy at our newfound friendship, a moment of reconciliation. I am sure Okike will be very pleased in her grave. Everything seems right again. But I am missing Grace. Egoyibo! The man who married her stole a decent part of my joy. In a moment of wool-gathering, I see us sitting on the tomb and laughing over my result. I would have revisited the scene of our affection. I would have strolled down the wooded village path, watching the striking cobras and listening to the chatter of sparrows. But after considering my badness—the iniquity of the bordello and the indignity of masturbation—I decide that, until I penance myself, I am too unclean for golden memories like hers.

"What kind of student hires someone to write their exam?" Machebe smirks. "How are you going to succeed at the university?"

I don't know how Machebe nosed out my exam deal with Amechi. He won't believe me if I tell him that I wrote the exam without anyone's help, so no need for that. Still, I have been pondering his second question myself, looking up the long, rough vista of the road to the university. By passing my GCE exam, I have only succeeded in grabbing my dream by one third. The other two thirds are waiting in the university beyond Edaga Hills. I still must climb that unforgiving height back to Oregwu with a degree all on my own.

Forty-two

I OPEN MY EYES. THE OIL LAMP IS TURNED LOW, BUT I am able to make out an outline in the doorway. I recognize my father's wiry silhouette as sleep flees from my eyes. He walks into the room I share with Machebe and settles on the only stool. He asks me to get a pen and a notebook and to write down what he says. I don't know if it is a coincidence or if my father has chosen a night my brother is absent from our room. Machebe has gone to help his master with the funeral of his mother. He will be spending a few nights there. It is a relief that he will be away and off my back for some time. I don't have the strength to fight him. He seems less full of vinegar since I passed my exam, but he still says things that glance off my past mistakes. It is around one in the morning when I check the time.

"The legend I want to pass on to you I am passing on because I have seen new signs of maturity in you. You have grown more mellow, enough to succeed with your exam. My father only passed this legend on to me when I had come of age; such an age when I understood things better. You may have heard scraps of it elsewhere or even from your mother. Women are not very good at keeping secrets from their children. It is a story that has the potential to erode your self-confidence or even provoke unnecessary aggression in you; hence, I forbade her from discussing it at home."

I do as my father says and reach for a pen and an exercise

book, worried by the somberness in his voice. I am sitting on a back chair, hunched over a small table. I am writing from the light of the oil lamp, in the singlet and boxers I sleep in. My father speaks in a low, clear voice. He is bare around his skinny upper half, his left palm cupping snuff, which he lifts into his nose with his right forefinger in measured quantities. He refills from a box kept handy. He fills the pauses in his clear, deliberate, and often-repeated sentences with snorts and sneezes. Once in a while a cock's crow tears through the silence of a fast-approaching dawn, which is how long his story lasts, the tale of how our community is named after one of the few men who was left after it fell to the slaving and intercommunal warring activities of stronger enemy neighbours. The territory had remained a slave route even after the end of the transatlantic slave trade, with internal slave raiders terrorizing the community. Captives were sold at the internal market, and many were forced into exile as the community broke up and scattered. The few survivors, who had set about rebuilding the village, went in search of protection and returned with a powerful protective medicine, Ezenwanyi, to safeguard them from total annihilation.

"That is the story of your ancestry," he says at the end of the story of Onoyima, who renamed himself Gbaghalu, and his wife, Obochi. "Now you know why people have called you names. You know now who you are. You know why I was not crowned the village head, because it is forbidden for a man like me, an outcast and a foreigner in the land of Ishiayanashi, to touch the arua staff with my taboo hands." He pauses. "And perhaps you should also know that your aunt Okike did not just drown: she committed suicide."

I shoot my father a wide, puzzled look, shocked by this disclosure.

"She committed suicide because Inyinya, the village choir-master, got her pregnant and rejected her. Inyinya and Okike were lovers. They had been secret lovers for some time. Inyinya would sneak to this house and spend long hours chatting with us, eating with us, and laughing furtively with us. He was liked by everyone in the family. He was a likable young man, famous in the village. He was doing well as a schoolteacher, the toast of every maiden in the village. Our family had been waiting for the day he would fulfill the promise he had made to Okike to take her as a wife. But then Okike became preg-nant by him, and a date was fixed for the wedding. Everything had to be rushed before the church found out about Okike's pregnancy; that way, Inyinya would not lose his position as choirmaster for committing the sin of fornication. But on the eve of the wedding, Inyinya sent word to the family saying he had backed out of their marriage plan."

I absorb the shock. "Why?" I can hardly hear my own voice.

"That maggot." My father spits a curse at Inyinya. "He was not man enough to take up his responsibility. He thinks us dirty, but he is filth itself, o ruruunyi."

I feel myself drowning with my father's revelation, the knowledge that Okike killed herself, and that the man for whom she died, Inyinya, still lives. I think of him walking to church with his hymn book tucked under his arm, a sweet song always taking a slow, melodious flight from his soft and treacherous mouth. He is married to a woman who has borne him children. I can feel my anger collecting at the far corners of my mouth like soapsuds.

"I was born into this caste just like you," my father says. "I watched my father talk in whispers and walk in sidles. I watched bullies snatch our pot of dinner from the fire while my father stood by and watched, while my mother wept and watched us go to bed hungry, and I hated my father for his weakness. I have observed you watch me with the same eyes that ask questions. I see hatred in your eyes for me. You think I am weak, and that I should have fought to reclaim what's my right. Like you, I determined to succeed where my father had failed. I determined to be strong where he was weak. I took on the most dangerous wrestlers in the land, the most dreaded of all, that people avoided for their ruthlessness, their talent for dislocating the opponent's waist. I did all that to prove a point, that I am not a weakling like my father, and to ensure that our village had pride of place in the community. The competition gave me my first hip injury. I did not get it from moulding bricks."

This comes as a surprise, too.

"My exploits as wrestler and masker made me popular in the village. I gained the confidence of the elders, commanded the admiration of young men, and became a great favourite of maidens who respected my talents, my stature, and my smile. At least I thought so." He laughs mischievously. "Nkwo was a pretty maiden I admired in the community. I fell in love with her for a sneer that never left her face, a sneer that would linger a little around her mouth, and then it moved up into her eyes. Somehow the sneer gave her the kind of no-nonsense look I liked in my woman. Because I was not a very confident person, I needed a woman who could balance that impairment."

I ponder the absurdity of my father's choice, wondering if my mother has such a quality.

"Nkwo was very beautiful: dark, shapely, and strong-looking. So, when my mother, your grandmother, started to talk about marriage, when she became obsessed with it, I told her about Nkwo. But my mother objected to my choice of a wife. She was not able to offer me a satisfactory reason why I should not marry her. So I insisted, but Nkwo's father turned me down. He humiliated me, telling me I was the descendant of a man who was cast away as punishment for a crime he committed, therefore not meant to enjoy full status as a member of the human race. That was the first time I became acutely aware of our caste."

He pauses to stretch himself, yawning and reknotting the wrappa tied around his thin waist.

"Today I have a son like you who is getting education," he says proudly. "I am pleased with myself, and with everyone. I am pleased with my compound—this mud-brick, crumbling four-roomed house and its rusty tin roof. I am pleased with the entire village, its red, fertile soil and tall trees with bright green foliage; its colourful, high-flying birds and stainless blue skies. I am pleased with everything in spite of the injustices done to me despite my contributions. However, I have one regret: that my family is divided in their faith. Have we not seen enough signs to make us realize that our rebellion against Ezenwanyi is why we are having some of these challenges?"

My father leans out the window to blow his nose, sullying the early morning air with the smell of tobacco. And then he talks about his sisters, who wandered off after a series of marital frustrations.

"They never returned, but it is possible they are alive and married with families wherever they are, and do not wish to come home in order to protect the secret of their caste from their spouses. It is also possible that they are dead. You are aware that Ogbom, your aunt, is separated, but you may not know that she made the mistake of loving a man from the other side. Her marriage was predestined to fail; it was against the wish of his family. She returned childless, forced to flee from the man by untold pressure from his family, even before he completed her marriage rites." My father clears the remains of his snuff with a few quick sniffs to his left palm. He rises and spits through the window. "I hope that you find your path in life, and, in doing so, also find your faith. It's my ultimate wish that we rediscover our faith as a family, and as a community."

I walk outside to stretch myself at the end of it all. It feels like a dead weight has been lifted. The village is clothed in silver. I sit on the tomb and gaze up at the bright and endless savannah of the sky. There are hills in the round yellow face of the moon. I can see their rugged outlines as clearly as I can see why my cousin Beatrice is an agaracha in Lagos. As clearly as I know that I was the fear that lurked somewhere in the heart of a woman, the undesirable seed that was sowed a long time ago at a shrine. And as clearly as I know why my father is a poor sharecropper. We are Ezenwanyi's outcasts. We are ohu ma. A cursed, minority caste. My aunt Okike tried to transcend her fate and paid the ultimate price.

The day finally unfurls itself, patches of shadows melting away, unveiling my mother's poultry clucking outside. Ihebube, a broom in hand, still half-drunk with sleep, is grudgingly sweeping the compound. Ebube is feeding the goats in their pen, two young nanny goats sent to my father by his son-in-law to nurture a new livestock. Usonwa is kindling a fire that sends smoke curling over the kitchen. My mother is standing at the mouth of the kitchen. She is shooing a troublesome rooster away from a cluster of chickens feeding on a handful of grains she has thrown out. The bully beaks a grey-feathered hen into a squawking flight.

How many more bullies are lurking out there? I compare my father's story—the story of my ancestry—with the story of the woman we buried in Anukwu, and I see their sameness. Mama Obodo had told me that Elizabeth-Marie founded Jehovah Kingdom Mission with Aaron, her husband, in 1981. "They died childless, as outcasts, and that's why you were hired to bury the woman. Only foreigners could bury her without repercussions."

When I asked Mama Obodo what would happen to their children, assuming they had any, she explained that they would inherit the status of outcasts, unless they agreed to perform rituals to cleanse themselves.

From what I later learned from my mother, it was not entirely Inyinya's wish to reject Okike, but he was up against unfamiliar forces, something my father had warned Okike about. According to him, neither Inyinya nor anyone in his family had offered an explanation when he suddenly backed out of the marriage. Just as no one had offered any explanation when my father was not made village head. The success of the act had been in the unspoken word. It drew its strength from the conspiracy of silence, and from superstition. You can't hold a man who prefers to remain closemouthed responsible for what he hasn't said. On our path, no one had dared to ask questions. The message was cryptically passed, and clearly understood in the same mood.

One thing had been palpable. In the midst of the hocus-pocus—my father's deep grunting, my mother's silent toiling, and the intense hate people who have no reason to dislike me visited on me—was a secret in the form of a family legend. It was hidden from me and my siblings for as long as our parents could conveniently manage it. But when your father is denied his right to the village patrimony, and your aunt impregnated and rejected by a man who beguiles her with the promise of marriage, you don't really need a family legend to put things in their proper perspective. I picture Inyinya conducting the choir, good-looking and multitalented, writer of beautiful hymns, arms moving with fluidity, carrying the choir gracefully on broad shoulders, and enjoying the admiration of a thrilled congregation. And I despise him with a skin-crawling loathing.

Forty-three

I TAKE A LONG AIMLESS WALK THROUGH THE EDAGA Hills to give my mind time to digest my father's story. My father tells me Ezenwanyi is also a goddess of fertility, for both humans and crops, and that's why the parishioners sneak to her shrine when their wombs won't hold a fetus or their hoes are denied rewards from the soil. He says that long before I was born, the missionaries had made attempts to destroy Ezenwanyi. They would set the shrine ablaze and watch it burn down to ashes. But what they did not know was that they only burnt her relics and idols, and not the soul of Ezenwanyi, which left the shrine even before they finished hatching their evil plot, slithering away as a snake and returning to inhabit the shrine soon after.

Chinua Achebe's *Anthills of the Savannah* preoccupies my mind as I walk the half loop of a savannah that I believe inspired the book's title, and then the novel recedes with a long vista of valleys and enfolding hills. I circle back to my father's stories of human tabooing, then to Biafra and the muffled voice of history.

The atmosphere is charged, crowded bars and restaurants dropping hints of wild celebration as I wander onto University Road. I can't seem to remember any occasion that calls for such jubilations. It is not yet Independence Day, and Christmas is gone. I approach a young man with knock-knees.

"We are celebrating Biafra!" he shrieks. "Nnamdi Kanu is

bringing Biafra home from abroad. To hell with MASSOB. To hell with the Biafra Zionist Movement. To hell with Nigeria. To hell with them all. It is IPOB and Biafra all the way, and this time success is not negotiable."

I ponder this. There have been hints of a powerful new group, the Indigenous People of Biafra, masterminded by a man said to be very young, wealthy, educated, connected, courageous, and powerful. I never gave them much thought. I became discouraged after Ikuku duped us. But now the news that this new group is becoming a reality excites me. I join the celebrations when I realize that I do not have to bother about paying for the drinks.

"They have already been paid for in cartons and are available to anyone who wishes to join in," Knock-Knees says.

We sing and dance to tuneless rhythms beaten with bottles. The drink enters our heads and drives us into the streets. More groups emerge. They come from east, west, north, and south. The crowds that come from the east and the south through Orba Road and Enugu Road merge at Ugwuoye and march towards the market in a great show of solidarity. Those coming from the north and the west through Techtonics Road and University Road meet at Odenigbo Roundabout. Both groups begin to push up towards Ogige market, stamping and chanting "Enyi mba enyi." There is chaos at Ogige market as the groups merge, the air thickening with their chanting, flags waving fervently: tricolours of red, black, and green charged with rising suns over golden bars.

"The red symbolizes the blood of our eastern brothers massacred in northern Nigeria and those who died during the war. Black is to mourn them, and to remember," Ikuku had explained previously to me.

We break into the market and begin to loot from stalls whose owners have not joined in the jubilation, as punishment for their refusal. There is scrambling as the stalls hastily shut down. Women and children are watching from their house-fronts and balconies. They are cheering the rioters, pushing the air with their fists and chanting the mantra in solidarity.

Suddenly sirens fill the afternoon air as the police arrive in a Hilux truck and fire warning shots into the air. They throw tear gas at the crowds to deplete them. We begin to haul stones at them. One of the police officers is caught on the nose. The sight of his own blood enrages the cop, who replies with a bullet that whizzes past my ear. A boy with a wide fore-head and a small obstinate mouth hauls a Molotov cocktail towards the police Hilux standing in front of the long NITEL Building. It lands next to the Hilux and rolls underneath the vehicle. A moment later, a deafening explosion occurs and a blanket of flame leaps into the sky. Maddened by the sight of the Hilux being consumed by great flames, the cops turn their guns on the crowd. They begin shooting randomly. The boy with a wide forehead leaps into the air like a paper towel, then crumbles back into the gutter, a bullet hitting and splitting his forehead and messing the tarmac with his brains. I take off as the women watching from their housefronts and balconies scream and retreat into their rooms, but a searing pain stops me dead in my tracks, and, tottering, I crumble into a gutter.

The pain I experience at the hands of a local bonesetter hours later is better imagined. I am pinned down by several hands, every searing touch bringing urine to the tip of my penis as the fractured shinbone is reset. The pain is more than flesh and blood can bear. Afterwards, I lie in the gloomy little room that I will share with two other patients in the coming months.

"Okukontike." My mother's tears rain down and soak her clothes for my headiness.

My father's thoughts I see in his eyes, written in grey lettering. "I warned you. Those who make themselves causalities should realize that Biafra can be achieved not through violent protest, but through dialogue and voting."

"You should consider yourself lucky that you only fractured your leg." Usonwa's voice is consoling. "I heard many people died."

The skull-splitting pain finally gives way to a dull ache punctuated by needles of it that remain there except when I am asleep. It is worsened by bedsores from weeks of lying in one position, the shame and agony of being lifted onto a bowl to stool, and the revulsion of watching the other patients do the same. But more than the pain of falling into the gutter and fracturing my leg is the anguish of not going to the university anytime soon.

Usonwa and Machebe take turns to look after me. Machebe's scolding crinkles in his eyes. The situation is far too serious for him to voice out his grouse, although he manages to give it expression in sideswipes: "I should be in the workshop learning new things, not here caring for you."

I try to read and even write when the pain allows me. One of the books I read is a novel by the famous black American author Zora Neale Hurston, *Their Eyes Were Watching God*. I like the way the book is written. The liquid flow of language. Could I ever write in that powerful way? I wonder as I resolve to write scraps of stories about our ancestry, and about my father's life. Although I have it all figured out in my head, after writing it down I get the sense of a scene where poultry scrounges for food with intense competition. My language is trash compared to Zora Neale Hurston's rhythmic Black American English. I figure I will never be able to write with a rhythm and flow like hers.

Forty-four

THE WORLD IS WHITE AND EMPTY WHEN I TAKE MY first few steps outside the bonesetter's sore little region. I walk with the help of crutches, my injured right leg heavy as a log, but I am happy to momentarily escape the acute smell of pain and Dettol. The matron steadily sprinkles Dettol disinfectant to kill whatever bacteria or germs are waiting in the shadows to infect wounds. The Dettol also drives away the odour of sores. I take more walks without Usonwa shuffling behind ready to offer her arms. Finally, I am happy to drop the crutches, even if I think the ground unsteady and ready to give way if I march too hard.

The first place I visit as soon as I have the full use of my legs again is the cybercafé at Ogige market, to apply to work there. I am not sure how much money I can make as a cybercafé assistant, but I'd be happy to bring smiles to the faces of people who come to check their results. I will try to save and repay my sister Oyimaja and Nnamdi Adaka. Besides, it sounds impressive to introduce myself as a cybercafé assistant, and Machebe might even treat me with a little respect.

I am also thinking of sitting the Joint Admissions and Matriculation Board exam, to try to get into the university to study sociology and anthropology. I began to read even more during my convalescence at the bonesetting clinic: novels, old newspapers the patients used as toilet paper, anything I could lay my hands on. I learned that looking at some people as having less worth is a social construct. I want to access more scholarly views on social segregation to try to overcome my complexes. Perhaps I can even carve out some recognition for myself despite my history and caste.

One day, I take a stroll towards the open country to clear my head. It has been a period of erratic weather, now windy, now sweltering, the trees nutty brown. My father was probably right when he said that our rebellion against Ezenwanyi was part of the problem. I find myself drawn to Ezenwanyi's shrine and its curiosities more and more. The attama is sitting in the thatch hut as usual, his face, in deep shadow, turned away from me when I walk in.

"Attama." I bow my greetings and walk in to sit on a bench as the old man indicates with a wave of his staff, the same bench I had sat on with my father to have my ancestral benefactress unveiled.

"A woman came to the shrine to dedicate her baby to Ezenwanyi," the attama begins to say in his usual chatty way, being a very conversational person. "The woman had come to terms with her infertility, and in order to protect the baby bequeathed her by her co-wife in a world full of evil, she decided to dedicate the child to Ezenwanyi." He pauses and shakes his head. "Whoever heard of such magnanimity from a co-wife? The child was a girl. She grew into a beautiful woman and got a suitor. Her suitor did not know that she had been dedicated to Ezenwanyi as a baby when he married her. The couple had a baby boy, but not another child came. When the man's father consulted a dibia to know what had sealed the young woman's womb, he came to the truth about his daughter-in-law's background. Having been dedicated to Ezenwanyi as a baby, the young woman had become Ezenwanyi's bride and possession. It would have cost the husband nothing more than to take her bride price to this shrine and perform a few rituals to put things right and reclaim his bride. But he wanted to be more Christian than the white man who introduced him to that religion. He would not budge even after realizing that the jealous goddess had taken away from them the power of procreation as a couple. And then the woman died. He had her buried at the churchyard. He had a second chance to put things straight when her remains were accidentally exhumed with her head untouched by white ants some years after her burial. He was supposed to rebury her exhumed remains at Ezenwanyi's grove, but instead he reburied her in a tomb that stands at the entrance to his house. The wrath of the goddess then fell on their only child and struck him down in his prime. What the man has failed to see is that he will be the next victim unless he comes around to perform the atonement rites. The deaths will not stop until his lineage is closed. That's how jealous and fiercely possessive Ezenwanyi can be." He pauses again. "These godheads are terrible and unpredictable beings, and people should avoid getting in their way."

I do not realize why the story of the infertile woman and the baby that became Ezenwanyi's "dedicate" strikes a note of familiarity until I am in bed and pondering my long dialogue with the attama. Although he had not mentioned names, I realize the young woman in the story must be Ehamehule's mother. I also learn that the arua staff is rooted in superstition and the few skeptics among the village elite live in dread of the infliction supposedly visited upon anyone who goes against the order of things. The deaths of my aunt Okike and Ehamehule's mother are two symbolically significant events with the potential to change the course of history. My mother's tears were, more than for Ehamehule's tragic end, for the memory of his mother, who, like my aunt Okike, was caught in the crosshairs.

"Good book you've got for yourself there."

When I look up from the book I am buried in at the cybercafé, where I now work, I see that the young man speaking is about my age. He has a husky voice, a finely boned face, and wears a new haircut that starts halfway up the sides and back. The haircut is more fitting than I have seen on anyone else wearing it. He's a National Youth Service Corps member; I can see that from his crested vest, khaki pants, and jungle boots.

"I am Chikelue." He extends a nut-coloured hand. His fingers are long slender pencils with strong pink nails.

"I am Dimkpa." The hand is warm when I stand up and take it in my own palm. He is a head taller as we settle into seats.

The book I am reading is a novel by Toni Morrison. It's about Margaret Garner, a runaway slave who killed her own daughter to prevent her capture and enslavement. We talk about the book, loudly because we are the only two in the cybercafé. He has read the book twice, and wouldn't mind reading it a third time. Reflecting on the story and my ancestry, I think if Obochi had had half Margaret Garner's courage, she would have done the same thing to her child. The intensity of her hate paraphrases the strength of the love he draws from her.

I like Chikelue, for the huskiness of his voice, and the well-formed words that spill from his rounded mouth and pert lips. He is at the cybercafé because he is having trouble with his scanner, which my colleague helps to fix. But he continues to come to the cybercafé to see me afterwards. We exchange novels and talk energetically about them. Eventually, I learn that his mother is from Ohodo, a town not too far from mine, and his father is from Imo state, and they both live in Lagos with his only sister. As a National Youth Service Corps member, he has a primary assignment at the University Secondary School, where he teaches economics. For the first time since Eke's death, I feel I have made a friend.

Forty-five

HOW SMALL JOY IS. I HAVE WAITED FOR THIS MOMENT, promising myself that the whole village will know if I pass JAMB, even if it means climbing to the top of Ugwu Asho Mountian and screaming it to the world. But everything I have planned—the wild celebration, the drinking spree, the ironed shirt, the chest-puffed-out-and-head-held-high stride—has faded into the smallness of pure joy.

It still surprises me how calmly I am taking my success. I score 230 marks in my JAMB and am offered admission by the University of Nigeria to study sociology and anthropology. It is as if my family has at last won a prize after many years of losses. My mother sings praises insisting that the God-of-Selected has done it for her, saying it in such a way that I wonder if the God-of-Selected is the same God all the other Christians worship at different churches. My father stirs like a wet fowl driven to the far corner of the wall with cold, but rising and shaking its feathers to the first stirrings of warmth from the fire tripod. He offers a libation to the gods in the secrecy of his room.

"But how will the family raise the money to train you in the university?" Machebe broaches the subject everyone seems to have been avoiding.

"I have saved some money, and I intend to keep my job as a cybercafé assistant on a part-time basis," I explain.

He nods.

•

The days following are busy, and I spend them shuttling between home and the university to pay my acceptance fee and familiarize myself with the campus. I have been there only once or twice since we used to trek out to fetch water and wash students' laundry as children. It radiates an aura of learning that intimidates me.

I go for a haircut at Aaron's barbering salon, which is veiled by a thin muslin curtain, before my departure to school. Aaron is the only barber in the village, which is probably why he doesn't care that his salon is dirty and dusty. A cracked mirror is screwed to the uneven plank wall. I have to sit on a rusty-backed chair and stare at a woolly pile of hair flaking with dandruff in a corner of the salon, hair begging to be disposed of, as Aaron works on me with gloved hands.

"We heard you are going to the university," he says.

He is a shabby man with narrow features, in an apron over a faded shirt. He has long black fingers he covers with dirty gloves. As he works, he nods his egg-shaped head to the scratchy tune playing from squat old speakers, music that seems to be quarreling with his screaming power generator.

"I am going to study sociology and anthropology."

"What's that?"

"I will be learning about culture and social structures."

He shrugs. "I will give you a smart haircut. Don't bother about the pay. It is my own little way of supporting you. You are going to be our first university graduate."

I thank him and shut my eyes to the caresses of his long gloved fingers, and as he rubs spirit into my scalp after cutting my hair, the evanescent spirit with an intensely cooling effect that tickles, reaching deep in my soul to soothe my troubled past and explore happier beginnings.

"Mind your book. Don't join cult boys" is his parting gift as I walk away from his salon.

On the day I finally leave for school, my mother bathes the parting with tears. "Be a good boy. Don't go there and join cult boys," she says in the same tone as the barber. "Remember where you are coming from. Mind your books. If you run out of food, come home; at least we will have something for you to eat."

My father's wrinkled face is blank. He seems to have done what is required of him—handing my future over to Ezenwanyi—and now he has no words to waste.

"Be careful." Machebe's hug feels obligatory. In his eyes I see a wavering light, a mix of envy and doubt, as I set off with my bag.

The green-and-ash gates, bearing the words UNIVERSITY OF NIGERIA, NSUKKA, usher me in. The campus is serene, shadowed by overhanging branches of tall trees standing in regiments, the roads stained with their purple-blue-yellow blossoms. Students weave forth and back, shimmering like thick populations of winged termites. Some sit in quiet corners with heads buried in books in their laps; others lounge under shadows in couples, glued together like swans, hands and tongues exploring every crevice. Water fountains spurt into the skies as though determined to cleanse the air of moral pollution.

The early days are full of the young and enthusiastic faces of the first-years, like mine, with eagerness in their strides. But rushing to classes in the hot sun and being crushed wall-to-wall during long lectures will wither their confidence, half deflating it like a balloon. Now I can look back and see the reason for Nwodo's outbursts. Life is not easy with students packed like sardines in hostel rooms, high tuition fees to pay, and costly books to buy.

Even now that I am finally poised to become the first university graduate from my village, I continue to feel held back. Sometimes I have nothing to eat for days on end. I still see Chikelue, who occasionally helps me with money, but this all stops when his National Youth Service ends and the time comes for him to return to his family in Lagos. I wish he'd extend his stay. He writes long and generous responses to the pieces of writing I share with him, making me feel less small, and making my future feel bright.

Forty-six

I WISH I HADN'T SPOKEN ABOUT EZENWANYI'S CAVE IN such glowing terms. I don't know about its healing powers any more than I know a fairy tale, even though my father has told me about them many times. But I feel indebted to Chikelue, and hope that he will be healed of his epilepsy in my village, where we are now headed together.

"I have had it since childhood," he confessed to me after we became fast friends. "I have been everywhere from medical doctors to palmists to prophets to herbalists in search of a cure."

Chikelue's story is heartbreaking. Sitting next to him as he drives, I steal glances at him, wondering about this monster that comes into him and leaves him hollow after it departs. After we parted ways at the end of his National Youth Service—Chikelue returning to Lagos while I continued my studies and writing—our correspondence became less frequent, and eventually I lost his contact information. I didn't hear from him until he called me five years later. By then I had finished at school, and his husky voice on the phone scraped my ears of the ants running around in my head. My father had invited this colony of ants when he said, "If you are not a failure, why can't you find work after leaving the university instead of sitting here roasting your buttocks in the ash heap writing trash?"

"Leave this boy be and stop pecking at him like he is bird-seed," my mother scolded him.

"Boy." My father sniggered. "Do you still call him a boy?"

Machebe sided with my father. "The rest of us couldn't go to school because you people wasted the family savings and even sold our only land to send him."

My heart would sink each time I heard their lamentations. Machebe had rounded off his mechanic apprenticeship. Usonwa had learned hair braiding at Ogige market. Ihebube and Ebube were finishing at primary school. If I had a job, I could support them all the way to the university. With nothing to do, life in the village became more boring than ever. I had no one to visit, with Eke long dead and the boys I grew up with all gone in pursuit of careers, leaving snuff-nosed old men and women in the village behind. It was so boring, I felt like running away. I'd sit on the tomb all day lost in day-dreams. I realized how much I missed Grace, remembering how we sat together on Okike's tomb during an evening of orange sunset, an evening when nature was profound with its paintbrush. I wondered about her family, her wealthy husband and round babies. Good for her. She wouldn't have gone any-where with a man like me.

What my father had called "writing trash" was my attempt to write our history. I had been working on the plot outline for the book when Chikelue and I parted ways. He had been very encouraging, even reading some pages and praising them at length. I had resumed work on the book to fill up the empty days after my Youth Service Scheme, determining to leave the village even if it meant sleeping under a bridge like the touts in Lagos. And then the phone rang and Chikelue's deep voice was saying, "My father wants his biography written. I recommended you." I had given up the hope of ever hearing from Chikelue again. My breath quickened with the expectation of seeing him after such a long time, and the thrilling knowledge that he'd not have recommended me to his father if he didn't consider my writing good enough.

Forty-seven

WE ARRIVE AT OGIGE MARKET, MY MIND FLYING BACK
to the horrors of the little cell in the mango grove. Chikelue
says the town has changed. It still looks the same to me,
though. It's been just five months since I left home to work on
Chikelue's father's book. The carcass of the burnt police Hilux
still lies in front of NITEL Building. The insignia of Biafra.
The ground is still crimson with the blood of those the police
murdered on the night I escaped with a broken leg. But the
fearless leader of the Biafran separatist group, the Indigenous
People of Biafra, the young and revolutionary Nnamdi Kanu,
has vowed that the government must pay for the spilled blood,
and freedom for the land of Biafra is not negotiable, in a statement that reads as follows:

> As they campaign vigorously for elections, you would think
> they are coming to grow the economy, enthrone justice, breed
> unity and tolerance, love for one another. No, they are com-
> ing to enthrone Hausa/Fulani supremacy, to reposition the
> security agencies by sacking all competent hands and replac-
> ing them with their kinsmen in order to drive their eth-
> nic domination of the south. The Fulani herdsmen will be
> armed and encouraged to slaughter us with impunity, and
> their masters will protect them. They are coming to ensure
> that my people are enslaved forever. Those who do not be-
> lieve me will soon see it happen before their eyes. The Fulani

will take over the entire south as a continuation of their age-long agenda to Islamize Eastern Nigeria. They will brazenly seize our land in pretense of creating grazing fields for the Fulani. Then the conquest will be complete, we will become their serfs forever.

"I broke my leg in that gutter," I say, pointing out the spot where it happened. "I was full of enthusiasm then, but now I am tired of their rhetoric."

"I do not think Biafra is mere rhetoric," Chikelue says. "I recognize a fair amount of truth in what the IPOB leader says. Biafra reserves the 'Remedial Right to Secede' in theory and in principle."

"It will not be achieved easily, assuming secession to be possible in principle." The intensity of my feelings roughens my voice. I think back to my National Youth Service in the north after my graduation from university. The experience helped me to understand our country better. The trouble with Nigeria was and always has been that of complex. You see it in every detail of your day-to-day interactions, from colleagues in the same orientation camp to the sugarcane vendor or shoeshine mallam on the street, those dangerous feelings of complex and insecurity, which triggered the pogrom that created the civil war.

"Besides," I say to Chikelue, "we have traitors amongst ourselves, greedy people and cheats who betray the ideals of this struggle."

Chikelue drives in silence as we both recede into our thoughts.

•

A scowl darkens Chikelue's face as we turn onto a dirt road riddled with potholes, the road to my village. I feel guilty each time the underbelly of Babydoll scrapes the hard surface of the village road as Chikelue negotiates a pothole. He says it feels like it is his heart, and not the car underbelly, that is being scraped.

I understand.

The car is barely two weeks old, a birthday gift from his father, George Emerenini. It is a sleek, black, sexy convertible Chikelue nicknamed Babydoll. The road is wet and muddy—it rained recently—and the tyres are rolling with a splosh that angers Chikelue and keeps the scowl on his face. Even when some naked children playing in a village square abandon their play and flee at the sight of the car, skittering away like little black beetles, it doesn't amuse him.

I remember Ogbareka and the hot chase he gave me for stealing his pods as we drive past his compound, how we went tumbling over farm ridges, getting snagged on brambles and nettles.

"Was he really going to cut you with the machete?"

"He looked mad enough to kill me."

Driving through village squares hemmed in by squat cement and mud houses, we finally arrive in our compound. We climb down, Chikelue walking around the car and inspecting his fenders and wheels streaked with mud. My eyes travel to the tomb, next to our old mud house, looking abandoned and unhappy. Devoured by woodlice, the windows are gaping at us with hollow, disquieting eyes. A door half wrenched from its hinges is left in its near wreckage like a big rotten tooth. The outer wall is barely hanging, looking like it will fall any moment. I can see the hump of the tomb beneath the avocado tree. The tree is losing its leaves, like an old man losing his hair, shedding on the grave over a long time. The grave is in ruins, covered in mud and grime: the debris of broken slabs.

My father is sitting in the shade of our umbrella tree, and my siblings, Ihebube and Ebube, are playing okoso a few yards away from where he sits. They are watching us with undisguised curiosity as we approach. I know they don't recognize me. The starched indigo brocade I am wearing fans out around me like a peacock's beautiful tail feathers.

Chikelue is frowning beyond them to the rusty roof and stark mud-red walls of our house in whose many cracks and gullies lizards and geckos have made their home.

I understand.

I have been in his family's mansion in Victoria Garden City. It looms white, like a snow-capped mountain, at the end of a long driveway edged with tall palms. I glimpse my mother peeping at us from the side wall leading to the kitchen behind the house under the rust-zinc eaves with a faintly suspicious expression. The sound of the car must have drawn her away from her chore, the same way the noise must have roused Usonwa from her weekend siesta.

Ihebube and Ebube, in their early teens, have grown taller. They race into my arms smelling of sweat and grime. My father draws himself up to his full height with a slight stoop. He is tying a dirty wrappa around his thin waist. It is loosely knotted at the groin, such that his pubic hair peeks out. His eyes are puffy, and the sag in his flesh tells me he has been drinking more and more ekpetechi, and he is fast ageing. He has gone completely grey. He comes forward gingerly with his shriveled arms splayed.

"Big motor car, that is. Whose is it?" he whispers, expectation tickling the hairs in his nostrils.

"It belongs to my friend."

My father withdraws, folding up like one of those millipedes that crawl around, when it is touched with a stick. Obviously he had mistaken the car for mine.

Usonwa flies into my arms. My mother hugs me tight to her bare shrunken breasts and chore grease. I stare at my mother's leathery neck and hair overcrowded with grey. I did not expect this hero's welcome. The parting had not been too warm when I left home. Usonwa is a woman now, having completed her apprenticeship, and runs her own braiding shop at Ogige market. Gone is the sharp, defiant look. She is wearing a skewed dress with yellow sunflower blooms embroidered on a faded black background. The dress, which she had worn before I left the village, hugs her tightly, outlining the graceful lines of her new curves. Her hair is braided, her beauty full and spilling. A short wrappa is tied around her slim waist as she walks around the compound swaying her hips, her braids swinging behind her like the tail of a horse. My father says that she inherited her height from him, and her lucent dark skin from my grandmother, my father's mother. Looking at her, I can't help but think of the swamp lantern that grows around the creek, attractive to the eyes with bright yellow blooms, but unpleasant to the nose, untouchable.

"Your dress is big and beautiful," Ihebube whispers to me.

"I like your friend's motorcar." Ebube giggles.

Chikelue is watching the drama of our reunion with discomfort. I ponder my family in contrast to his. I am my parents' first son, their third child. Chikelue is the baby of his family. He holds a bachelor of science degree in economics and a master's degree in computer science. He has a sister, and he is heir to an inheritance running into hundreds of millions. My father looks frail and old, whereas his father is a large, hairy man who reminds me of a wooly bear, a man so large he must look like a fallen tree trunk when he is sleeping. He is bald while my father has a knot of hair like a white skullcap. His mother is a small, pretty woman who wears a huge wig and lays a neat, jewel-laden little hand on the shoulder of his son's friends when they visit the mansion. My mother is scrawny and greyed, and her hair flakes with dandruff. His mother uses nail polish and a pink blusher. Sometimes there are black clots of mascara on her eyelashes when she is fatigued. Her perfume combs the hallway, her voice having the same effect in my ears as the languid piano music always tinkling from the mansion's hallway speaker, but my mother's cologne is a pungent cassava effluvium. The odour is stronger around the kitchen, where the fermented sieved cassava, wrung of water, lies thick in a bowl.

Machebe is not home.

"He is still at the Mechanic Village," explains my mother. "Take your friend into the house for lunch.

I lead Chikelue into the cold, bare-walled room with crooked forms and an old wooden table. The earth floor smells of termites, and of fungus growing in wet, hidden corners. Chikelue looks around the room and swallows his spit politely. I completely understand. The mansion has a retinue of household staff keeping it clean and sweet, a large sitting room with big leather seats, and potted flowers in vibrant colours.

My mother pokes her head in and says, "I have a message for you."

I know she wants a private moment with me. It is only a polite way of calling me aside for one of her endless whisperings. I had caught her eye earlier and seen the clouds gathering in her face, like a sky heavy with rain. My mother lives in the fear that one of us children will get himself into trouble one day and the police will come looking for him with their Hilux trucks and guns.

She pulls me to a corner. "Who is he?"

My family knows about a certain friend of mine who has been helping me, but they have never met Chikelue until now. I tell my mother the truth: I am not as big as my garment. I have a job writing a biography, and Chikelue is my oga's son, and a close friend.

The clouds fritter away and the sun breaks through in my mother's face. She moves about as if some tight knots have been loosened, calling out to my siblings to come help her make food for us in the kitchen. My mother makes aribo with empty ohoyi soup. She serves it in the metal plates she uses to serve food to our important guests. It is served on the table that is dark and glossy with accumulated dirt. Chikelue declines to eat the heavy black paste plucked and dunked into plain, watery soup that stretches from the plate to the mouth. Again I understand. This food is muck compared to the mansion's continental dishes, like the eggs Benedict with creamy hollandaise sauce served in breakable plates, which we had for supper the previous night.

"Shall we go and see the cave?" I note the eagerness in Chikelue's voice.

"I have barely swallowed my last morsel."

"I know." His voice is edged with impatience. "But I want us to check into a hotel in town after we have been to see the cave. We will head back to Lagos in the morning."

We had agreed to pass the night here in my family house, but Chikelue seems to have changed his mind.

This, too, I understand.

Forty-eight

I FOLLOW CHIKELUE'S EYES TO IHEBUBE AND EBUBE. They are walking round the car and smiling at their reflections in its glittering body as we step outside to go to Ezenwanyi's cave.

"You may look at the motorcar, but do not touch it," I say to them, surprised that at their age they still slobber over a motorcar.

My father is still sitting under the tree. "Should not a poor old man like me have a little something for a sip?" he says to Chikelue, his eyes milky with expectation.

I feel a rush of blood to my face.

"Sure, Papa, but why not?" Chikelue counts off some crisp notes from a bundle and hands the money over to my father.

"Agunnia. Akunwata. Akunatakashi." My father grabs the money with both hands and calls Chikelue the praise names people call any young man with money to throw around.

In extended appreciation of the money my father breaks into egara, eulogizing Chikelue; it is accompanied by a series of wild movements combining nimble foot thrusts with delightful springy jumps and precise hand gestures—a flare of athleticism you would never picture a man of his age executing. I see nostalgia in my father's eyes, a longing for a certain time in history when he embodied the dazzling spirit whose metallic costume of bright buttons catches mirror reflections, a time when he was the masker of Echaricha maa, whose face

317

is defined by horizontal linear radiations of white thread and motions marked by a poetry of body movements, the masquerade with a lofty plume everyone rushes to the village square to watch on the day of Omabe Festival.

"Back then your father was in his prime, strong and graceful. He was the toast of the village women," my mother would say every time she retold the story before she became born again, sparks of memory brightening in her face. Behind that wistful smile a frown at history, time, and habit that eroded his qualities was thinly disguised. I'd remember those evenings that my father would stagger home from his bricklaying work smelling like a jar of ekpetechi, his eyes red and glazed, his trousers wet and muddy, a halting and lisping quality to his voice, and his pockets empty.

My father's masking exploits inspired my thesis at the university. First, I had considered studying the arua mythology, influenced by the conspiracies against my father. I thought it would be interesting using my family as a case study and studying the myth surrounding the arua, the belief that if my father or any member of his caste touched the arua staff, there would be fatal consequences. But then I remembered my father's words, the night he told me about our ancestry: *I have one regret. That my family is divided in their faith.* I decided to write about my father's belief in traditions in contrast to my mother's extreme Pentecostal views and condemnation of Traditional African Religion. "Mushroom churches are sprouting everywhere," I wrote, "but of the mushrooms few are edible."

I notice that Chikelue is in a better mood after watching my father's footwork. He also shares money out to my mother and siblings in generous proportions. I am not sure if my father still makes bricks, and looking at him, a rag of himself whose height—though no longer as erect as it used to be—remains the only vestige of a certain poignant time in history, a time when he used to have bulgy pectorals and the best pair of calves in the village, I think not.

I suddenly remember his sister, my aunt Ogbom, who performed her trademark legwork at Nkwo square on the day of the Onunu festival in honour of the ancestral mother Nkwo, to the cheering of a large crowd. My father had said that Igba Echi unlocked open doors, bringing sound health, wealth, good suitors, and a home full of children. Ogbom's case turned out different for obvious reasons.

I feel an intense longing to see her. I mention this to my friend.

"We will make it snappy." Chikelue is impatient to get to the cave.

On our way out, we pass through my aunt's old hut.

"Is it you, Dimkpa?" Ogbom says.

I embrace her, feeling her scrawniness.

She looks pasty-faced. Age has dug depths in her cheeks. Her shock of hair is a small patch of white on the dark cloud of her head. The burden of time that dug chasms in her cheeks weighs down more heavily around her neck, with its mass of wrinkles and taut veins. Ogbom was never large, but now she is an old, shriveled rag of a woman. Inscriptions that resemble Arabic are tattooed on her shrunken arms. I have always seen her as a sad woman. I think of her failed marriage with a man outside of her—our—caste, and I squeeze her hand.

We talk with her. She asks a few questions, sometimes being drowned in her forgetfulness, her voice a sonorous tremble.

"I saw the fire in your eyes as you left for the city, blazing like red-hot charcoal, and I knew you were ready to pluck success from the land of the spirits. I have been proved right."

"My friend from the city would like to see your footwork and hear your egara," I say to her. Ogbom earns gifts from people for her skill as a griot, a repository of oral tradition.

She laughs toothlessly, and I see a shy old bride. The musty smell of age fills the air.

"Your aunt is old. Can she still lift her ragged, weak legs in legwork?" she says.

Normally, she requires a stimulant, a shot of ekpetechi to put her in the mood, or anything that stirs up poignant memories, especially of the happy early times before her failed marriage. Chikelue sets her off with money, a bunch of clean banknotes. Ogbom is bewildered; instantly, she breaks into a cantillation and slowly works herself into the mood, her voice shaky at first, and her mouth trembling around the words. Bit by bit she gathers the limbs of her voice until it wraps itself around the lyric like a braid. Ascending in variation, her voice then picks up a sonorant quality too amplified for a woman of her age. Now in her element, she thrills us with egara and omaganga, a flowing combination of footwork accompanied by the clear resonance of her voice, one of my best vocals ever. Surprisingly she carries the burden of age lightly, still retaining that gracefulness of carriage, that swing of movement that only a few women of her time and age could perfectly execute in that flowing sequence that catches light. I know that in the night, though, in the loneliness of her world when everyone is asleep, Ogbom will intone slow threnodies in a voice that echoes the depths of her sorrow.

After leaving Ogbom's house, Chikelue and I walk through the narrow, rocky track that links the cave and the village. The village is covered in lush green farmlands with bright cascades of cornsilk. Okra flowers are perching on their plants like yellow butterflies. Sparrow hawks are wheeling high above the valley, wings splayed, bodies given totally to the will of the wind as they explore and savour vast spaces.

"It is a beautiful country."

I am glad Chikelue likes the countryside. Walking along the outer wall, we enter the quiet grove with caution. The cave still lies crusted at the basin of high rock bluffs despite a few rains. We settle on a shelf of rock. I laugh, a guffaw that wakes echoes in the cave, and instantly water begins to trickle from the rocks. I yell out. The cave yells back at me. The water leaps to our amazement. It is not the first time I have come here to sit on steps cut into the rocks by the goddess to yell with the hope that she might spill her water and heal the world. We came here uncountable times when we were children, yelling ourselves out of our minds for nothing. But now the water leaps in excitement, and a huge waterfall drops off the last shelf of rock and thunders down into the bottom of the cave. The more I yell into the cave, the higher the water leaps. Chikelue is watching with wide eyes. He is now on his feet, yelling, too, and, yelling and yipping together, we set off a magnificent cascade and a fine ricochet of echoes, water pouring from all the openings, lashing onto the rocks and thundering to the bottom of the cave.

"Hurrah!" Chikelue is saturated with pleasure.

At last we tear ourselves away from the cave. We climb up the hill to the full panorama of palm trees dotting a rust-coloured village below. We savour the magical moment back in the cave, a moment staggering and euphoric. And then we begin to walk home with the sun setting on us, painting the sky in watercolours and crayons.

"Is the moon rising tonight?" Chikelue says.

"I will ask my mother."

"I will pass the night and watch the moon," he says.

I hide a chuckle.

Forty-nine

THE MONSTER TAKES OWNERSHIP OF CHIKELUE ON our way home in violent jerks and spasms. It knocks him down. He kicks out, throwing wild punches in retaliation. He chews his tongue and lips until blood and saliva dribble down the corner of his mouth. His body is like steel when I try to help him. The monster holds him captive for about ten minutes. And then it frees him as he gulps air into his lungs and succumbs to a quiet stupor.

"I am sorry," I say, overcome with guilt as he regains consciousness.

He answers with a nod, too tired to utter words.

We walk slowly home against the encroaching darkness, taking a different route back, a longer route, because we want to get into the village after dark to hide Chikelue's stained white gabardine shirt and hair covered with dirt. This illness demystifies him, taking away the timber in his voice, and the pride that stands in his eyes and squares his shoulders.

My mother has lit her ochanja when we arrive home. "The moon will not be rising," she says.

Outside, the night sky is set with stars, but the cold is piercingly hostile, and we sit over dinner in the mildewed warmth of the room. The seats are set closely around the table in a square illuminated by the dancing yellow flame of my mother's ochanja. My father shares a seat with my mother. His body is shielded in his thick, dirty awuru, and his face is dark against the mushroom of his hair. My mother's wrappa is thrown around her shoulders to keep the cold at bay. Machebe is sitting next to Usonwa, his broad chest bare. His arms are short, thick, and bunched with veins from lifting car engines. He is eating quietly, stretching his rough and callused workman's hand to pluck food from the large dish on the table. Ihebube and Ebube are protected from the cold in layers of dirty clothing. They are scoffing greedily as if competing with each other. The dinner is unusually rich.

"It is a special meal to celebrate your homecoming." My mother glances at Chikelue with a rueful look.

Chikelue once again refuses her cooking and instead eats the hamburgers he brought from the mansion in a slow and disconsolate way. He has changed from his stained white gabardine into a thick ash turtleneck sweater. It is a long, long night ahead, and he will have to take his bath in our bathroom with its palm-frond walls and a wet floor covered in sickly green moss. He will have to scoop water from an iron bucket with cupped hands and throw it over his body. In his father's mansion, he sits in a tub and indulges himself in a warm, luxurious bath flowing from the hot-water tap. In my father's chicken coop, he will sleep on a naked mattress after the ordeal of the iron bucket, and dream of the duvets and Armani coverlets of the mansion.

"My friend is very sick." I open up to my father about Chikelue's illness and our experience in the cave after my mother and siblings have gone to bed.

"Ndo," he says to Chikelue, his mood suddenly pensive.

My father explains that what we saw in Ezenwanyi's cave might not happen again for another generation to come. According to him, we only needed to splash ourselves in the great waterfall, soaking ourselves in it long enough to benefit from its ritual ablutions. Its deep spiritual nourishments.

"You will take him to the attama in the morning to see if there is something he can do to help him," my father says. "I shall provide you with a cock to offer him."

I stir and open my eyes. Chikelue's form is outlined against the wall in the blue light of his mobile phone. He is sitting up, his knees raised and his arms wrapped around them. He has his back against the wall. A mosquito is caught in the blue light in a slow and heavy flight. Another one drones in my ear and my clap is rewarded with a thick red sludge in my palms. I don't know why Chikelue would want to blame me for his being caught up sleepless in the cold, dark night of my small village. The dinner my mother made was the best she could have offered an important visitor, but Chikelue had preferred to eat hamburgers from the mansion. I sit for a long time trying to figure it out. Chikelue is full of life and yet so sick? But why come to the mythical cave in my village backwoods to seek healing? I think I understand. This is not Chikelue; this form looking small and vulnerable is the dignified hypocrisy of the "new world." But I am much indebted to Chikelue, so deeply I cannot hold his rudeness against him.

We spend the rest of the night sitting up, nodding, and slapping at mosquitoes. I resolve not to rest or close an eye again in sleep until this sickness is chased out of him, this sickness that has defied medical knowledge. We rise at the crow of the first cock and leave for the shrine to see the attama.

"He is the custodian of Ezenwanyi's cave," I explain to Chikelue on our way.

We have with us the cock my father has given us. The village is still silent and full of darkness. At this time of the winter solstice, the nights draw out and it doesn't get light until later in the mornings. We make our way to the shrine, the same clearing in the grove, the same grim thatch shelter curtained with ribbons of appliqué cloth of different colours. We enter without our footwear, as is customary. It is still the same inside the shrine. There is still a half-buried clay pot on the earth floor near a small hollow in the ground, but it is no longer the same attama, the same old man sitting with his face in deep shadow. The old attama has passed on, and a new attama has assumed his position and is already sitting by the light of an oil lamp as if he were expecting us.

"He will take a bath in the water," the new attama says after we have explained the symptoms of Chikelue's illness.

He is a lanky, soft-spoken, somnambulant-eyed seventeen-year-old boy who treats us impassively and touches things distractedly in the shrine. He inherited the priesthood of the deity at the age of sixteen. "That boy has left too much in ruin," my father had said of him.

"That's all?" I ask the boy.

He raises his sleepy eyes to look at me. "He will return to the shrine for a final ritual. He was destined to be favoured. Eziyi was in a benevolent mood. You were at the cave yesterday."

I don't know if it is a statement or a question from the off-hand way he says it, but I reply, "Yes."

"What you saw in the cave, many men have lived and died craving to see."

We wait to hear more, but the priest resigns himself again to silence and that enigmatic habit of touching things around the shrine.

We set off to the cave with him leading the way. He is dressed in khaki shorts and a sober brown shirt. His walk is evocative of a moth's. At the cave he asks that I wait around the mouth while he leads Chikelue in. I sit in the grass to wait. I think of Chikelue's sickness and the attama's erratic ways. The scenery is full of earth-coloured anthills and trees with foliage looking like the thick afro hair of a man. And then I pace about to release the tension cocked into me like beer, ready to spill over if shaken and uncorked.

They spend a long time in the cave. The splashing of water tells me Chikelue is having the bath. The chill of each scoop that falls on him stings my body. At last Chikelue climbs out of the cave fully dressed and we walk back to the shrine where the ada of Ezenwanyi, a wizened old woman, is summoned by the priest for the final ritual. My father had said that before so many women like my mother abandoned Ezenwanyi for their so-called Christianity, whoever had held the position of ada had headed the governing council of women who oversaw the caretaking of Ezenwanyi. They kept the shrine clean and fined members who broke their rules. Most of these women eventually left to join the Catholic community, leaving an inactive group with a few skeptics, but the ada has been as consistent in her duties as she is unwavering in her faith.

It is daylight by the time the ada of Ezenwanyi arrives. Chikelue is asked to remove his shirt. We watch the attama slay the cock into the hollow in the ground. He performs a libation, muttering incoherent words, immediately after which comes a loud rustling sound in the bush behind the shrine.

"Eziyi is about to make his appearance," he says to warn us

ahead of the appearance of Ezenwanyi's serpent. My father has told me about it.

Eziyi approaches with a sound like a boiling sea wave. Every eye in the shrine is fixed on the thick undergrowth now shaking with vigour. Fear seizes us as the fabulous serpent with an enormous head, complete with combs and wattles like a full-grown cock, looms into view. We cringe from the chilly stare of the serpent as it swings its massive greyish body into the shrine, raises its head, and hisses loudly. I have never witnessed a scene so terrifying. Now I can see the serpent closely, scarlet about the face, with an artistic arrangement of cowries running along its serrated cockscomb down to the back of its head. The shrine resonates with the voice of the ada rising and falling in a well-rehearsed cantillation. At the sight of the serpent, she leaps up then glides back and forth in a fluid sequence of movements, her face radiant and yellow, and the tempo of her voice rising correspondingly with the fluidity of her footwork. A startled silence rules the shrine in that brief moment while she pauses and anoints the serpent's great head with a powdery substance crushed from yellow chalk in her hand. Suddenly, the serpent begins a long, slow withdrawal, sliding out of the shrine into the bush to complete the process.

"You may now go. You are healed," the attama says, then adds as an afterthought, "If in three days you do not suffer a relapse."

Chikelue is shaking with trauma. He drops some money, an entire bundle of it, on the earth floor, and we hurry out of the shrine and head home. Once he has calmed down, he looks like a new creature, pride back again in his eyes and in his walk. The success of his healing ignites a smile, his round cheeks dimpling and making his pert lips more feminine.

Fifty

WE DRIVE TO THE UNIVERSITY IN THE AFTERNOON IN search of a sculptor to make a statue for Okike's tomb. Chikelue is playing loud music on his car stereo as we cruise into a lonely campus. It is always like this when students go on vacation, leaving the hostels sitting like bored old men gazing at a barren housefront view, and trees and their shadows leaning away from each other like isolated lovers. The green campus shuttles are noticeably absent. We drive to the faculty of arts, where a gallery of artwork is on display, passing by the general studies building with a sense of nostalgia. I had been in the building countless times for lectures.

"A village of a mute tribe." Chikelue whistles as he pulls up by the side of the road.

We come down from the car, and walk towards a big muscular man. He is bare to his loincloth, a giant who dwarfs us as if we were toddlers, though he is pulling a muscle to break the chains cuffing his great wrists, held high above his head, an action that forces him down on one knee. A short, dark boy with an afro haircut pauses in his work to talk to us while the giant stares away with only the whites of his eyes. Next to him, a large antelope escapes at an easy lope.

"I want a statue for my aunt." I reach for the photograph of Okike in my breast pocket and pass it to the artist. My mother had exhumed the photograph from our household detritus. "I want something really special."

"It depends on your pocket." The sculptor is perching on a high stool, putting finishing touches on the giant's nose.

"Money is not a problem," Chikelue chips in, rubbing the giant's long, sinewy arms and a gritty torso coloured like cement.

While we bargain, the sculptor and I, Chikelue wanders off to admire the loping antelope. We settle for twenty-five thousand naira when he wanders back.

"Here is half payment." He hands the money to the boy. "You get the balance on delivery."

The boy collects the money, pockets it.

"What's your name?" I ask.

"Chinedu Ugwuja, Department of Fine and Applied Art, 300 level."

"How soon are you going to fix it?" I ask.

"It will be ready before the end of the month."

"If I don't come, someone else will take the delivery." We shake hands and exchange phone numbers. "I want a good job."

"You will get it."

We walk back into the car and drive off. I was thinking of Machebe when I told the boy I would send someone to pick up the statue. I will talk it over with him and see if Machebe could use any of the cars he works on at the Mechanic Village to come fetch it. We drive back home past Uwakwe's shop. He is seated outside with chin cupped in hand, in frayed singlet and boxers, looking into the emptiness of the afternoon. We stop to speak with him. He looks aged, with streaks of grey in his hair and on his chest.

"I am happy to see you again." He stretches a coarse hand to shake mine, his angular face broadening in a grin.

"How's business?" My eyes wander to the inside of the shop. The shelves are empty.

"You don't bury a man who is still breathing," Uwakwe says with a shrug. "That's the improper thing to do."

We settle on Uwakwe's crooked bench, which evokes a flood of memories. I notice the way he is stealing curious glances at Chikelue, so I introduce them.

"What has been happening?" I ask.

"They silenced the people with their guns." Uwakwe seems to speak with effort. He looks sick and emaciated. "I heard they are now plucking young men out of their homes and killing and disposing of their bodies in secret. It is their way of weakening the opposition. They are afraid of another war. But they either accept us or they let us go in peace. You cannot stamp a man to the ground and expect him not to cry out."

The mood in the village is low. I can feel it, the growing sense of trepidation and hopeless longing that Uwakwe's melancholic figure symbolizes.

"That sounds like ethnic cleansing." Chikelue whistles.

We sit for a long time in brooding silence. And then we drive away. Back in my father's compound, we spend the afternoon sitting on the bonnet of the car, playing loud music and watching a sunset's orange landscape.

We leave for Lagos the next day, a bright Saturday morning full of sunshine and long shadows. The university town rolls away in green hills and fluffy white clouds like young chicks huddled together. Chikelue had phoned his parents and told them he was coming back healed.

"I am excited. And anxious. I can't wait for the three days to elapse," he says.

He is playing a gospel tune: Patty Obasi's "Ezinwanyi Di Uko." He hardly plays gospels, but he is crazy about R&B, about R. Kelly and Boyz II Men, and he likes to sing tenor along with Wanya Morris. "That voice, Wanya Morris's catching tenor, is unrivalled," he'd say while singing along.

But now it is Patty Obasi who is singing in his sleepy, un-hurried voice. How I like the song, I muse. How the slow-ness of the music blends with motion and rolling tyres. When Patty Obasi sings "Ezinwanyi Di Uko," I think of birds and brooks and nothing else. After a long, bumpy drive on a pot-holed road, we arrive at Nine Mile Corner with its slow traffic and the scent of okpa. We buy canned Coke, chilled, and hit the potholed Enugu/Onitsha Expressway. If Chikelue turns left, we will head towards Anukwu, the land that drank Eke's blood, but we drive straight up past Awka, with the old whiff of bronze and hot metal wafting through. And then we enter Onitsha, bustling Onitsha, with a faint imperial aura in the air. Niger Bridge looms into view, an oriental gait calling up memories of broken bridges. As our car tyres are rolling away against metal, the calm voice of a female broadcaster filters from the car radio. The voice alights from a commercial to report the bombing of an army base in the Lake Chad region, the third of similar attacks in one week. The soft voice trails off again, giving way to a blasting pop music.

At Umunede, we stop to eat garri and egusi soup.

Chikelue swings the car into the long drive edged with palms, and Ahmed, a dark, lanky, hilarious Housaman in a milk-white caftan, throws the gate open and smiles at us with teeth stained rust-red with kola. We climb out of the car. Ahmed, excited, scurries around to get our luggage and take it inside. He grins and bows so many times I can't help but laugh and feel slightly irritated at the same time. The mansion's floodlights are on. They brighten the surroundings and emphasize the whiteness of the house against a solid black background. Beyond the blackness the sea stretches and extends forever. The garden is blazing with sweet William, and Star of Bethlehem, and frangipani blossoms. We walk into a chandelier-illuminated lounge full of people.

Chikelue's parents have planned a surprise celebratory reception dinner for him, attended by his uncles, aunts, and family friends. The party blossoms with our arrival. More guests, all looking glamorous, arrive and stretch their jewel-laden hands to hand Chikelue bouquets of flowers. They touch his cheek with their own cheeks like white people.

"Congratulations."

Fifty-one

TIRED FROM TRAVELLING, WE GO TO BED EARLY. THE moon has risen. I spend a brief time on the back balcony, a solitary figure gazing as far as I can over the waters, savouring the faint iodine smell of the sea and thinking about George Emerenini's biography. I have collected his genealogical data and finished with the thesis. I intend to spend the next couple of months here working on the book. I can hear mountain-high waves crashing against the sea wall as I rejoin Chikelue in bed. The tide is still wailing as the party draws to a slow end. I can hear the guests leaving, cars starting outside, and the gate opening and closing. And then Chikelue's mother comes into the room to check on him. We pretend to be asleep. She leans over him to kiss his forehead.

"Good night, Papam," she whispers, smelling of champagne, sweat, and tiredness.

This action is repeated twice before we finally fall asleep, of her coming in softly, standing in what seems a quiet reflection and deep thankfulness for a lost-and-found item, and then leaning over to wet Chikelue's forehead with a kiss and a softly whispered "Good night." We lie side by side under lime-green Armani coverlets as if we had all along been siblings. I imagine how Chikelue's mother would frequent his grave with tears and flowers if he were to die of his strange illness. I wake up to see her again walking quietly out of the room and shutting the door behind her with a soft click. I can't help but

THE LIQUID EYE OF A MOON

admire this act of motherhood. This beauty of motherhood. I lie awake for a long time thinking of Eke's mother with a cold clutch to my heart.

We are left out of the morning prayers, perhaps to give us enough time to rest. I can hear Chikelue's mother singing in a loud voice, thanking God for saving him: Imeela Chineke muo . . . I can hear Dili, the housemaid, calm and dutiful, making breakfast. I can hear the vendor arriving.

"Good morning, sirs," Dili says as we come out to the lounge room. She always bends her knees when she greets. Her hair is cut short, her gown a light shade of red against her dark skin.

The room is impossibly clean, no traces of last night's party—no half-eaten plates of food, half-drunk champagne bottles, or dirty glasses. Household staffers are moving about briskly, nodding or genuflecting.

While Chikelue is having some private time with his mother, I watch the play of sunlight upon the water from the back balcony. The sky is flushed with the gold of a new dawn. The air smells clean, and the sea seems lulled after last night's tides. When Chikelue finally shows up at the balcony he is in a low mood, with a palpable sense of dejection. He invites me to take a stroll outside.

"This is the third day of the sacred bath." He heaves a deep sigh as we walk towards the garden past a light green fabric awning sheltering more than half a dozen cars. "I can't believe I am cured. You saved me, Dimkpa, so no one has a right to interfere."

He makes me feel even. "You saved me first. My father was impossible to live with, especially after my youth service. A few weeks after returning home, he was already hounding me to go get a job. He always had a partner in my brother. It became unbearable, and then you came into the picture, but I don't blame him. He sold our only heritage, a piece of land, to pay my fees."

We walk by the garden.

"No one has a right to interfere," he reiterates.

I am lost.

"I have a bad feeling." His voice is shaky, growing faint.

"You have had a long and tiring week," I say.

"Yes." He leans over to admire dewdrops on white frangipani blossoms. "I wanted you to be the brother I never had. I wanted us to live as brothers. We should reclaim the land your father sold and help him acquire many more lands, as many as he wants. We should build them a bigger house in the village, and give them a better life."

He leaves me speechless, more confused than ever.

"That cobra!" he says with a shudder as we step into the lawn. "I had to shut my eyes tightly while it slithered all over the place. The memory still makes my flesh creep."

"It will go away in no time, the trauma."

He plucks a hibiscus bloom and sniffs at it. And then he laughs, a dry laugh. "That boy, the attama; he is something else, the image of nonchalance."

"It was foisted on him. He never wanted it. The priesthood of Ezenwanyi is passed on to male firstborns. The boy inherited it from his father at the age of sixteen. He was born an only son in the twilight of his father's life."

"No one has a right to interfere." The hibiscus bloom slips out of his hand to the ground. He makes a huge task of picking it up. "Why didn't you tell me about ohu ma?"

I take two quick steps back.

A black bird, a crow, arrives on top of the fabric awning.

Crows are harbingers of evil in my village. I turn from the bird in time to see Chikelue slide to the ground. And then he is kicking violently and rolling around. I watch him, stunned, as he gets caught again in the familiar bloody struggle. I grab hold of him and manage to drag him under a hibiscus bush, holding him tight until the daemons take leave of him in a spurt of blood that slithers down his chin. Panting from exhaustion, I wipe sweat from my forehead and throw glances up at the balcony to see if anyone is watching us. The house is full of people. Chikelue and his family occupy the top floor. The ground floor is reserved for the household servants. His father has a coterie of staff who occupy the large cream-and-brown duplex on the other side of the large compound. He is a big importer of plumbing materials and electronic gadgets. So the compound is crawling with human ants, but we are well out of sight. The same building also houses the library that George has equipped for me, a downstairs cloakroom I use as a study to write his biography. He is going into politics.

This relapse in Chikelue's health must be hidden from his family. No one must know what happened this morning, not after the party last night. It will give his mother a heart attack. A plan is already shaping in my mind, to sneak Chikelue into his room after he recovers, help him with a bath, and try to sneak him out. We will hit the road again and continue our quest for a cure. He is out for about twelve minutes. And then he stirs and opens his eyes. More crows are arriving on top of the awning. There are so many of them, perhaps fifty or a hundred, making an uproar all over the awning, and over the roof of the house.

•

In another half hour we are back to the road. What went wrong? The question rages in my head, unanswered, as Chikelue fires away at the car engine. We must get to the attama as fast as possible, the lanky boy, master of the crowing crested cobra, to get an answer to this question. If he can't furnish us with an answer, we will ignore him and further our quest.

"No one has a right to interfere," Chikelue hisses again from the driver's seat. "My mother and I had a talk about you, and about my healing. When I mentioned Ezenwanyi she recoiled. The colour drained completely from her face. I have never seen my mother look so agitated. She told me about Ezenwanyi's outcasts. She says you are cursed and forbade me from associating with you or anyone related to you to avoid a curse following me. I insisted, and we argued. She went hysterical and threatened to kill herself if I disobeyed her."

It is beginning to make sense.

"I have never disobeyed my mother, but no one has a right to interfere in the friendship between you and me."

I entreat him to slow down: "Be careful." He is driving too fast.

"I don't care," he snaps.

I fear for our lives. At the rate we are travelling, Chikelue could lose control of the wheel. There is no emotion in his countenance. He looks calm in the face of imminent death.

"No one has a right to interfere. We have come a long way," he reiterates.

I stare ahead, wondering at what the cruelties of life are capable of doing to a man, deciding I will go with Chikelue to the ends of the world, the farthest reaches of the universe, as, moving with terrific speed, he grips the wheel tightly, fury in his right foot, the gas pedal floored like a long-standing enemy that must be crushed even if it takes two lives to achieve that purpose.

I reach out and grab the wheel. The car careers dangerously across the road as I wrestle it from Chikelue. The engine wails and the tyres plead the course of the car. The tarmac spreads then lengthens. A long truck zooms past and leaves Babydoll dancing in the wind, missing her by the whiskers. I clench the wheel tighter, because I am taking back my life, our lives. They had our poor little lives all figured out for us. My father could not be village head. My mother starved us, her children, to pay tithe. I have lived my life trying to be the person Machebe and my father wanted me to be. And I had to put my family history aside to write the biography of a rich man. Chikelue has driven all his life, and I am only a rookie, I know, but I am taking over the wheel.

And that's how things will stay.

Acknowledgments

In writing the book, I drew on many sources. Words and phrases like "deity wives," "ethereal entities," and "medicine" draw from Nwando Achebe's beautiful piece *Igo Mma Ogo* (The Adoro Goddess, Her Wives, and Challengers—Influences on the Reconstruction of Alor Uno, Northern Igboland, 1890–1994).

I would not have written this book without the support, encouragement, and love of friends and family.

I wish to thank my wife, Amaka, for her patience while I spend hours to myself writing; to my younger brother, Jonas, for helping with family bills when it mattered most; for believing and investing in me, Chris Ngwu occupies a special place in my professional life; and to Ejiofor Ugwu, for his early mentoring that changed my perception of art.

With gratitude, Robert Lopez, for your constant inspiration. Jeffery Renard Allen, Joy Baglio, and Mary Adkins: your support and motivation played a key role.

Special thanks to my agent Annie DeWitt for believing in me, to Leslie Shipman and Mary Alice Stewart, and everyone at the Shipman Agency. My editors, Kendall Storey and Molly Slight, for your competence and patience while we walked down the rigorous path of editing. To the Catapult crew: Wah-Ming Chang, Megan Fishmann, Vanessa Genao, Elizabeth Pankova, Dustin Kurtz, Na Kim, Nicole Caputo, Rachel Fershleiser, Kira Weiner, and everyone who had a hand in making this dream a reality, I say thank you. Whatever errors that are found in the book are all mine.

For the offer of a fellowship when it mattered, I am grateful to the IIE Artist Protection Fund and Arkansas International Writer-at-Risk Residency Program. Thank you, Alison Russo and Mary Margaret. Specially to Padma Viswanathan and her husband, Geoff Brock, for their incredible mentorship, for making my fellowship a valuable and memorable one.

I am grateful to my MacDowell and Vermont Studio Center friends: Rebecca Reuter, Greg Tebbano, Chaya Bhuvaneswar, Dennis McFadden, Kwong Kwok Wai, and Juleen Johnson.

Thanks to my friends in Fayetteville for making it my second home and always being there for me: David and Laura Jackson, Bill and Laura Spear, Gabrielle Idlet, Austin Wilkins, Laurie Marshall, Heather, Jody, Sharon and Charles. Elizabeth Muscari and Bill Spear, for always reading my drafts and giving inspiring feedback.

I got my first computer from MacDowell: they gave it to me when they learned I had never had one. Thank you, David Macy, for making my dream come true.

And in memory of Haruko Tanaka: rest in peace.